Guardians of the Apocalypse Book One:
You're Never Ready for a Zombie Apocalypse
a novel by Jeff Thomson

Copyright 2018, Twisted Synapse Books, West Haven, UT
Library of Congress 1-6160010181
All rights reserved

Cover Art created by www.rockingbookcovers.com

The idea for this story was suggested by the scenario posited in John Ringo's *Black Tide Rising* series; (Baen Books, Wake Forest, NC). As such, there are similarities: both are Military Theme Zombie Fiction, both take place in a marine environment, and both involve a viral outbreak. The plot, characters, locale, branch of service, and focus are all different. Some of the science is the same, but science is science, and you can't just make stuff up. Having said that, the author believes in giving credit where credit is due, so thank you Mister Ringo. Well done, sir. You can find his books on Baen.com and Amazon.com

Thanks also to Mr Lane Keely, and Ms Lisa Hillman, for being beta readers, along with an extra special thank you to Mr Jim Barber for his continued support and assistance in my writing efforts. Your literary death, when it comes, shall be epic.

Feel free to contact the author: twistedsynapsebooks@gmail.com

This book is dedicated to the men and women of the United States Coast Guard: past, present, and future. You do an incredibly difficult job, with incredibly few thanks, and are the butt of jokes from all the other services, but in my eyes (and in this book) you guys rock.

This is in many ways a love letter to the people I served with. Sorry, but *with whom I served* sounds far too pompous. The Grammar Nazis may feel free to kiss my ass.

I have "borrowed" the names of some of those people, because they are immortal in my heart, and so I thought I'd make them immortal in reality. You guys (and women) deserve it. You *earned* it.

For Frank Rosseler and Gus Perniola, just flip-flop the last names. Sorry guys, couldn't resist.

The actions, thoughts and most of the literary personalities of those great people are of my own creation. I hope they don't mind. As for the other names, I made them up. Any resemblance to anyone living or dead (or a zombie) is purely coincidental.

I served on two icebreakers and two of the older 180 buoy tenders. Having never been on any of the newer 225's, and because their configuration is *For Official Use Only*, I am unfamiliar with their layout. Also, my years aboard the ships I did serve on was a long time ago, and my memory ain't what it used to be. So, yes, I'll admit it, I made up a bunch of shit. Also, I took certain liberties with the rating designations, and the manning and organization of the LEDET and TACLET. Call it Artistic Licence, or simply say that I liked it better the old way. Don't bother telling me that such-and-such a compartment was on the Port side, not the Starboard side, or that the New Guard is different. I don't care.

I took the same liberties with some of the geographical details, as for example: there isn't an actual pier in Midway Harbor, but I put one there, anyway. It's good to be the King. My world, my rules. Deal with it.

Fair winds and following seas, shipmates.

1429Z18MAY

FM: COMCOGUARDISTRICTFOURTEEN, HONOLULU, HI

TO: CGC KUKUI (WLB 203)
   CGC SASSAFRAS (WLB 217)
   CGC SEQUOIA (WLB 215)
   CGC ASSATEAGUE (WPB 1337)
   CGC GALVESTON ISLAND (WPB 1349)
   CGC KISKA (WPB 1336)
   CGC WASHINGTON (WPB 1331)

CC: COMCOGUARDPACAREA, ALAMEDA, CA
   COMCOGUARDSECTOR HONOLULU, HI
   COMCOGUARDSECTOR APIA, GUAM
   COMSTA APIA, GUAM

SUBJ: POMONA VIRUS

1. SUMMARY

     A: POMONA, A MAN-MADE VIRUS, RELEASED VIA AIR
     BORNE, BLOOD BORNE AND CONTACT VECTORS, AND
     WHICH HAS NO KNOWN CURE, HAS BEEN DECLARED A
     WILDFIRE EPIDEMIC BY THE CDC. IT HAS BEEN
     DETERMINED TO BE TWO SEPARATE VIRUSES.

     B: THE FIRST MANIFESTS AS A VIRULENT, BUT
     OTHERWISE NORMAL STRAIN OF THE COMMON COLD,
     CAUSING AN UPPER RESPIRATORY INFECTION. THIS IS
     BOTH AN AIRBORNE AND CONTACT PATHOGEN, AND
     IS CONSIDERED HIGHLY CONTAGIOUS. NORMAL COLD
     REMEDIES AND OTHER PREVENTIVE MEASURES HAVE
     BEEN DEEMED INEFFECTIVE DUE TO THEIR INABILITY
     TO TREAT THE SECOND VIRUS (SEE BELOW).

C: THE SECOND VIRUS, WHICH MANIFESTS 2-5 DAYS AFTER THE ONSET OF UPPER RESPIRATORY SYMPTOMS, IS A NEUROLOGICAL BLOOD PATHOGEN, SIMILAR TO RABIES, THAT ATTACKS THE HUMAN BRAIN, DESTROYING THE FUNCTIONALITY OF THE FRONTAL LOBE, WHILE ACTIVATING THE AMYGDALA - THE SO-CALLED "LIZARD BRAIN." SYMPTOMS OF THE SECOND VIRUS INCLUDE, BUT ARE NOT LIMITED TO: DELUSIONAL BEHAVIOR, SEVERE PARANOIA, REMOVAL OF CLOTHING, LOSS OF LANGUAGE ABILITY, LOSS OF HIGHER ORDER BRAIN FUNCTION, AND EXTREME VIOLENCE, WHICH INCLUDES BITING.

D: THESE BITES ARE HIGHLY CONTAGIOUS AND SHOULD BE AVOIDED AT ALL COSTS. TIME FROM FIRST BITE TO ONSET OF NEUROLOGICAL SYMPTOMS IS 1-3 HOURS. EXTREME CAUTION IS ADVISED.

E. THE FIRST CONFIRMED OUTBREAK OCCURRED APRIL 1ST, THIS YEAR, AT THE POMONA JUNIOR HIGH SCHOOL, POMONA, CALIFORNIA.

F. CDC HAS REPORTED THE SPREAD OF THIS VIRUS THROUGHOUT THE ENTIRE WORLD. CDC, WHO, ETC., HAVE BEEN UNABLE TO STABILIZE THE SPREAD, OR CONTROL ITS EFFECTS.

G. AN ATTENUATED VACCINE HAS BEEN PRODUCED, USING INFECTED SPINAL TISSUE FROM HIGHER-ORDER PRIMATES, BUT THE SCARCITY OF SUCH NON-HUMAN PRIMATES HAS MADE WORLDWIDE DISSEMINATION OF THIS VACCINE FUNCTIONALLY IMPOSSIBLE.

H. ATTEMPTS TO RESTRAIN AND TREAT VICTIMS OF THIS EPIDEMIC HAVE PROVEN TO BE INEFFECTIVE.

I: RULES OF ENGAGEMENT: STUN, TRANQUILIZE, TRANSPORT TO SECURE FACILITY (SEE ENCLOSURE 01 BELOW) REMAIN IN EFFECT.

2. ACTION:

A. COMPACAREA HAS ORDERED ALL D-14 USCG SHIPS TO ALPHA STATUS.

B. ALL LEAVE IS TO BE CANCELLED. ALL CREW IS TO BE RECALLED. STOP LOSS IS IN EFFECT FOR ALL RATES AND RANKS, FOR THE DURATION OF THE EMERGENCY.

C. YOU ARE DIRECTED TO LOAD FUEL, STORES, DISASTER SUPPLIES, AND AMMUNITION. COORDINATE WITH BASE COMMAND, SAND ISLAND, FUEL POINT, PEARL HARBOR, AND/OR NAVCOM APIA, GUAM.

D: YOU ARE DIRECTED TO BE UNDERWAY NLT 0800 LCL 19 MAY.

E: SEE ENCLOSURE 02 FOR DEPLOYMENT DIRECTION.

F: ONCE ON STATION, HOLD IN POSITION AND AWAIT FURTHER ORDERS.

1

"Fuck me sideways," OS2 Bill Schaeffer, sitting in the Radio Room of the US Coast Guard Cutter *Sassafras*, said, in what most people would consider a casual tone. Anyone who knew him, and knew his laconic manner of speaking, however, might be alarmed.

He leaned back in his chair and read the message again. All was not well. Not even close.

He'd watched the news, knew of the Pomona outbreak. The CDC announced it three weeks ago, using carefully-worded political doublespeak, saying nothing but speaking volumes. It hadn't seemed real, somehow. And he'd seen the original reports of the outbreak, the body bags being brought out of the Pomona Junior High School on stretchers, the families wailing and crying and hugging each other for support. That *definitely* hadn't seemed real - just familiar.

How many times had scenes of mass death been played out on national television, over, and over, and over again, with those same images: stretchers, emergency workers, families, and with *A Community Shattered* in bold headlines, scrolling beneath it all? Only this time, there hadn't been any guns involved. This time there hadn't been the NRA to stop anything from being done about it. This time it was the anti-vaccine morons.

Pomona had only been the first. Those same images, those same scenes of death played out as twisted sequels to the original, in school after school, after school. Whatever crazy fuck did this, used children to spread the virus.

Bill couldn't help the comparison to *Apocalypse, Now*; to the scene where Brando talked about the VC hacking the vaccinated arms off the village children. The logic was deadly simple and deadly effective. Even after the virus spread, even after it had become an epidemic, what were people supposed to do: not hug their sick child?

The cold virus came first, and it was a nasty bugger. Some shook it off, many didn't.

The respiratory infection lasted a few days to a week, followed by a day or two of relatively good health. Then the fever would hit, carrying with it a microscopic passenger that attacked the human frontal lobe, taking away all higher level cognition, and leaving behind it a pissed off, insane and violent monster with an eerie resemblance to the standard Hollywood zombie - except, they weren't dead.

Bill heard the rumors: people going crazy, cannibalism, "treatment centers" more like some twisted nightmare from a Nazi Death Camp than anything useful, or helpful, or sane. He'd even seen signs of it in Honolulu.

Two days ago (was that all it was?) he'd been out picking up beer and snacks for the party he and his roommate, BM1 Jones, were throwing at their apartment, over by Pearl Harbor - just a normal Saturday night. He'd been choosing between pretzels and tortilla chips, and had finally decided upon both, when he heard: "Help me! Help me! The bugs! All the fucking bugs!" followed by...*growling*.

Of course, he'd known he hadn't actually heard what he thought he'd heard. He hadn't heard growling. No way, Jose. He hadn't heard anything like growling - except, he had. But it was impossible! People didn't growl. People never growled. But then he'd heard it again, and this time it had been closer.

He'd peered around the snack aisle, towards where they kept the tequila (which he remembered he was supposed to pick up). Jonesy loved him some tequila, and there would be no small amount of bitching if he forgot it. The thought passed through his head like a will-o-the-wisp, to be swept aside when he realized he was watching a middle-aged man in what was left of a Hawaiian shirt, remove his board shorts.

Forget that the guy was far too old and knobby-kneed to be wearing board shorts, in the first place. Forget that he was dropping trou right there in the liquor store, in front of God and everybody. What Bill couldn't forget, hard as he tried, was the look of insane rage on the guy's face.

With a keening of such lunatic malice as Bill never wanted to hear again, the lunatic charged. Fortunately for Bill, but unfortunately for the man with anger-management issues, the middle-aged exhibitionist hadn't quite finished taking off his shorts. They'd still been down around his ankles, and sent him straight to the ground with a splat.

From around the opposite corner of the tequila shelves, a police officer, in full riot gear appeared, took one look at the situation, then dropped on the still-snarling tourist It took place in barely more than an instant.

Bill watched in detached fascination as the cop pulled an Eppy-pen from a pouch at his side, flipped off the protective cap, then jabbed it into the still-struggling man's thigh, pulled flex cuffs from a belt pouch and secured the man's hands as the drug began to take effect.

The cop had looked up, then, and said: "Nothing to see here."

"Right," Bill had replied, and promptly headed to the checkout counter, paid for the beer and snacks, and left the store, forgetting the tequila completely.

Two days ago. Only two days.

Even with the news reports and rumors and the wild speculation at the party that night (and yes, Jonesy had bitched about the lack of tequila), the entire idea of what was laughably being called a zombie apocalypse remained just an idea - and a screwy one, just on the face of it.

Forget the technical conversations about how it couldn't be a zombie apocalypse, because the people weren't dead and could not, therefore, be zombies. Forget the signs that this whole thing was bigger than what the official word was making it out to be. Bill could even forget (or maybe just push aside) the incident at the liquor store. None of those things made it seem real.

But this message, and its order for all the buoy tenders and patrol boats in the entire District to get underway...? *That* shit was real.

He clipped the message to the SECRET board and picked up the phone.

2

"Don't give me any zombie apocalypse bullshit," Harold insisted, as he tossed a heavy box of lettuce up the brow to MK2 Frank Roessler. "Because there's no such thing as fucking zombies."

Harold F. Simmons, jr., was a tall and thin nineteen year-old African American Seaman in *Uncle Sam's Confused Group.* Most days he was happy about this. Most days, his face carried an expression of perpetual mirth - just not today, and certainly not while discussing the current *NON*-Zombie Apocalypse.

"You're obsessed with this not-a-zombie thing, Harold. What else can you call crazed, homicidal naked cannibals?" Frank asked, catching a box of broccoli from the young man and tossing it further up the brow. He was also tall, also thin, in his early twenties, with short, dark brown hair and the beginnings of a receding hairline. His face carried a sardonic grin as he sweated in the late morning sun.

They were taking on stores - *lots* of stores - which was weird, because up until today, they'd been scheduled to go into Charlie Status, which meant they weren't supposed to be going anywhere. But first thing this morning, before Harold even had his first cup of bug juice (he hated coffee, and the powdered drink carried a shocking amount of sugar guaranteed to give even the most sleep-deprived person a rush), they announced the change in status. And then came the pipe every junior enlisted hated:

"All E-5 and below lay to the pier to load stores."

A general cry of "What the fuck," went up on the mess deck, like the wailing of a siren (or a big bunch of babies, as Harold was sure his BM1 would say), but it changed nothing. They'd still had to tromp out to the pier to start lifting and toting. They hadn't even stopped to hold morning muster, just "Turn to ship's work." Everybody grumbled, everybody bitched, but it did about as much good as it usually did - which is to say, none at all.

And then word spread they were getting underway to go turn the "Box of Death," out off of Kauai for an undisclosed period of time. No reason was given, but everybody knew: *Pomona.*

The most definitely *not* zombie virus had been circulating for about three weeks, by this point. Most had seen the signs: naked, crazy people running down the street, growling and trying to bite other people, was hard to miss, and just so *wrong.* "Don't dare get bit," was the most common suggestion. Like he needed to be told something so obvious.

Word from the mainland was worse. The last time he'd talked to his father in Philly, his father said there were riots and fires, and that the police had set up warehouses - fucking *warehouses* - to hold the infected, because there wasn't a damned thing else anybody could do with them.

"How the Hell should I know?" Harold asked. "Zombies are the living dead. These fuckers never died." This was true enough. Pomona usually didn't kill its victims outright; it just drove them out of their goddamned minds.

The radio waves and the Internet were filled with wild conspiracy theories about who caused it. Some asshole had even suggested *Black Lives Matter* created it to take down Whitey, which was idiotic, because it was taking down black people every bit as much as white, or brown, or yellow, or whatever color you wanted to name - truly an Equal Opportunity virus.

But people wanted someone to blame, and so the conspiracy theories spread like wildfire. There was even one - told first by some Talk-Radio nutjob on *InfoWars* - that Obama and Hillary created it as revenge for having been beaten by Trump.

None of it mattered. Figuring out who caused it wouldn't change a thing, because Pomona was as real as it got, and it had changed everything.

"So what do they have?" Frank asked. "Mad Cow?"

"That's right, Frank," BM1/OPS Socrates Jones said from his supervisory post alongside the brow. "They're nothing but naked, human, flesh-eating Mad Cows."

3

"A little less bullshitting and a lot more sweat, please," Jonesy said. Socrates (Jonesy) Jones was tall and well-built, with the sun-washed face and squint-crinkled eyes of a man who'd spent almost a third of his twenty-seven years of life at sea. He wore the Tropical Dress uniform: a short-sleeved, light blue shirt over dark blue dress pants; his shoes shined and his ribbons adorning his chest, making him look like an honest-to God war hero. All a facade, of course. He was no hero, in spite of the four rows of three ribbons, topped by two more singles, a Cutterman's Pin, a Diver's Pin, and a Tactical Law Enforcement Badge.

He was the Officer of the Day, put there, he suspected, because none of the Wardroom assholes wanted to deal with loading stores. They might have actually had to work for a change. Couldn't have that!

"Come on, Jonesy," Harold said. "What do you think it is?"

"I think you need to shut the fuck up and turn-to ship's work," he replied. "And don't call me Jonesy when I'm the OD. You know better than that."

"Aw, come on, Jonesy," Harold said. "Lighten up."

"You're in the military, Harry," Socrates said, knowing full well hos friend hated to be called "Harry." He checked the clipboard he was holding, as if it served some purpose, which was silly, since the CS1 would be signing for all of the stores. "At least *try* to act like it."

"Yes sir, Petty Officer Jones, sir!" Harold said with an exaggerated salute.

Jonesy coughed into his fist. It sounded strangely like "blow me." He scanned up and down the dock to see if there were any other higher ranks. Most of the officers and senior enlisted were cool, but there were always a few assholes. Best to be safe.

Harold and Frank, and at least half a dozen of the other poor bastards who were now straining to get the stores up the steep gangway and into the ship, had been to more than one party at Jonesy's apartment that he shared with OS3 Bill Schaeffer. The parties weren't strictly supposed to happen, since Jonesy was a senior Petty Officer, but, number one, the Coast Guard wasn't as strict about rank as the other services;

number two, he and Bill had become instant roommates because of limited housing availability, even though pairing a Third Class with a First Class wasn't strictly supposed to happen, either; and, number three, Jonesy didn't really give a rat's ass about rank. With a crew of less than fifty people (including officers), who were often sent to the ass-crack middle of nowhere, the *Sassafras* had far too few people from whom to choose as friends. Jonesy took them where he found them, regardless of their rank.

He started his Coast Guard career as a Deckie aboard an icebreaker on the Great Lakes. Breaking chunks of ice off the superstructure with a wooden mallet, scraping, painting, messcooking, and other forms of groveling subservience generally relegated to the bottom of the military food chain, had not appealed to him, and so he put in for Quartermaster School. At that time, Quartermaster (QM) combined the equivalent of four Navy ratings: Quartermaster (navigation), Signalman (SM, visual signaling and communications), Radarman (RD - self-explanatory), and Operations Specialist (OS, a sort of Navy catch-all that meant the poor bastard was condemned to be stuck in a windowless, locked compartment called the Combat Information Center - CIC). In the Coast Guard, however, it just gave him one more thing to deal with - like he needed more.

His first unit as a QM3 was a buoy tender in Alaska - one of the older 180-foot variety, which had since been phased out. He enjoyed the Hell out of it. But then some Headquarters Half-Wit decided it would be a brilliant idea to combine Quartermaster with Bosun Mate (BM), which covered basic and advanced seamanship, small boat handling, and all things deck-related on larger ships. If Jonesy wanted to become a Bosun Mate, he would have become a Bosun Mate, and so he began casting about for some other job he could do within the Coast Guard.

At around the same time as the transitional cluster fuck, inevitable of all bureaucratic changes, they began talking about creating a new rating, specializing in Tactical Law Enforcement. It was to be a demanding job, and certainly not dull, so Jonesy volunteered. Thus, he was transferred to the Maritime Safety and Security Team (MSST), and sent to the Special Missions Training Center at the Marine Base on Camp Lejeune, where he received training in Advanced Combat Marksmanship, Close Quarters Combat, Progressive Breaching, Vertical Insertions, Underwater Port Security, Explosive Detection with Canine Teams, and Tactical Boat Ops.

Shortly after he graduated second in his class (over a full dozen Marines, which pissed off the Master Gunnery Sergeant to no end), and emerged as a fully-fledged Coast Guard Ninja, he discovered the MSST was being phased out, and so he found himself transferred to the Pacific Area (PACAREA) Tactical Law Enforcement Team (TACLET). Shortly after arriving there, some other Half-Wit (presumably not the same one) decided it would be a really good idea to attach a TACLET to a Polar Icebreaker, and so he was sent to the Cutter *Healy*, then prepping to depart on a four month deployment to the Arctic. They still hadn't officially created the new rating yet, and so he went aboard as a BM2/OPS, just filling in his time requirement to be advanced to First Class.

Upon returning to their home port of Seattle, he discovered cooler and more rational heads had prevailed and decided that, no, a Polar Icebreaker really did not need a TACLET, at which time, he was transferred to the District 14 TACLET, in Honolulu, now as a BM1.

A week after his arrival, there was an...*incident*...that landed him on Administrative Leave. Shortly thereafter, the BM1/OPS aboard the newer, 225-Foot buoy tender, *Sassafras*, pulled a truly boneheaded move, which landed him in Leavenworth Prison, and left an open billet with no immediate replacement available - until the *Powers That Be* thought of Jonesy.

So convoluted had been his career, with so many changes and upheavals, he now considered himself to be an SN QM BM SM RD OS Coast Guard Ninja Brain Surgeon. He'd added the Brain Surgeon bit because, why the Hell not?

He'd been aboard for six months, and had found himself a home on the ship, and a family in the crew. He was happy - more or less. And then, wouldn't you know it, a zombie apocalypse happened. *Dumb fucking luck.*

A Government Vehicle rolled to a stop thirty feet back from the truck they were unloading. Jonesy didn't think anything of it. Mucky Mucks had been coming and going all morning. It might be Duke, he supposed, but the man shouldn't be back from Hickam Air Force Base for another twenty minutes, even with the insane way he drove. He thought of the person being picked up there, and wondered at the Murphy's Law of it all.

Said person was a boot Ensign, sent to replace the one who'd moved up to Bull - not a big deal in the Grand Scheme of things. Jonesy had dealt with plenty of newbies straight out of the Academy.

The new Ensign was a female - also not a big deal. He didn't have any trouble taking orders from a woman. It was a bit odd, in that *Sassafras* had only one other female crew member in her short history: another officer, three years ago. He'd never met the woman.

The other new buoy tenders all had female enlisted on board, but for some reason - either because of a foul up at the yard which built her, or an idiotic error at the Headquarters Planning Unit that had commissioned her - none of the crew berthing compartments on *Sassafras* had been fitted with a private head and shower. The Coast Guard was pretty open-minded about most things, but unisex showers wasn't one of them. They'd been scheduled to retrofit the aftermost four-man (sorry, four *person*) compartment during their Charlie maintenance period, but then the zombie apocalypse came along and all such plans had flown right out the damned window.

None of those things gave Jonesy a moment's pause. What did was precisely *who* that female Ensign was. *That* was simply too goddamned complicated, so he shoved it from his mind.

"Don't make me have to get official, Harold," he said. "You know how the XO gets about this military bullshit. He'll have me put your ass on report for insubordination, I'll have to do a shitload of paperwork, and that would piss me right the fuck off."

The Coast Guard, unlike the other Armed Forces, only seemed to be military when they weren't otherwise too busy doing any of a dozen different missions, from Search and Rescue, to Law Enforcement, and Drug Interdiction, to Marine Environmental Protection, Customs, Immigration, Homeland Security, Port Security, Boating Safety, or - every now and then - Aids to Navigation, the primary purpose of their ship. Just the way Jonesy liked it.

Yes, you needed discipline. Yes, people needed to follow orders. Yes, you should show respect to your superiors, just as they should show respect to those junior to them, but he preferred it to be mutual, earned respect, rather than a simple matter of doing what you're told. Far less bullshit that way.

He was about to expound on this to his African-American friend, who - though an accomplished smart ass of the highest order - had nonetheless gone back to the work of tossing produce up the brow, when he looked down the pier and saw who was getting out of that Government Vehicle.

This should be interesting, he thought.

4

Molly Jean Gordon, Ensign, United States Coast Guard, the ink barely dry on her commission, looked up the pier toward the black hull and white superstructure of the USCGC *Sassafras*. She was of medium height, with short-cropped golden brown hair beneath her Combination Cap.

She looked soft and feminine. She wasn't, and many a cock-sure Midshipman had discovered this to their great detriment during her four years at the Academy; none of which mattered now.

She saw the produce truck and the line of uniformed men passing the stores up the brow, and thought: *My first ship. My first crew*, with no small degree of swelling pride. And then she saw Socrates Jones.

You've got to be kidding me, she thought. *Why him? Why now?* Her heart, which had been filling with a mixture of pride and anticipation and anxiety and nervousness and a sense of impending adventure, sank, like the *Lusitania*.

Socrates Jones had been an...*indiscretion.* Her first, truth be told, though she hadn't been a virgin by any stretch. Past dalliances had been under the usual circumstances: making out in the back seat, playing spin the bottle, a half-remembered, rather intoxicated prom night, and a few assorted bits of fun while at the Coast Guard Academy. Socrates had been something else, entirely.

The first indication he might be something more than a passing fancy happened while she was living, and he was stationed up in Alaska with her Uncle John. He was a young QM3, only twenty-one at the time, fresh out of Navigation School, and to her, he seemed like something out of Greek mythology. She'd been sixteen, for all of three months, and was, for the first time in her life, smitten.

The crush had been harbored in absolute secrecy - the secret not divulged, even under the duress of pillow talk, after they'd "hooked up," almost five years later. It had been *so damned easy* to fall into his arms - regardless of the impropriety.

He had been a BM2 by then, just one of the people who trained her in bridge watches and celestial navigation aboard the USCGC *Healy*, the polar icebreaker on which she had spent her Cadet Summer, between Junior and Senior year. And what a summer it had been!

The *Eagle*, the Coast Guard's very own tall ship, was the prestige posting, but the *Healy,* homeported in Seattle, was the one everybody wanted. It went places, not the least of which was above the Arctic Circle, but also, San Diego, Puntarenas, Costa Rica, through the Panama Canal, to Curacao, in the Netherland Antilles, then San Juan, Puerto Rico, Boston, Halifax, in Nova Scotia, Bergen and Tromsö, in Norway, Thule, Greenland (okay...that wasn't so great, but it *had* been an adventure), then over the top of North America, through the Northwest Passage, down through the Bering Straight, and back home to Seattle.

Four months, seeing some of the most beautiful places in the world, including one night near the ice edge, above the Bering Sea, where she witnessed a spectacular, multi-colored, sunset worthy of the most psychedelic Pink Floyd concert. It lasted four solid hours. Jonesy shared it with her, holding hands on the ship's fantail at two in the morning: *magic*.

And, okay, she'd also had a torrid affair with an enlisted man. In retrospect: not the best idea. But while it was going on, it had been *astounding*. And now he was standing there next to the brow leading to her very first ship.

Dumb fucking luck.

She hesitated, frozen in mid-step, then chided herself for looking like an idiot, steeled her nerves, and strode up to him.

"Ensign Gordon reporting aboard," she said, thrusting her order package into his hand, while trying not to drop her garment bag, which threatened to tip her sideways. She brought her hand up in a salute, half a second before realizing he held a clipboard in one hand, and she had just shoved her orders into the other, making it impossible for him to return the salute.

She heard a snigger from one of the men loading stores off to her side, and felt sure her face must have turned all the colors of that Arctic sunset. Not according to plan!

"Shut your pie hole, Harry," Jonesy barked, without taking his eyes off her. He tucked her orders under the arm holding the clipboard, and snapped a military salute. "Welcome aboard, ma'am." His face carried a neutral expression, but his hazel eyes (which had always made her knees weak) were filled with mischievous delight.

Damn him, she thought. *How dare he? How dare he look at her that way? How dare he look so damned good?*

BM2/DECK Duke Peterson, her chauffeur from Hickham Air Force Base, came strolling up behind them, carrying her sea bag and carry-on. Thoroughly Scandinavian, she thought, with blonde hair and corn fed, ruddy features - pure Minnesota, unless she missed her guess. And she *was* trying to guess - desperately - trying to think of anything other than Socrates Jones.

The sea bag was heavy, as she well knew, but the bruiser of a guy could have been carrying a paper cup full of daisies, for all it seemed to affect him. The Bosun Mate placed the bags on the pier at their feet and smiled at Jonesy.

"Got her here safe," he said.

"Didn't run anybody over?" Jonesy asked.

"Wanted to, but I figured she was an Officer and probably wouldn't like it."

"Duke, here, is a notorious driver," Jonesy said to her. "Just be thankful he didn't pick you up in The Scull Mobile.".

"Don't hate the truck," Duke replied, with a touch of wounded pride.

Molly had no idea what they were talking about, but she relaxed (a bit) at the familiar comradery passing between the two shipmates. If they were comfortable enough around her to joke, then maybe this wouldn't be a *complete* disaster.

"There was that old woman, on the approach to the bridge," she said. "I thought she was a goner, for sure."

"Nah," Duke waved it off. "Missed her by a mile."

"Would have been worth serious points, though," Molly replied.

Duke grinned at Jonesy. "At least she has a sense of humor."

"She does indeed," Jonesy replied, passing the clipboard to Duke, once he'd removed Molly's orders from the paperwork chaos in his left hand. "You get to take over. I'll get her checked in." He looked at the sea bag and carry-on at their feet. "I'm going to steal Harold."

Duke nodded and shrugged. "Harold! Job opportunity," he barked in fine bosun fashion.

"What now?" the young man said, still tossing boxes of produce.

"Get your ass down here and grab the Ensign's sea bag," Jonesy ordered. Harold's shoulders slumped in obvious displeasure. "Secure that attitude, or Duke will find something unpleasant for you to do."

"I can think of three or four things," the bosun agreed.

"I'm doing it," Harold said, sliding out of line and down the brow.

Jonesy looked at Molly and smiled. "Can't get good help these days," he said, then picked up her carry-on and shouted "Make a hole!" as he worked his way up the brow and onto the ship.

5

"Semper Gumby, Gus," QMC John Gordon (retired) said, as he made his way up the brow of his ship, the M/V *True North*. She was an ex-Canadian Coast Guard buoy tender - one hundred and eighty-nine feet of what used to be red-painted, rusted hull. Now it was re-plated, repainted a deep blue, topped by a white superstructure, and refitted into a decent, ocean-going yacht. He, on the other hand, looked as if he had been enjoying his retirement just a bit too much. His once lean frame, topped by short-cropped gunmetal gray hair, had developed a decidedly un-military beer belly, and his lined face needed a shave. "Semper fucking Gumby."

The expression was a play on the US Coast Guard's motto: *Semper Paratus - Always Ready*. It meant, *Always Flexible*, and described their current operational status, to a tee.

A robust fifty, he wore black cargo pants and a blue tee-shirt adorned with the caption: *I haven't had my coffee yet. Don't make me kill you.* He retired from the Coast Guard after twenty-five years, settled into a pleasant existence teaching nautical classes at the local state college in Astoria, Oregon, joined the local PTA, and looked forward to an easy, middle-class life.

Until he won the lottery.

The prize had been a staggering nine figures, after taxes. It felt unreal then and still did now, almost a year later. Of course, he'd done what any true sailor would do with a sudden infusion of ridiculous amounts of money: he'd bought a boat. And because it had been an insane amount of money, the "boat" had been a full-on ship.

The ludicrous windfall was now going to save the lives of himself, his family and a few of his friends.

"Yeah, John," Gus replied. "I know...Semper all the way. But Jesus! We have everything we need. Why don't we just throw off the lines and get the Hell out of here while the getting's good?"

Gus Perniola, a retired MKCS and long-time friend, was helping John load the last of the medical supplies. He stood maybe five-ten, and carried a shape best described as "round," though it was the type of round found on older bikers with whom people would never consider messing, even though his face held a pleasant, happy expression, and his head was topped with fuzzy white hair and adorned with an equally white beard - kind of like Santa Clause meets the *Sons of Anarchy*. He was one of the very few people John told of his escape plan.

"Because," John said, balancing the enormous, blue and white First Aid Kit (its manufacturer boasted it contained "everything you need, except an operating room") while struggling to open the Quarterdeck hatch. The dogs on the hatch were brand new and the action felt stiff as Hell. "We don't know how long this thing's gonna last." With a metallic *CLUNK*, he managed to swing the dogging arm open, and they climbed through. "It could be weeks, it could be months, it could be years."

Pomona had arrived in Astoria eleven days ago - at least that's when the first victim went apeshit, ripped off his clothing, and attacked a UPS guy who'd had the extraordinary bad luck to arrive at the man's house at exactly the wrong time. UPS Guy got bitten and, in his turn, went apeshit, three and a half hours later, killed a doctor, an orderly, two patients in the ER, and injured five assorted nurses and staff at the hospital - two of whom now resided at the local "Treatment Center," in a disused warehouse near the port. The cops put the first poor bastard down with extreme prejudice.

Things had gotten worse since then, but John, while concerned, was not anxious to sever all ties with civilization just yet. There were plenty of things to do, not the least of which was to pay a call on their former shipmate, Gilbert Farcquar, at his gun store. He wasn't looking forward to it. The guy had been an asshole when they served together, and time had not improved him.

"I'm well aware," Gus said. "And still don't see why we don't get the Hell out now."

They made their way down the starboard ladder to the tiny medical office, where Marcie, John's (long suffering) wife busied herself stocking the cabinets with a variety of illegal narcotics, such as morphine. Having a shit pot of money made "legal" a relative term.

"Precisely because we don't know how long it's going to be," John replied, exasperated. He dropped the First Aid behemoth on the desk with a thunk, then leaned in and kissed his wife on the cheek. "How many times do we have to go through this? No point in falling back on our stores until there's no choice."

"Yeah, well, I'd say the hundred or so cases of infected people and the three times as many deaths and injuries tell me we absolutely have to," Gus insisted. The figures were exaggerated, but it hardly mattered.

"As long as we're careful, no we don't," John said, turning to Gus and pointing toward the small refrigerator, into which Marcie placed a tray of opiates. "Because, my friend, in case you've forgotten, we have vaccine."

6

Christopher Floyd glanced at the e-mail and chuckled. *Well, well,* he thought. *Serves those greedy bastards right.*

He was a tall man, thin, with pale skin and the hint of dark circles under his eyes. His brown hair was short and not quite combed. His clothes were neat, however: white lab coat over a dark blue collared shirt and black slacks. He fingered the keyboard on his laptop and typed an uncharacteristic "Thank you," on the return e-mail. "No," he added, and hit *send*.

He chuckled again.

The original e-mail read: *CDC says a secondary booster is required: 31 millicuries. Optimum time period is three weeks after initial booster, but must be given within 45 days. Eighteen percent infection rate even after primary and initial booster. Need gel powder. Do you have any left?*

He looked at the boxes stacked next to his desk. Three hundred pounds of polyacrylamide gel powder were in them. He'd lied to the "friend" who sent the e-mail. He felt no remorse. No such thing as friends in a zombie apocalypse.

He deleted the e-mail and sat in his empty classroom, thinking. He often did this, though probably shouldn't, since thinking was what landed him at Oregon State - Astoria . Well, thinking, and then doing. The doing was what got him in trouble.

It could have been worse. He could have gone to jail, though very few people knew what he'd done - what he'd *tried* to do. The Dean at Stanford wanted to avoid a scandal, so nothing came of it, but now he was stuck in the hinterland of wannabe bohemian granola chicks, purveyors of modern herbology and chemistry, white guys in dred-locks, and shitkicking former loggers, unemployed, thanks to liberal protests about clear cutting. It wasn't exactly Purgatory, but it was pretty damned close.

He'd been a PHD candidate, once upon a time. He'd been a lot of things, once upon a time, including what many would consider a "Mad Scientist." His PHD in Microbiology was...*cut short*..., but on top of it, he held Master's Degrees in Biochemistry, Microbiology, Neurobiology, Psychopathology, and Psychopharmacology, as well as Bachelors Degrees in Chemistry, Biology, Psychology, and Art History. The last had come about because of the one and only time he had allowed himself to dally with a female. It had not ended well, and he had loathed Art History, but he still ended up with the piece of paper. And so (Art History not withstanding) he had earned the distinction of *Mad Scientist.*

He liked the moniker, although most people meant it as a pejorative. Most people were morons, in his estimation. Judging by IQ points, this was demonstrably true. His Stanford-Binet score was one-seventy-nine, beyond the top of the scale, with ninety to one-hundred-nine being average. He'd always been smart, and (to him, anyway) the rest of the huddled masses squatted just above the level of drooling idiocy. Didn't make them bad people, *per se*, but it meant he usually had to dumb things down for the dullards so they'd understand what were simple concepts.

The classroom door opened and three of those dullards entered. He could remember one of their names - the second through the door, a young man named Thomasine. Not a bad mind - not a particularly good one, either. In front and behind him were a young black man, and a young white woman. Their faces were familiar, since they both attended his Bio 343 Seminar. He hadn't cared to learn their names, and only knew Thomasine's because it was so unusual.

"Got a minute, Professor?" The young man asked.

"A minute," Floyd replied.

They took seats at three of the desks, the other two looking to Thomasine. He cleared his throat. "Uh, we'd like..."

"Let me guess," Floyd interrupted. "You're not here to ask about the homework." He hadn't assigned any. What would have been the point?

"No, sir," the boy replied. "It's about the virus."

"Of course it is," Floyd said, and of course it was. Pomona was the only topic on anyone's lips these days.

"Could you..."

He waved the question off. "It's actually two viruses: a variation on the common cold rhinovirus, and a rhabodovirus, similar to rabies. The first, causes an upper respiratory infection, the second, destroys the brain."

When word of the virus first leaked out, twenty-four hours before the official announcement by the CDC, while the rest of the world lay blissful in its ignorance, most of the major organizations (First World governments, too big to fail banks, technological corporations, and - of course - pharmaceutical companies) wasted no time preparing for what even then seemed the worst case scenario. Oh, they soft-soaped it a bit, saying there was always a chance to stop the outbreak from turning into a global-killing pandemic, but in their heart of hearts, they knew the world's goose was cooked. And so steps were taken, all the while maintaining the facade of international cooperation.

One of those steps, taken by a large tech company in the Pacific Northwest (which shall forever remain nameless) was to hire every microbiologist and biochemist they could lay their hands on - at least all those known to have a certain moral and/or ethical flexibility. And so they called on one Associate Professor Christopher Floyd, and dragged him neither kicking, nor screaming, nor protesting even a little bit, out of the obscurity of the Pacific Northwest hinterland.

Not exactly. He hadn't left Astoria, hadn't left the college, but they had set him up with a lab (in a disused warehouse near the City Wharf), with all the bells and whistles and equipment he wanted, and they paid him in gold - half up front, half upon delivery of the vaccine. The moment he delivered the last of it, they seized all his equipment, all his supplies, and unceremoniously dumped him out onto the street. They neglected to make the final gold payment.

And now, they didn't know about the Secondary Booster - or if they did, it was too goddamned late. Served the fuckers right.

Treating the common cold portion of the outbreak was child's play, and rather beside the point. It became evident from the start, the cold bug was merely the pathfinder for the neurological pathogen, paving the way for it through the respiratory infection it caused. The coughing and inflamation led to bleeding of the lungs, which gave the blood-bourne neurological pathogen a way in. And that sucker was a right evil bastard.

It cooked the human brain in such a way that all higher function was not just impaired, but eliminated - permanently. Even if (and it was one gigantic motherfucker of an if) they found a way to stop the spread of the virus, those inflicted with it were beyond hope or help, because there was no cure.

It didn't just cook the brain; it played with it first, causing delusional behavior, which took many forms. The most common of those was a lovely little mind fuck called *Delusional Parasitosis*. The high fever would cause the sensation known as "prickly heat," which felt like tiny insects crawling on the skin. The cooking brain would then interpret this sensation as *actual* bugs crawling all over the delusional victim, causing them to rip off their clothing in an effort to rid themselves of the imaginary infestation. There were other delusions, ranging from simple memory loss, through dementia, and right to extreme paranoia, but the bug thing was by far the one most manifested.

That, in and of itself, would have been bad enough, twisted enough, but the neurological pathogen didn't stop there. While it was destroying the frontal lobe, it also jacked up the lizard brain - the prehistoric remnant of humanity's savage progenitors. In short, in turned them into vicious, violent, insane animals with no morality, no remorse, and no compunction against killing and eating (if no other food source were available) fellow humans. Mad Scientist though Christopher Floyd happily was, even he thought that was some fucked up shit.

"We know," the woman said, with the insipid know-it-all superiority of pampered youth. "But how did it happen?"

"And what kind of asshole would use it to infect kids?" the black man said.

"A genius," Floyd replied.

"What?" the young woman sputtered with righteous indignation.

"Spare me the outrage," Floyd said, cutting her off.

"You admire the asshole," the black man said.

"Consider the logic," Floyd said, dreading the slow process of making these thick-headed students understand. "Whoever did this either did it for fun, or by design. The complex nature of the viruses, the fact they were genetically engineered, and the logistics of disseminating them throughout the world, all indicate design. Design indicates both a goal, and a plan to achieve that goal." He paused to let the ideas sink in.

They (FBI, CIA, DHS - pick your Alphabet Agency) traced the source of the outbreak at Pomona Junior High to bulk food cans - the kind distributed to all large organizations, such as the military, prisons, and, yes, the public school system. They found traces of both the cold and so-called zombie viruses inside, as well as outside the cans. They traced those cans to *Darwin Industries*, owned by one Mr. Duncan Darwin, who seemed to have disappeared. The fact the man also owned *Darwin Genetics,* and *Darwin Pharmaceuticals*, pretty much sealed the deal. Not that it did any good. The entire world was still fucked.

"If Pomona was the one and only outbreak, the one and only place the virus appeared, then this would have been a simple act of terrorism. Logic, therefore, dictates the goal must have been to destroy human civilization." He looked at their faces. Thomasine showed a glimmer of understanding, the girl continued her moral outrage, and the young black man just looked pissed. None of them spoke.

"There are almost seven billion humans on this planet. Each and every one has their own agenda, each and every one has their own dreams, their own likes and dislikes, their own beliefs. The need to procreate is one of the very few things we all have in common." He paused again to let them digest, then dropped the logic bomb. "What vector could be more efficient than children?"

Everyone involved knew that to slow, let alone stand a chance of stopping the spread, would mean vaccination. Thanks to the anti-vaccine idiocy of the Tea Party, however, the "V" Word was not easily bandied about. Coupled with the fact the only readily available source of antibodies was live, infected human beings (which meant committing murder), and suddenly millions of short-sided, misinformed, ignorant Americans were protesting the one and only thing that could stop the pandemic.

Luckily, Floyd had acquired (through mutual acquaintance) a source at the Portland Morgue, where they had been taking bodies from the *Treatment Centers* (a Devil's Euphemism, if ever there was one) and incinerating them. The "source," would intercept a chosen few before sending them to the crematorium - for a fee, thus cutting Floyd's profit margin. At least he hadn't needed to do any actual killing. As long as the...*subject*...had been dead less than twelve hours and had not been subjected to extremes of heat or cold, the virus bodies remained viable.

The problem then became producing enough vaccine in a short enough time frame before it was too late. As such, the growth or cloning methods of attenuation were out of the question. The process took months, and even the rosiest scenarios only gave the world weeks. This meant using the modernized version of the Pasteur Method: extracting viable virus bodies from a living (more or less) host, passing them through a separation medium, treating them with the proper dose of radiation, adding de-ionized water in the proper amount, and then injecting it into the waiting Corporate arms. This brought up a logistical problem.

He looked at the stacked boxes again. *Chance favors the prepared mind.* The moment he'd heard of the virus and the vaccine, he'd placed an order for as much gel powder as he could get his hands on. The tech firm had supplied him with enough to create the primary dose and booster for all their chosen recipients, but Floyd thought long term, even then, and the powder was the one consumable ingredient not available at almost any drug store.

His mind had always been quick, his memory, photographic. The latter, enabled him to obtain his nine degrees before his twenty-sixth birthday. The former, allowed him to see just how fucked the human race was going to be. He saw the progression as if some cosmic professor charted it out on a white board: announcement, disbelief, anger, finger-pointing, denial, protest, depleted resources, panic, doom, aftermath. His particular interest had been in numbers seven and ten: depleted resources, and aftermath.

He knew there would be howls of protest over the source of the antibodies, which would slow public production (though not the clandestine production for the corporations, who wouldn't care). This slowed production would lead to wider spread of the virus, which would, in turn, lead to panic when the morons realized they were doomed. This panic would cause a run on the market for the consumable products necessary to create the vaccine, which would have already been depleted

by those who had the wherewithal and moral ambivalence to hire people
like Floyd, and so he had planned ahead.

He looked at the stacked boxes again, thought of their contents
and smiled. He hadn't paid for it himself. Polyacrylamide gel powder
was expensive stuff. Luckily, the College had a credit card. Of course,
things would go badly if they received the bill before he managed to get
away with the fruits of his foresight, but plans were already laid to make
his escape this very night. Christopher Floyd planned ahead.

"So what do we do?" Thomasine asked.

"Run," Floyd replied.

"Just like that?" The young woman asked. "Drop everything and
run?" She and her sanctimonious attitude were getting on his nerves.

"Just like that," Floyd repeated, then thought better of it. "Before
you run, find a cabin up in the mountains, away from any populated
areas. Bring as much food and water as you can, then barricade yourself
inside."

"Then what?" Thomasine asked.

"Wait."

"Till Hell freezes over?" The black man said.

"Till the plague is over," Floyd replied. "Till the zombies die
out."

"And when will that be?" The young woman asked, the derision
evident in her voice. He wanted to slap the little bitch.

"How the Hell should I know?" He snapped. He'd had enough.
"I'm busy," he added, pointing toward the door. "Feel free to let it
smack you in the ass."

The woman bolted to her feet, working herself toward what Floyd felt sure would be a righteous retort, but Thomasine grabbed her arm, and pulled her toward the exit. He, at least, seemed to have enough active brain cells to grasp the situation. He might survive, with a little skill and a lot of luck. The other two wouldn't last a week. They left without another word.

Professor Christopher Floyd was okay with that. He was also okay with the knowledge that the selfish corporate bastards would just about now be finding out they hadn't made enough vaccine. They needed a secondary booster, which needed to be filtered through the separation medium of polyacrylamide gel, which was now in severely short supply. He looked at the boxes and started to laugh. He was sitting on a gold mine.

7

"It's about time you got here, Jones," LT Rick (the Dick) Medavoy said in his slightly nasal and always annoying voice as Jonesy entered the Wardroom. He'd just gotten word the XO wanted him at this meeting about five minutes ago. He'd been back on the Quarterdeck supervising more supply loading - something he'd been doing all damned day long - and the XO knew it.

"Sorry," he said, not meaning it, then added "sir," as a sort of afterthought. In his opinion, LT Medavoy, their Executive Officer, was an asshat fucktard with delusions of grandeur, though this was just his opinion. Others had expressed worse opinions, but since Jonesy was a senior petty officer, he couldn't agree or disagree - officially. Didn't stop him from thinking it, though.

Gathered around the long, rectangular dining table in the Wardroom were the XO, the Engineer, CWO4 Chuck Kincade, the Bosun, CWO2 Eric Larson, the Comms Officer, LTJG Craig Bloominfeld, the Supply Chief, SKC Duane Robinson, and, sitting next to the only open chair, ENS. Molly Gordon. Jonesy did not see ENS. Mark Ryan, his OPS Officer, but then, he hadn't expected to. The kid (he looked younger than the eighteen year-old boots straight from Cape May) had flown out on leave just last night.

"Well hurry up and sit down," the XO snapped. "Ensign Ryan won't be with us."

"Is it true his plane went down?" Bloominfeld asked. The two were close friends.

Medavoy hesitated for the briefest of moments, as if checking to see if he had any actual humanity inside of him, then, having found none, said: "That's the word we got," and flapped his hand as if waving away a gnat. "Let's get this meeting started."

He pointed to Molly and said: "Introduce yourself."

"Molly Gordon," she replied, in what Jonesy thought was a small voice. He knew she had to be nervous as Hell.

In the first place, the XO was a dick (so his name was not just a happy coincidence), and he felt sure the bastard had done his level best to intimidate the crap out of her in the hour or so since Jonesy dropped her off at the Ship's Office. In the second place, everything about this situation was new to her: the ship, its officers, the fact they were rushing to get underway in response to a zombie apocalypse... Anybody would be intimidated by it all.

"I'd say I was looking forward to all this, but under the circumstances..." she said, squaring her shoulders and making eye contact with each person around the table in turn.

And in the third place, Jonesy thought, she's baring up pretty well, all things considered. There was a reason he'd liked her when they were on the *Healy*.

Yes, he had known her from his days in Alaska, and yes, he had liked her then, even though she was both jailbait, and the niece of his QM1, but that was beside the point. And okay, he had really liked her butt, he thought, in the interests of full disclosure to his own psyche. She *did* have a really nice butt. *However*, she was also intelligent and funny and cool and, as it happened, a real badass on the sparring mat, which was how their affair started, in the first place.

The thing about standing watch in the middle of the night in the middle of the ocean, is that you end up with lots and lots of time to either wax selfish in the dark-clothed self-absorption of a ship's bridge, while the rest of the crew is dreaming sailor's dreams, or you can talk (albeit quietly) with the other people on watch. And so they had talked. And in talking, they discovered each had been into martial arts during their respective childhoods.

He hadn't known this about her before - hadn't really thought of her as anything but a cute kid before (primarily because of her *persona non nookie* status as his boss's niece), and found it rather compelling when he did find out. One more thing they had in common.

She had learned *Krav Maga,* the Israeli fighting technique developed by Imi Lichtenfeld, during his defense of the Jews in Czechoslovakia in the 1930's. Jonesy, on the other hand, had the great fortune to be living in Santa Monica as a kid, and so had access to the *Inosanto Academy,* where he trained in Filipino *Kali* and *Escrima,* as well as bits and pieces of *Jeet Kune Do,* the art created by the immortal Bruce Lee, and then passed to Dan Inosanto. Jonesy liked to boast he'd been given the honor of having his ass royally kicked by Dan Inosanto, himself.

Okay... bullshit. He wasn't anywhere near good enough to spar with The Master. He had, however been good enough to spar with Molly, who successfully kicked his ass the first time they met on the mat.

This might have been because, during the match, he'd been trying to cover the unsightly bulge in his sweat pants all the tussling with a really good-looking woman had caused, but she'd still kicked his ass. One thing led to another, however, and the temptation had just been too damned, well, *tempting,* so he put the moves on the not yet commissioned cadet, and the rest, as they say, was history.

Technically speaking, they violated all sorts of regulations againt fraternization, but the *Healy,* with its mixed male and female crew, had been a big, red, *Love Boat,* adorned with a Coast Guard racing stripe. The Command wisely kept to the adage *Never give an order you know won't be obeyed,* and so everybody turned a blind eye to the many and varied hookups during their deployment.

But now she was here, sitting next to him again, and he could smell her scent, and feel the warmth and nearness of her body, Jonesy had to admit (if only to his innermost self) that their four month trip to the Arctic had been more than just a hookup.

Gulp, he thought, then turned his attention to the meeting.

"Did you run into any...difficulties...during your flight?" LTJG Bloominfeld asked. He was an affable officer: tall and thin and (prior to the insanity of their current situation) only concerned with getting flight school, the odds of which were now slim, indeed.

One plane crashed, they knew for sure, when apparently one of the pilots turned and went zombie during the flight. The plane ended up spread all over a field in Pennsylvania. Another flight simply disappeared. One minute it was there, crossing the Atlantic; the next, it was gone. And now, apparently, the flight from Honolulu to San Francisco, carrying one of their own, had crashed. No survivors.

"None," Molly replied. "They gave us all nasal antibody tests prior to boarding." She paused to let the information sink in. "That means I'm not infected, in case anybody was wondering."

What she did not include, could never include on penalty of going to prison for capital murder, was that the nasal tests were for common cold antibodies, not the blood pathogen. If they'd tested for the blood pathogen, she would have lit up their tester like the Vegas Strip. It would have done so because she, unbeknownst to almost everyone everywhere, had been vaccinated with attenuated vaccine, made from the spinal chords of infected human beings.

Conflicted, thy name is Molly. On the one hand, the antibodies coursing through her bloodstream and giving her immune system the necessary target to fight off the neurological pathogen, originated in the spinal column of what had once been a live, vibrant human being with a family and a future and dreams and all the other life-stuff she, herself took for granted. That person had been killed - murdered - to provide vaccine. On the other hand, the vaccine kept her from turning into a naked, raving, homicidal lunatic, so...

The assembled officers and chiefs (and Jonesy) didn't actually sigh in relief, Molly thought, but she did detect the slightest relaxing of tensed shoulders around the table.

She supposed she should feel guilty, as well as conflicted. In the first place, she'd just come aboard, just met these people who would be her shipmates (Jonesy notwithstanding), and who would need to trust her, and she was starting out by hiding something monumental about both her character and her physical well-being. In the second place, she was in possession of knowledge that could very well save their lives, and she had no intention of ever telling them about it. Because, in the third place, if they knew, they'd probably arrest her on the spot for conspiracy to commit murder.

She would debate her lack of guilty feelings later. In the meantime, she was keeping her mouth shut.

"They've been talking about closing both Portland and Seattle to air traffic," she continued. "The jury was still out, but it could happen any time now."

Jonesy sensed a certain wariness in her voice, but he supposed it could just be the stress of the current situation. He was delighted and impressed to see her power on, regardless.

"Whidbey Island was still operational," she added, referring to the Military Airlift Command field at the combined Army and Air Force base.

"Yeah, well, welcome aboard," SKC Robinson said. He was a very large, very in shape black man, with a deep, sonorous voice. "God knows we need you, what with Mr. Ryan..." His voice trailed off.

"Yes, yes," the XO said. "I'm sure we're all saddened by it," he added, not sounding the least bit bothered. "But we have more important matters to discuss."

Bastard, Jonesy thought. Everybody liked Ryan. Hard not to. The kid had been eager and helpful, and willing to learn. He'd gotten a lot of ribbing when he became the senior Ensign, after Bloominfeld made JG, but he'd taken it all in stride. The "promotion" (a military in-joke, if ever there was one) to Bull Ensign made him OPS Boss, but it hadn't gone to his head.

The same could not be said for Rick (the Dick) Medavoy.

The fucktard positively delighted in the power of being the *Executive Officer*. In the Navy, he'd have been just another fucking Lieutenant - just another zero to be bypassed if you wanted to get anything done. But in the Coast Guard, and with a crew of only seven officers and forty-one enlisted, being a Lieutenant meant something.

Some managed the power just fine. Jonesy suspected their CO, LCDR Russell Sparks, had been a decent LT. He made a decent skipper, and wasn't a martinet like some of the power-mad assholes he'd met. Medavoy, on the other hand....

"We're scheduled to fuel at the Pearl Harbor POL at 0300 tomorrow. We need to be underway not later than 0030," the slimy bastard continued.

There goes a good night's sleep, Jonesy thought. What else was new? Having duty the day before getting underway always sucked. This went double for getting underway in an apocalypse.

CWO4 Chuck Kincade said: "Actually, they decided to send the barge over, so we won't need to get underway. Same time, though. 0300."

"That would have been good information to have before the meeting," Medavoy snapped.

The man liked to rule by intimidation. This worked with the junior officers, and certainly worked with the enlisted, who had no recourse against whatever fucked up thing the asshole dropped on their poor heads. The same could not be said for Chief Warrant Officer Kincade.

"I got the information just before the meeting," he said, with barely-disguised contempt. He was in his early forties, with mousy brown hair and eyes, and an expression that always made Jonesy think he was suffering from constipation. "And you didn't need to know about it until the meeting." He said this last with a tone of challenge in his voice. But then (discretion being the better part of valor) he continued in a conciliatory tone, shrugging. "Figured you had enough on your plate, so I didn't bother you with it."

Kincade stopped short of apologizing, or of seeming in any way contrite, and Jonesy admired him for it. The XO, on the other hand, did not seem placated (if his sour expression was any indication), but there wasn't a whole lot he could do. Warrant Officers were commissioned by an Act of Congress. Medavoy might be the Big Fish in a two-hundred-and-twenty-five-foot pond, but against Congress, he wasn't jack.

Medavoy glared for a moment, as if trying to regain his dominance, saw it wasn't working, and then, with a near-growl, said: "Where are we on stores?"

The question was barked, and Jonesy knew perfectly well at whom the dog yapped: BM1 Socrates Jones, junior-most person in the room. If the self-important prick couldn't throw his weight at a Warrant, then he'd just take it out on the enlisted pukes. The knowledge pissed Jonesy off, and, being the ornery, contrarian son of a bitch he had always been, he decided on a bit of passive resistance.

"Oh! You're asking me," he said, in mock-surprise. He shrugged. "The stores are coming in, the crew is loading them up the gangway." He shrugged again. "What else is coming or where we are, as far as completely loaded, I have no idea." He looked around the table, his eyes falling on the none-too pleased XO last. "Nobody bothered to give me the information. The trucks come in, I get them unloaded. Beyond that, I haven't got a clue." This did not make Medavoy happy, but there wasn't anything he could do about it, either. The facts were as Jonesy had stated them. Nobody had felt he needed to know. He was okay with that. If the XO wasn't...?

The XO stared at him a moment longer, then turned his baleful glare on Chief Robinson. "Well?"

"How many trucks have we unloaded?" Robinson asked, looking at Jonesy.

"Two," he replied. "One of produce, and the other of canned goods, which they're working on now."

Robinson nodded. "We have another one of meat, which should be here..." He looked at his watch. "...any time now. And then we've got pallets of disaster supplies coming this afternoon." He looked at CWO2 Larsen, the Bosun. "We'll need to pop the buoy deck hatch."

Eric Larsen was a medium man: medium height, medium weight, medium looks. If you looked away from the guy, you might forget what he looked like. He nodded. "We also have the ammo load coming in at 1700," he said. "And while we're on the subject...Judging from the manifest, it looks like we're getting ready to go to war."

"How so?" Medavoy asked.

"We're already fully loaded," he said. "With what we have coming in, we'll have twice our normal compliment."

"And?" the XO snapped.

"And isn't it about time we discussed the elephant in the room?" CWO4 Chuck Kincade said.

"Which is?"

"What's our mission, sir?" Jonesy asked.

8

"Your mission," Captain Clark Winstead said to the assembled officers, "is threefold." He looked pale and nervous. And he kept flicking glances at his boss.

Rear Admiral Charles Deguine normally looked like the male subject of the painting *American Gothic* - an impression that belied his bright mind and good nature. Now he looked distracted and flushed, and...*scared*.

None of this boded well for LCDR Russell Sparks, Commanding Officer of the USCGC *Sassafras*. He looked the way a skipper should: tall and strong and confident, although *confident* was not what he felt at the moment.

The Captain continued. "First, preserve Force Continuity. We're not going to do anyone any good if we don't remain operational." They were assembled in the District 14 Conference Room - a long, narrow office space, with the required nondescript white walls, unimaginative framed posters of sailing ships, and the ubiquitous motivational screeds about teamwork and perseverance. Included in the meeting were the skippers of the *Kukui, Assateague,* and *Galveston Island.*

"Second, conduct Security and Search and Rescue as needed. There are a lot of people in boats heading out to sea in an effort to escape the plague. As usual, about two-thirds aren't going to be experienced. Accidents will happen. Because there is panic, and because panic breeds chaos, there will be people more than willing to take advantage. Stomp on it - hard. Zero tolerance of piracy."

Zero Tolerance? What the Hell did that mean? Free fire? Kill 'em all and sink their boats?

"Uh, sir...?" LCDR David Gaffney, CO of *Kukui* began. He was a small man, with sandy blonde hair and alarming blue eyes.

"And before you ask," Captain Winstead interrupted. "Yes. Prosecute with prejudice." He paused, cast another worried glance at the Admiral, who thus far had remained mute, though he squirmed in his seat. "We can't officially say it's open season on pirates, but you're going to be out there on your own, and we're going to have our hands full here." Another glance at the Admiral, who seemed about ready to climb out of his own skin. "Use your best judgement."

Vague orders with unrestricted power...Not a good precedent, Sparks thought, but as usual, he kept his own council. Best way to do things. Coast Guard commands afloat were independent by their very nature, what with operating in remote areas, reacting to conditions at the scene, and the only real supervision coming from a voice on the radio hundreds, if not thousands of miles away. Of course, you were up shit creek if you screwed the pooch, but as long as you got the job done, all sins were usually forgiven. Usually.

"And third, Disaster Response. We don't know - nobody knows - how bad this is going to get. We don't even know if Honolulu will remain viable."

That one word: *viable,* spoke volumes.

Sand Island, in Honolulu Harbor, was their home base. The District Office, itself, was housed in the Federal Building in downtown Hono, but everything else was on The Island, which housed the ships, the small boat Station, the Communications Station, and the District Command Center, along with the Logistics Command, Office of Aids to Navigation, the Marine Environmental Response Team (MERT), the Tactical Law Enforcement Team (TACLET), and Sector Honolulu. The Air Station, with its compliment of HH-60 helicopters and two C-130 airplanes, was over on Barber's Point. Toss in the Air Force Base at Hickam, the Army Base at Schofield Barracks, Marine Base at Kaneohe, Navy Base at Pearl Harbor, the Submarine Base, and various other military installations spread throughout the Island of Oahu, and what you had was one heavily armed piece of real estate.

If the Captain was questioning whether or not Honolulu would remain viable...?

"And the infected?" LT Gary Rhiannon, skipper of the *Assateague* asked.

Winstead flicked his nervous eyes toward the Admiral, who was scratching his arms and chest, and wore an almost feral expression on his flushed face. The man moaned.

"Rules of Engagement are...uh..." the Captain began to say, but then the Admiral let out a howl, and started to tear at his uniform shirt. The fruit salad of ribbons popped off his chest and bounced across the table, knocking a water glass into Winstead's lap.

There was a moment of stunned immobility, as the sheer irrationality of the situation sank in, before everybody seemed to act at once, thrusting up and away from the table, tossing chairs aside in their haste to get the Hell away from their insane Flag Officer - a scene straight out of Bedlam.

The thought *he's turning* flashed across Russell Sparks' forebrain as he bounced against the wall and nearly tripped over the chair Rhiannon had just vacated. Everyone was up, everyone moved in seemingly every direction at once, except for the Yeoman First Class, who'd been taking the meeting minutes. She sat, dumbfounded and frozen, a look of both confusion and horror on her face.

"Move, damn you!" Sparks yelled at her, but too late.

The Admiral leapt, teeth flashed, and Sparks heard the flesh on her neck rip, as a fountain of blood spurted through Charles Deguine's snarling mouth. A jet of it arced across the table, right into Captain Winstead's face. He jerked back, as if to avoid what already happened, and smacked his head against the far wall with an audible *thunk*.

The others hesitated to act, either from shock, or years of ingrained obedience to the military hierarchy. They all looked toward the Captain for guidance, but the Captain just stared and blinked at the blood coursing down into his eyes.

Move, you idiot, a voice shouted inside Sparks' own brain, and he lunged toward the snarling Admiral. He had always considered himself a *man of action* - whatever the Hell that meant - and so he'd acted, and the result was to be tangled up on the ground with a one hundred and ninety pound, fifty-eight year-old screaming animal, who had once been the District Commander.

The keening mass of arms and legs and snapping teeth (even there, in extremis, Sparks couldn't bring himself to acknowledge the word *zombie*) felt like he held a pissed off banshee in his arms. "Help me, Goddamnit!" he shouted, as teeth snapped a scant half-inch from his fingers, which were slick with the still-spurting blood. His free hand grabbed the man by what little hair he had on his head and yanked the snarling mouth away, as somebody - Chambers, from the *Galveston Island*, he thought - piled onto his back.

Out of the corner of his eye, Russell saw the pointed and shining toe of a neatly polished dress shoe pulverize the Admiral's nose, pull back, then do it again, and again, and then it was over. The man stopped struggling, as if some internal switch had been flicked to *OFF*.

A door opened somewhere off to his right. The screaming began.

9

Jonesy leaned against the shore tie transformer that gave power to the Sass when in port, and watched the poor enlisted pukes lugging heavy cases of frozen meat from the truck to the brow and onto the ship. His head hurt. He felt like his ass should hurt, as well, since the XO had shoved a gigantic pile of horseshit up it at the end of the meeting.

"The mission is to do whatever the fuck you're told to do," Medavoy had snapped, in answer to Jonesy's question. This hadn't set well with the others seated at the table in the Wardroom, but they all knew the XO, and so knew challenging his asinine response would only lead to far more trouble than it was worth. Even Jonesy had refrained from sarcasm, which he thought showed remarkable restraint.

He hadn't liked the XO from the moment he'd walked into the man's small office and saw the derision upon the bastard's face as he flipped through Jonesy's service record. All a show, of course. Medavoy had known who he was. Everybody on The Island knew who he was. Hard not to, after the M/V *Haika Maru.*

It had been a freighter, filled with illegals, mostly women, mostly very young women, and no small amount of heroin.. Fairly routine, as such things went. But then one of the assholes pulled a gun.

He shoved the memory away. *Best not to dwell on it*, the shrinks repeated, over and over, and over. About the only intelligent thing those psychobabble weasels said.

It had been a good shoot. Everybody knew it. And he had been cleared - officially. But in the Blame Game of political bullshit, they couldn't just leave well enough alone, and so he'd been placed on Admin Leave.

This left him in the limbo of Administrative dipshits who couldn't make a decision if their lives depended on it, and so he sat, doing nothing, going nowhere. Of course, if you had to be in Purgatory, Honolulu was a pretty damned nice place to be, but the feeling of uselessness grated on his psyche. The seemingly endless time led to idle hands, which led to frequent trips to the liquor store. His liver hurt, thinking about it.

And then BM1/OPS David McGinness (his predecessor on the *Sassafras*) did something incredibly stupid, and the billet on the Sass came open. *When God closes a door, he opens a window, or some such bullshit*, he thought, as he shifted his lean to a more comfortable position on the transformer.

This was not a religious thought. Jonesy had no religious thoughts. Not that religion was a bad thing, *per se*, but it wasn't - and never had been - his cup of ecclesiastical tea. He believed in...*something*...just not what they taught in Sunday School.

All of which was rather beside the original point, which was the rat-bastard-ness of one LT *DICK* Medavoy.

LCDR Sparks, whom Jonesy had known when he was a LTjg, had personally approved the transfer, but Medavoy (ever the asshole) hadn't been happy. He thought that a TACLET member of the Armed Forces of the United States who dared to actually use the weapon he'd been issued, and who'd been placed on Administrative Leave following his psych eval, had to be crazy, and, therefore, was not to be trusted. This distrust had been evident from Day One, Moment One.

A siren blared in the distance; just background noise, the urban song of city life, barely worth the electrical energy to pass the knowledge between his synapses, but some tingle of instinct tickled Jonesy's spine. He dismissed it, and tried to go back to his intellectual cataloging of the many and varied faults of the Sass's XO, but then he heard another siren. And another. And another.

Then he saw the column of smoke.

Honolulu was beginning to burn.

10

1954Z18MAY
FM: COMCOGUARDPACAREA
TO: USCGC POLAR STAR (WAGB 10)

SUBJ: POMONA

1. SUMMARY:

> A. AS DISCUSSED IN MSG 1341Z16MAY, THE VIRUS HAS
> BEEN DECLARED A WILDFIRE OUTBREAK BY CDC.

> B. AN ATTENUATED VACCINE FOR THE
> NEUROLOGICAL PATHOGEN HAS BEEN DEVELOPED,
> BUT ONLY IN LIMITED QUANTITIES, DUE TO THE
> INADEQUATE SUPPLIES OF NON-HUMAN HIGHER
> ORDER PRIMATES FROM WHICH TO DRAW VIRUS
> BODIES.

> C. THERE IS, HOWEVER, NO CURE. ONCE THE SUBJECT
> REACHES FULL NEUROLOGICAL STAGE, THE DAMAGE
> IS IRREVERSIBLE.

> D. INFECTED TREATMENT CENTERS HAVE PROVEN TO
> BE A STOP-GAP SOLUTION OF LIMITED UTILITY.
> SECURITY AT THESE CENTERS HAS BROKEN DOWN IN
> MOST URBAN AREAS.

> E. EVACUATIONS ARE IMMINENT.

2. ACTION

> A. YOUR RULES OF ENGAGEMENT REMAIN THE SAME:
> DISABLE, RESTRAIN, SECURE.

B. DEADLY FORCE ONLY AUTHORIZED IN EXTREMIS, WHEN LIFE OF SELF OR OTHERS WOULD BE THREATENED BY NOT USING DEADLY FORCE.

C. USE YOUR BEST JUDGEMENT.

D. AS VIRUS IS HIGHLY CONTAGIOUS, AND AS YOU AND YOUR CREW HAVE NOT BEEN EXPOSED, YOU ARE DIRECTED TO PROCEED TO APIA, GUAM, UNDER STRICTEST NBC PROTOCOLS, TO TOP OFF FUEL.

E. DO NOT TAKE ON ANY OTHER STORES, AS PACKAGING MAY HAVE BEEN CONTAMINATED.

F. TAKE UP STATION IN POSITION: 14-7-25N/177-12-34W TO ACT AS FUEL AND SUPPLY POINT FOR HEC AND OTHER COGARD SHIPS AS DIRECTED.

G. AWAIT FURTHER ORDERS.

H. GOOD LUCK.

Captain Gideon Hall, Commanding Officer of the four hundred foot Icebreaker, *Polar Star*, stared at the message in disbelief. It seemed absurd, if not outright insane.

Head to Guam for fuel? They still carried half of their one-point-three million gallon full load. They hadn't even bothered to arrange for fuel in Australia, to which they now apparently would not be going after the two month deployment in Antarctica.

Speaking of which, they'd been OUTCONUS for six goddamned months. And now, PACAREA wanted them to go sit in the middle of nowhere, in the middle of the vast Pacific Ocean to act as a gas station for other ships? With no liberty for the crew after two months in the ice?

In a Zombie Apocalypse?

He hadn't wanted to use the "Z" Word, but what the Hell else could you call hoards of naked, screaming, violent former humans who wanted to take a bite out of you, if not zombies?

Hadn't seen any direct signs of it himself, and there hadn't been any reported cases before they left McMurdo, but that was three weeks ago. A lot had changed.

Polar Star was fitted with a satellite Internet Receiver. It didn't work all the time, due to the remote locations the ship tended to traverse, and because the Pacific Ocean was really damned big and their ship was really damned small, but it did work sometimes, so they had seen some of the videos, which hadn't seemed real. The general consensus among the crew was that it must be an elaborate hoax, but this soon went the way of the Dodo, once it came under the intellectual scrutiny of anyone with active brain cells. If it had been a hoax, it would not have been *everywhere* you looked.

There wasn't one Social Media Site, one News Site, one Government Site that didn't carry almost nothing but mention of the Pomona Virus. Even some of the retail sites had gotten into the act, offering survival kits and other Apocalypse Supplies.

It was, therefore, real.

It must be bad, if PACAREA was ordering full Nuclear, Biological, and Chemical protocols. They must be thinking worst case scenario, if they were ordering *Polar Star* to take station and wait.

They think the world is going to fall.

The thought flashed across his mind, and then was quickly shunted aside. Couldn't be. The whole world couldn't fall. Impossible! And yet...

He picked up the phone and called the bridge.

"Bridge, Norton," the Nav Watch, BM3/OPS Charlie Norton answered.

"Have all officers assemble in the Wardroom."

11

Jonesy couldn't see anything but the smoke, off to the east, but there was a lot of it. *Somewhere on Kapiolani Boulevard*, he thought. *Maybe King Street, but probably Kapiolani. Ala Moana Mall...?*

The location didn't make much difference in the grand scheme of things. Long ago, he adopted the attitude: if it didn't effect him, he didn't care - one of his many defense mechanisms: a weapon, like his sarcasm, to combat the general fucked-up-ness of life. The fact this attitude lay at odds with his current occupation was an irony he tried not to examine. *Cognitive Dissonance is your friend...*

He tore his eyes away from the column of smoke and glanced toward the chain of enlisted scum who were supposed to be loading stores up the brow. Instead, they were staring at the burning city.

"Quit skylarking," he barked, fully aware of his goose being far better than their gander. "Those stores ain't going to load themselves!"

He felt a mild - *very* mild - pang of guilt for being such a dick, but the crew knew he was just playing the part. At least he *hoped* they knew it. Whatever the case, they got back to work.

He was about to turn away and resume his contemplation of the mass-conflagration on shore, when his eye caught sight of Molly. She stood up on the bridge wing - *his* bridge wing - and stared into the distance. Thinking of her as he paid no attention whatsoever to the unloading, made him feel...conflicted. She was an officer; he was enlisted. *And never the twain shall meet, as they say (whoever the fuck THEY are)*, he mused.

The bitch of it was, he liked her. Love was an easy enough thing to fall into, at least for him. He'd done it plenty of times. Of course, those times almost always involved far more alcohol than was either safe or sane for the average wildebeest, but that was just a detail. Endorphins were released by neurotransmitters in response to a biological imperative, or so he'd read. Sounded like bullshit then, and still did now, but it fit, he supposed.

He'd felt the fluttering of the heart, experienced the pleasant distraction of adoring the *feminine divine*. It was fun, and usually resulted in his getting laid, so, all to the good. However; love was a piece of invariably-ending-in-disaster cake, and he'd *liked* Molly.

The simplest relationship in all of human interaction was the one between two heterosexual males. There were no rules, no expectations, no stony silences if one forgot the other's birthday. They didn't ask you to talk about the relationship. They didn't give a damn about the relationship. It just was. It existed simply because two individuals wanted it to.

If you like each other, if you enjoy each others' company, you hang out together. Maybe get a few beers. Maybe watch some form of athletic activity. Maybe get shitfaced, falling down drunk and sing loud and off key until the neighbors call to complain about all the caterwauling. What you do not do - ever - is burst into tears and blubber about not fulfilling each others' needs. You are friends. Nothing more. Nothing less. You certainly do not tell the other they should never call, never write; that they should walk away and never turn back, because the relationship "just won't work."

And so now he was back to the sour feeling in his gut. And the pain in his ass.

He blew out a sigh, ending in the ever-popular word: "Fuck."

Something caught his eye. More like some *one:* a single figure staggering down the pier toward him. *Is that...the Captain...?*

It was. Jonesy broke into a run.

"Get the Doc out here!" He shouted, over his shoulder. "And the XO!"

12

The Captain looked...*wrong.* Jonesy couldn't immediately identify the nature of the wrong-ness, but he felt it, nonetheless. LCDR Sparks was still a good distance down the pier - close enough to be recognized, but not with any detail. He was staggering, however, and that was enough to make this urgent.

The man was covered in blood. His face was clean; his uniform was anything but, and it was ripped in three or four places. Jonesy got close enough to see Sparks' face: white and hollow-eyed, with apparent shock; but the CO held up a traffic cop's hand to stop him.

"Don't come any closer," he said, his voice raspy and unsteady, as was his balance. He swayed in place, jerking slightly, not quite with any rhythm, as if his entire body twitched with nerves.

For once in his life, Socrates Jones had no idea what to say. The man - his Commanding Officer, a man he admired and even liked (as much as anyone could be said to feel the emotion for someone so exalted as a ship's Captain) - was a mess of blood and shock and unreality.

This shit didn't happen. Forget the craziness about it being a zombie apocalypse. That had its own brand of unreality. Forget the entire world as he knew it coming undone in a wave of madness. This was an absolute crack in the framework of reality.

"Captain...?" Jonesy asked.

"Get the XO," Sparks said.

"He's on the way, sir," Jonesy replied. "What...?"

"The Admiral, he's..." the man began, but then Doc Harris came running up to them. "Stay back!" Sparks shouted this time, and then he crumpled, his body folding in on itself as he fell to his knees. "Don't come any closer," he said again.

"To Hell with that!" Harris said, striding up to him.

He took the Captain by the arm and tried to pull him to his feet, but Sparks was dead weight. "Help me, Jones!" Harris yelled.

"Don't you dare!" Sparks said, his voice suddenly becoming firm and commanding. "Doc, get away from me. I could be infected."

"What the Hell is going on, Petty Officer Jones?" The annoying nasal whine of Medavoy's voice rang out behind Jonesy, as the man himself came puffing up to them. "What...?"

"Dick, good..." Sparks said, finally allowing Doc Harris to help him to his feet.

"What happened, sir?" the XO asked, in his very best ass-kissing voice. It made Jonesy want to puke, every time it reared its sycophantic head.

"The Admiral...*turned*," Sparks said, his voice betraying the shock already writ large upon his face. "We had to...kill him."

The news hit Jonesy square in the gut. *Kill the Admiral? What kind of bullshit was this?* He shook his head. *Didn't matter.*

As if a switch flipped inside his head, a cold, rational calm fell over him. This was reality. This was black and white, either/or. Forget the questions, forget the uncertainty, forget the unreality of the basic situation, and deal with it.

"What do you need done, Captain?" He said.

Doc pulled Sparks over to the Government vehicle Duke had used to pick up Molly, and leaned him against it. The Captain rubbed his face with both hands, then pulled them away and looked at them, as if they belonged to someone else.

Doc Harris took him by the wrist to check his pulse. Jonesy couldn't tell what the pulse was, of course, but the expression on Doc's face told him the answer was not good.

"Captain?" LT Medavoy asked. He sounded nervous. Of course, he usually sounded nervous, Jonesy thought - at least when the bastard wasn't living up to the phallic symbol of his first name.

Sparks blinked and looked first at Medavoy, then Doc, and finally Jonesy. "We're losing it," he said, finally.

The remark had so many potential meanings Jonesy couldn't begin to count. Had they lost "it," and gone nuts? A distinct possibility, given both the general sense of impending apocalypse and the battered and bloody condition of the CO's uniform. His own grip on sanity was feeling a bit tenuous at the moment, but he didn't think it was what the man meant.

So, what was "it?" The base? Sand Island? Oahu? The entire fucking world?

"Not sure how much longer things are going to last," Sparks continued. "Word from the mainland is bad. Los Angeles is overrun. San Francisco is almost there. New York, Philadelphia, Miami, Atlanta... The news from everywhere is bad." He said this while staring at the ground, though Jonesy doubted the man was even seeing the concrete pier. "They haven't evacuated Washington, D. C., yet, but it's coming."

"And Hawaii, sir?" Medavoy asked.

Sparks looked up at him and grimaced. He shrugged. "We've been ordered to get underway," he said, as if the answer was obvious - which, in a way, it was.

"What happened at the Staff Meeting, sir?" Jonesy asked. Medavoy snapped him a dirty look he caught with the corner of his eye, but ignored.

"The Admiral turned, full neurological, and started biting people. We tried to subdue him, but..." He let the thought drift, and just shrugged, instead. He shook his head, as if to clear the memory, then took a deep breath and drew himself up. "LT Medavoy, you are to lock the ship down. Nobody on, nobody off. Issue filter masks to all personnel, and get the rest of the stores on ASAP, then pull in the brow."

He looked at Doc Harris. "They've discovered large doses of Vitamin C can inhibit the cold virus. Inhibit the cold, and it stops the respiratory infection, the lungs don't bleed and the neurological pathogen doesn't take hold. Sometimes. It's not much, but... Not sure how you're going to do it - maybe force feed the crew orange juice. Do the best you can."

"Yes, sir," Harris said.

The CO looked last at Jonesy. "Jonesy," he began, and Socrates was taken aback to see him approach the next order with...what...? Regret? "The rules of engagement have changed. Control and containment are not viable. Once the person reaches full neurological, the only thing you can do is terminate."

Jonesy had always heard the cliche of the color draining from someone's face. He'd never seen it, and never felt it. Until now. The color drained from his face. He couldn't see it happen, obviously, but he felt as if someone had opened a valve in his head and drained all the blood from his skull.

Terminate? What the fuck? And why the Hell is he telling me?

He knew the answer, of course. He was the obvious choice, the *only* choice, but it didn't change the situation away from one gigantic bitch of a shit sandwich.

"Get with Petty Officer Peterson, and make sure," he said, and made as if to reach out to Jonesy, but then pulled back and brought his arms to his chest, as if holding them away from the temptation to touch anyone else - to *infect* anyone else. "Make fucking sure you avoid getting bitten," he said. His voice was quiet, though urgent, but he might as well have yelled it through a loud hailer, for the impact of his words. The man never swore - never - and he certainly never dropped an F-Bomb, but he had then. Jonesy paid attention.

"The bites are extremely infectious. If you get bitten, there's about a ninety-nine percent chance you'll turn. And Jonesy," he said, his voice taking on an even more urgent tone, which Socrates hadn't thought possible. "You can't turn. This crew is going to need you - maybe more than anyone else on board."

His eyes softened, and Jonesy saw the regret in them again. And it was regret - the gut-wrenching regret of someone whose job it is to order someone else to do something both completely necessary, and completely horrible. "You're a strong man, Jonesy. I've seen you. I've watched you. You joke a lot, and you're way too much of a smart-aleck, but there's a strength to your character few other people I've known possess."

He hated praise - almost as much as he hated getting his ass chewed - and he especially hated praise in front of witnesses. But this time, in this circumstance, he didn't feel the flush, didn't feel the embarrassment, didn't feel anything, other than a cold, hard resolve.

"You're going to need that strength Jonesy," Sparks said again.

"Yes, sir."

"You're going to want to be in full rig. No exposed flesh. Don't get bit."

"Yes, sir."

"Captain, sir," Medavoy said. "Are you putting him in charge of our security?" It was said with the proper degree of respect - Medavoy would never smart ass the CO - but Jonesy could hear the underlying tone of incredulity, as if the very idea of Jones - an enlisted man - being in charge of something so vital as the security of the ship and her crew was ludicrous.

Fucking asshat, Jonesy mused.

"Yes, XO, I am," the CO said. "He and Peterson are the only ones even remotely qualified for this. And Peterson is, well..."

"Duke will be alright, sir. He acts crazier than he is," Jonesy assured him.

The Captain nodded.

"But, sir," Medavoy protested.

"Those are my orders, Lieutenant," he replied, in no uncertain terms. "And Jonesy..." He sighed. "I'm sorry to put you through this. But it's got to be done. All your lives depend on it."

"*Our* lives, sir?" Jonesy asked. It seemed ridiculous, incongruous, to be having this conversation, with all its dark connotations, under the sunshine and soft breezes of one of the most beautiful places on the planet. Okay...Sand Island was a bit of a shit-hole, but Oahu wasn't, Hawaii wasn't. In any case, the alternative of not continuing this conversation, of not forcing some structure onto the abject insanity of the very real possibility he would be called on to kill one or more members of his own crew, was to dwell on that possibility; to swim in the idea of it, to drown in the horror of this new reality. And so he kept talking.

"*Our* lives, sir?" Jonesy repeated. "Not yours?"

Sparks didn't answer at first, just turned to gaze out at the harbor. His eyes once again held that blank look. Finally, he sighed and said, in a near-whisper: "No. Not mine."

"Captain?" Medavoy said. There was real alarm in the man's voice.

He turned to look at them again. "I could be infected," he said. He gazed down at his bloodstained shirt. "I probably am."

"We can give you the antibody test, sir," Doc Harris said, a note of panic creeping into his voice. "Then we'll know."

Sparks shook his head, then looked at his watch. He had to rub at the crystal face to clear it of blood. "I was exposed less than two hours ago," he said.

"It still might present," Harris argued.

Sparks shook his head again. "Can't take the chance."

Jonesy felt the shift in Medavoy, could almost hear the gears clicking and turning at the realization of what the Captain's words meant. *He* would now be the CO. He peered at the man out of the corner of his eye. Goddamned if the bastard hadn't puffed out his chest.

"Sir, does this mean...?" The arrogant prick began.

He's happy about it. He's glad the CO could be on the verge of turning into a mindless, insane, naked ball of arms and legs and gnashing teeth. What a fucking asshole!

The Captain nodded. He didn't look happy about it. He didn't look happy about anything. "I'm trusting you, Lieutenant," he said. "Take care of my crew."

This last was said with true steel in Sparks' voice, as if failing to follow his order would result in grave consequences. Jonesy suspected *grave consequences* were exactly what they would be, should LT Rat Fuck not do what he was told. They would come from the grave, because that was surely where LCDR Russell Sparks was headed.

13

"Want to tell me again why we're doing this?" Teddy Spute asked, for what John Gordon felt sure had to be the tenth time.

"No, I really don't," John replied. He looked at his friend in the passenger seat. Teddy was a wiry, skinny, small ball of energy, with salt and pepper black hair and deep-set eyes which, in the right light, seemed almost as black as what his hair used to be.

"Do it anyway," Teddy said.

"You know we have vaccine, right?"

"Yes!" Teddy smiled.

"And you know where it comes from, right?"

"Yes." Teddy's voice wasn't so enthusiastic, this time, and John really couldn't blame him.

When his "colleague," (a loose term, at best) at the college had first approached him about the vaccine, and had then explained to him how it was obtained, John had been appalled. Human spines? Human beings? The very idea had been out of the question almost before the question had been asked.

But then he thought about it, and about his family, and about his friends. The CDC declared the effects of the neurological pathogen were irreversible. Once a zombie, always a zombie. It didn't make the killing of human beings to create vaccine less abhorrent, but (when coupled with concern for family and friends) had made it more palatable. And so he agreed to Christopher Floyd's "terms."

Which was why they were headed to the Oregon State - Astoria campus to steal a dental x-ray machine.

14

"Okay, now, you know we don't trust this guy, right?" Gus asked. They were parked in the alley behind *Farcquar Guns and Ammo*. The air was cold, even though official summer was days away, and he was wearing a light grey jacket over a long-sleeved blue shirt.

"Yes, Dear," Jim Barber replied. He was a burly, stocky man with a full head of dark hair and a full beard; in his fifties, like Gus, and John, and nearly everyone else who was about to become the crew of the

M/V True North. He wore jeans and a flannel shirt, untucked over his belt line.

They'd already had this discussion, several times. He'd known Gilbert Farcquar since their days on the *Polar Star*. It seemed like centuries ago, but was only fifteen years. The man was a squirrely, untrustworthy little pudfucker then, and time had not changed him. They still saw each other occasionally (Astoria, Oregon, not being the biggest town in the world), and each occasion had left Jim feeling in serious need of a disinfecting shower.

They could have been friends, he supposed. They both shared fairly hard core conservative values, but Jim's were based on the Constitution, and Gilbert's were based on God only knew what. The shit that came out of the man's mouth was so divorced from reality, they may as well have been discussing different planets.

"Are we going inside, or just sitting here enjoying the ambiance of this alley?" He asked.

Gus shook his head. "I don't like it," he said. "But I guess it's gotta be done." He made as if to open his door, then stopped and looked at Jim. "Don't we already have enough guns? Hell, you've got your own arsenal."

This was true - the arsenal bit, anyway. Jim had four shotguns, including a Saiga, five hunting rifles, including a World War II vintage M-1 Garand, and ten handguns, including two Colt 1911 .45's, four Baretta 9mm, two S&W .44 Magnums, a .22 target pistol, and the S&W .38, tucked into its holster behind his back. But no, it wasn't enough.

"No such thing," he said. "Hello...Zombie Apocalypse."

The general absurdity of the current situation still hadn't sunk in. He understood it, at a gut level, anyway, but intellectually, it was damned hard to wrap his head around.

He'd never considered himself a "Prepper," (a sub-set of humanity convinced the end was truly nigh, and the shit would hit the fan any day now) but he did like to keep himself prepared. He had a stash of disaster supplies, including MREs and other freeze-dried foodstuffs, and a general shitload of other items one would need in a bad situation, but he had never been able to bring himself to go full-on commando.

He did know a fair number of people who had (Gilbert Farcquar being among them), but in general, they were too damned silly to take seriously. Most, he suspected, were just "playing soldier." And not a single Goddamned one of them was prepared for a Zombie Fucking Apocalypse.

"Let's go, if we're going," he said, and opened the car door.

15

Jonesy, now decked out in full tactical gear, including tactical uniform and boots, ballistic armor, knee and elbow pads, with gloves tucked into his harness, and holding his helmet under his arm, watched from the flying bridge as the crane lowered the buoy deck plate back into position, then climbed back down the ladder and entered the bridge. The first thing he saw upon entering was Scoot, standing at the chart table, staring at a rectangular piece of columned paper, set into a frame.

Scoot was BM2/OPS Ricardo (Ricky) Scutelli, Jonesy's twenty-two year-old right hand man. He was medium height and build, with dark hair and eyes, and the olive complexion of his southern Italian ancestors.

The paper he contemplated was the Watch, Quarter, and Station Bill, upon which all members of the crew were listed by billet, along with their assigned positions for evolutions such as Duty Section, Special Sea Detail, General Quarters, Shipboard Firefighting, etcetera. Why he should be looking at it remained a mystery.

He looked up as Jonesy entered, eyeing his rig. "Bold fashion statement," he said.

"It's what all the best ninjas are wearing this year," Jonesy replied.

"I'm assuming you have a reason for it...?"

Jonesy paused for a moment. *You can't turn. This crew is going to need you - maybe more than anyone else on board.* The Captain's words - and their implication - swirled around in his head. He might have to kill his shipmates. He might have to kill Scoot.

"You don't want to know," he said, finally.

"Secret Squirrel shit, then," Scoot said.

"What the fuck are you doing?" Jonesy asked, eyeing the Watch, Quarter and Station Bill.

"You know," the BM2 began. "I've been looking at this thing and I can't for the life of me find where I'm supposed to go in the event of a zombie apocalypse."

"Very funny," Jonesy said, dryly.

"I thought so."

"You thought wrong," Jonesy said. "Did you get all the tracks laid down, or have you been too busy fucking off?"

"Done and done," Scoot said, patting a stack of nautical charts on the chart table with one hand, as he replaced the WQS onto the wall with the other. The tracks were the course lines they'd be following, once they got underway. They had the Electronic Chart Display on the bridge, but Jonesy remembered what Chief Gordon (Molly's uncle) always said: *Paper doesn't break*, and so he insisted on paper chart backup to the electronic versions. His boys weren't too thrilled, but he was in charge, so he just didn't care.

"Box of death. What fun!" Scoot said, and let out a short, dry cough.

"Did you hear about the Skipper?" Jonesy asked, ignoring the cough, and praying to the God he didn't believe in that it was just something caught in his friend's throat.

"You mean that Lieutenant Fucktard is now the CO?"

Technically speaking, Jonesy should probably ream Scoot's ass for such a disrespectful attitude, but number one, he was too damned tired, and number two, he had himself to blame for it.

As to the first, this had been one bitch of a long day, filled with more emotional ups and downs than any sane man should have to deal with without benefit of alcohol. The Captain's condition, and subsequent abdication, were just the tip of the iceberg - which meant this particular iceberg was one whorey mother of a chunk of ice. Toss in seeing Molly again for the first time since their not-pleasant breakup a little more than a year ago, the fact Medavoy was now the Big Kahuna, and the dawning reality that they were in a real, By God Zombie Fucking Apocalypse, and what appeared was one FUBAR situation.

As for the second, well, he had to admit he'd called the XO "Lieutenant Fucktard" in the presence of junior people before. He knew he wasn't supposed to, knew it went against all good order and discipline. But the weasel *was* a fucktard. To deny this clear fact, was to lose credibility with one's subordinates. Jonesy had always at least tried to ameliorate his sin by saying: *You ain't gotta like it, you just gotta do it.* As solutions went, it was pretty pathetic, but it was also true.

He knew he'd have been shit-canned for such lapses in discipline faster than yesterday's Pork Adobo in any of the other services, but he wasn't in any of the other services. He was in the United States Coast Guard - *Uncle Sam's Confused Group* - and he was both damned glad and damned proud of it.

The phone rang.

"Bridge, Jones," he said, after snatching it from its cradle on the center console.

"Get your ass down to the Wardroom, Jones," Medavoy snapped on the other end. "Now."

Case in point...

16

"Do you know what a millicurie is?" Christopher Floyd asked, in response to John's question of why, exactly, they needed to steal a dental x-ray machine. They were in the Professor's lab/classroom at the college. Several lab tables, covered with test tubes, Bunsen Burners, and various other chemistry-type items of which John had no clue, were arrayed in a rectangle in front of a standard rectangular desk. It was dark, since the mad scientist kept the light off (for security reasons - or so he said) but John could still make out two large crates on one side of the desk, as well as a dozen smaller boxes stacked more or less neatly on the other.

"A sexually ambiguous pop group from the late Eighties?" John answered, meaning *Milli Vanilli*.

"How amusing," Floyd said, not amused at all.

"Didn't they get caught lip-synching, or something?" Spute asked.

"A millicurie," the professor continued, ignoring the pathetic attempt at humor, "is one thousandth of a curie."

"Glad we cleared that up," Spute said.

"It refers to the rate of decay of certain radioactive isotopes, and is used as a unit of measure," Floyd explained, clearly making no effort to hide his contempt for having to explain what he thought should be simple enough for the common low-grade moron to understand.

John had never liked him. To his knowledge, no one at the College did. Presumably he had a mother and/or father who didn't find him infuriating enough to strangle the life out of, but maybe not. In any case, the man knew how to make vaccine, had made it, had given several doses of both primer and booster to John, and was thus the savior of John's family and friends, so liking the man dropped in significance.

"And it has what to do with x-raying people's teeth?" John asked. He had worked his way over to the desk and was examining the cardboard boxes. One of them was partially open and revealed gallon-sized blue plastic bags. "What's all this?" He asked, pointing.

"Polyacrylamide gel powder," Floyd said, walking up to John and none-too gently escorting him away from the boxes. "It will allow me to make more vaccine." He pointed to the two crates on the other side of the desk. "Along with the centrifuge and scanning electron microscope." He turned and pointed toward a door John had not noticed, which apparently led to a closet. "And in there are test tubes and assorted equipment I will need for the procedure." He looked back over at John. "I'm assuming you can provide a blender?"

"Virus margaritas?" John asked.

"Grinding infected spinal tissue." Floyd replied, his expression becoming more irritated by the moment.

"And the x-ray machine?" Spute asked. He stayed in the middle of the room, afraid to move lest he knocked something over and made it explode.

"We can do without it," the professor said, pausing in his reply for effect. "If you want me to make vaccine guaranteed to make you turn into a zombie."

"We're already vaccinated." Spute said. "Why do we need more?"

John stared at Spute, amazed at the level of his friend's stupidity. "How much do you think vaccine will be worth, numbnuts," he snapped, "in a world overrun by zombies?"

"Ah!" Spute said, the understanding dawning upon his face. "Greed I get. Science...not so much."

"And besides," John said. "This was part of the deal to get our vaccine."

"And if all that is finally cleared up," Christopher Floyd said, wheeling a dolly out of the closet. "Let's get this stuff loaded into your truck so we can steal the x-ray machine."

17

"Failing to prepare means preparing to fail," Gilbert Farcquar said from within the darkened confines of the back of his gun store. He was a short man with a full beard, apparently grown to compensate for his male-pattern baldness.

"Sure, sure," Gus said. "We'll print up a greeting card, if it makes you happy."

"What would make me happy," Gilbert said, moving aside to let them enter, "would be going back to my dinner."

Jim Barber guessed the dinner in question had to be weenies and beans, if the undercurrent of stale flatulence was any indication. The smell battled with the heady aroma of gun oil filling his nostrils' He loved that smell - the oil, not the flatulence. He had, however, never liked Gilbert. He had never trusted Gilbert. He always felt certain Gilbert had been picked on as a child, and his dick-headedness was a natural extension, as if he were trying to compensate for past slights the way his beard compensated for his bald head.

Still, the man let them into his gun store, at night, in a zombie apocalypse. Had to count for something.

This was the thing about shipmates, Jim thought. Liking each other didn't matter. The shared misery and danger and adventure and joy and sometimes terror of being on a ship at sea together, created a bond unlike most others in the civilian world. You trusted each other - of necessity - particularly on a Coast Guard ship, because of their small crews. It might be different on a Navy ship with several hundred in her crew, but Jim had known the name of every single person on every single ship he'd ever sailed, and even long after he'd served with these people, he still had their back. They were shipmates, past, present, and future.

Still, the guy was being a prick, and a shared bond didn't mean he had to let it slide.

"You agreed to this meeting, Gilbert," he said, with a touch of menace in his voice. He didn't usually like to intimidate people, even though he knew he was capable of it. In Gilbert's case, he was more than willing to make an exception.

The intimidation worked. Gilbert shuffled his feet, then turned them away from his meager rooms at the back of the store, and led them into the store proper.

They followed through a long corridor, separated from the main retail area by a thick curtain. The walls of the corridor had been turned into a series of alcoves, with various items arrayed in them. Jim saw several types of sound and flash suppressors in one, a shelf unit filled with various flashlights and chem lights and helmet lights in another, and a gleaming object, mostly covered by a thick cloth in a third. This one drew his attention.

"Is that a minigun?" He asked in awe.

Gilbert paused and looked back over his shoulder at them, then glanced toward the multi-barreled bringer of death. "Yes it is. My pride and joy."

"Isn't it illegal?" Jim asked.

"Not if it was manufactured before the Brady Bill went into effect, back in '86. As long as it was registered before then, which this was, it is one hundred percent legal," Gilbert replied. "God Bless America."

"What kind of ammo?" Jim asked.

"7.62 X 51, NATO," was the answer. "And it burns through it like Congress through a dollar."

"Dammit!" Jim said, with true admiration.

"If you're quite finished gun-geeking..." Gus said, bringing Jim back to the reality of just how impractical a minigun would be in the current situation.

For one thing, 7.62 X 51, NATO, wasn't a civilian shooter round. It could still be obtained, but it wasn't as easy as, say, 9mm, or .203. Secondly, it required a shitload of the difficult to get ammo, just to keep the hungry beast fed, since its rate of fire would burn through a case load in about three minutes, thus turning the glorious minigun into a big-ass paperweight. And third, Jim doubted Gilbert would part with it willingly.

They continued into the main, public part of the store. The center portion was filled with racks and display cases filled with the various and sundry accessories to gun-nuttiness: Camo clothing and combat boots, freeze-dried foodstuffs and MRE's, shooting gloves, hats, backpacks, tents and assorted camping gear, and otherwise useless geegaws meant for the weekend shooter, rather than the hardcore survivalist. Anything lethal, or even mildly dangerous, was kept in locked glass cabinets at one end, near the cash register, or on locked shelves behind the counter.

"So what is it you want?" Gilbert asked, lifting part of the counter and pushing through the gap to stand behind the display cases. He closed the gap, thus separating himself from the other two men.

"Ammo," Jim replied. ".45 and 9mm, 30.06,.308, and 12 Gauge."

"And .357 Magnum," Gus added, since he owned a Colt Python, currently tucked into a holster beneath his shirt.

"Anything else?" Gilbert scowled, derisively. "You want maybe some cluster bombs or Napalm?"

Jim raised an eyebrow. "No. We're cool."

"You're fools, is what you are," Gilbert snapped. "If you haven't loaded up by now, at this stage, then you're shit out of luck."

"You don't have ammo?" Gus asked, worriedly.

"I have plenty of ammo," Gilbert replied, the contempt evident in his voice. "Just not anxious to part with it for a couple of idiots who left it to the last minute."

Jim thought he had a point. This was rather late in the game to be arming up in a zombie apocalypse. Then again, it had only started a couple of weeks ago. It's not like the average Joe stocks enough ordinance to stave off hordes of flesh-eating assholes as a matter of habit.

At first, he hadn't taken it seriously. A zombie apocalypse? Get real! Then he hadn't wanted to believe it. Then the evidence left no choice but to believe it, and he had been concerned with other things, like getting himself and his wife to safety, and getting his daughter, Stephanie, who was studying psychology at NYU, the fuck out of New York.

He thought she would resist and hang on, with tooth and claw, to her independence. In the end, however, she'd come willingly, enthusiastically, as ready to get the Hell out of there as he was to have her back in the relative safety of Astoria.

He came to discover the reason was the warehouses NYPD had set up as "Infected Treatment Centers." An ambitious (possibly suicidal) reporter for the *New York Times* had gotten into one of them with a concealed camera. What the pictures - broadcast that very night on every channel in the Five Burroughs - had shown, looked like Buchenwald on steroids. Dante, himself, couldn't have imagined a more Hellish scene.

And so he had left ammo well down on the list of priorities. He shouldn't have, and he knew it, but then, he had quite a bit more than the average Joe. For example, he had three thousand rounds of .38, for the pistol he had tucked into a holster at his back. But then again, there was never enough ammo for a zombie apocalypse.

"We're willing to pay a premium," Gus said. "We have gold."

"At this point, ammo is more valuable than gold," Gilbert replied, as if the suggestion of being paid with something as paltry as gold fell beneath his dignity. Jim really didn't like him.

"We have vaccine," Gus said, his tone almost pleading.

Gilbert's eyes *gleamed*.

18

"You're out of uniform, Petty Officer Jones," Medavoy said as Jonesy entered the wardroom. The voice was filled with contempt, as if Jonesy were some shit-covered worm he'd just stepped on - or so Jonesy thought. "Aren't you the OOD?"

"Yes, sir, I am," Jonesy replied, hoping his *"sir"* held at least some of that same contempt. "And the last order the CO gave me was to rig up," he added. "So I'm rigged up. The only thing missing is a sidearm, but I need BM1 Hurdlika to make it official, and he's been busy loading weapons and ammo." Hurdlika was the Master At Arms.

"You are not going to go armed!" the XO (and Jonesy steadfastly refused to give the man any higher recognition than his official title) snapped.

Jonesy took a seat at the table and stared at the bastard, ignoring the others - especially Molly. She sat next to the only empty chair, and so once again, he had to sit next to her. The last damned thing he needed was to be thinking about the jumbled-up feelings he had for an officer he could not have anything personal to do with.

"The CO said the Rules of Engagement have changed. Deadly force is authorized." He now had every eye at the table fully focused on him. "If I can't draw a firearm, what am I supposed to use? Harsh language?" Even before the slam left his lips, he knew it was a bad idea, but he couldn't help himself.

"The Rules of Engagement have not changed," Medavoy retorted. "There has been no message traffic, no communication from Headquarters."

"Actually, sir," LTJG Bloominfeld, the Comms Officer, said, tapping the message board on the table in front of him, "The order was received about twenty minutes ago."

"And why am I just finding out about this now?" Medavoy snapped.

"Because I only got it in my hand ten minutes ago, sir," Bloominfeld said, his voice a combination of both nervousness and resolve. Forget Medavoy being the sudden Captain. The XO of a ship - particularly one as small as a buoy tender - was damned-near God to the junior officers. One bad FITREP, one negative word in the service record, and any hope of flight school or grad school, or command afloat on a Patrol Boat, or any of a dozen other possibilities were tossed right out the window. And Medavoy used that power like a club.

"Your incompetence is duly noted," Medavoy said, "and it's no excuse."

"The fact remains, sir," Jonesy cut in. He didn't give one single flying fuck what the asshole could do to him - with the CO gone and possibly dead, and with the looming possibility he might have to kill his shipmates, might even need to kill his friends, and the lunatic reality that they were in a zombie by-God apocalypse - and so he threw caution to the wind and sent it sailing toward Shanghai. "The Rules have changed. Infected are to be terminated."

He heard a small, barely audible gasp next to him, from Molly, but he ignored it.

"Am I supposed to do it with my bare hands?" He let the insolent question hang there for a moment, before adding a derisive "Sir."

Medavoy stared at him, his face going from pink to red.

Maybe the fucker will have an aneurism, he thought, and the thought didn't bother him in the slightest. He was probably going to have to kill somebody - maybe today, maybe tomorrow, maybe half the goddamned crew. He had no problem at all starting the festivities with LT Dick Medavoy.

"Hold on just a minute here," CWO4 Kincade, the Engineer, said. "You want to let the rest of us in on what's going on?" The question was directed at Medavoy, who continued to stare at Jonesy.

"The CO was infected," HS2 Donny (Doc) Harris said from the far end of the table. Jonesy hadn't noticed he was there. "Or at least he thought he was." The focus of the entire table shifted to the young man, whose eyes were hollow with shock. His light blue uniform shirt carried a sideways "J" of smeared blood, just above the left breast pocket. "His last orders were for Jonesy to take charge of security, to...terminate, if necessary." His voice was a flat monotone. He paused before continuing, as if he didn't want to say what came next. "He then turned over command to the XO."

"And as CO," Medavoy said, with a look of satisfaction on his rodent face, "I'm saying you will not go armed on this ship, Petty Officer Jones."

"But–" Jonesy began. LT Fucktard cut him off.

"That's final," he said. "Is that clear?"

Jonesy leaned back in his chair and stared at Medavoy in disbelief. There was a shitstorm coming, the like of which had never been seen or experienced by anyone in the room, aboard the ship, or on the entire planet, and Jonesy didn't even have an umbrella.

19

The minuscule parking lot behind the Medical Sciences Building was dark, adding to John's general sense of unease. They'd managed to load all of Floyd's stuff from his lab/classroom into the back of the rental truck (and it was a back-breaking lot of stuff) without getting caught pilfering what John was sure couldn't be Professor Christopher Floyd's personal scanning electron microscope, centrifuge, and mass spectrometer, but it had been a near thing.

The Department Head, Professor Douglas Pemberty, who should by all rights have gone home hours ago, had bumped into them - literally. Spute just finished shoving the final box (which happened to contain miscellaneous glassware that could, conceivably, belong to Floyd) as deep as it would go into the truck, and pulled the sliding door closed, when Pemberty rounded a corner and bumped right into John, who, to his infinite chagrin, had almost screamed.

"Excuse me!" the man sputtered, then seemed to realize he had no idea who John was.

The faculty at the College wasn't large, but the departments rarely mingled, so John, who was part of the Extended Education Department, had never met the Department Head of Physical Sciences. He'd never met any of the teachers from the department, except Floyd, and that was only because Floyd heard John owned an ocean-going ship. The College's resident mad scientist had then put two and two together, saw they equaled a way to escape the zombie plague, and then approached John with the proposition, which led them into this farcical situation.

"Who are you, and what are you doing here?" Pemberty asked, his tone brusk and authoritative.

"Good evening, Douglas," Floyd had said, rounding the side of the truck. "What brings you here so late?"

"Ah! Floyd!" the man exclaimed. "Forgot some of the budget summaries in my office. The Dean has asked for a full accounting, in case..." He let the sentence peter out.

John knew what "in case meant." Everybody, from the College Administrators, to the Mayor of Astoria, the Chief of Police, and even (presumably) the Dog Catcher, and every other mucky muck in between was making sure all their ducks were in an appropriate row, should the worst happen and they needed to evacuate. He could have told them they were wasting their time. The goose of the United States of America was cooked by the microscopic evil of the Pomona Zombie Virus.

"Yes," Floyd had answered. "I'm picking up a few of my personal items," he said, then added: "In case."

Pemberty eyed the truck. "A few items...?"

"I also have several things in storage downtown," Floyd replied, the lie seeming to roll off his lips. At least John thought it had been a lie. He did not want to be stuck cleaning out the man's storage locker on top of all this clandestine skullduggery. "Papers and such from my days at Stanford."

Oh!" Pemberty had exclaimed, impressed by mention of that prestigious university. Backwater college professors tended not to be from top-shelf schools - more bottom shelf, or even stuck in some cobweb-filled closet, instead of a shelf. "Yes..." The man seemed flummoxed, and had been about to leave when he paused and looked at John, Spute, and Floyd with sudden suspicion. "I found an invoice for three hundred pounds of polyacrylamide gel powder, charged on the department credit card," he said. "You wouldn't know anything about it, would you?"

Floyd shook his head, a puzzled look on his face - the picture of confused innocence. "That's used for cancer research, isn't it?"

Pemberty had shaken his head. "Some. But mostly Immunology."

"No, sir. Haven't used any of it in years." The lie again slid off his lips like a snake over glass. John was clearly going to have to watch the guy, if he could lie so convincingly. Even John had been convinced, and he had been more or less certain the gel powder was, if not outright stolen, then certainly missapropriated.

"Very well," the academician had replied. "Are you coming to the staff meeting tomorrow?"

"Wouldn't miss it," Christopher Floyd, consummate liar, had replied.

"See you there," Professor Pemberty had said, and then - finally - walked off.

And now they were skulking around the back of the Medical Sciences building, in the dark, and John was hoping against hope their run-in with Pemberty hadn't used up all their luck for this night of criminal activity. They were going to need it.

He was alone, in the first place. It was dark, and he was acting as lookout for this bit of Grand Larceny. *Make that Breaking and Entering,* he thought, looking at the crowbar in his right hand, as if it had just appeared there with no conscious effort on his part. They had used it to pry open the back door of the building, had, in fact, nearly wrenched the door knob completely free of the door with it. The fact there hadn't been an immediate shrieking of some security alarm, seemed a miracle. Still, B & E was, after all, a crime, and if the cops came, their gooses would be boiled, fried, sauteed and slow roasted in jail, if they were caught. And if they were in jail during a zombie apocalypse, then they would either starve to death, when everybody else evacuated, or be eaten, if the zombies overran the jail. Neither option seemed good - or survivable.

He calmed his fears. With the tipping point so near, the police were, in the first place, focused on more important things than stolen dental x-ray machines, and, in the second place, were busy dealing with insane, naked, homicidal victims of Pomona. Or so he hoped.

He jumped at the sound of something clattering off in the distance. *A dog. Nothing but a dog*, he thought, his heart feeling as if it were beating a John Bonham drum solo. *Please dear God, let it be a dog...* The sound came from the right side of the building. His once-calmed fears decided a vacation would be a good idea, and a crawling sensation emanated from the vicinity of his nut sack, then exploded into his chest when the back door banged open and Spute and Floyd stumbled out, wrestling with a large and cumbersome machine strapped to a dolly.

"Little help!" Spute grunted. "This fucker is top-heavy!"

John headed toward the door - or started to - when a zombie came staggering around the corner of the building, and saw Spute and Floyd.

It was male, naked, and covered in blood. At least John felt certain it was blood. It looked like black gunk in the darkness, but since it was all over the zombie's face and spread down its chest, John held no illusions about its actual source. And it was clearly Samoan. Samoans came in two sizes: large, and *you've got to be fucking kidding*. This Samoan-turned-zombie was the latter. It howled - a sound made of equal parts keening wail and deep, animal growling - and lunged forward, right at Spute.

20

"Vaccine...?" Gilbert said, his voice taking on an oily quality Jim didn't like one bit. He rolled his fingers on the glass counter top, as if he were tinkling the keys of an imaginary piano. "Do tell..."

Jim had argued against the idea of offering vaccine in trade to anyone - least of all to Gilbert Farcquar. Mere possession of it was a crime, since its source material came from the spinal chords of formerly living human beings. Granted, those human beings had turned into slobbering, drunk-looking, naked, homicidal lunatics, but they were still - at least in the eyes of the legal system - humans, and, therefore, subject to all the protections of the law. Possession of the vaccine was, therefore, accessory to capital murder, and so the fewer people who knew they had any of it, the better Jim liked it.

He considered Gilbert to be about as trustworthy as a crystal junkie. If Gilbert saw an advantage in screwing them, he'd be on it like a meth whore on her drug dealer. And Gilbert owned a lot of guns.

The man's attention focused on Gus, Jim took the opportunity to reach behind his back and release the hammer strap on his holster and tuck the back of his flannel shirt into his belt. Better to be safe, than sorry.

"Two doses," Gus said. "Each, of primer and booster, for all the ammo we want."

Gilbert sucked air through his teeth, as if the thought of this deal pained him. "Ten," he said. "Of each type."

Gus' eyes flicked toward Jim. They were only carrying eight vials: four of primer and four of booster - the last of their supply, although John was picking up the scientist who made them, so presumably they were going to get more. Still, to leave themselves with none...

"Three doses," Gus countered.

"Twenty," Gilbert sneered, and Jim was quickly getting sick of the prick. He was tempted to clock him over the head and see if it made the bastard negotiate a little better, but Gus carried on in good faith.

"Four doses," Gus said, then added: "Final offer."

Gilbert tilted his head sideways and gave a small negative shake - almost a "no," but not quite.

"You know anywhere else you can get it?" Jim asked.

The man's eyes shifted and narrowed. "I've...got a source."

They'd been shipmates for three years, back in the day, and the thing people tended to have when underway was time - lots and lots of time - on their hands, while spending twenty-four hours a day trapped inside a steel shell in the middle of a vast ocean, in which to do lots and lots of nothing.

Some people read. Jim had once read the entire multi-volume set of Winston Churchill's *History of the English Speaking Peoples*, cover to cover. Some watched movies. A few played weeks-long games of *Dungeons and Dragons*. Gilbert Farcquar had played poker.

Jim had played against him, more than once, and Gilbert Farcquar was a terrible poker player. He almost always lost, for the simple reason that he couldn't bluff for shit. He had a tell: his eyes would narrow and shift, exactly as they had just done. The bastard was lying.

"Bullshit," Jim said.

Vaccine had started out at fifty bucks a pop, street value, but as each day progressed, and as people became more and more panicked about the so-called "zombie virus" that was not stopping - was, in fact, accelerating, as more and more and more became infected - the price kept rising. The last Jim had heard, the going rate was five hundred per dose of primer, and seven-fifty per dose of booster.

Capitalism in action, Jim thought. He was a Capitalist, through and through, but even he considered it highway robbery, especially since almost nobody was accepting cash at this point. The dollar had descended in value as social values spiraled deeper and deeper into the chaos of a world speeding toward the tipping point.

"We've got the most valuable currency in this economy, Gilbert, and you know it," he said. "We're offering you a fair deal. Take it or leave it."

Gilbert's eyes shot daggers at him for the briefest of moments, then returned their gaze to Gus. "Let me see this vaccine," he sneered. "I want to test it."

When vaccine first began to circulate (*Christ, it was only a couple weeks ago*, Jim thought), everybody got into the action - even drug dealers, who produced everything from colored water to actual high-grade vaccine that proved indistinguishable from the stuff coming out of the corporate labs. A way needed to be found to test it, and so some entrepreneurial person quickly developed, and then mass-produced vaccine test kits. One of the bigger Pharmaceutical companies dropped a shit-ton of money on the inventor, and in less than a week, had them spread all across the United States, where they were sold at every drug store, convenience store, and liquor store. Jim had even seen them on display at a *Starbucks*.

Gilbert slid down the counter and pulled open a drawer at the far end. Jim tensed, thinking the asshole might be going for a gun, but he only pulled out one of the brightly covered packages, emblazoned with the label: *True Test*. He placed it on the glass in front of him. He also, Jim saw, left the drawer open.

Gus pulled a small cloth pouch out of his jacket pocket and laid it on the glass counter. It clinked, as the glass vials of vaccine came together. He undid the drawstring and removed one clear bottle, about an inch-and-a-half high and three-quarters in diameter, then placed it in front of Gilbert. It sat there, gleaming in the florescent light of the gun shop, looking like nothing more than an ordinary bottle of medicine, like insulin, except for its lack of a label. He pulled a hypodermic, its needle capped in plastic, out of the opposite pocket, and set it next to the vaccine.

Gilbert stared at it for a moment, not moving. He sniffed in a lung full of air, then blew it out like smoke from a cigarette, as if steeling himself. Jim didn't like this one bit - especially when he saw the man's eyes flicker toward the open drawer.

Finally, he picked up the hypodermic, uncapped it with his teeth, then picked up the bottle and eased the needle through the wax seal at the top. He pulled back the plunger just a bit, enough to withdraw a few tiny drops of the clear liquid into the hypo reservoir, then set the bottle back on the counter and brought the needle to the open test kit. This stuff was worth more per ounce than gold, and he wasn't going to waste a single drop.

Depressing the plunger, he shot the vaccine into the small plastic bowl at the indicated spot on the kit. All three of them watched the clear liquid flow through the channels as the medicine passed over the test strips, or whatever the testing medium might be.

None of them knew exactly how the thing worked - like most things in life - but they still retained the certainty that it would. That's the way life in an ordered society had always been: things did what they were supposed to do. It didn't matter if the people using them hadn't the slightest idea how they did what they did, like computers or TV sets or microwave ovens or the internal combustion engine. These things worked. They always had, and they always would, and each and every one of them woke each and every day in the certainty this simple fact would never change. They didn't question it. They just accepted the fact and moved on with their day. Pomona was about to teach them just how naive they all were, but not yet, not yet.

The thing - whatever it was - in the appropriate place turned a bright blue. All three men leaned forward to stare. Gilbert slid the package the kit had come in around, so he could read the instructions. Blue meant *positive for Pomona booster*. He smiled. Gus smiled.

Jim would have smiled, but out of the corner of his eye, he caught the movement of Gilbert's hand toward the drawer. He eased his own hand behind his own back and gripped the butt of the .38.

In a flash so fast it even took Jim by surprise, Gilbert pulled a big damned handgun out of the drawer, cocked it, and pointed it an inch from Gus' eye. Gus froze. Jim didn't.

"Give me everything you've got," Gilbert said in a rush. "Now god damn it!"

Jim pulled his own gun, cocked it, and stuck it right into Gilbert's temple.

"You're gonna want to rethink that."

21

"What the fuck is he thinking?" Jonesy raged.

Molly stood beside him on the Flying Bridge, watching as the sun went down on what had turned into a very long and terrible day. That it was also her first day on her first ship as an Ensign in the United States Coast Guard had not escaped her. And what a day!

She looked at Jonesy, at the man she had...what? Loved? No... Not that. Not loved. Liked, then. Liked enough to have given him her body - willingly - more than once. But that was something she could not - would not - dwell upon.

They had known each other for quite a long time; since Alaska, five years ago, when she had been sixteen, and he had been maybe twenty, or twenty-one. He had seemed such an unattainable goal back then. He was absolutely unattainable now - by law, if not by actual fact or...desire? She couldn't think about that, either.

In any case, Jonesy was now as pissed off as she had ever seen him, and she couldn't blame him for it one bit. The XO - sorry, CO, now - was an asshole, and a dangerous one, to boot.

"How am I supposed do my job?" Jonesy asked. Molly couldn't answer.

"I may have to kill some of these guys," he said. "Do you realize that?" He turned and stared at her. "Does he?"

"I don't think he much gives a damn, Jonesy," she said, and mentally kicked herself for saying it. She was an officer, damn it! She was *never*, under *any* circumstances supposed to bad-mouth a superior. She had a momentary, and crazy-absurd vision of herself as a *Harry Potter* house elf, banging her own head against the steel railing as punishment for disobeying one of the cardinal rules of officer-ship. But she was damned if she would disagree with Jonesy. Not on this.

Medavoy was clearly, indefensibly *wrong* in refusing Jonesy the ability to arm himself, when it was abundantly, dreadfully clear he was right. He, in all probability, would have to kill one or more of his - and now *her* - shipmates, and you only needed open eyes and access to a TV set to know it.

Scenes of chaos, mayhem, and brutal violence that would have given any Hollywood movie an R-rating, had been playing out on the nightly news of every city of any size all over the entire world. Thousands were dying every day. And those were just the images shown on TV. The ones out on the street, seen with actual eyes, and not camera lenses, were far, far worse.

And of course, the Powers That Be in the governments of all the nations of the world had been playing it down, so as not to create a panic, but everybody with active brain cells knew: it was coming apart. And so, therefore, Medavoy knew. And yet, he was acting in a way contrary to good sense and the safety of the crew to which LCDR Sparks had given him command.

Maybe that was it. Maybe he was so afraid of his tenuous hold on this new command, thrust upon him in extremis, he feared the possibility of losing it to armed insurrection.

And there it was: the pop psychology she had loathed in her classmates. As each year of psychological study had progressed, along with the command responsibilities thrust on them as part of the curriculum at the Coast Guard Academy, and the *you are superior* attitudes the Academy fostered in its future officers, her classmates had seemed to grow more and more pompous in their certainty. They understood the workings of the human psyche, better than anyone, ever. And they proved this, day after day, by psychoanalyzing any and everybody with whom they came in contact, snapping off psycho-babble diagnoses like homilies from Hallmark.

It had been bullshit then, and it was bullshit now. Which did not mean she was wrong.

Jonesy sighed. "What am I gonna do, Mol?" he asked, then seemed to realize what he'd just said and where he currently was. "Sorry...I meant Miss Gordon."

She didn't answer right away, and didn't chastize him for the clear lack of military decorum. She didn't even look at him, at first.

Instead, she stared at the dark grey non-skid deck at her feet. "You know how Uncle John is always coming up with pithy sayings, like he was a walking motivational poster?"

Jonesy didn't answer right away, then suddenly, a snort burst out of him like hilarious gas. She supposed the correct term would be *chortle*, but his had seemed darker, somehow, as if tinged with despair. Or was that just more psycho-babble?

"Yeah," he laughed. "He was always making lemonade out of tangerines, or some stupid thing like that."

"Exactly," she chuckled, and favored him with a smile. "Anyway, he used to say you can only deal with what's in front of you, and only with the tools you have at hand."

Jonesy nodded. "That sounds like John."

She shrugged. "It's probably what he'd say to you now."

He thought about it for a moment, his shoulders still tense with anger, but then they seemed to ease - if only a little. "He probably would."

"In other words," she said. "Go find yourself some tangerines."

He laughed and nudged her shoulder with his elbow, then seemed to think better of it and stepped away toward the ladder off the Flying Bridge.

"And maybe a baseball bat, while I'm at it," he said, and headed below.

22

The giant zombie charged, and John didn't even think. If he had, then he'd have hesitated, and if he hesitated, the six-foot-seven, four hundred pound monster would have been on Spute in seconds.

The second problem (the first being the mammoth zombie, itself) was John had no gun. Of course, a gun would have just pissed the behemoth off, so more to the point, he had no rocket launcher. What he did have was a crowbar. He took two running strides, brought the crowbar from around his back, as if he were bringing it up from last week, and with an overhand swing that would have made Venus Williams weep, he slammed the claw end of the bar smack into the side of the zombie's head.

Gigantor-zombie lurched and recoiled from the blow, yanking the crowbar out of John's hand. It hung there, swinging slightly, embedded in the thing's skull. And the zombie kept moving. Blood flowed from the terrible wound, adding to the blood spread all over the thing's face, as it staggered. But it kept moving.

Spute had frozen; Floyd had not, and so the dolly upon which the dental x-ray machine perched, was now spinning in a circle, as one of them moved and the other didn't. And the zombie kept coming - slower now that it had an iron bar stuck in its head, but still moving.

"Move, you idiot!" Floyd shouted, as he bitch-slapped Spute on his left cheek. It did the trick.

As Zom-zilla reached out its dinner plate-sized hands to wrench Spute's head off his neck, they - and the dolly - spun aside, the x-ray machine nearly crashing into a million pieces onto the concrete, but was saved when John darted forward and shoved it upright.

The zombie kept coming, though there seemed to be something wrong with its vision, because it kept right on going in the direction it had been, *through* where Floyd and Spute had been moments before. It bounced off the entrance alcove wall, hitting it with its right shoulder, and did a slow turn, as *I've got an iron bar in my brain* finally registered, then it fell over backwards into a hydrangea bush. It lay there, twitching, for a moment, and then was still.

Silence fell over the bizarre scene. John heard nothing - not even the thudding of his own heart, so he thought it might have stopped - but then with a rush in his ears as the blood flowed back up into his stunned head, he heard it pounding, right where it was supposed to be.

"Fuck me!" Spute said.

John looked at Spute, who looked back at him. His friend's face seemed to be made out of bleached and worn paper. But when John looked over at Floyd, he saw something disturbing and different.

Professor Christopher Floyd was staring at the now dead and blood-covered former human being with an expression of keen interest. *This guy really is a mad scientist,* John thought. He was interested - *fascinated* - by it, rather than being scared witless and in serious need of a new pair of underwear.

John, himself, felt a combination of fear, nausea, guilt, and adrenaline-fueled exhilaration. All those feelings swirled around in his head and his heart as he tried not to think. He had just killed a human being. Granted, it had been a human being the size of a '52 Buick, gone stark, raving mad and trying to kill his friend, and the freak show Christopher Floyd was turning out to be, but still human. What he didn't feel, couldn't feel, would *never* feel, was fascinated. And yet there was Christopher Floyd, contemplating the remains, as if it were an interesting science experiment.

"Fuck me!" Spute said again.

John snapped out of his reverie. "Fuck this," he said, grabbing Floyd and pulling him away from the dead zombie. "Let's get out of here."

23

Gilbert Farcquar lay on the somewhat dusty concrete floor of his gun store's back room, trussed like the proverbial Christmas turkey, with zip ties, instead of string. Christmas turkeys weren't ordinarily gagged, either, but Jim had insisted, and Gus had not argued.

Gus Perniola stared at the pistol in his hand that had so recently been pointed at his eye. It was a big fucker - a Ruger .44 Magnum, to be precise - and the round barrel had seemed like staring into a planet-sized black hole. And yes, it was loaded. He had never been closer to death, and he never wanted to even be in the same zip code, ever again.

"There's a keypad on the gun vault," Jim said, coming back into the room. "We need the code." He stood over the prone, and furious form of their former shipmate. "I'm going to remove the gag."

"You can't do this!" Gilbert spat, as his mouth became free of the gun oil-covered rag they'd used.

"We did do it, Gilbert," Jim said, his voice calm and even "Deal with it and give me the vault code."

"Go fuck yourself!"

Jim replied by pulling the .38 from its holster behind his back. He cocked it and placed it against Gilbert's bucking knee.

"Jim! Wait," Gus said, staring at the tableau with more than a little unease.

He hadn't had enough time to process what just happened. First, there was the gun pointed at his eye. Then there was Jim's gun pointed at Gilbert's temple. Then there was the knife's edge tension of the standoff, as Gilbert added two and two and realized with certainty, Jim would pull the trigger if he so much as twitched. Jim had stood back then, and ordered Gus to find the zip ties and truss the gun store owner up like the proverbial dinner. He had done so, mechanically going through the motions as the dawning realization of his own mortality flashed across his mind.

Gilbert had pointed a gun at his eye. The asshole had pointed a gigantic fucking pistol at his fucking eye.

Gus pulled the hammer back with his thumb, stepped forward, and said: "Let me do it." He jammed the barrel into Gilbert's knee. "Motherfucker was going to shoot me."

Gilbert's eyes had been wide with rage before. They were wider with panic now. He gave them the vault code.

"We can't leave him tied up like that," Gus said, heaving a case of 12 gauge into the back of Jim's SUV. They were once again in the dimly-lit back lot of Gilbert's store.

"Sure we can," Jim said, adding another case to the growing pile of ammo.

"He'll starve," Gus protested. He had been perfectly willing to blow the asshole's kneecap off (or at least he *thought* he'd been willing, and more importantly, *Gilbert* thought he'd been willing), but letting the man slowly starve to death seemed a little harsh.

Jim stood and stretched his back. The ammo cases were heavy, and neither of them were young any more. "He's in a store filled with knives and other assorted sharp objects," he said. "He'll be okay." He thought about it for a moment, then added: "But we had probably better be long gone by the time he gets loose."

The realization hit Gus of just what they were doing. Illegal didn't begin to describe. If they were caught...

"Jim..."

"Too late to back out now," his friend said, apparently knowing him well enough to guess what had been going through his mind. What's more, Gus knew he was right.

In the first place, this was a zombie apocalypse. Life as they knew it was well and truly over. The world was toast. In the second place, they were planning to get underway in just a few hours. They were not planning to come back.

The finality of it hadn't sunk in. Maybe it would later. Or maybe not. Maybe he'd just repress it all. Maybe he'd need a lot of alcohol to make it happen.

He'd quit drinking six (or was it seven?) years ago. He didn't have a problem with it, beyond the usual one. Hangovers tended to get worse as he got older. He'd quit because he got bored with it. Do anything often enough, and even the most entertaining things could become tedious. But maybe an apocalypse would make it fun - or necessary - again.

He didn't want to think about the "necessary" option. But still...This situation was hard to ignore.

He and his wife, Joanne, had packed up their house, finishing just this morning, which could explain why his back hurt. Or maybe he was just old. Either way, it had been surprisingly easy to sort through what was junk and what wasn't. Most of it had been junk.

The comedian, George Carlin, used to do a bit about the need to buy a bigger house so you had a place to hold all your stuff. And they had a lot of stuff. Carlin also said that your things were "stuff," but everybody else's things were shit. That had not turned out to be true. Gus had been astounded at the incredible load of shit filling his house. It was everywhere: every closet, cabinet, nook, and cranny - and almost all of it had been useless in an apocalypse.

He thought about it as they made their way back into the building and toward the vault.

He'd found Chia Pets (never used), and tea cozies, and a wide assortment of woodworking tools he'd bought with the best of intentions, but only used once or twice. He doubted a gadget for making scroll work on wooden planks would in any way be useful in the current world. He had all sorts of gadgets designed to do all sorts of things. All were pointless now.

They'd had a fondue set. Where had they gotten that? *Why* had they gotten that? He *hated* fondue. All of these were bits and pieces of seventeen years shared together, and all of them were now useless.

They'd never had children. Never seemed to be the right time. Sad... But at least they didn't need to worry about them like, Jim, or John, or half a dozen other of their soon-to-be shipmates. But they had taken their motorcycles. Those would be useful. He'd also packed his one remaining box of fine cigars. It was half-full. He doubted he'd find a replacement.

He hefted another box of ammo - 30.06, and heavy as fuck - and headed toward the SUV.

Jim, on the other hand, went into the back room, where Gilbert lay.

They pulled out of the alley, checking to be sure the coast was clear. Gus looked at the pile of cases in the back.

"Did we really need to take half of his ammo?" He asked. They'd removed half of the man's store of 12 gauge, .357, .45, 9mm, .308, and 30.06, and Gus's back felt every ounce of it. The SUV bottomed out as they drove over a speed bump.

"Call it carrying charges," Jim said with a dismissive shrug.

Gus nodded. "And the minigun?" He'd been shocked, then mildly angered when Jim appeared at the back of the store with Gilbert's "pride and joy."

Jim hesitated, then replied: "Fucker shouldn't have pointed a gun at you."

The logic seemed unassailable. Or maybe Gus was still pissed off about his near-death experience. In any case, he didn't argue.

"Did you leave the vaccine, at least?" Gus asked.

"Yes, Dear," Jim said, a note of derision in his voice. "I'm an asshole," he added, "not a thief."

"I somehow don't think the police will care about the distinction."

"Probably not," Jim agreed.

"Then we'd better be long gone when they find out."

"Yes, Dear," Jim said. He picked up speed.

24

"He said what?" BM2/DECK Duke Peterson asked, incredulous. They were in the Bosun Hold. BM1/DECK Dennis Hurdlika and SN Harold F. Simmons, jr., were in there with them.

The compartment looked - and smelled - the way the interior of a ship should look. At least Jonesy always thought so. Line of various sizes, and made from various substances (cotton, nylon, hemp, etc.) sat arrayed in spools at the back of a long steel bench lining most of the port bulkhead. Vices, and bolted down, conical (phallic) fids, used for working with line in all sorts of ways, also in varying sizes, sat at either end.   Cages lined the starboard bulkhead, filled with all the accouterments a good sailor would need, from giant wrenches and fire axes, to chem lights and flashlights and helmet lights, to hard hats and Big Fucking Hammers. There were chains and block and tackle rigs of every size and configuration; tarps and canvas and sail cloth; buoy lights and buoy batteries, neon orange, red and green dayboards, and solar panels, and everything needed to repair or build various Aids to Navigation. And there was a locker, painted dark blue (the others being institutional grey), labeled: *LE GEAR (LE* standing for *Law Enforcement).* It - more than just the ability to commiserate with other victims of LT Medavoy's asshole-ness - was why Jonesy had come down there.

"He said we can't have firearms," Jonesy said again, though he hardly needed to. Once was enough to convey the bad news.

Duke stared at him in disbelief. He, like Jonesy, was rigged up in full LE gear, sans helmet, which sat like a disembodied head upon a gunmetal grey desk at the aft end of the Hold. "What are we supposed to use? Harsh language?"

Jonesy nodded and pointed at Duke. "That's exactly what I said."

"Fucking idiot," Harold swore.

"What was that, Seaman Simmons?" Hurdlika barked. If senior Petty Officers weren't supposed to badmouth superiors, junior enlisted absolutely weren't.

"Uh! Errr... I meant Duke," Harold said.

"Fuck you, Harold," Duke said, then returned his attention to Jonesy. "How are we supposed to..."

But Jonesy waved him off. "I've already gone down that road," he said. "It leads to nothing but being more pissed off." He shook his head. "What we need to do is deal with what's in front of us." He cast a sideways glance at Hurdlika and Harold, sizing up whether or not they could be trusted. He should have saved the effort. He knew they could be. "We need to go around him."

"You mean arm up, anyway?"

"No, numbnuts," Jonesy replied, his tone friendly. "Not unless we want to get court martialed."

"And Medavoy would," Hurdlika said.

"What then?"

"He didn't say anything about batons, or knives, or tasers," Jonesy said.

Duke smiled. "Ah! I begin to see your evil plan." He looked at Hurdlika. "You've got the keys."

The BM1 looked between the two of them, hesitating. This was a big step in a potentially nasty direction. Then again, it was the *right* step. He pulled out his keys and headed towards the blue locker.

"Uh...this might seem like a stupid question..." Harold began.

"And it would differ from the rest of your questions how?" Duke asked.

Harold coughed into his hand. It sounded oddly like *fuck off*. "Why do you need to be armed up in the first place?"

25

The M/V *True North* was alive with activity. Stores were being put away and secured against the inevitable rocking and rolling in the vastness of the Pacific Ocean. Engines were being taken through their pre-start checklists. Dinner was being cleared away, young children were being put to bed, and a dozen other things were being done by a dozen other people, as the ship prepared to sail off into the proverbial sunset. The actual one had displayed its light show and disappeared hours ago. This was how Samantha Gordon, age sixteen, and utterly, irrevocably depressed at the thought of any of it, managed to slip over the gangway and disappear into the night.

Her life was over - nothing more, nothing less. She would never see her friends again. She would never go to the mall, or sneak into the cinema to catch a forbidden-by-law R-rated movie. She would never see a concert at the Astoria Center. *Green Day* had been scheduled to play there. She even had two tickets - a birthday present from her Dad, a little over three weeks ago. She'd wanted a car, of course. Sixteen was the magic year, after all. And he had planned to get her one. She'd taken and passed the driving test the next day, and they had even gone to the dealership to shop a couple days later, but then they announced the Plague. And so now it was concert tickets she couldn't use and a life she would never have again. *Happy Birthday...*

She'd had the entire concert scenario worked out, too. *Green Day* was old, but still considered cool, without being trendy. They were even (in certain circles to which she could only dream of belonging) considered *edgy*. But that wasn't why this whole affair was such a suck-fest. It was a gigantic ball of *suck* because she had been planning to ask Justin Blaisdell to go with her. In the scenario she created with loving, painstaking, fever-dreamed care, there had been *kissing*.

Justin, of course, was why she slipped away.

She knew she had to go back. Her father would tear the city apart looking for her, and there would be an endless series of *Parental Moments* inflicted upon her, over and over again, for however long their voyage to wherever they were going would last. But Justin was supposed to be at The Park tonight. And so she went, into the night, in the dark, past curfew.

Edgy...

26

Twenty-two days earlier, and three days before the CDC announced the Pomona outbreak, Brian J. Reeves, sales representative for *ChromoSolve*, a high tech genetics firm, based in Portland, Oregon, traveled to Los Angeles for a conference with potential buyers for their latest product, *AccuChrom*, a next gen system for modifying seed corn to grow in arid environments. He'd traveled by air.

At check in, he had touched the automatic check-in screen to save time, then headed to the TSA checkpoint, where he touched the plastic bin that hadn't been cleaned since God knew when, into which he placed his keys, coins, laptop and shoes, and then removed them after going through the scan. He leaned on the scanner's conveyor to put his shoes back on, touching it with his left hand.

During the flight, he touched his seat, his seat belt, the tray table, the plastic cup, mini bottle of vodka, and can of tomato juice for his Bloody Mary. It was only ten in the morning, but it must have been cocktail hour *somewhere* in the world. He paid for it with cash that had, in turn, been change for the cup of convenience store coffee he'd bought on the way to the airport. The coffee had tasted terrible.

In between the purchase of the coffee with a twenty he'd gotten in change at the bank, where he broke a hundred the night before, and the time he paid for his Bloody Mary, the money he'd used changed hands four times. He gave the money to the flight attendant, touching her hand in the process. He had no idea who she touched after that.

He, however, touched the car door on the cab he took from the airport, the seat inside the cab, and the money he gave to the driver, and then the money and receipt he received in exchange. He also touched the door to his hotel, the hotel registration desk, the hotel clerk's hand, when he handed over his Amex Black credit card, the elevator button outside the elevator, and then the floor button once he'd gotten inside. He touched the room key, which in turn had been touched by an unknowable number of others, and the room door handle, both outside and inside of the room.

And he went right on touching things, all day long: in the cab to the buyer (representing a consortium of investors from Dubai and Macao), at the buyer's office building and in the buyer's office, at the restaurant, where he had an excellent steak he couldn't finish because his appetite was strangely muted, and on and on, and on for another two days, before he finally drove his car back into his driveway at home in Astoria, Oregon.

His wife and three children were there.

He felt more or less fine for e few days, except for the lackluster appetite. He didn't give it a second thought, though. He always suffered from horrible jet lag.

It had never lasted so long.

Truth be told, he hadn't felt right since before he'd gone on his business trip - a day before, come to think of it. On that day, he'd attended a Father/Son event at Ronald Reagan Middle School, with his middle child. He'd tried and failed to make eleven year-olds care about genetics. They'd eaten lunch at the cafeteria. It had tasted bland, institutional, and just a touch odd.

Three days after his return from Los Angeles, he awoke feeling like something the cat dragged in, chewed up, then yacked out as a fur ball. He couldn't ever remember feeling so terrible. Between the coughing and the fever, he didn't leave his bed for two days. During one of his many naps, the CDC announced the Pomona epidemic. He hadn't paid attention. He'd been too sick.

His wife, who neglected to mention the plague to him, feeling he had enough to deal with, continued to go to work at the florist shop she owned, and the kids continued to go to school. Then they, too, got sick.

On the seventh day - now fifteen days after his trip to Los Angeles - he began to feel better. Not perfect, by any stretch, but good enough that he'd been able to keep down a small bowl of tomato soup. It reminded him of the in-flight Bloody Mary, though it contained no alcohol. Odd he should think of something so insignificant, but this could be passed off as side-effects of the low grade fever.

Three days later, the fever spiked. Two hours after it reached its peak of 105, Brian J. Reeves was no longer human - at least not in the sense of what was considered normal human cognition and behavior before The Plague.

His wife and children were now dead, though he didn't know it. He'd been there when it happened, but nothing had registered. The lights had been on, but nobody had been home. Nobody, except the black dark rage-monster that rose up inside him, blotting out everything and everyone who had ever mattered to him, or ever would.

His middle child, a boy, had died from the fever. Brian hadn't noticed. He'd been too busy killing and (over the next few days) *eating* his other two children, and his wife.

He'd been trapped inside the house. The concept of closed door, plus door knob, plus turn door knob, equals open door, was so far beyond his capacity, it might just as well have been quantum mechanics, or origami, or scrap booking; all of which were simply beyond his comprehension.

His neighbor solved the problem for him.

Three days (or it could have been three weeks, for all Brian knew) after he'd finished killing his family, Veronica Marsinski, whom he and his wife had loathed, because she was such a snooping little bitch, had come-a-knocking. Nobody had answered her knock, and so she just invited herself in. It was the last time she would ever do anything so rude.

He hadn't bothered to eat her, since he was full, following his family feast, but he'd still ripped out her throat with his teeth. Her blood now mingled with his family's, all over his face and neck and chest and arms and hands. He did, however, stop to drink the last of the water out of the downstairs toilet bowl before heading out the conveniently open front door.

Now, he walked the dark, post-curfew streets. Or rather, he stumbled and staggered, as if intoxicated, since his motor function had been impaired, though not as completely as had his higher brain function. Had anyone seen him, they might have mistaken him for a drunk - except for the fact he was naked (which could have been passed off as inebriation) and covered in blood (which could not) - but nobody did.

He banged into a wooden sign, almost falling ass-over-tea-kettle down the hill upon which the sign sat, but he somehow managed to retain his feet by grabbing and holding the wooden rectangle for support, leaving a bloody hand print upon the upper left corner. He groaned, growled, and headed past the sign and into the trees.

The sign, though he could not read it, said: *Grosvenor Park.*

27

John, Spute and Floyd pulled their rental truck onto the pier bare moments ahead of Jim and Gus in their heavily-laden SUV. They each got out of their respective vehicles - all of them, except Floyd, a bit creaky, since breaking, entering, burglary, and lifting and toting were such a younger man's game. But casual passers-by, ignorant of their recent activities, would have only seen five men moving with purpose toward a ship that itself was a bee hive of activity.

The five men met at the foot of the gangway.

"We need to leave," both John and Gus said at the same time.

John and company had just *removed* several hundred thousand dollars of scientific equipment and supplies from the College, where John had killed a man with a well-placed crowbar. Gus and Jim had just cleaned out half of the ammo stores from a place where the gun store owner now lay trussed up like a turkey on the floor. Being elsewhere when the police discovered their crimes would be a good idea. There was only one problem.

Marcie Gordon called down to them from the head of the gangway.

"John, have you seen Samantha?"

28

John Gordon wove the SUV through the streets of suburban Astoria, searching for his daughter. He was going to kill her, if she wasn't already dead.

The idea, the possibility, she might actually *be* dead - or worse, ready to turn into a raving zombie, like the hulking behemoth at the

College - froze his insides like an ancient glacier, it's ice ten thousand years old. What the Hell could she have been thinking?

It's a zombie fucking apocalypse! Let's party!

He was going to kill her.

He'd always considered himself a good father. He wasn't a brute. He wasn't a drunk (most of the time). He tried not to be an asshole. He did his best to keep their mother, his wife, Marcie, happy. He'd always heard this was the key: keeping Mom happy, and he had done so, for the most part. He hadn't pestered his children: Samantha, sixteen, going on thirty, and David (Davy), a bright ten year old, whose mind worked so fast sometimes it scared him. He hadn't picked at them, constantly, as if nothing they ever did could ever be good enough, like his own father had.

Henry Gordon had been a prick. That was the kindest thing he could have said about the man. No wonder John left to join the Coast Guard the day after he turned eighteen. Doing so, left his younger brother, Charlie, alone to take the brunt of the bastard's animosity toward the world, and take it he had.

Charlie had been a great kid: always cheerful, always warm, always funny in a way John could never be. It was a kind sort of funny: never at anyone else's expense, never dark, never biting. How he'd retained it during the three years he'd spent alone under that fucker's roof after John left, John would never know.

He'd been happy for Charlie when the kid won a scholarship to Stanford, and even happier when he'd met and then married Ashley Jane Wilkes. Their father had not come to the wedding. He hadn't been invited.

And then Molly came along, all dimples and sparkling eyes. The word *precocious* got used so often about everybody's children that it ceased to have any real meaning, but Molly was precocious in spades. At four, she'd learned how to read; at six, she was performing Sixth Grade math; and at ten, she'd won the State Science Fair for her age group by doing an ingenious thing with mice in a maze that John, to this day, still didn't understand.

Then the accident happened.

There were moments in life, seared into the memory like a burn scar, with a cruelty so vast, so cold, and so absolute John had never again been able to believe in a loving God. Moments like the time Harriet Gordon - John and Charlie's mother - committed suicide by hanging herself in the garage. John found her. He'd been eight years old. Her suicide note had been an apology to her children. It hadn't said a word about their father, and the heartless bastard hadn't said another word about her, either, as if she never existed.

John still had the occasional nightmare about the day he found her. It had been terrible, heart-wrenching, and unforgettable. But it was nothing compared to the day he heard about Charlie.

John had just made Chief. The Chief's Mess on the Cutter *Planetree* sponsored the traditional Kangaroo Court, accusing him of everything from brigandage to buggery, all the while plying him with alcohol in front of two thirds of the entire crew at *Rosie's Bar and Grill*, in the unlikely town of Pelican, Alaska. It was unlikely, first, because the entire town had been built on stilts and sandwiched between the waters of the inlet and the mountain behind it, and second, because *Rosie's* was a place that had to be seen (and experienced) to be believed. The walls and ceiling and long wooden bar were covered with well over a thousand signatures. The rule was, if you wanted to sign your name, you had to first drop trou, as explained by the plain wooden sign: *Drop Your Pants and Party.* And party they had. It had been epic.

He'd awoken at noon the next day with a hangover so horrible, his eyelids had hurt, and when he stripped to take a shower, he discovered the signatures of a dozen of his shipmates in magic marker upon his bare butt. No memory of how they'd gotten there, any more than he had one of getting back to the ship at the end of the night. He'd been sitting in the mess, nursing a cup of coffee, when the Messenger handed him the telegram.

We regret to inform you of the tragic death of your brother and his wife. STOP. *Car accident.* STOP. *They are survived by their daughter, Molly Jean Gordon.* STOP *You have been designated executor.* STOP.

Everything had stopped, as abruptly as if he had been in the car with Charlie when the drunk slammed into them head on - including his hangover. He'd sat there, slumped behind the mess table, frozen like the permafrost earth in the high Arctic, feeling nothing. His brother, who had survived their father with his kind humor intact, who had excelled at Stanford, who had married a wonderful woman and fathered an amazing child, who had the world at his feet and a life full of potential ahead of him was dead.

The pain came a day later - brutal, crushing, all-consuming pain, He'd hidden it from Marcie as best he could, but it had still come out -

lashed out - at odd times. She had borne it well, had borne him well; had been his crutch, his solid wall against which he could lean. Davy, their son, hadn't even been a year old at the time, but Samantha had been a mischievous six, full of jokes and loving silliness. She had been his light in the darkness. Even more than his wife, his daughter helped him find the way home. And now she was out there in the zombie-haunted darkness.

STOP

He stared at the Stop sign through the windshield, his foot having depressed the brake without his conscious brain telling it to do so. The SUV sat at the crossroads corner of Grove and Juniper. To the right, he knew, was the Mall, but it was late, already after ten, so it would be dark and closed, given the Police-mandated curfew. To the left, Grove snaked its way through one of the ubiquitous housing developments built during the boom in the first few years of the Twenty-First Century, before the economy crashed and burned. Half the houses had never been occupied. Ahead, Juniper dead-ended at Grosvenor Park. He knew kids sometimes (often) went there to smoke weed, and makeout, and do all those things their parents never wanted to hear about for as long as they lived, mostly because they, themselves had done it when they were teenagers. He eased the SUV forward.

Samantha was there; he just knew it, in the Park, at night, in the dark, after curfew, in a zombie apocalypse. He really was going to kill her, because the pain of that long ago telegram had been so immense, so overwhelming, so deep and lasting, that the thought of having to go through it again, to feel it again, to have to live with it for the rest of his life if she had done something so stupid as to go out partying in a zombie motherfucking apocalypse was just too goddamned much to bear.

His foot pressed down on the accelerator.

29

BM2/OPS Ricky (Scoot) Scutelli leaned against the chart table on the *Sassafras* Bridge, trying to control his spinning head. He was sick - had been sick - for the better part of a week now. And he was scared.

He'd gotten through the worst of the coughing and spitting of blood over the weekend, at the off-base apartment he shared with his wife, Maria. She had not been there, thank God. She had flown to the mainland to visit her sick mother in Cleveland, eight days ago. He hadn't heard from her in four of those days. During their last conversation, she told him she was feeling sick.

Communications between the Hawaiian Islands and the mainland of America had been spotty, due to the sheer volume of calls passing back and forth. It didn't take a genius to figure out the topic on every caller's mind: Pomona. Everybody knew about it. Everybody was scared about it. A significant portion of everybody had it, in one form or another.

Scoot knew he had it, knew his wife had it, and her mother, and... and... And he was scared.

He'd never been more scared of anything in his entire life. Everybody was shitting in their pants, whether they had gotten the cold or not, which was why he'd kept his own illness a secret. With his wife gone and possibly dying, he needed something to hang onto, and that something was his other family: his shipmates. If the command ever found out he was sick, they'd put him off the ship, and send hm to Base Medical, where he'd be alone, except for all the other people slowly being driven insane by the zombie virus.

On the upside, he was feeling better, his spinning head notwithstanding. There was hope in that. This was an odd disease - whatever it was. Not everybody got it. Not everybody who got the cold passed onto the neurological stage. So maybe he wouldn't, either. Maybe his wife wouldn't. Maybe everything was going to be okay. Maybe he'd get through feeling like shit, get better, and move on to carry out whatever mission was assigned by the United States Coast Guard.

He chuckled at the absurdity of this last thought, shook his head to clear out the rest of the cobwebs, and went back to working on the underway checklist. He wasn't - and never had been - the flag-waving *Simply Semper* kind of lifer one occasionally found on Coast Guard ships.

Scoot called it the *Military Disease*: a malady created when individuals were thrust into a position where there was no choice but to subvert their individuality and become part of a cohesive team. It wasn't natural, in the modern era, with its Reality TV and Social Media and texting and Blog sites and a hundred different ways to remain utterly self-absorbed on a day-to-day basis. Some people adapted - or, rather, simply ignored it and pressed on - but others were consumed by it, and yet seemed to thrive on it, turning them into that which he and Jonesy and most of the people he'd met during his time in the Guard hated. Either way, it still wasn't natural. The human mind and body rebelled against anything unnatural - like, say, the Pomona virus, or, say, the bullshit generated by assholes who took all the military shit too seriously. People like LT Dick Medavoy.

Scoot exited the pilothouse and climbed up the ladder to the Signal Bridge to visually check that both radar antennae were rotating on the mast as they should be. They were, but instead of ducking back inside, he glanced down onto the pier, where he saw two people - a woman and child - being escorted onto the ship by their new CO. They were carrying luggage.

Medavoy held an Officer's Call, a little less than two hours ago, to brief the crew on their current mission. He'd told them they were to take position between Oahu and Kauai and just wait. For what, he hadn't elaborated, but he hadn't needed to. Everybody knew: *wait for the end to come*. And after...? : Pick up the pieces, Scoot supposed. But the plan was all rather vague - probably because nobody knew what was going to happen.

The result of that uncertainty had raised the inevitable questions about the crew's families living in Hawaii. What about them? What would happen to them? And could they be brought on board and evacuated?

Medavoy had said: "No."

And now the motherfucker was bringing his own family on board.

What an asshole! Scoot thought. And then he coughed. His head swam. Maybe he wasn't getting better, after all. Maybe none of them were, or ever would...

30

Samantha could feel her heart coming apart, shattering into a million pieces, right there in the middle of Grosvenor Park. Justin Blaisdell was kissing Cheyenne Drummond.

Cheyenne Drummond, all blonde hair and blue eyes (Sam's own hair was naturally a mousy brown, and so she died it jet black - about the way her heart felt at the moment), and a bra size larger than her IQ, (she contemplated her own mosquito bites, then dismissed the thought as being far too depressing). In school, she'd been Sam's *frenemy* for years: the kind of girl who seemed to be a picture-perfect friend, right up until the moment Samantha turned her back, and then Cheyenne would stick the knife in and *twist*. She'd made the mistake of confessing her crush on Justin to the scheming little bitch in a moment of ill-considered self-delusion, just last week.

And now Cheyenne Drummond had her tongue halfway down Justin's throat, and his hand was firmly planted on her conniving ass. *Crack! Crunch! Shatter!* Her heart fell to pieces.

As if the universe hadn't already done enough damage, they had an IPOD station set up with external speakers and siting on the park bench, in front of which they were swapping cooties. At least she hoped it was cooties, at the very least. The music they were listening to was - wouldn't you know it - *Green Day*. Of course it was. *Crack! Crunch! Shatter!*

SNAP!

At first she thought the sound had been just another internal explosion as her soul was being crushed, but then she realized she'd heard it with her ears, not inside her head. Somebody else was out there.

31

Brian J. Reeves, former sales rep for a company that had no more meaning to him than did the mosquitos buzzing in the night air, and current psychotic, naked, blood-covered, rage-filled zombie, snapped a twig under his bare foot, where it caused a one inch cut that left splotches of blood in his footprint. He didn't feel it - or if he did, it didn't register.

What did register was the sound of...*something*. The something, as it happened, was music, but it might as well have been explosive flatulence, for all it made any difference. All he understood was noise, somewhere ahead, beyond the trees (which could just as easily have been sky scrapers) in which he stood. The sound angered him. That emotion couldn't have been explained, either, but it mattered even less than the mosquito that landed on his cheek and began to feed.

What mattered was the *rage.*

32

John pulled the SUV into the parking lot of Grosvenor Park, backed it into a slot by the groundskeeper's building, and shut off the engine. There was a car he didn't recognize, some foreign job, parked a few dozen feet away. It had several stickers of brand names he'd never heard of, plus one of a skull, in the corners of the tinted windows, and one on the bumper that said: *My Child Beat Up Your Honor Student.* He doubted the car belonged to a parent.

He knew Samantha was here - or so he kept telling himself. The question was: *where.* It wasn't a big place, like Central Park in New York, or Golden Gate Park in San Francisco, but it may as well have been. The night and the park were dark, and she could be anywhere.

And there could be zombies.

He picked the .357 off the passenger seat and looked at it. When Marcie asked the question of whether or not he had seen their daughter, John hadn't hesitated, hadn't thought about calling Sam's friends' houses, and certainly hadn't thought about calling the cops - not with two truckloads of stolen contraband sitting on the pier. He'd simply pushed Jim out of the way and gotten into the still-running SUV.

He'd shoved it into gear and started to pull out, then slammed on the brakes. "Gun!" he'd yelled, and Gus handed him the cannon he now held.

He'd never fired a Magnum of any caliber before, and had only fired a revolver of any type once, when he'd successfully killed a tree branch with a .32. He'd fired automatics, of course. The Coast Guard had still been using the .45 when he went through boot camp. He'd scored expert. He had liked it so much, he'd bought one for himself - a Colt 1911. It was traditional. It felt good in his hand. And if he hit somebody in the pinky with it, it would knock them flat on their ass.

Then the Coast Guard had shifted to the 9mm, supposedly so they'd have ammunition commonality if there were ever another World War - or some bullshit. He really couldn't remember the reasoning, and really couldn't give half a shit, at that particular moment. What he did remember was that the 9mm was a lousy replacement for the .45. A Nine may or may not knock a person down with a single round. Probably not, come to think of it.

He hadn't brought the Colt with him to the college. They had already been committing Burglary and Breaking and Entering, and Grand Theft. He hadn't wanted to add Armed Robbery to his list of crimes, so he'd left it in its locked case aboard the *True North*. It wasn't going to do him any good there, but after the incident at the college with the super-sized zombie, he was damned if he'd go unarmed ever again, and so he borrowed the big-ass pistol from Gus.

As he got out of the SUV and headed into the Park, he hoped the Magnum was as good as the 1911. If anybody got in his way or threatened or hurt Sam, he wanted to put the motherfucker on the ground.

33

Samantha watched in broken-hearted anguish as her fantasy of kissing Justin got sucked into the slurping, disgusting mouth of Cheyenne Drummond. She hated that bitch. And she wasn't feeling too friendly toward Justin. In fact, she kinda hoped Cheyenne had Herpes.

Her dream of diseased justice popped like a thought balloon when she heard another SNAP, off in the distance, this time to her right. Then she heard another. And another. And another. Whoever it was out there had brought friends.

When she saw the first of them - a naked man, covered in some kind of paint, or something - she was shocked. Not every day you see a naked man wandering around in a public park. Maybe in New York, or someplace like that, but not in Astoria. When she saw the second, then the third, then the fourth - all of them naked, and all of the men - her broken heart began to pound and her spidey sense began to scream.

She'd heard about the "zombies," of course. Who hadn't? The rumors were flying like the Wicked Witch's monkeys, and they ran the gamut from the sublime to the ridiculous. She'd thought the one about them being naked had been ridiculous. Now she wasn't so sure.

They hadn't seen her - at least she didn't think they had, and she wasn't going to test the theory by yelling or something equally stupid. But they had seen Justin and Cheyenne, a fact demonstrated when they all began to converge on the pair. She thought about calling out then, thought about shouting a warning, but something - maybe some sense of self preservation, or maybe - *GULP* - a sense of *revenge*, held her voice in check.

And then Cheyenne saw them. And when the first of them reached the park bench and grabbed the girl by her long, golden blonde hair, Cheyenne began to scream.

34

John was ten feet from the SUV when he heard the scream. He stopped in mid-stride, unsure of where to go or what to do - but only for a moment. The scream had come from a woman. Or maybe a girl. Or maybe Samantha. He ran back to the still-running SUV (the thought of turning it off hadn't occurred to him) yanked open the door and threw the truck into drive - then realized he was pointed in exactly the wrong direction.

He spun the steering wheel hand over hand, jamming it all the way to the left, and stomped on the gas pedal. The power steering whined in protest, and he did not care. There was a dog-crap disposal box on top of a stanchion on the opposite side of the road. He also did not care when he took it out with the right rear quarter panel. Jim could bill him.

The SUV jolted over the curb as he shot across the grass and toward the sound of the scream. The truck bottomed out, and John realized, in an offhand way, that the back was still full of ammo. The wooden cases bounced and crashed together, but he drove on.

He switched on the brights and the small service road leading from the groundskeeper's building appeared out of the darkness. He shot toward it, jolted off the grass and onto the road, and floored the accelerator. The truck hit forty when he saw a clearing to his right. He braked hard, swung the wheel, then braked again when he saw the hellish scene in front of him.

Four naked men were tearing apart - literally tearing apart - two fully-clothed people: one boy and one girl. His heart felt like it had been hit with a baseball bat, and a moan of pure anguish escaped his lips.

No! Oh please Dear God, if you exist, NO!

He didn't believe in God - hadn't believed in any kind of benevolent higher power since he found his mother hanging in the garage, all those years ago. But at the moment, he was willing to grab anything - any straw, any lifeline - for it not to be his little girl getting slaughtered before his eyes.

A rage filled him, so deep, so pure, so white hot, it seared his heart like phosphorus, consuming it, cremating it, as one thought cavorted across his mind, like some crazed demon from Hell: *Kill... Kill... KILL!* He slammed his foot down on the accelerator, vision tunneling toward a pinpoint aimed at the motherfucking zombies.

Just before his eyesight zoned down to nothing but the horror in front of him, his last bit of peripheral vision caught movement off to his left. Even so, he might have ignored it in his lust for violent revenge had two things not happened: some minute portion of his brain registered the girl being ravaged was a blonde, and the movement off to his left screamed:

"DADDY!"

The SUV skidded to a stop on the damp grass, then hit a hole big enough for a gopher the size of a poodle. His body jerked forward, and only the unconscious defensive move of throwing his arms in front of his face stopped him from cracking his skull on the steering wheel. The cases in back crashed and crunched against each other, with a sound of splintering wood and the unmistakable tinkling of brass spilling out and bouncing against who knew what else was back there.

Dizziness swept through him, either from the sudden impact, or from the unbridled relief of hearing his little baby's voice, but he shook his head to clear it and damn near threw out his spine turning around to look. She was there, running toward him, an expression of pure terror frozen on her face.

"DADDY!" She screamed again, then stopped dead in her tracks and began to point.

Two of the zombies had apparently tired of the massacre at the park bench and decided to investigate the screaming. They lurched forward, in a staggering, shambling run, right at Samantha.

His hand slapped at the passenger seat, where he'd tossed the gun when he jumped back into the SUV. It wasn't there.

"Fuck!" he shouted, scrambling to find the gun. He looked between the seats. Not there. He looked behind the seat. Not there. He looked in the floorboard. Not fucking there! Panicked, he dove across the passenger seat, slamming his head against the far door, as he craned his neck to see if the damned thing had fallen to that side. Where the fuck was it!

His left hand scrambled for the seat to throw his weight back toward his own side of the vehicle, but it slipped, nearly spilling him into the foot well. Then he saw it. The shiny polished metal barrel was just poking out from beneath the seat. With a cry of anxiety and relief and anger at his own clumsiness, he grabbed at it, but it wouldn't come. The fucking gun was stuck.

"MOTHERFUCKER!" he screamed, pounding the seat with his right hand as his left grabbed the barrel and yanked. It stuck for a moment, then jerked free, the sudden release spilling him into the foot well again. He didn't care. He had the damned gun. And now he was going to use it.

He heaved himself back onto the drivers' seat, transferred the pistol to his right hand, and pulled at the door handle. Nothing happened. The door was locked.

He slapped at the lock release, nearly ripping the fingernail off his middle (FUCK) finger, then yanked at the handle and shoved the door open, spilling himself onto the ground.

John often enjoyed slapstick humor. He was a huge *Three Stooges* fan - had even attended a midnight *Stooge-Fest* just last year. But now was abso-fucking-lutely NOT the time. He stumbled to his feet.

"Daddy?" Samantha said, in a surprised voice, eyeing the large weapon in his hand.

The brief idea she had never seen him with a gun before swam through the murk of his overloaded brain, but he shoved it down.

"Get in the truck," he said, then turned to face the two approaching zombies.

"Daddy?" she said again. It seemed to be all her shocked mind could produce.

"Get in the Goddamned truck, Samantha." She stated at him in disbelief. He never swore around his kids - never - and it dawned on him, she had to have heard him through the open window, screaming profanity as he was coming unglued, looking for the gun. With all of the other mental malfunctions the night had piled upon her, this latest incongruity had simply hung her up and froze her in place. But, again, now was not the time.

"MOVE YOUR ASS!" He shouted. It did the trick. As she scuttled in through the driver's door behind him, he cocked the pistol, took aim at the closest zombie, and opened fire.

Turned out, the Magnum worked just fine.

35

The scuttlebutt throughout the ship was in high performance mode as the final preparations for getting underway were nearing completion. While checklists received their last notations, and the last of the stores were secured for sea, the general consensus on the *Sass* was that Jonesy and Duke were prepping to "deal with" anyone who turned zombie. Opinions differed as to what, exactly, "deal with" meant, but it seemed clear it didn't bode well for anyone who succumbed to the neurological pathogen.

They all knew what was happening out in the world, had all watched it unfold on TV and in Social Media, and they knew it was bad on toast. People were dying out there - some of them people they knew: family, friends, and even (as in the case of Ensign Ryan, who had died when his plane went down) shipmates.

Word was (fairly well confirmed) that anyone who went neurological was as good as dead, even if they didn't get put down. The virus caused irreparable damage to the brain. There was no coming back from it. And once you went zombie, you were better off as a corpse, because when you turned, you might just eat one or more of your friends.

Being sailors in what was (up until Ms. Gordon's arrival that morning) an all male crew, and thus more than a bit sick and twisted, the black, gallows humor had been flowing thick and furious all day. Hardly an hour went by without two or three people pointing at two or three other people and saying: "Look out! It's a zombie!" And the typical followup would be to suggest the accused should start by munching on the accuser's asshole, which, in turn, would be expanded into a discussion of the solid waste coming from said orifice, and thence, naturally, to the current status of the corn they'd had for chow at lunch, which would then conclude when somebody or another finally made a suggestion far too disgusting for any of them to bare, at which point, the perpetrator of this breach of decorum and anything resembling good taste, would then be pelted with whatever might be at hand.

One comedic genius suggested they have a George Romero, *Night of the Living Dead* zombie movie marathon, to which another half-wit suggested to CS1 Gary King that he make up a batch of Tripe, to simulate a zombie feast. Gary himself, a thirty year-old, ebony-skinned excellent cook, with a calm demeanor, remained above it all, in spite of being on the Mess Deck - center of more gossip than any girl's locker room. He simply ignored the suggestion and carried on making his specialty: spinach lasagna. He knew it was Jonesy's favorite, and had decided to make it, instead of the pork adobo originally on the approved menu, because he figured his friend would need at least one good thing to happen this day. Jonesy, himself, quickly got labeled with the name *Petty Officer Khevorkian*, after the assisted suicide Doctor. Duke remained simply Duke, but, then, they always knew he was kind of screwy from the word go, and took great pains to point that out, over and over again - just not in front of either one of them.

One look at their uniforms, complete with body armor, knee and elbow pads, helmets, face shields, knives, batons, and (so it was rumored, though not confirmed) tasers, and it didn't take a genius to figure out somebody - maybe several somebodies - were going to have a very bad day. Few, however, were either brave or stupid enough to confront them about it.

One of those few, a short and ruddy-faced Electronics Technician with ginger hair named Terry Proud, long known for his near-complete lack of tact, saw Duke grabbing a cup of coffee on the Mess Deck and simply couldn't resist. "Hey, Duke?"

"Yeah?" Duke asked, the expression on his face amiable, as usual.

"What do we do if you and Jonesy go zombie?"

The assembled crowd of people fucking off on the Mess Deck (instead of doing something more constructive) drew a collective breath and waited for some revelation of things to come. Would Duke confirm or deny what had become known as *Zombie Plan Alpha*: *Death to anyone who turned*? Inquiring minds wanted to know.

"Well then, Terry," Duke replied, no longer amiable. "If I were you, I'd start running." And so saying, he left the compartment without another word.

OS3 Bill Schaeffer, Jonesy's roommate, had been sitting off to one side, by himself, as was his habit. It wasn't that he was anti-social, or anything along those lines. He just didn't think he needed to fill the air with idle chatter about stupid shit. But he also was no great fan of cruelty, which was, in essence, what he'd just witnessed. From Jonesy and Duke's perspective, this situation had to suck.

"Proud," he said, disgustedly, getting up and starting to walk away. "You're an asshole."

"Yes, sir, I am," said Terry Proud, proudly. The assembled crowd laughed.

Fun times at the Dawn of a Zombie Apocalypse, Bill thought, leaving the Mess Deck.

36

After killing the two zombies (one of their heads exploded from the point blank impact of the .357 bullet), John had scrambled into the SUV and drove the flying fuck out of there, before the other two zombies, still engaged in mauling the two kids at the picnic table, could react and head their way. Once out of the clearing and onto the road near the groundskeeper's building, he slowed to a less insane speed, returned to the access road, and headed out of the park.

He drove on in silence for the same reason he'd tried to ease out, rather than scream out of the park, once the immediate danger passed: Samantha was curled into a ball and had jammed herself into the corner created by the edge of her seat and the door. He could hear her whimpering, and the sound broke his heart.

He stared through the windshield with blurred vision he couldn't, at first, explain, until he felt the tears rolling down his own face. His little baby nearly died. More than any other thought he'd had any of the days since making the decision to evacuate, this fact filled him with anxious resolve. They needed to leave, right now. They needed to get as far away from there, and as far away from anything remotely resembling what just happened as fast as they possibly could.

But first, he had one more important thing to do.

He scanned their surroundings, surprised to see they were back at the crossroads. The night around them seemed still and quiet. More to the point, their location left them with at least thirty yards of empty space in every direction, so nothing...*unpleasant*...could come upon them without warning. Granted, it placed them in the middle of the intersection, but there was no one in sight, nor did he think there likely would be, anytime soon.

He braked to a stop, put the truck in park, and undid his seatbelt, then turned in his seat and looked at his daughter.

"How ya' doing, sweety?" He said, softly.

She twitched, but otherwise didn't budge.

"Sam, honey... Are you okay?" He knew it was a monumentally stupid question the moment it passed his lips. Of course she wasn't! She gave a tiny, almost imperceptible shake of her head. "Yeah, I know. Dumb question, Dad," he said, laughing at himself. "But that's my job, isn't it? To ask the stupid questions, act like a clown and keep you entertained." She shook her head again, this time more visibly. "That's me - Dad, the Circus Clown. Buffoon for hire. Still haven't got the knack of making balloon animals, though. Shame really," he shook his head, as if sad at his incomplete knowledge. "I'd really like to learn how to make that giraffe walk."

"Dog," she said, in a small voice.

"What's that?"

"It's a dog, dummy," she said, picking her head up and wiping her eyes. "You walk a dog, not a giraffe, you goof."

"You sure it's a dog?" He asked. "Not a two-toed tree sloth?"

She chuckled. "You're an idiot," she sniffed.

"Yeah, but you love me anyway. So what's that make you?"

She stared at him for a moment, then slid across the seat and into his waiting arms. "Your daughter," she said.

That's right, he thought, trying with his hug to express the inexpressible depth of just how much she meant to him. *Absolutely goddamned right.*

"Does this mean I'm not in trouble?" She asked, snuggling.

"Oh, no. You're totally doomed," he replied. "The payment will be high," he added, kissing the top of her head. "And it's going to take a very long time to pay off."

37

"Be careful with that!" Christopher Floyd shouted, watching as the net-covered pallet of scientific equipment was lowered into the hold.

Lane Evan Keely, age forty-nine, balding, wearing glasses, and feeling every moment of this long night, sat in the crane doghouse and briefly contemplated dropping the load the remaining twenty feet onto the steel deck below. He wouldn't really do it - probably - but that didn't stop him from wanting to. This "mad scientist" John picked up was a jerk.

Lane had been a real Bosun Mate during his Coast Guard career, not one of those half-assed ones created when the Guard, in its infinite lack of wisdom, combined the rate with Quartermaster. Taking one group of people who were masters of all things Deck related and mashing them together with another group of people who were masters of all things OPS related, then tossing them higglelty pigglelty into one position or another, regardless of experience and training, had been an exercise in madness - at least in his opinion. That it had worked - sort of - was more a testament to the men and women in the rank and file than a verification of the bureaucratic wisdom of the clueless officers who planned it. And so, his real Bosun Mate status and experience was offended by this new guy's meddling in something he had done countless times throughout his career. He knew what he was doing. He doubted the professor could say the same.

Still, he just smiled and nodded, and kept doing what he knew.

"Three feet," Mick Fincham's voice crackled over the radio, and Lane slowed the descent. "One foot," the voice said from the depths of the hold. "Down." Lane paid out an extra three feet of cable, then released the controls and sat back.

Mick was an odd duck, or so Lane thought. He'd been a Machinists Mate on one of the many ships John had served on, and had only arrived two weeks ago, so Lane didn't really know him. What he did know, he wasn't sure he liked. The guy was a dog, for one thing, sniffing after every woman he saw - including Lane's wife, Janine. She'd flicked him aside in her friendly way, and he went without argument, but it still stuck in Lane's gut. He'd have to watch that guy.

"Clear," Mick called from below, and Lane began to reel in the cable.

He looked down onto the pier where Spute stood next to the one and only remaining pallet. *Hallelujah,* he thought, panning the crane arm right, until the hook hung directly over the load, feeling relieved the night's work was almost done. But then he saw Jim's SUV rolling up the pier and remembered it was loaded with ammunition. His heart sank. His body ached. He lowered the hook to Spute.

"I do so love my job," he said to no one who cared.

38

John looked at the lightening sky to the East as he waited for the crew to assemble on the fantail. The last of the stores had been brought aboard and secured for sea, the last pre-trip checklist had been completed. They were as ready as they were going to get.

He looked at their faces. Everyone was there, except for Gus and Mick, who were down monitoring the running engines. Their faces were drawn, their eyes were red and bleary from sleep deprivation. He knew the prudent thing would be to wait until everyone had at least a little sleep. But with the sun slowly rising and the tide just beginning to go out, and the question of whether Gilbert Farcquar had managed to escape his bonds and could be - at that very moment - talking with the police, now sounded like a really good time to get the fuck out of Dodge.

"Before we go any further, does anybody have any questions?" he asked.

"Uh, yeah," Bob Stoeffel said. They called him Bob-Bob, because three simple letters, *B-O-B,* wasn't enough to describe the huge man. He had once tried out for the Milwaukee Brewers, but didn't get picked up because he wasn't fast enough. He could hit, though. Whenever they played softball, every time he swung a bat and connected, the *boom* could be heard a mile away.

"Where are we headed?" He concluded his question. Several of the others perked up. John hadn't explained the details of the plan, beyond getting out of Astoria and away from the plague.

"We're going west," John said. "Toward Hawaii," that produced a few smiles, but there were still looks of confusion and uncertainty. Why would Hawaii be any better than anywhere else? "Several reasons," he continued, checking them off on his fingers. "The weather is okay here, now, but we don't know how long we're going to be gone, so we're better off heading to where we know the weather is good, all year round." He ticked off another finger. "Islands are going to be the safest places to go on land, because there won't be as many people..." he could see looks of scepticism, "...once we get away from Hawaii. If we find one where there are no infected people, we'll be golden, as long as nobody else shows up."

He ticked off a third finger. "My Niece, Molly is out there, in the Coast Guard, on one of the new buoy tenders. She's been vaccinated, and she's smart and capable." He looked at Marcie, as if for confirmation, and she gave him a smile. Then he ticked off the final finger. "There will be other Coasties with her, and if we've got to ride out an apocalypse, I want the Coast Guard around me." That, perhaps more than any of the others, seemed to satisfy the assembled crew. The men were all retired Coasties. Most of the women and children had spent their lives in a Coast Guard family. They knew the people, knew their training and their strength, and dedication.

John could see he'd convinced them. Now to get going before anybody had a chance to second guess their decision.

"If everybody could please form a circle..." he said. He half expected bitching, moaning, groaning, and an untold number of good-natured aspersions against his character, but everybody was too damned tired. They did as he asked.

He looked at each of them in turn: Marcie, Samantha and David (who looked as if he might actually be sleepwalking); Lane and Janine, whose kids (a boy, 23, and a girl, 19) elected to try and sit this plague out in Alaska, where they now both lived with families of their own; Spute and his girlfriend, Clara, who only started dating a month before the plague was announced; Jim and his daughter, Stephanie, and his wife, Denise; Gus' wife, Joanne, her salt and pepper hair a mess of frizzy split ends after the heat generated by the galley dishwasher; Bob Stoeffel, whose wife had died of the fever two weeks ago, a scant three days before they'd gotten the vaccine, and their twelve year-old son, George; and Jason Gilcuddy, who had never found a wife, though he had - according to him - looked under every nook and cranny, whatever the Hell that meant. All of them were his friends, except Clara, whom he didn't really know. She'd been happy about getting the vaccine, though.

"Here's the weird part," John said. "Everybody hold hands." They did, though a few of them sniggered, and Jim raised an amused eyebrow. "Most of you know I'm not the least bit religious..." There were several nods around the circle. "But there's no sense in tempting fate, so I'd like to offer a prayer." Both Marcie and Samantha, on opposite sides, gave his hands an encouraging squeeze. He bowed his head. "Lord, the sea is so big, and our ship is so small. Watch over us and guide us safely to our new home, wherever that might be, ere journey's end."

"Amen," several of them said in response.

"Okay then," John said. "Let's get underway."

39

"Fuel barge is away," Scoot called from just outside the port Bridge door.

Jonesy turned to LT Medavoy, who had by now reached new pinnacles of crew loathing with the dick move (pun absolutely intended) of bringing his family aboard after he'd expressly forbidden the rest of the crew the same right, and saluted. "All checklists are complete, sir. The ship is ready to get underway."

The new (though still unofficial, since no message had come down from District Headquarters about the Change of Command) CO nodded, then turned to LTjg Bloominfeld, the Conning Officer, and said: "Single up all lines."

Bloominfeld turned to BM3/DECK Richard Masur, a short, squat young man, who wore what, to the uninitiated observer, might look like industrial hearing protection headphones with a large plastic microphone, but anyone who'd ever served on a ship would know they were sound-powered phones, designed to communicate even if the ship lost all power. With the exception of his mop of strawberry blonde curly hair, he looked like the nickname of every ship's Deck Force: a deck ape. Most people who knew him would say he acted like one, too. His billet for Special Sea Detail, was phone talker for the Anchor Detail and line handlers.

"Single up," the Conning Officer said.

"Single up all lines," Masur said into the microphone.

Jonesy knew without looking that men on deck, fore and aft, were bringing in the first of the doubled lines mooring the ship to the pier, thus completing the intricate dance, borne of hundreds and thousands of hours of training, practice, and experience. This was a good ship, in Jonesy's estimation, and a great crew. He didn't like them all, but he knew them all, and trusted them all with his life. That's what it meant to be part of a ship's crew.

He looked at brand new Ensign Molly Gordon, standing next to him at the chart table, which was laid out with the paper chart of Honolulu Harbor. She stood ready to plot the navigational fixes that would begin moments after they left the pier, with information coming in from the radar, where Scoot stood looking down at the activity on the forecastle, and from the port and starboard wings, where BM3/OPS Eric Hebert and BM3/OPS Jack Ross stood ready to provide visual bearings to known fixed objects; as, for example, the red light standing atop the bollard at the end of the pier to which they were moored. Jonesy would be taking in the information through his own set of sound-powered phones, writing it down, adding further information from the GPS, then passing it to Molly; each individual acting as part of a whole, the result of which was that they would not just know, but be able to *prove* exactly where they were at the moment the fix was taken. This, too, was part of the dance.

Advances in electronic navigation, as well as the ship's Dynamic Positioning System, made it technically unnecessary for them to do what they were doing, but Jonesy's attitude was that electrical things can stop working. The pencil Molly would be using to plot the fix wouldn't; or if it did, all she needed to do was sharpen it.

He looked at her face and suppressed the urge to laugh. She looked so serious, so determined to do a good, professional job on this, her first time getting underway on this, her first ship as a commissioned officer of the United States Coast Guard. But at the same time, he could see beneath the demeanor and to the young women trying her damnedest not to smile. Strip away all the officer shit, all the military shit, all the professional shit, and when it came right down to it, this shit was fun.

Until you thought about why they were doing it.

When Jonesy sounded the ship's whistle to announce to anyone with ears that they were underway, he couldn't help but see the glow of numerous fires, as Honolulu burned. They were getting out just in time. Question was: would there be anything left to come back to?

40

LTjg Amy Montrose, age twenty-three, with dark hair and eyes, shaded by her blue ball cap, exited the interior of the *Polar Star* onto the starboard Quarterdeck and went in search of her boss, the Assistant Operations Officer. She was an athletic woman of the not-quite graceful sort; more like a weightlifter than a runner, though she looked more like the latter than the former. General consensus of the crew (who thought she didn't know this, but were wrong) was that she was likely to beat the crap out of anyone who crossed her. It wasn't true, but she spared not one bit of energy to disabuse them of the idea. It gave her an interesting sort of "street cred," she thought. She found who she was looking for on the Boat Deck, just forward of the rectangular red bulk of the LCVP (Landing Craft Vehicle and Personnel) leaning on the rail and slowly - very slowly - smoking a cigarette and staring out to sea.

LT Steven Wheeler, who was (as he told everyone at every opportunity) from *Baaston* (meaning Boston), which, according to him was the Center of the Known Universe, was ever-so slowly smoking that cigarette, because he knew the number of available cigarettes in the world had suddenly become finite. No world meant no tobacco farmers, which meant no cigarette companies, which meant no more cigarettes. So he was savoring what he had while he could.

He was thirty-five, tall and stocky, and had gone to OCS, after working his way up to QM2, having not entered the service until he was twenty-three. When the announcement was made about combining QM and BM, he decided he would much rather be an officer. Amy liked him, though she wasn't quite sure why. He was one of those people it was hard *not* to like, in spite of (or maybe because of) his brusk manner and brash personality.

"Mistuh Wheeluh," she greeted him, intentionally saying his name with a Boston twang.

"Amy," he said, smiling, and tossing the thoroughly-smoked cigarette butt over the side. "What's the haps?"

"I'm actually here with something of an official question," she said, smiling in return.

"Oh, do tell."

"It's in my capacity as Morale Officer." One of her duties (and the Junior Officers always had a multitude of them - far more than their superiors) was to evaluate crew morale and see that it never got below a certain level, though that level had never been clearly defined. The previous AOPS, LT Gardella, left the ship in Australia, by helicopter, a mere three weeks before the plague was announced. He hadn't known how to define the level, either, but suggested anything over and above the crew being ready to mutiny was a good goal to maintain.

Wheeler frowned, slightly. "Go on."

"In a word, sir," she said, "it sucks."

"Not happy with the end of civilization, are they?" He asked. Three days had passed since the orders came down to head toward Guam, top off their fuel tanks, then take station in the middle of the Pacific. Once there, they were to...*wait*. Just sit and do nothing as the world fell apart.

"No, sir, they're not," she said, crooking half a smile at him. "Neither am I, now that you mention it."

"It is a kick in the crotch, isn't it?"

"I don't think I'd have put it quite that way..."

"Yeah," he said, waggling his eyebrows at her.

"They've lost everything," she continued, ignoring his crudity. "Their families, their country, their world..."

"Yeah," he said again, no longer smiling.

"I think we need something - some event - to jolt them out of it," she said.

"I somehow don't think the Captain will go for letting them get falling down drunk, so... Talent Night?" He suggested, referring to a shipboard tradition where the crew showcased their general lack of talent for the amusement of all.

"Bit more than that, sir."

"Oh?"

"I was looking at the chart last night," she said, smirking as he theatrically rolled his eyes at her. Junior Officers "looking at the chart," or anything even vaguely related to independent thinking, was a long-standing joke among all the military services. In the Coast Guard, however, given their numerous missions, enormous Areas of Responsibility (the Pacific Area alone covered eleven million square miles), and ridiculously small numbers, it was essential that those same Junior Officers do exactly what the jokes were there to mock. Still, they couldn't be allowed to get too cocky, and so the jokes remained.

"I am suddenly very afraid," he said, returning her smirk.

"Of course you are, sir," she replied, in mock seriousness.

"Go on."

"Couldn't help but notice that, with just a little creative navigation, we could cross the X." The "X" was an imaginary spot in the Pacific where one could cross the Equator at the International Dateline. Many sailors had crossed one or the other, but far less had crossed them at the same time. It would, in fact, be an event - especially when combined with a "Crossing Ceremony."

Crossing Ceremonies were also a long-standing tradition, though historically they had been far more about hazing than about ceremony. As such, they had been frowned upon in recent years.

"I think we should have a full on crossing. All the disgusting bells and whistles," she said.

"You realize you would be included in that ceremony?" He asked. They had crossed both lines individually, on the way down, but because of the political incorrectness of the hazing aspects, had simply held a barbecue up on the flight deck, renamed "Non-Skid Beach."

"I do," she said, a bit nervously. Tales had been told of Crossings past that weren't so subdued. Most thought the lurid descriptions of the "old salts" who had been through them were just a load of hyperbolic bullshit to scare the boots. They were wrong, but didn't know that.

He pondered the idea for a moment, slowly nodding his head. Then he smiled.

"Let's wake up King Neptune," he said.

41

"Jonesy, wake up!" Seaman Joey Siemen said, shaking him. Seaman Siemen had taken so much ribbing about his name, every single day since arriving at boot camp, that he'd just gotten used to it. But it made no difference to him at the moment.

Jonesy cracked the eye on the right side of his head (the one on top, since he was lying on his side) and stared at him. "What?" He growled, then glanced at the clock on the small desk next to his rack. 2326, it said.

He ordinarily shared the compartment with ET1 Carlos Hernandez, but the Electronics Technician had gone TAD to a school for some twidget bullshit Jonesy didn't understand, and so he had the compartment to himself and didn't have to listen to the bastard snore.

"It's Scoot, Jonesy," the young man replied, and he suddenly noticed that the kid looked...*frightened*. He sat up.

"What about him?"

"He's on the Mess Deck," Seaman Siemen said. "There's something wrong with him."

Jonesy stood, wearing only underwear and a white tee-shirt. He grabbed for his gear. "Go wake Duke.," he ordered. "Tell him to rig up and meet me there."

The "something wrong," was BM2/OPS Scutelli stripping off his clothing in the middle of the Mess Deck. The compartment was relatively empty, at that late hour, but not entirely. The people scheduled for what was called the Midwatch were gathered there to eat midrats (midnight rations) that were to sustain them while standing watch until 0345, and then beyond, since they wouldn't be crawling out of the rack three hours later to eat breakfast.. So there were people there to witness Scoot's "strip tease;" kind of like the reverse of that dream where you're in front of a class, naked - only for real.

Harold F. Simmons, jr., was there, drinking bug juice, along with DC3 Mike Kiepelkowski (Ski, to everyone - every ship had a "Ski").

They were sitting at their table in open-mouthed shock. CS3 John Ryan stared through the serving window, an expression of mixed amusement and horror on his face. MK2 Frank Roessler had been sitting at a table with ET3 Terry Proud (who didn't have watch, but had decided to grab an extra meal, anyway). They were now standing as far away from Scoot as they could get. He was howling.

Scoot looked really, *really* pissed off. He twitched and blinked, looking around as if unsure where (or who) he was. And then he launched himself at Terry Proud.

Jonesy was still strapping on his tactical rig as he reached the top of the ladder leading up from Crew Berthing. He wore the same uniform he'd had on since talking with the Captain (the *real* Captain, as far as he was concerned): black LE tactical, with boots, gloves, and helmet, body armor, emblazoned with the words: *US COAST GUARD* on the chest plate, plus the tactical harness that held two retractable LE batons, a large Gerber knife in a sheath, and a small holster containing the taser that he'd kept hidden in one of his cargo pockets, in case Medavoy got too curious. He had an additional blade - his dive knife - strapped to his right calf.

Conspicuously absent from the rig were any firearms. The idea still pissed him off. As he headed down the passageway toward the Mess Deck, he had the undeniable feeling he was going to need at least one.

He hadn't even turned the corner to the athwart ships passage that led to the Mess when he began to hear...*screaming*. He broke into a run.

42

Clara Blondelle, Spute's recent girlfriend, age thirty-eight, with bottle-created hair so red it was almost purple, stood on the bridge of the *M/V True North* staring out into blackness. She sort of saw the ocean out in front of her, certainly saw the fore...*thingy* at the front of the boat (it's a *ship*, Clara - ships *carry* boats - *whatever...*) But not another damned thing. She was tired, she was bored, and she was more or less thoroughly unsatisfied with her boyfriend.

Well... That wasn't *entirely* true. She was quite satisfied that his friends had provided vaccine. That had - quite literally - been a lifesaver. But the rest of it...? Don't think so.

Teddy was a nice enough guy, she supposed, and good enough in bed - at least for a zombie apocalypse. What was that thing...? Any port in a storm? But he wasn't the *head* guy - the Man in Charge. He was just another underling. Just another also-ran, like all the rest of her lovers had been. Why couldn't she ever find the Top Dog? Why was it always the Lap Dog, instead?

She didn't have an answer. But she did have *ambitions*.

The *actual* Man in Charge, John, was out of the question. Too married. Too bad. That Mick Fincham character was fairly yummy. He could butter her buns, quite nicely. But he was just a dog - not Top, not Lap, just Dog. And while it might be fun to go there, at some point, ultimately, it would lead nowhere, and she'd had enough of nowhere, thank you very much. Jim Barber was an interesting brute, but far too grumpy, and she got the distinct feeling he didn't trust her. Bob Stoeffel, now... *There* was a tasty morsel, if ever she saw one. And a widower! Might be nice to console him. But, then, in the end, he's just a cook. Lane Keely? Too *normal*. And too married. Gus Perniola? It'd be like screwing Santa Clause. That Gilcuddy guy was far too needy, and the Professor? No F-ing Way! No Bride of Frankenstein for her. Guess Teddy will have to do.

For now...

Sooner or later, they would get to someplace new. They were headed more or less toward Hawaii - at least that's what John had announced, although he'd added the caution that they probably wouldn't be going to Maui or Oahu, or any of the decent islands, because of the plague. But they would certainly be going to *some* island, sooner or later. They would have to, since their boat (*ship,* dammit - *whatever*) couldn't carry an infinite amount of supplies. Sooner or later they would find some slice of civilization. And sooner or later, she'd find a suitable replacement for Teddy Spute.

She was ostensibly up there on the bridge to stand watch as lookout. John had more or less required the spouses, girlfriends, and *children*, for God's sake, to help out on watches. Said it was a necessary thing, and it would give them something to do, since there was no telling how long they'd be out there, and sooner or later they'd get bored. Couldn't fault him. She was already bored, and it had only been three days.

She was supposed to be up above on the Flying Bridge, or whatever they called it. But Teddy was up there, "shooting the stars," whatever *that* meant. So he had asked her to come down and monitor the radar (nothing - absolutely nothing - for miles and miles and miles), and the radio (ditto...)

But then, the radio crackled.

"...Anybody out there monitoring sixteen?" a male voice called out of the black.

She didn't really know how to use a radio, but she had *seen* people using it in the three days since they left Astoria. You pick up the hand-thingy, press the button on the side, talk, say "over," when you were done talking, then let go of the button so you could hear the other person talk. Seemed simple enough. The red readout thing said: "16," so all she really needed to do was press a button. She was bored, so why not? She picked up the microphone.

"Hello...?"

43

Blackjack Charlie Carter, was thirty-five, tall, and lean, with jet black hair and a face so lined it could have masqueraded as a cracked desert floor   The recently "promoted" Captain of the motor-sailor *Daisy Jean*, heard the voice crackle over the radio and smiled. It was not a pleasant smile. He turned to his underling and said:

"Joe-Boy, hone in on that signal and find out what direction it's coming from." The man (man-child, really, couldn't have been more than seventeen) instantly did as he was told, going to the Radio Direction Finder above the small chart table and spinning the knobs. Blackjack

Charlie really liked having "underlings." They had been necessary during the evacuation, that was for sure.

Five days ago, they had been at Soledad Prison. Things had been going to shit for about a week before that, with both inmates and guards getting sick. Then the food trucks stopped coming. Then the Mess Hall had been closed, after three convicts turned and started eating one of the guards. The jailhouse humor-mill suggested it was normal behavior for the three, since they had all been in for either Aggravated Assault (two of them) or Manslaughter, but no one at the prison seemed willing to take the chance, and so they went into lock down. Then the riot started.

The word *bedlam*, long-absorbed into the English language, had taken on its own meaning, but it was derived from an insane asylum in Old London that, from all reports, had been really, *really* bad. The post-Fall riot at Soledad was worse, and it gave Blackjack Charlie the opportunity he needed, so he'd grabbed a few of his closest *associates* (calling them *friends* would've been too much of a stretch) and headed for the coast.

Didn't take a genius to figure which way the wind was blowing: out to sea. He *was* a genius *and* a former Merchant Mariner, and so he led his band of miscreants to the affluent confines of the San Francisco Yacht Club. There, they found the *Betty Jean*. It had not been unoccupied.

The owners (a husband and wife in their late fifties) proved willing enough to let them come aboard. Of course, the sawed off shotgun Blackjack had shoved in the husband's crotch had been rather persuasive. The two of them now resided somewhere in the Pacific Ocean.

The couple had stocked well: plenty of food, plenty of water, plenty of fuel. They'd also brought along a healthy stock of extremely good booze. That was becoming a problem. Most of the eight man crew he'd brought out of Soledad were now shitfaced. The problem would work itself out when the booze ran out, but unfortunately, it wasn't their *only* problem.

The *Betty Jean* had a more than adequate supply - *for two people*. He had eight people, and not a single goddamned one of them was particularly well-disciplined. They had, after all, been in prison. Impulse control was clearly not their strong suit. So this problem would soon become acute, unless they found themselves another boat.

He smiled again, and put on his least intimidating voice.

"Hey! Glad to hear another human voice," he said into the radio. "Where are you?"

44

Jonesy turned the corner onto the Mess Deck and into *carnage*. Terry Proud lay crumpled in the far corner. Blood shot from his neck like a busted lawn sprinkler, spraying Frank, who was hiding under a table in an effort to get away from Scoot, who was trying to see what other parts of Terry he could rip to shreds.

He slid to a stop on the terrazzo deck and stared.

"Fucking do something Jones!" Ski shouted from the opposite corner to Jonesy's left.

That snapped him out of it. He dropped the face shield on his helmet, pulled the taser from its holster, and advanced on Scoot. He knew the taser would only be a temporary solution, but temporary would be good enough for a start. Thumbing the device to ON, he stepped up behind the naked back of his BM2 and pressed the trigger. Two electric probes shot out, trailing thin wires, and stabbed into the flesh between Scoot's shoulder blades. They crackled with twelve hundred volts of electricity, and the newly transformed zombie shipmate jerked in spasms as the signals in his brain went haywire,

Any normal human being would have dropped and begun to vibrate like a dying cockroach. Scoot, however, was no longer strictly human. He twitched, let out a scream of more rage than pain, then spun and launched himself at Jonesy.

The former friend/current zombie slammed into him, toppling them both into, then over the bolted Mess table at Jonesy's back, and sent them crashing to the deck. Jonesy's breath left him like a spurned lover, slamming the door on his ability to take in oxygen. Gnashing teeth tried to take a chunk out of his face shield, as clawing hands tried to remove his kidneys through his abdomen. Jamming a forearm beneath the biting chin, Jonesy shoved with everything he had, and rolled the raving naked lunatic off of him and to the side. Planting his foot on the Mess Table stanchion, he thrust his leg straight and sent himself sliding head first on the supposedly non-slip deck, worn smooth by the tramp of thousands of feet in the three years since the last time the flooring had been replaced.

It shouldn't have worked, the terrazzo should have been too coarse, but the fact the crew had been too damned busy to maintain the decking might have just saved his life.

The maneuver put his steel-toed boot in striking distance and he kicked Scoot square in the nose, pulverizing it with a blood spraying crunch. Again, this should have incapacitated his opponent, if not killed him outright, but again, it seemed, zombies were made of sterner stuff. He (it) scrambled onto its knees and crawled toward Jonesy like some insane Pekinese, howling its rage and bloodlust.

Duke arrived then, hesitated as he took in the insane tableau, then swooped in and grabbed the screaming freak in a choke hold from behind. This should have ended the fight. The burly Bosun Mate had been tossing calves around on his family's Minnesota dairy farm, pretty much since he could stand. A mere human being was but a rag doll, in comparison. Not this time.

The screaming ball of rage thrust upward from its crawl and backpedaled its feet, slamming Duke into yet another Mess table. Duke fell. The zombie didn't. It spun and clawed at the (thankfully) lowered face shield on the LE helmet, found it impenetrable, and slid its hands downward to Duke's throat.

Jonesy had regained his feet by then. It the nanosecond it took for the electrical connections in his brain to zip back and forth between its synapses, he realized that a taser hadn't fazed it, a shattering kick to the nose hadn't stopped it, and Duke's heretofore unbreakable choke hold had held like wet tissue paper, and so only one option remained: deadly force. In a move he had practiced countless times in training, though never actually used in the field, Jonesy pulled one of the batons from his harness, snapped it out to its full length with a flick of the wrist, and side-armed it through the air to connect with Scoot's head, just below the left ear.

He wasn't supposed to do that - ever - wasn't supposed to take a head shot with the baton - wasn't supposed to go anywhere near the head, by law. But the law had changed; merged from the street and into the jungle.

It worked. It killed the zombie. It ended his friend's life.

45

Spute dialed in his final sight with the sextant. *Aldebaran* would make five stars - plenty enough for a good fix.

They had GPS, of course, but John correctly said the system could go down at any time, given the state of the world. When it went down, if they didn't have some other means to navigate, they were lost., and the Pacific Ocean was really damned big. As luck would have it, however, he, John and Jim, were all old-school navigators, and could all perform celestial navigation.

It took him a while to figure it out, back in the day, and his brain had actually *hurt* learning it, but learn it he did, and now, by God, he was using it. Made him feel like a real Old Salt.

Plenty of people who didn't have the slightest idea of what they were talking about, believed you could only shoot the stars at morning and evening twilight, when the rising or setting sun revealed a solid horizon. They were wrong. Any time of night would do, as long as you could see a solid line in the distance. All it required was a good eye, a clear night, and a relatively calm sea. Spute had all three, and now he had a five-star fix to reduce and then plot. He looked forward to it. Civilian life had been turning his brain to mush.

Oh, it had been good enough. He'd had a decent job as a Surveyor, that paid well and kept him out of doors and not chained to a desk in some dreary office filled with ass-kissing sycophants trying to impress the "boss," who wouldn't know his ass from a hole in the ground. He'd bought and (mostly) paid for a pretty nice house, and he hadn't saddled himself with a wife and kid to make him do any number of things he didn't want to do.

Who the fuck wanted to change shitty diapers? Not Teddy Spute.

He put the pen and notebook, on which he'd written the sight information, into his shirt pocket, cradled the sextant carefully in one arm, and used the other to descend the latter to the bridge deck. It was a nice night. The temperature was pleasant, the sea was calm, the breeze was just strong enough to be fresh without threatening to rip his clothes off.

Speaking of which, he smiled as he thought of ripping Clara's clothes off - with or without the assistance of a nice, stiff breeze - and giving her something else stiff to think about. She'd been a delightful find at a bar near his house, where the pickings had been slim, indeed - until she walked through the door.

She'd been wearing a low-cut blouse, insanely tight white pants that showed her black thong to delicious effect, and four-inch come-fuck-me-pumps, lifting her ass in such a delectable way, he simply had no choice but to hit on her. And it worked!

He smiled in anticipation as he palmed the bridge door handle and stepped inside.

"...What we'd really like to find is some vaccine," the male voice crackled over the radio.

In a frozen moment when he could have said something, could have done something, but didn't, he saw her lift the radio microphone to her lips, take a breath, and say: "Oh, we've got plenty."

He rushed to the radio set, jammed his finger into the OFF button, and said: "What the fuck did you just do?"

46

Molly stepped from the Mess Deck to the Buoy Deck and into darkness. It wasn't entirely dark. A sliver moon cast its long shadow upon the sea off to starboard, and the wave tops - what little waves there were - sparkled with the silvery light. And then there were the stars: thousands upon thousands of tiny dots spread across the velvety dark.

At first, she wasn't quite sure what she was looking at. Then it dawned on her: she was gazing at the spiral arm of the Milky Way; a concrete piece of the actual Galaxy, arcing away to infinity. They had to be at least two hundred miles from the nearest source of man-made light.

Nothing blocked the majesty of Mother Nature, in all her glory. She stared upward in wonder, barely breathing. A feeling of calm eased into her, filling her heart and soul and mind and body.

And then she remembered what brought her into the darkness in the first place, and her eyes came back down to Earth - which in this case took the form of the Buoy Deck. Jonesy was not there.

After "dealing with" Scoot, he had disappeared. She called his room, but had gotten no answer. Most enlisted rooms didn't have phones, but the First Class Petty Officers did; the design department apparently having decided that it might be necessary to get ahold of senior enlisted at any time of day or night without having to blast their names all over the ship via the 1-MC.

He hadn't been in the First Class Lounge, the Crew's Lounge, or on the Mess Deck (where CS3 John Ryan had been given the unenviable task of cleaning up all the blood), and she started her search on the bridge, where BM3/OPS Eric Hebert none-too-happily stood an extra two hours of watch. Scoot had been his relief. Under normal circumstances, Jonesy would have taken over the Midwatch, but nobody - not even LT Medavoy - had even whispered the idea. BM3/OPS Jack Ross would come on watch two hours early, though he didn't know it yet.

So there remained but one place Jonesy could be: out on deck. Of course, at night, at sea, in the dark, out on deck was a pretty damned good place to hide. There were spots a person could sit quietly and you'd walk right by them. Or maybe trip over them.

She glanced up at the raised platform of the forecastle, but dismissed it as a possibility, and turned to climb the starboard ladder to the boat deck. The idea that he might have come out into the darkness because he wanted to be alone crossed her mind, but she dismissed that as well. Friends don't let friends dwell on the fact they just killed one of their shipmates.

This brought up an interesting and uncomfortable question: were they friends? They had been friendly, to be certain. *Understatement*, she thought, feeling a burning flush rise from places within her body upon which she did not want to concentrate. She reached the top of the ladder and drew in a deep breath.

The climb hadn't robbed her of oxygen. She could run up and down the ladders and run several laps around the deck before becoming even mildly winded. But maybe, just maybe, the question of their friendship - their *relationship* - might have robbed her of her usual confidence. The idea, quite frankly, scared the crap out of her.

So, yes, she paused for a deep breath to steel her nerves. Partially out of nervousness, and mostly out of a desire not to trip, fall, break her neck and roll over the side into the depths of the lonely ocean, she moved forward, past the hulking shadow of the RHIB in its cradle, through the aircastle, and toward the fantail.

The white of the superstructure glowed in the warm night air. Outside, on its surface, an orange life ring, stenciled with the words USCGC SASSAFRAS, hung from the bulkhead, just forward of a long fire axe in a cradle, its blade covered in a leather sheath to protect it from the corrosion of salt spray. Inside lay the DC Shop, the Dive Locker (a closet, really), and the Survival Gear Locker, with its cargo of empty Survival Suits and piles of Type 3 PFDs.

Why, exactly, she was contemplating the layout of the aft portion of the 01 Deck might have been a mystery, had she been prone to self-delusion. She wasn't, and so she knew why: to keep her mind from dwelling on certain thoughts and implications that would only serve to complicate the living Hell out of her life. Surviving the zombie apocalypse was going to be complicated enough.

She sensed him before she saw him. What magic is it that enables one person to feel the presence of another? What sixth sense floats across the ether until it touches some sympathetic tendril emanating from the other person?

Molly did not normally wax esoteric in this manner. Lately, however, life had been anything but normal. From the greeting at home after she graduated from the Academy (*Welcome home, Molly! Now roll up your sleeve so I can inject you with zombie vaccine*), to the apocalyptic reason for it, and through seeing Socrates Jones (of all damned people) on arrival to her first unit, and all the zombie-craziness in between, normal had packed its bags and sailed to Aruba.

All of which was bullshit, she mused, pausing in the deeper, shadowy darkness of the superstructure. She could see him now, sitting on a bollard, with his chin resting on crossed arms upon the starboard rail, staring out to sea.

A plethora of *girlish* feelings swept through her at the sight, and it pissed her off. Damn him! Damn his good looks and charming manner and witty repartee. Damn his calm acceptance of her do-not-call-me edict at the end of the Arctic trip, the previous summer. Why hadn't he pined away for her? Why hadn't he curled into a ball of human misery and wallowed in his loneliness? And why hadn't he called her, dammit?

She was scared, and she was nervous. Both things pissed her off. And one thing about Molly by-God Gordon, was that when she was pissed off, she bulled ahead. Damn the torpedoes!

She took a strident step forward, then froze. What the fuck was she thinking? The poor guy just killed his friend. What was she going to do: charge in and start bitching at him? *Huge points for compassion, Moll*, she chided herself. *Get a grip!*

Should she even be out here? Should she just go away and leave him to what had to be really long thoughts? What right did she have to interfere? She teetered on the horns of this latest dilemma, balancing on the knife edge of some metaphor for which she had no clear definition. She was stalling. In the end, however, he decided it for her.

"Ms. Gordon," his honey-whiskey voice floated out of the darkness.

She was caught. And being caught, she did the only thing she could and walked aft toward him.

"How did you know it was me?" She asked, as she arrived.

"Your perfume," he said, not looking at her. He patted the empty bollard beside him.

"Did I lay it on that thick?" She asked.

He chuckled. "No."

"Is it that distinctive?"

Yes," he said. "And no." She sat beside him, taking great pains to not touch the skin of his well-muscled arm. "Who else, among the crew, would be wearing perfume?"

"Ah," she replied.

"Okay...Maybe Harold," he said.

"Well, you took a chance and it turned out to be right," she quipped, sounding far more glib than she felt.

"Yay, me!"

They lapsed into silence - or, at least, as much silence as one could have when sitting on the deck of a ship, directly above the churning propellor that was propelling them ever-box-ward in the *Box of Death*, toward...what, exactly? She knew the technical answer, of course. They were patrolling a point on the chart of the North Pacific, a hundred fifty miles offshore and roughly equidistant between Oahu and Kauai. What they were supposed to do beyond that remained a mystery, but it was a question for another time.

"So..." She said, finally. "Whatchya doing?"

47

Two decks down and about a hundred feet forward, Seaman Apprentice Tommy Barnes, of Akron, Ohio, whose sole ambition growing up had been to learn how to surf, twitched in his bunk. He still hadn't learned how - the Banzai Pipeline being no place for amateur surfers - but it hardly mattered, now. It would never matter.

He'd felt like shit all day. He hadn't told anyone, however. Mrs. Barnes hadn't raised any idiot sons, and only a real idiot would have mentioned feeling sick. Not with *Petty Officer Kevorkian* around.

He slept now. His dreams - if he had any - weren't significant enough to interrupt his slumber. He was, however, feeling feverish.

Two four-man staterooms up and one over, on the port side, YN3 Gregory Haversham rolled over and snorted. He'd been feeling feverish, as well. And his skin felt irritated. Not bad, not enough to be worrisome, but enough to notice. A spasm rippled through the muscle of his right thigh. He stirred, let out a slight moan (that may or may not have sounded a little bit like a growl), then slipped back into the Land of Nod.

In the next compartment forward, CS3 Eric "Manny" Manoa, all six-foot five and two hundred-fifty pounds of him, farted. This was nothing new. His gaseous expulsions were legendary on two ships, the Recruit Training Center at Cape May, New Jersey, and the Culinary Specialist A-School, in Petaluma, California. What *was* new - really new - was the fever.

One deck up and almost directly above the flatulent cook, BMC Bernie Adams, alone in his stateroom, thanks to his exalted rank, lay awake, reading. He wasn't really seeing the words, however. Truth be told, he hadn't comprehended a single goddamned sentence in the last ten pages.

He was worried. *Oh, Hell, be honest, Bernie. You're scared,* he thought to himself. He coughed, tried to muffle the sound, as if not hearing it might somehow eliminate the possibility of what it could mean, failed to do so, and collapsed into a coughing spasm that felt like his left lung might explode. He groaned to a sitting position and hacked a disgusting goober into a tissue he'd grabbed from the box on his night stand.

The box wasn't secured for sea, he noticed. *Bad Bosun Mate,* he thought, then glanced at the crumpled tissue in his hand. It was smeared with blood.

48

"Whatchya doing?" Molly asked.

"Performing brain surgery," he replied with his usual dry humor. "Can't you tell?"

She leaned her elbows on the rail and joined him in staring out to sea. The water sparkled with reflected starlight. There was a splash off to her right.

"Flying fish?" She asked.

"Either that, or *Cthulu*, the Beast from the Depths," he replied. "Can't decide which."

"You're just a bundle of sunshine, aren't you?" Their conversations had always tended toward the sarcastic, pretty much from the moment they met. *Great minds thinking alike...*

He didn't respond, and she didn't press. They sat there in silence. It wasn't uncomfortable.

That was something else they had fallen into right away: companionable silences. So many people felt the need to fill the air with useless chatter. It had always annoyed her - possibly because it interrupted the chatter going on inside her own head. One more thing in Jonesy's favor. She shoved that thought to the side so hard it would have fallen overboard, if it'd had an actual body.

Finally, after about three minutes, he broke the silence by asking: "Did you hear how I came to be on this ship?"

"Not exactly."

"After the *Healy*, when the Powers That Be finally realized how truly pointless it was to have a TACLET on a Polar Icebreaker, PACAREA sent me to D-14."

"That was nice of them," she said, to fill in the conversational gap, thus giving lie to her earlier observation about companionable silence.

"Oh yeah," he laughed. "Here, Jonesy. Have a nice little Hawaiian vacation."

"You should fire your travel agent."

He thought about it for a moment, then said: "He's probably a zombie by now."

"Bundle of sunshine," she repeated, as a squadron of frightened butterflies took flight in the pit of her stomach.

"That's me," he quipped.

She gave him a moment, then said: "You were saying?"

He took a deep breath, then continued his tale. "A week after I got here, we received intel on a freighter out of the Orient. Human trafficking, drugs. Nice bunch of guys." He reached into his front shirt pocket and pulled out a roll of lemon-flavored throat lozenges. He took one, then offered the roll to Molly. She declined.

"My team had the crew under guard, back on the fantail," he said, popping the glorified candy into his mouth and shunting it off into the depths of his cheek. "And we were just starting the pat-down, when one of the assholes pulled a gun. Didn't even think about it. I took the shot."

"I...heard about it," she said.

"The entire fucking Coast Guard heard about it," he laughed. "Not exactly an everyday event."

She gave her own grunting chuckle, but didn't otherwise respond, not wanting to interrupt.

He glanced at her, then resumed staring out to sea. "You know, I looked it up on the Internet. Typed in '*Coast Guard Involved Shooting.*' You know what I found?"

She shook her head, but doubted he'd been expecting an actual answer.

"Nothing. Not a single goddamned entry, except for a series of stories about a murder several years ago, up in Alaska. For all I know, there's *never* been one." He gave a short, breathy chuckle, and shook his head. "I am a man outstanding in his field," he added, his voice dripping with irony. "And that's certainly the attitude the Shooting Board took. What a cluster fuck!"

"I can imagine," she said.

"I doubt it," he replied, not unkindly. "Three Admirals and half-a-dozen Captains, and every last goddamned one of them just had to make a speech, with me sitting in a chair in the middle of the room." He shook his head and snorted in obvious disgust. "It was like watching a bunch of Republicans at an I-Hate-Hillary Convention - with me as Hillary."

She stared at him, open mouthed, and said: "That must have been..."

"Gangs of fun," he said. "And ultimately pointless. Every member of the boarding team swore under oath, they'd have taken the shot, if I hadn't." He shrugged. "And then there were the helmet cams. Every team member wore one, and everybody with eyes could see it was a good shoot."

"But of course, it wasn't that simple," she said, knowing there had been more to it. She'd read the reports, seen the videos on the news, and had been right in the Rumor Control Pipeline at the Coast Guard Academy.

"Yes and no," he said. "Yes, because after all the posturing, the evidence was overwhelming."

"And no because...?

"No because they couldn't just leave it at that."

"Naturally."

"Ain't life grand?" he chortled. "And so I got to spend some quality time with the Psychological Trauma Team!" He gave his breathy laugh (that contained no humor in it, whatsoever) again. "Imagine your brain getting gangbanged by Oprah, Dr. Phil, and the entire cast of *The View* - not a single damned one of whom knew what the fuck they were doing."

"Yikes!"

"As I said," he quipped. "Gangs of fun."

"And...?" She knew the basic details of the story, at least what she'd been able to filter out from Rumor Control, but hearing him talk about it gave it a sense of immediacy and personality that no scuttlebutt nonsense could ever achieve.

"I should have lied to them and told them what they wanted to hear."

"But you didn't."

He looked at her and shrugged. "I don't lie."

She stared at him, cocking an eyebrow.

"Oh, I bullshit with the best of them," he said, in response to her obvious disbelief. "But that's different."

"I see," she said, dripping with sarcasm. "You'll have to explain the difference to me sometime."

He chuckled again and resumed. "Anyway, when they asked what I was feeling, I told them the truth."

"Which was?"

"Nothing," he said. "I felt nothing."

She stared at him again, the shock clearly reflected on her face.

"Don't get me wrong," he said, holding up a traffic cop-like hand to stop her protest. "It sucked. Well and truly." She kept staring at him. "I'm not a sociopath." He shrugged yet again. She couldn't decide whether the gesture annoyed her or was simply a manifestation of his boyish charm. "Simple matter of black and white," he continued. "Kill him, or he kills somebody else."

She stared at him a moment longer, at his eyes, which held that damnable charm and, at the same time, deep down, a sense of vulnerability that threatened to melt her heart. He wanted her to believe him. *Needed* her to believe him. She nodded and gave him a slight smile.

"You get it," he said. "At least intellectually," he added, as if in response to her narrowed gaze. "But they decided I wasn't wrapped too tight - or way too tight, not sure which. And so they pulled me off the Team. Called it a 'temporary stand-down.' Couldn't even call it a suspension - which is what it was. And so they put me on Admin Leave."

"Bastards," she said, softly, meaning it.

"And since the whole thing was far too public (thanks to somebody in Public Affairs releasing the helmet video, when they weren't supposed to), they couldn't very well kick me out after they cleared me. Couldn't even say I was crazy, because that would make it seem like they cleared a lunatic."

"The media would have loved that!"

He laughed. "I actually got chased one night. Thought I was going to have to do a Lady Di." He shook his head, and she could almost see the memory flashing over his hazel eyes.

"But then some celebutante got busted for drunk driving, for like the third time, and my fifteen minutes were up." He didn't look one bit sorry for the loss. "So there I was, off the Team, with nothing to do, and nowhere for them to put me, and no idea of what to do with me. And then Providence came calling."

"Oh, do tell!" she said.

"The BM1/OPS on this thing," he said, patting the rail, "went and got himself arrested for trying to ship a kilo of Maui Wowie home to Indiana, or wherever, and suddenly, there was this huge opening for a BM1."

"And the rest is history," she finished - or thought she had.

"And the music swells, and I walk off into the sunset."

"And right into a zombie apocalypse," she said.

"Ain't life grand?" He gave her his most charming smile. He wasn't doing it on purpose - at least she didn't think so - but it melted her heart anyway.

*Danger, Will Robinson...*she said to herself, falling back on her own storehouse of personal sarcasm to fight the urge to take him in her arms and give him a big, wet kiss, right on the lips. *Danger! Danger! Do something! Say something! Resist!*

Out of desperation, she settled on a verbal kick to the nuts: "And now...?" She could tell by the sudden darkening of his expression that her jab had hit home.

He shrugged. "And now I feel nothing again." He sighed, looked like he was about to shrug for the umpteenth time, seemed to realize he'd been doing it a lot, and let his eyebrows shrug for him. And then he said: "Black and white."

"How bad was it?"

"It sucked. Full-blown neurological. Wild eyes, gnashing teeth, growling. Certainly not puppies and kittens."

"But you're okay?" she asked, ignoring the danger signals and placing her cool hand on his well-muscled forearm.

"Yeah, I am, actually."

"So what are you doing sitting alone out here in the dark?" She asked the obvious question.

He pointed out to sea with his chin. "Look out there," he said. She did. "What does it make you feel?"

She thought about the question. And she thought about why he'd asked it.

Her degree at the Academy had been in Psychology, so she acted in fine Shrink fashion and turned it around on him. "I don't know," she said. "What do you feel?"

"Peace," he said quietly, and she felt the answer in her own heart. "I feel peace. I feel like this is where I belong."

She folded her hands on the rail and laid her chin upon them. "Uncle John talked about that. Said it was the mark of a true sailor."

"Said the same thing to me when we were up in Alaska, four or five years ago."

"He likes you," she said.

"I like his niece," he said, and she felt his answer right square in her heart.

Time to put a stop to this.

She stiffened and sat up. "Stop," she said. "Don't do that."

"I'm just saying..." he smiled.

"Well, don't," she snapped.

He looked at her a moment longer, then said: "Fine. Have it your way." Her heart sank, as he looked back out to sea. *Careful what you wish for*, she thought. "Anyway, I'm out here to soak up as much peace as I can." He looked at her again, and his expression wasn't the least bit charming. "Because I think things are about to get a whole lot worse."

49

OS3 Bill Schaeffer keyed his entry code into the door, heard its distinctive click, and entered the Radio Room. He was glad he had the watch this morning. He hated funerals, and a funeral at sea for two of his shipmates - one of whom had turned zombie - would have been a far too depressing way to begin the day. Plus, he was feeling just a bit...*paranoid*.

The familiar faint smell of ozone wafted into his nostrils, as OS1 Carlton Bertram (Bert) spun in his chair and looked at him with mildly bloodshot eyes. "You're early," his immediate supervisor said, glancing at the clock on the bulkhead, which read zero-seven twenty-five. The eight-to-twelve watch ordinarily began at a quarter till the hour, so technically he was, in fact, early, but that was generally not something for the guy he was relieving to grouse about - especially coming off the dreaded four-to-eight watch in the morning.

Dragging your ass out of the rack at three-thirty to sit in an enclosed compartment with no windows, listening to static and not much else, was universally hated by all. But there was something more going on here. Bert looked...*nervous*.

"Are you complaining?" Bill asked.

The man stared at him for a moment, then seemed to relax. "No," he said. "Early is good. There's a lot to brief."

"I'm all ears," Bill replied, deadpan, taking a seat at the second of two bolted-down chairs.

"Lots of chatter all night long," Bert said. "Lots of news. All of it bad." Bill cocked an eyebrow at him, but said nothing.

"The BBC has been reporting from all over the world: Paris, Budapest, Bremerhaven, Cairo, Rio, Singapore City..." he consulted a handwritten list on the console. "...Osaka, Shanghai, Mexico City, Lima... All gone."

"Gone?" Bill asked, incredulous.

"Fallen to the Infected," Bert clarified. "No communications. No word," he gulped. "Last word out of Mexico City was cut off by screaming." Bert's face had turned a sickly white. "I heard it all."

"Fuck me."

"It gets worse," he said, and a terrible chill started in Bill's scrotum and moved upward toward his heart.

"Worse?"

"Worse," Bert repeated. "New York has fallen. They blew the bridges to Manhattan about an hour ago. Washington, D. C., is being evacuated," he said, his voice gone cold and dead. "All the politicians, anyway." He tried a faint smile, but it didn't work. "No great loss, there." He tapped the *Top Secret* board. "List of all the main players and where they're evacuating to. About half of them have confirmed arrival."

"And the other half?" Bill asked.

"No word yet," his boss said. "Don't know, don't really care. We have bigger problems." Bill cocked another eyebrow at him. "Ford Island has fallen, and the word is, Sand Island won't last much longer."

50

OS2 Amber Winkowski, brought the last of the bottled water into the Comms Room and set the dolly on the deck next to the rest of it with a sigh of relief. Sixteen cases of water, in total. She hoped it would be enough. "That's all I could get my hands on," she said, straightening her sore back. She was twenty-eight, not tall, and her short, frizzy hair was tied into a pony tail and tucked beneath her blue US COAST GUARD COMMSTA HONOLULU ball cap.

Sports Illustrated would not be inviting her to grace the cover of its *Swimsuit Issue*, and that was just the way she liked it. She was just Amber: not tall, not petite, and hippy - both in her Bohemian/Feminist attitudes (her car sported two bumper stickers that proclaimed: *US Out of my Uterus*, and *Sorry, But I Was Too Busy Leaving My Husband, Killing My Children, and Practicing Witchcraft to Care* - a twist on a truly idiotic televangelistic proclamation by Pat Robertson), and the fact that her backside wasn't small. She didn't care. The pretty girls, the ones that had been prom queens and cheerleaders, and the object of unrequited teenaged sexual fantasies, always seemed to get hooked up with shitheads. They were used. They were liked for what others hoped they could give them, whereas Amber was liked for being Amber - just the way she liked it.

What she didn't like was the jackass who would be her companion for who knew how long.

OS3 Jackson Grabon, age twenty-two, stared at her, but said nothing. He hadn't helped her at all, even though he would benefit from her labors every bit as much as she would. It would be the difference between survival and dying of thirst - or of hunger, since she had also brought in three cases of MRE';s and another two of industrial-sized canned goods. And yes, she also remembered to bring a can opener. He seemed oblivious about this, as, Amber mused, he had always been oblivious about most things. He just sat there munching on the remains of a ham and egg MRE. The detritus of its packaging lay haphazardly on the console. He belched.

Even if he doesn't turn, she thought. *I might have to kill him.*

51

"I could kill the stupid bitch," John snapped.

"I know," Spute said in a placating voice. The two of them were on the Bridge. Clara was back on the Flying Bridge, though John had been tempted to toss her over the side.

"What the fuck was she thinking?"

"I don't know, dude," Spute said. "I didn't exactly bring her along for her brain power."

"Yeah!" John spat. It was almost a yell. "And her nice ass might just get us killed."

Spute woke him up with a phone call bearing the news that Clara had "inadvertently" let slip they had vaccine - over the fucking radio! *Inadvertently, my left nut!* John thought. *How could she have been so stupid?*

He took a deep, calming breath. It had no effect, whatsoever. He looked out the rear Bridge window at the yellow ball of the rising sun. It sat a full diameter above the horizon.

How much longer did they have? How much longer before pirates descended on them?

52

Blackjack Charlie looked into the lightening sky. "We wait till dark," he said, making up his mind. They had to be careful, had to do this right. If they did, they would be golden. They'd have vaccine. If they didn't...?

Such thinking would only lead to trouble, he thought. At the very least, he must never speak it aloud. He nodded to himself, then turned to Old Joe.

"Sober everybody up. Put them to bed. Tie them there, if necessary," he told the man. "And lock up the rest of the liquor." The last damned thing he needed was a bunch of drunk fuckers messing this up.

Old Joe nodded, but didn't move. Blackjack Charlie sighed.

"Now would be good," he said, making shooing motions toward the door leading below.

"Right boss," the man said in his gravelly voice. And then he left.

Old Joe wasn't really that old, being maybe ten years older than Joe-Boy, but having two men in the same gang with the same name could get confusing. Having two men in the same cell block could be confusing, for that matter, and that's where the nicknames had been created.

Joe-Boy, barely seventeen, had been tried as an adult after beating his own father to death with a baseball bat. Maybe the guy had it coming. Blackjack didn't know, didn't care. He'd wanted to call the kid Shoeless Joe, after the White Sox baseball player, but most of the people on the block could barely remember last week, let alone several decades before they were born.

Old Joe had been doing a dime for Armed Robbery. The two of them arrived on the same prison bus, and wound up together on C-Block, though in different cells. The nicknames had been picked and agreed upon by the general consensus of people who couldn't give two shits about much of anything, and they stuck. "Blackjack" Charlie Carter's moniker had come in the same manner, though his had been far easier to grasp by the general population.

He'd carried a blackjack for years, having discovered the utility of the leather filled pouch of tiny ball bearings during his travels as a

Merchant Mariner. There had been that Chinese asshole in Shanghai, and that Australian fuck in Melbourne. They tried to mug him, thinking he was too drunk to be much trouble. He *had* been drunk - both times (hilariously so in Shanghai) - but he and his blackjack proved to be far more trouble than either bastard counted on. He left them both in need of a headache remedy, but it was the pimp in San Francisco that got him the nickname.

That douchebag busted in on him while he was banging one of the guy's hookers. Fucker hadn't even bothered with him. Just marched right in and started smacking the girl around. So Charlie had taken his trusty blackjack and taught the guy a lesson. Bit too good of a lesson, unfortunately, because the useless piece of shit died from it. *That* got Charlie sent to Soledad. The nickname had been a no-brainer.

He was going to need all of his brains now, though, stuck, as he was, on a boat filled with drunken idiots in the middle of a zombie fucking apocalypse. But that was okay. He had plenty of brains to spare. And tonight, if he could keep his band of misfits sober, he would have the means to ride this shit out. And with a little luck, he'd be riding it out in style.

53

"Sorry, but no," Captain Gideon D Hall said. "We can't divert."

LTjg Amy Montrose stood next to LT Wheeler in the Captain's office/stateroom, and tried not to slump her shoulders in disappointment.

They hadn't been able to talk directly to the CO until this morning, but both had been certain he'd okay the proposed Crossing Ceremony. Apparently, they'd been wrong.

"The idea has merit," The Captain agreed. "But until we get to Guam and top off the tanks, we're on a schedule." He tapped the message board on his desk. They both knew what it contained. "With everything falling apart, we can't delay." He looked pointedly at each of them. "We need to get to Guam before it falls."

A symphony of fear played *Toccata and Fugue in D Minor* along her spine. What the original Phantom of the Opera theme had to do with the current situation, she had no idea, and was only speculating on it to take her mind away from the stark reality of their uncertain future. She was babbling internally - the worst kind of nonsense - and it irritated her to no end, but she struggled to maintain a placid expression on her face. *Nothing to see here, folks...* Nothing, that was, except the slow and continuous decline of human civilization.

"Yes, sir," LT Wheeler said. Amy said nothing.

CAPT Hall leaned back in his chair. "You are absolutely right about crew morale, Ms. Montrose. We need to do something." He sighed, looked at the overhead, and rubbed his face.

He looked tired, she thought. They all looked tired. Or maybe it was shell shock. One moment the entire crew had been looking forward to a great liberty call in Fremantle, the seaside city near Perth, Western Australia. And the next...? The world had turned sideways. They weren't going to the land of beer and barbecued shrimp. They weren't going to get the rest they'd earned after two months in Antarctica. They weren't going to go home - ever, in all probability. No more United States. No more pizza and football on the TV. No more Reality Shows, or sitcoms, or movies of the week. No more movies, other than whatever DVDs the crew had brought with them. No more Mom's Apple Pie.

No more Mom.

Their families were dead. Or if they weren't they soon would be. Everybody knew it, though everybody was going to great lengths to avoid getting anywhere near the subject. The words: *family, home, mother, father, sister, brother, girlfriend, wife, boyfriend, husband*, and any other permutation of the concept of missing loved ones had been struck from the English Language, so far as the crew of the *Polar Star* were concerned. What they saw around them right now - each other - was all they had, and maybe all they would ever have.

"Tell you what," the Captain said, interrupting her intellectual descent into depression. "Have the Bridge Gang lay out tracks from Guam to the X. We'll do the Crossing Ceremony after we're done refueling."

"Yes, Sir!" LTjg Amy Montrose said, brightening.

"We'll need to do something before we have to park in the middle of the ocean and wait."

Those were their orders: Take station and wait for either contact from higher, or communications from the High Endurance Cutters that had been patrolling the Pacific before the Fall. Just sit there and wait, as the world fell apart around them.

54

"Good fix on the hour has us right on track. Time to turn, twelve minutes," Jonesy said, tossing the Speed Wheel (a circular sort of slide rule for calculating time, speed, and distance) onto the chart table. He had the watch, along with CWO2 Eric Larsen, the Bosun, Seaman Siemen, the helmsman, and Harold F. Simmons, jr., the lookout. BM3/DECK Masur had the BMOW, but he was off doing rounds. Everyone else, except the watch in Radio and the watch in the Engine Room, was back on the fantail, attending the funeral of ET3 Terry Proud, and BM2/OPS Ricardo Scutelli.

Jonesy gladly relieved Jack Ross, one of his Thirds, so that he could attend. Jonesy, himself, had no desire. Forget that he caused one of those deaths. Forget that the crew had been looking sideways at him in his full LE rig since before the fight on the Mess Deck. Forget that the last damned thing he wanted to do was listen to their supposed Commanding Officer make a speech. He had no desire to go to the funeral because he had no desire to go to *any* funeral, ever again. He had already been to far too many.

"We will be coming right to two-seven-zero, and continuing the Box of Death," he said, completing his report.

The "Box of Death" was so named because: (A), it was a box, in the middle of the ocean; steer a particular course for X-amount of time, turn ninety degrees, then steer that course for X-amount of time, turn ninety degrees again, etcetera, etcetera; and (B) because it was mind-numbingly, brain cell killing-ly dull. Ordinarily, it was used as an LE maneuver to take station in a particular area where high value targets were suspected, and cruise around till one of them shows up. In this case, they were on station to...*wait*. For what, no one was really sure. End of the world? Something obvious happens to change their status? Or maybe (and this was becoming increasingly unlikely) for new orders.

"Very well," CWO2 Larsen said, his normally bland face looking somehow frozen.

He's in shock, Jonesy thought. And why not?

They were screwed - well and truly fucked like a three dollar crack whore.

The crew didn't trust him. But maybe that wasn't it. They feared him, and wasn't that a royal kick in the balls? He'd been many things over the years: friend, clown, teacher, student, asshole, certainly, but feared? No. Never. But they feared him now. He could see it in their eyes. He could sense it, from the way conversations would suddenly stop when he came near. They were afraid of him.

But trust came into it, too. They didn't trust each other. One of their number had already turned homicidal. Who would be next?

55

"...We commend their bodies to the deep," LT Medavoy said, intoning the time-honored salute to fallen sailors.

MK2 Frank Roessler bowed his head with the rest of the crew, then watched in silence as the two shroud-covered bodies of Terry Proud and Scoot slid over the side and into the depths of the Pacific Ocean. The ship was still moving, and so the ripples from where the bodies entered the sea were soon lost from sight. Frank had always thought you stopped the ship for this sort of thing, but for whatever reason, the XO (*sorry, CO*) had directed one and all to keep steaming. Seemed disrespectful, somehow. One more reason for the crew to dislike the bastard, he thought.

Since the man brought his own family aboard after telling the crew they couldn't bring theirs, the talk had gotten more and more nasty. But, after all, it was just talk, right? It could never get beyond talk, right? He should be sure - should be *damned* sure - nobody would actually mention the "M" Word, but they were all in uncharted territory here, so he wasn't sure of a single damned thing. This was a whole new world, and it wasn't a nice place. Was mutiny really that far beyond the pale?

"Ship's Company, Atten-shun!" LTjg Bloominfeld barked. He was now the XO, since he was also now the highest ranking Commissioned Officer, after the CO. They'd been at Parade Rest throughout the ceremony, but now everybody stood to attention - more or less. It certainly wasn't parade ground, but not a single damned one of them had done anything remotely parade ground since the day they left boot camp. It just wasn't the way in the Coast Guard. Not that they weren't military, nor that they didn't feel a love of country, or whatever the thing was that stirred the patriotic part of the human soul or psyche, or whatever the fuck it was. Not one of them had marched or done close order drill, or the manual of arms, or any of that shit since boot. They were just too damned busy, under normal conditions, and so they were all out of practice.

And these were not normal conditions.

Bloominfeld looked around to make sure everybody followed his order, seemed a bit surprised that they had, then said: "At ease," and they all sort of slumped into a more relaxed position. "Gather round," he added, and the crew shuffled forward to form a human arc in front of the CO. They were all there, except the watchstanders, and everyone was wearing their best Tropical Dress uniform - even Duke, whom Medavoy had ordered to get out of his LE rig.

Frank wasn't sure if that was a good move, or a really, really bad one. On the one hand, nobody needed to be reminded that there were two people on board whose specific job was to "deal with" anyone who turned zombie - least of all at the funeral of someone who had. On the other hand, any one of the assembled crew could, themselves, turn at any moment, thus proving the need for those two men.

Nobody said anything. There were no smart ass remarks or jokes, or whispered comments of any kind. The only sound was the sea and the churning propeller beneath their feet.

They all look stunned, like a gaggle of concussed geese, Frank thought. *And they look scared.*

He was scared, for sure. He was damned near shitting in his pants. Okay...maybe not. He didn't think he was in any actual danger of needing to change his shorts, but it was a matter of degrees. He was spooked, and he didn't mind admitting it - at least to himself.

He'd been there on the Mess Deck during the attack - had seen what the full neurological looked like. He didn't want to see it again - ever. Not much chance of that, though, was there?

"This is a sad day," Medavoy said. "We all feel the loss of our shipmates."

"Motherfucker didn't even slow down," Masur muttered next to Frank. There were several quiet grunts of agreement.

"But we should take heart in the accomplishments and contributions they made. And we should resolve to carry on the mission, as they would have done."

"About now, Terry would be farting," Ski said, on the other side of Frank. This produced a few chuckles.

Frank gazed at his shipmates in a surprised sort of wonder. They were trying so damned hard to make this seem normal. But nothing was normal. Not a single goddamned thing. And the forced jocularity clearly covered the one question none of them could escape: who was going to turn next?

And then they all received the answer.

"Bugs! All over me!" Doc screamed, tearing at his uniform shirt, and all Hell broke loose.

56

"Hold this!" Jonesy said, thrusting the sextant into Harold's hands. They were on the Flying Bridge: Harold as lookout and Jonesy taking a sun line, when they heard shouting from back on the fantail - lots of shouting. "If you break it, you bought it," he added, leaping down onto the Signal Deck.

He'd just reached the bottom of the ladder at the bottom of the steps leading from the Bridge Deck, when Mr. Larsen popped his head out the Bridge door.

"I'm going!" Jonesy shouted.

"Go!" The Bosun shouted in return, tossing Jonesy's helmet to him. He'd left it on the chart table, since it made using the sextant functionally impossible.

Jonesy fumbled the catch, almost dropping it over the side, but managed to grab it by the chin strap just in time. It swung and smacked him in the elbow pad as he turned to race aft. He bounced off the RHIB sponson in his uncoordinated attempt to don the helmet while running, but it was on his head when he reached the end of the superstructure and entered into a scene of absolute chaos.

Shouting members of the crew were running in every direction - several of them directly toward him. He spun to avoid colliding head on into Medavoy as the man sped away from the melee.

"Deal with this, Jones!" the CO shouted, as he scampered past.

"Working on it!" He said, ignoring the fact that the Commanding Officer was running away from the danger threatening the crew of his ship.

Much of the crew were clustered on the port side, since the battle was happening to starboard, but along the way, FN Douglas Carney had fallen, and YN3 Greg Haversham had tripped over him, knocking down

SA Tommy Barnes, who was trying to get up as Jonesy shot past. CS3 Manny Manoa bulled his way through the smaller crowd surrounding the fight, took one look at Jonesy, then headed in a different direction.

"Doc's gone nuts!" The big man yelled, then shoved CS3 John Ryan out of his way. Ski, Frank Roessler, Molly, LTjg Bloominfeld, and CS1 Gary King bobbed and weaved around Duke, who struggled with the writhing forms of HS3 "Doc" Harris and BM2/DECK Masur - the sole member of the fight not wearing a dress uniform.

Masur stood pinned against the towing windlass, pushing back against Doc, who was trying to eat Masur's face. Duke was trying to get his forearm around Doc's throat in a choke hold, but the wirey young man-turned-raving animal was writhing and jumping and seemingly oblivious to the big Bosun's efforts.

"Move!" Jonesy shouted, and pushed his way into the action, just as Doc chomped down on Masur's arm.

Masur screamed, as a chunk of his flesh flew out of Doc's mouth, and a copious amount of blood streamed out of the wound. Doc's head flew backwards, as he ripped at Masur, and smacked Duke square in the nose. Blood squirted from both nostrils as Duke staggered from the impact. But the movement of Doc's head gave Masur just enough room for a roundhouse punch that connected with the new zombie's chin, and snapped his head sideways with a violence that should have torn his head off, but it barely seemed to faze the raving maniac.

What it did do was give Doc/zombie a sudden view of Jonesy off to his side. Like an animal distracted by a shiny object, Doc whirled and charged, just as Jonesy was bringing a baton out of its sheath, knocking the weapon from his hand and sending it spinning across the deck.

Off balance, Jonesy stumbled back, struck the bollard he'd been sitting on the night before with the inside of his knee, and fell sideways to the deck with a clang, as his weapons struck the steel decking. Doc lunged forward, but then something happened that utterly surprised everyone - even the new zombie.

Many of those who had run to the supposed safety of the port side had returned at Jonesy's arrival, like a convoy of motorists slowing down to view a grizzly accident, their faces filled with both fear and a sick fascination. But their expressions changed to shock and wonder as ENS Molly Gordon, the new boot officer - the new *girl* - strode into the fray, planted the ball of her left foot, and spun with her right to send an amazing spinning kick directly into the side of the charging zombie's head.

A chorus of "Holy shit!" spread throughout the crowd, as Doc staggered from the blow, tripped over the figure of Masur (who was curled onto the deck, cradling his bitten arm and moaning in pain) and fell against the towing windlass, smacking the side of his head against the lip of the windlass barrel. He/it didn't fall to the ground, since most of his/its body was leaning against the machine, but he/it did stop his frenetic, violent scrambling that made it so hard for Duke to come to grips.

The burley Bosun wasted neither time, nor opportunity.

When Doc first began to turn, he - as usual with this plague - started by trying to rip his own clothes off. But with first Masur, then

Duke rushing forward in an attempt to subdue him, he never got the chance to finish the job. As a result, he still had his pants on, and what remained of his dress uniform shirt still covered the man/zombie's skinny chest.

Duke shot forward, grabbed his shipmate by the back of his belt and what was left of his shirt collar, then lifted him bodily over his head, took three steps to the far back end of the fantail, and pile drove the former Hospital Corpsman over the side. Jonesy joined him at the aft rail just in time to see the churning water from the prop wash turn briefly, shockingly red, as the giant propeller chewed him into chum, then continued its rotation. The sound of the machinery beneath their feet never changed pitch.

"Man overboard!" somebody shouted from the crowd.

"Don't bother," Jonesy said, turning to face the crew. "He's dead."

57

LT Richard Medavoy steeled himself before entering the Captain's (his) Cabin. He'd just run from the debacle on the fantail. Worse yet, the crew had *seen* him run, like a coward; the most despicable failure he could have committed.

He knew what they said about him behind his back - had always known, since the Academy days, since before, since grade school and high school, when the bullies had taken the utmost pleasure in calling him by the shortened version of his name: *Dick. Dick-Head, Dick-Face, Dick the Prick, Dick-Breath, Dick-Stain;* on and on and on, the names had fallen on him like bricks, singly or in job lots, crushing him beneath their weight.

If they could only see him now...

Now that he was a coward.

But I wasn't running away! Honest! I was running to...

He stared at the door and jerked his head, as if to remove a flying insect. None of that mattered. He had bigger problems.

He opened the door.

"There you are, Richard. Where have you been? I've been waiting for you. I was worried, so worried, and I heard no word at all, nothing at all. Why didn't you tell me, tell me, tell me that it would take so long?" Marissa - *Manic Marissa*, to be precise - his wife, said in a rush of words, not pausing for breath. That was always the first sign of her manic phase: the blurted speech and repeated words. The second was the wild look in her eyes, like the caricature of a mad woman, only real, and certainly no joke. The third was her constant pacing - always pacing, around and around and around, ceaseless, like a Great White.

"It's okay, Marissa," he said, in a calm voice. "I'm here now."

He didn't know which he hated more: *Manic Marissa*, or *Morose Marissa*. Probably the former, come to think about it. At least the depressed Marissa didn't talk all the time. She rarely talked at all in that phase. He found it kind of peaceful, in a disturbing way.

"The boy, the boy, the boy, he's sick, so sick, there's something wrong, wrong, wrong. You need to do something! Do, do, do something!"

But there was nothing he *could* do. At least, nothing any father *would* do - ever.

His eight year old boy (only eight), Carson, was more than just sick. He had *THE FEVER*. And LT (*Dick-Face, Dick-Breath*) Richard Medavoy knew *exactly, precisely* what that meant. He had just seen (*run away from*) what comes next.

58

"Okay, so what's next?" LT Steve Wheeler said to the assembled "Crossing Council." They had convened in the Wardroom, both as a way to keep their plans secret from the uninitiated pollywogs, and to give the junior enlisted members of the Golden Shellback fraternity a bit of a status bump by allowing them into Officer's Country, where few of them had ever been, except as messcooks. "We've got the King and Queen, we've got the Wog Talent-less Show, we've got the garbage being stored for the Whale's Belly... What else?"

They were still twelve hours out of Guam, the NBC gear had been brought out of storage and prepped, the fuel hoses were distributed and tied down in place; there wasn't a whole lot else to be done, and LTjg Montrose had been right. The crew needed a morale boost, and so he had convened the Council.

They could have been to Apia, by now, if they had run the turbines, but those things sucked up fuel like mad, and they ran on JP5 Av-gas, same as their two HH-65 helicopters, and they hadn't gotten confirmation from Guam about its availability. They probably had it, since the island's military base also had helos, but they couldn't be sure till they got there, and this was no time for uncertainty, so they had taken the slower, diesel-fueled method.

"The Baby?" OS1 Rudy McGuinn suggested, referring to the third (and by far most disgusting) member of the Initiation triumvirate of King, Queen, and Baby. This brazen individual was always the largest member of the Initiated crew, whose belly would be covered in things most normal people would not even want to consider. The initiates face would then be rubbed in this revolting concoction before finally standing before the King's Court to determine their worthiness to become a Golden Shellback.

"Who should it be?" LT Wheeler asked.

"Dave Ablitz," BMC Stevens suggested, and this was met with uproarious laughter. The First Class Yeoman in question was quite large, and hairy as an ape. He would be disgustingly memorable as the Baby. At the moment, however, he was not in attendance, even though he was one of the few who had actually been through a full Initiation. The motion was carried and he was elected in absentia. That's what he got for not attending the meeting.

"Slave auction?" BMCM Philip C. Wolf suggested. He was, without a doubt, the saltiest bastard on the *Polar Star*. He had made more deployments, logged more nautical miles, been to more liberty ports, and seen more sea time than all of his bridge gang put together. People didn't even bother with the DECK or OPS designator when referring to him. He was the Master Chief. This might be the Captain's ship, but that was *his* Bridge, three decks above their heads, and no simpering, touchy-feely Headquarters pussy fart was going to change the fact.

The "slave auction" had been a tradition in the Crossing Ceremony since the Master Chief was in diapers, and so LT Wheeler didn't want to dismiss the idea out of hand, but the racial implications of it made just about everybody cringe. Plus, Wolf scared him. He suspected the man scared every officer, with the possible exception of the Captain, who was himself an "Old Salt," in addition to being a Mustang.

The auction put the polywogs (or simply *wogs*) who had never crossed the line up for sale to any crew member who had, making said wog the slave of his or her purchaser for the entire day prior to the Ceremony. The money went to the Morale Fund, and the auction (a morale event in itself, filled with raucous hilarity) had always raised a lot of it, but as with the hazing aspects, it had fallen out of favor.

"I'm afraid the Captain won't go there, Master Chief," Wheeler said, and several of the others around the Mess table - including the XO, CDR Carl Swedberg - nodded in agreement.

"Not a chance," LCDR Lawrence Stubbelfield agreed. "Sorry, Master Chief." The Operations Officer was soft spoken, though competent, and friendly, in a detached sort of way. He was of mixed race, his father being white, and his mother, black, and both of them clearly tall. He stood six-foot-four when he slouched, and looked not unlike Kareem Abdul Jabbar - though not exactly like him, either.

Wheeler had come to *Polar Star* to replace him, arriving in Sydney just before she went down into the ice. The Lieutenant Commander had been scheduled to fly out of McMurdo, but first one, then a second, and finally a third C-130 had been unable to land due to weather. Two other flights had gotten in and out, but both of them were full, and so he had been slated to depart when they docked in Fremantle after two months in the Land *Really* Down Under. One zombie Apocalypse later, and the *Polar Star* now had two OPS Bosses. Wheeler had taken the AOPS position that would ordinarily have been a junior officer, but he didn't mind. The two of them got along well enough, and he had no complaints - at least none he cared to voice to anyone.

Master Chief Wolf muttered something which may or may not have been an aspersion against the CO's masculinity, but Wheeler ignored it. The XO raised an eyebrow, but said nothing. He was definitely afraid of the Master Chief.

"What about the Fashion Show?" YN2 Lydia Claire asked. She was a short blonde woman in her early twenties, a Southern Girl, with a dry wit, who always seemed to wear a half-smile on her face. Everybody liked her. This was her second deployment to Antarctica, and would have been her last, if not for the zombie apocalypse. They had done a modified Crossing Ceremony on the previous trip, which didn't include the Whale's Belly or the slave auction, or the more adolescent of the traditional accouterments, and it had been little more than a glorified pizza party, but it *had* included the Fashion Show.

The Fashion Show put male wogs in drag to parade up and down the Mess Deck for the amusement of all. Accusations of latent closet homosexuality aside, it had always been a fun part of the festivities. Wheeler wrote it down.

"Yeah, but how can we get the female crew members involved?" MST3 Michael Paladin asked. He was a slim young man, about the same age as Lydia, with reddish blonde hair and glasses. The Marine Science Technician was a likeable, unassuming guy who had come aboard just prior to the last deployment, and so he, also, had crossed the X.

"Like the Drag Kings?" EM1 Greg Lamonski (Ski, naturally) asked, referring to the female-to-male drag show. "That could be amusing."

He was right, Wheeler thought, it would be amusing, but he suspected Ski thought so for different reasons. The man was a notorious slut, whose escapades at the many legal brothels of Sydney were legendary. It might be a non-issue (if not a reason for veneration) in an all-male crew, but with a mixed crew, the specter of sexual harassment had always hung about the man's head, and so any idea that came out of it was suspect. They would need to tread carefully.

"I'm all for it," Lydia said, favoring the assembled Council with a full smile.

Or maybe not... "Take an informal poll of the other females, Lydia. I don't want to harsh anybody's vibe, but I don't think we need to be crossing any lines *inside* the ship." Wheeler temporized.

"Good call," CWO4 Robert (Bobby V) Vincenzo agreed. He was a salty bastard in his own right, and no one to be trifled with, either. If he liked you, you were golden, if he didn't... You might as well just resign yourself to being in Hell for the length of your tour on the ship. He was in charge of the Deck Force, which contained four females, all of whom were wogs. The last damned thing he needed was a gender controversy. Wheeler knew the very thought of it pissed the man off, but Bobby V was not an idiot. "Damned political correctness complicates everything, but we can't ignore it."

The Initiation had been a time-honored tradition at sea for centuries. Sailors from navies all over the world engaged in it, often with relish, sometimes with violence (before the modern era of common sense in such things). The violent aspects had changed as the centuries turned from Eighteen to Nineteen, and the more grueling aspects went by the wayside, but it had still been not the least bit politically correct. It was disgusting, it was juvenile, it was a total mind-fuck, and there were always one or two idiots who took it too far (there were assholes in every crowd - just a fact of life), but it was also, above all, *memorable*. No one who had ever been through it forgot it, for as long as they lived.

Crossing the line was something maybe one percent of the population in all of human history had done. It *needed* to be marked with some ceremony; it *deserved* to be memorable.

But then the Age of Political Correctness - that destroyer of all traditions, no matter how necessary - descended upon the sea going services of the United States, and the Initiation went the way of the Dodo. It was a testament to both Captain Hall, and the utterly fucked circumstances in which they found themselves, that the old traditions were being restored. This did not, however, mean they weren't going to hedge their bets, just in case. As impossible as their circumstances seemed, there was always the possibility civilization would pull out of the dive before it was too late. To not think so would be to admit hopelessness.

"Right you are," the XO chimed in. He'd been staying out of the conversation, much like the CO had stayed out of the meeting, not wanting to restrict the general entertainment value of the festivities, even though both of them had crossed all of the lines at one time or another in their careers. These included the Equator (Shellback), the International Dateline (Golden Dragon), the Arctic Circle (Bluenose, or Polar Bear - depending on who you asked), and the Antarctic Circle (Emperor Penguin), along with the Golden Shellback, which they were discussing, and the Order of the Ditch, for going through the Panama Canal. The one thing they - and a few other members of the Council - had done, but which did not come with a Crossing Certificate, was circumnavigating North America, by going Over the Top, through the Northwest Passage. The *Star* had done it, so had the *Healy,* as well as a couple of the Canadian Icebreakers, but few others had in history. Okay, some submarines had done it, but nobody cared about those sneaky bastards, and in any case, there was no certificate for it. "But as long as *all* of the women agree, then by all means, let's do it."

"Okay, then," Wheeler said. "Fashion show. What's next?"

59

"You know I gotta do this, right?" Jonesy asked, tightening the zip cuffs around Masur's wrists.

Jonesy, Duke, and Frank Roessler were still on the Fantail with Masur. The rest of the crew had gone below, but they remained. After treating the gaping wound in Masur's arm as best they could, they brought out a canvas deck chair, so their shipmate could at least be comfortable. They flex cuffed him at ankles and wrists, and stayed with him to wait until the end.

"Yeah," Masur said. "Can't believe the fucker bit me."

"Seriously," Duke agreed. "You had to taste terrible."

"Blow me," his fellow Bosun Mate replied.

"Don't Ask, Don't Tell is over, dude," Frank said. They were trying to keep it light, but it wasn't working. Jonesy thought it felt more like standing around somebody's death bed, which, in a way, it was.

"Anything we can get you?" He asked.

"I could really use a bottle of Cointreau," Masur answered, referring to the upscale orange liqueur. It was all the man drank, and he drank it a lot.

"If I could get you some, I'd even drink it with you," Jonesy said. "Though how you can stomach that shit is beyond me."

"Years and years of practice," the man replied.

"Years and years of masochism," Frank said.

"The masochism comes with the hangover in the morning," Masur said with a chuckle. "You remember that night in Pago Pago?"

They all remembered many nights, in many places, like American Samoa, Maui, the Big Island, Roratonga, Truk, and that one insanely inebriated golf tournament on Midway; their lives together streaming by in one memory of drunken debauchery after another. But none of them said a word.

They fell into an uncomfortable silence, waiting. Jonesy's heart felt like a rock in his chest. The deaths of Scoot and Doc had both been in the heat of battle, but this one would be cold and premeditated. He glanced at Masur, then looked away, trying not to notice the additional zip tie hanging loosely around their friend's neck, its tail jutting out behind him. It was there in case they had to strangle him. The moments ticked by.

Finally, Masur took in a deep breath, and said: "Fuck this. Let's get it over with." He struggled to get out of the chair, but being retrained at wrist and ankle made this impossible. "Get me up," he said. "Bring me to the rail."

They did as he asked, the reluctance showing in each of their faces.

"Do me a favor, Jonesy," Masur said. He stood facing out to sea, waiting, with his back - mercifully - to them all.

"Anything," he replied. He could feel tears welling up in his eyes - not quite sliding out, but there, ready to fall. Sunglasses concealed the evidence. He adjusted them to make sure.

"Make it quick," Masur said. "And none of this strangling bullshit. That'd take too long."

Jonesy closed his eyes as his heart sunk into a cold, bottomless pit. But then it was replaced with a deep, equally cold anger. *Why me? Why does it gotta be me? Fuck no! Abso-fucking-lutely not! I won't do it!*

Another part of him, however, the Arctic center of his being that had enabled him to shoot the human trafficker, to kill his friend, Scoot, to live his life before any of this began, in spite of all the crap and loneliness, and loss and separation he'd had to endure before finding his home among the Coast Guard misfits, came forward into his psyche and said, *Bullshit. You can do it. And you will.*

But then the whiny little inner bitch voice retorted: *He hasn't turned yet. It would be murder.*

This was true enough, on the face of it. Masur wasn't a zombie, or whatever the fuck you became when you went full neurological, so he would, in fact, be killing a sentient human being. But he'd been bitten. They had no vaccine. Turning was inevitable.

There could only be one real answer:

It would be mercy.

He opened his eyes, the expression on his face as cold and immobile as a stone effigy, then reached into his harness and pulled out the baton. He sensed, more than saw Duke and Frank step to the side, but he did not look at them, did not truly see them, or anything, for that matter, except the spot on Masur's neck, just below the right ear.

There is a cluster there, called the brachial nerve. Hit it with just the right touch, and anyone, no matter how big, will drop to their knees - assuming they're human. Hit it a bit harder, and they'll be unconscious when they hit the deck. Harder still, and they'll be dead, as the signal between brain stem and central nervous system is interrupted, and the survival mechanisms of the body forget how to function.

He flicked his wrist and the baton extended with a metallic *SNICK*. Masur flinched at the sound. Somewhere deep inside, Jonesy noticed this, but something deeper, closer to the center of his being, ignored it, and moved his body to take a firm stance, come up on the balls of his feet, cock his torso to the right, and then bring all the kinetic force of legs and body and arm into the swing.

By the time Duke and Frank eased the body of their friend and shipmate over the rail and into the sea, Jonesy was halfway back up to the Bridge.

Silence greeted him there.

Hebert had taken over the plot, BMC/DECK Bernie Adams had the conn, and SN John "Mad Dog" Kennedy had the helm. They all stared at him. No one said a word.

He strode to the telephone on the bulkhead next to the chart table and dialed.

"Ship's Office, Petty Officer Haversham," the voice on the other end answered.

"Yeah, this is Jones. I need the Social Security numbers for Doc Harris, and BM2 Masur. It's for the log," he said, then looked at Chief Adams, whose face had turned pale. "Both are deceased."

60

Frank entered the Mess Deck, followed by Duke, and was confronted by a gang of blowhard gossips more severe than any old time beauty parlor. For one thing, they were sailors at sea, which meant there were no secrets, as there was no privacy. Secondly, they were agitated and pissed off, because, third, they were in the middle of an absolute shit storm, they knew it, and they were looking for someone to blame.

"Fucker ran away - *ran away*, god dammit!" FN Craig Moncrief said, and received numerous nodding heads in reply. MK3 Carlos Martinez, who looked to be the senior guy in the compartment before Frank and Duke showed up, said nothing. But he, also, nodded

"And what was that bullshit about bringing his family aboard?" SN Jim Borgeson asked.

"Yeah," the tall and lanky Fireman said. "We should do something about it."

"You secure that shit right this fucking second, Moncrief!" Frank spat, getting into the young man's face.

"Come on, Frank," Martinez soothed. "You gotta admit this is bullshit."

"I don't give a damn if it's the biggest pile of shit in the history of the Coast Guard." He pointed at Moncrief. "What he just said is mutiny, and if you didn't have your head so far up your own ass, you'd have done something about it."

"Okay, okay," Martinez said, backpedaling while still sitting at a mess table.

Frank glared at the rest of the assembled junior enlisted. "You all should know better, especially now. Aren't things fucked up enough for you assholes? You want to make it worse?"

"Easy, Frank," SNCS George DeGroot said.

"Fuck easy," Duke snapped, before Frank had a chance to reply. "We just had to kill Masur, you dumb motherfuckers! There isn't a single goddamned thing easy about any of this!"

The crowd fell silent.

Masur had been a popular guy, even if he was a self-avowed asshole. So had Doc, in the same way all ship's Corpsman were. The loss of both of them at once, on top of losing Scoot and Terry Proud, and the word about Ensign Ryan's plane disappearing, combined to fall like a ten-ton buoy anchor on them all.

But this was a ship at sea, and these were sailors, and Coasties to boot. No news - however dire - could stop the flow of bullshit humor.

"Did you see Miss Gordon?" Borgeson asked.

"Fuck, dude," Moncrief replied. "Remind me to never get her pissed off."

"Seriously," SA Eddie Sanders said, grinning from the far side of the compartment.

"Was kinda hot, though," Martinez added, and Frank couldn't disagree.

61

"If this was a Western, I'd be the old codger saying I've got an itch at the back of my neck that says we're in Apache country," John said, closing the Nautical Almanac with a snap. He ripped the piece of paper from the notepad he'd used for his calculations, crumpled it, tossed it into the trash can, and added: "Sunset is in about two hours."

Jim scanned the horizon with binoculars. "That's when I'd do it," he said. "Right at sunset."

"You always were a bit of a pirate," John said, joining his friend at the Bridge windows.

"Shiver me timbers," Jim said, dryly. "Left my parrot at home, though."

"And a bit of a fuck up."

Jim replied with a look of pure sarcasm. "Yeah, well, I'm not the one who let Spute bring that skank aboard."

John sighed. "Nobody's perfect." He pulled a second pair of binoculars from one of the felt-lined boxes bolted to the forward bulkhead and brought them to his eyes. "Lets get all the families below, and lock all the exterior hatches." He had installed electronic locks on all of them during the refit. They could be accessed by either a key card, or the key fob John carried in his pocket. "And then lets get armed up. You, me, Mick, and maybe Bob-Bob." Bob-Bob was Bob Stoeffel, so named because such a large man couldn't properly have just a three-lettered name.

"Gus, too," Jim suggested.

"Really?"

"You should have seen him at the gun store."

"Do I want to know?" John asked.

"Plausible deniability," Jim replied.

"Ouch."

"Yeah, well..." Jim shrugged. "Give Lane a gun, too. He's a good man."

John sighed again. "Fuck," he said, sadly. "The mighty battle-tender *True North*. Who'd have thought?"

"Brave new world," Jim replied.

"Bad new world," John countered.

"No," Jim said. "It's really just the same old world - on steroids." He walked over and peered into the radar screen. "You know, Ben Franklin had it wrong."

John gave him an odd look. "Non-sequitur alert."

Jim ignored the jibe. "Ben Franklin's quote about the only sure things being death and taxes? He left one thing out."

"Which is?"

"There will always be assholes," Jim said, still looking at the empty radar screen. "And I'll bet you there's one of them out there, right now."

62

Blackjack Charlie Carter glanced at the radar screen and smiled. The faint blip was still there, right at the edge of the screen, and right where it was supposed to be. They'd been shadowing the contact for hours, since they'd followed the DF plot to the most likely location.

The *Daisy Jean* was a shade over twenty-five nautical miles out, and the contact was at the edge of the twenty-five mile ring, which meant it had to be pretty big, otherwise they wouldn't pick it up. The *Daisy Jean*, on the other hand, was not big, so the other boat probably couldn't see them on radar.

Probably...

And so he'd been darting in and out of range just long enough to confirm they were still there, then heading back out another five miles. He spun the helm to starboard and goosed the throttle to give them a bit more speed.

He should have the sails up, since fuel was limited, and if they didn't snag the other boat, he had no idea when they'd find more of it. But the sail cloth had radar reflective tape sewn into it, and raising them would increase their profile, and the jig would be up. That would fuck them before they even started.

The other ship could be a fancy yacht with a handful of rich bastards on it, or it could be a freighter with a full crew. He leaned more toward the former. The stupid bitch he'd talked to could only be some rich fucker's trophy wife. No professional crew would be dumb enough

209

to put her on the Bridge. *But maybe...* He didn't know, and so their only hope was to catch them by surprise.

He smiled. It was not a pleasant smile. Small children would be scared by it. If everything worked the way he'd planned, the surprise wouldn't be pleasant, either.

63

Captain Hall set MOPP (standing for Mission Oriented Protective Posture, yet another military gobbledygook acronym) Level 2, when the *Polar Star* was fifty nautical miles out of Guam. This meant everybody on board had to put on the NBC (Nuclear, Biological, Chemical) Hazmat suit and over-boots, but not the mask and gloves, and all non-essential personnel had to lay below to their NBC billets. These consisted of holds and other interior compartments without direct access to the exterior of the ship.

He also set Condition ZEBRA, throughout the ship. Ordinarily, while underway, Condition YOKE was set, which meant, all watertight hatches and doors were closed and dogged, but personnel could still move about the ship without bothering the people who were running it to get permission to open a damned hatch so the messcook could get powdered bug juice from dry stores. ZEBRA meant personnel *did* have to bother the already busy people up on the Bridge for permission. Fortunately, the bug juice had already been prepared.

He increased to MOPP Level 4 when the ship was twenty nautical miles out. Everybody had to wear the whole enchilada of suit, boots, hood, gas mask, and gloves. It was hot, it was uncomfortable, and many thought it was overkill, but nobody had either the balls or the poor sense to voice that opinion.

The suit by itself was uncomfortable enough, while still being more or less bearable. It wasn't booty shorts and a tank top, by any stretch of the imagination, and there were at first many sarcastic remarks about what a bold fashion statement everybody was making, but all-in-all it wasn't too bad. The addition of the mask and gloves, however, made life miserable.

The suit, designed as it was to protect the wearer from all sorts of nasty airborne contagions, didn't breathe. It stank of plastic and protective chemicals, and made the person sweat as if they were sitting in their own personal dry sauna. But as long as the mask was off, the poor unfortunate stuck in the suit could still draw breath. When it was on, and when the poor unfortunate was locked into an interior compartment, and when, further, the Captain set Condition Circle WILLIAM, and closed off ventilation, just before the tugs out of Guam hooked on to pull them into harbor, it became cruel and unusual punishment.

This, at least, was the opinion of YN2 Lydia Claire. It was, honestly, the first time she regretted becoming a Yeoman.

The civilian equivalent of a Yeoman would be somebody in Human Resources. In the Coast Guard, it was, essentially, a nine-to-five job. The billets were usually land based, which gave them the opportunity to have something resembling a normal life, while still serving their country, but even on a ship, the job was pretty much nine-to-five (or, rather, 0800 - 1600). They didn't stand underway watches, they didn't have to drag their butts out of bed at some obscene hour, and they sat behind a desk all day. It was nice, it was routine, and it was the easiest way to slide though the day while still enjoying the benefits of an adventure at sea, without having to work too hard for it. It was a necessary job, because no propellers turned without administrative support, but in the grand scheme of life aboard ship, it was pretty cushy - until the CO set MOPP Condition 4.

Since she was a Yeoman, and didn't stand watches or have a Special Sea Detail or Fueling Ops billet, or any of the other added extras of a life aboard ship she had thus far avoided, in MOPP Level 4, in a suit that didn't breathe, in a compartment with no ventilated air, she was in Hell. So were the rest of the Yeoman and Storekeepers.

"I'm having the time of my life," YN1 Dave Ablitz said next to her, the sarcasm coming through loud and clear, even though his voice was muffled by the gas mask.

"I can barely contain my enthusiasm," she replied.

They were sitting side by side on a wooden crate, labeled: *Dr. Robert Stephanopolis, National Science Foundation, Woods Hole, MA.* She had no idea what it contained, but assumed it was something Doctor Bob had either used or collected while down in Antarctica. He was no longer aboard, the scientists having all been flown off as the ship passed near Adelaide, South Australia, after coming up out of the ice.

He's probably dead now, she thought with a pang. *Or turned into a zombie.*

Polar Star's primary mission had been to cut a trail through the ice so freighters could deliver the necessary supplies to the Navy Base in McMurdo, Antarctica. Conditions were so extreme, and the weather so unpredictable, that the only way to deliver enough material for all of the US research stations to be supplied through the insane winter, was to bring it by ship in the summer. While many freighters were equipped with icebreaking hulls, few were actual icebreakers, and so the *Polar Star* went down every year.

Antarctica was one of the few truly unexplored places on the planet, so they also brought scientists, from Woods Hole, The National Science Foundation, Scripps Institute, the USGS, and other places, with them to conduct experiments and gather samples that required a floating platform. The scientists were a pain in the ass, and went by the pejorative nickname of *Beakers*, but Doctor Bob had been liked by one and all. And now he was either dead, or worse.

"I think I'm melting," Dave said.

She could only imagine - and then instantly regretted having tried. Dave Ablitz was a large man, though by no means fat. With his large frame and hairy body, he looked quite a bit like a gorilla, even though he had a heart like a Golden Retriever. He'd been a defensive lineman in high school and college, but injured his knee, and so lost his scholarship, and then (in a sequence of events far too complicated for Lydia to even want to understand), he'd become a prison guard in Los Angeles County. It had not been to his liking, so he joined the Coast Guard.

Since Dave was so large and so hairy, the idea of what he would look - and smell - like when the suit finally came off, filled Lydia with sincere revulsion. Of course, she wouldn't be smelling like a daisy when her's came off, either, come to think of it. They sat there in shared misery, knowing they were stuck for the duration, condemned to watch others leave the stifling confines of the Forward Hold to go out into the air and perform the duties that she and Dave had so happily avoided - until now.

The hatch opened with a *clunk*, and LTjg Amy Montrose, her face barely recognizable beneath the mask, entered and said: "We need three volunteers to act as runners."

Lydia's hand shot up.

64

Jonesy walked onto the Mess Deck, grabbed a tray, and shuffled to the serving window as the line of hungry Coasties slowly made its way to the promise of food at the end of a long day. As a First Class, he could, technically, skip to the head of the line, but he'd always thought it was bullshit when he was more junior, and so couldn't justify doing it now. Rank did have its privileges, but that didn't mean he had to exercise them every time.

Talk in the compartment was subdued, instead of being the usual raucous conglomeration of a dozen different conversations going on at a dozen different tables, as sailors talked shop, or bitched about their day, or their boss, or talked eagerly about the next liberty port. Jonesy had, on occasion, thought it seemed rather like a family dinner, only larger. The basic conversations were the same. Only the details were different. This *was* a family - *his* family.

He reached the serving window, and could smell the aroma of herbs and spices which meant CS1 Gary King had whipped up a batch of his famous Spinach Lasagna - Jonesy's favorite. Gary himself was serving.

"Made this for you, Jonesy,"" Gary said, sliding a square of cheesy, garlic-y goodness onto the tray, and adding a perfectly toasted piece of garlic bread.

"Thank you, sir," he replied touched. *Just like a family...*

EM3 Dan McMullen bumped into him from behind on his way to drop his own tray in the scullery.

"Sorry, dude," the Electrician said. People bumping into each other was just something you had to get used to on a ship. In the civilian world, this would have been an unusual event, but at sea, it was an everyday occurrence. Jonesy barely noticed. He'd been focused more on the impending lasagna.

"Better watch out, Dan," SN Borgeson said, from his table close to the serving window. "Petty Officer Kevorkian might take you out."

Yeah... Just like a family, Jonesy thought, his appetite vanishing. *A really dysfunctional family.*

He looked at his tray, sitting on the counter in front of the window, then looked at Gary. The cook's eyes held complete understanding.

"Fuck," Jonesy said, almost in a whisper, and then he turned and walked away, leaving the tray behind.

"Take over serving," Gary said over his shoulder to SNCS George DeGroot, who had already begun the task of cleaning the galley. He was pissed. Insensitivity was something you just got used to in the military. It went hand-in-hand like morning muster or any other part of the daily routine. But as with all things, it could be taken too far.

He stalked out the door to the port passageway, turned at the vestibule just aft of the buoy deck and entered the Mess. He had a temper, did Gary King, and he knew it. He'd gone to great lengths over the years to control it. His wife had helped in that regard.

She was dead now. Probably.

He made his way to the serving window, picked up Jonesy's abandoned tray, and took it to the scullery, trying to curb his rage. It worked. By the time he turned to face the crowd, ice had formed in his veins. He stood in front of Borgeson, but didn't look at him.

"How's everybody feeling?" he asked, his voice calm.

"Great chow, Gary," MK3 Danny Morey said.

"Nobody feeling feverish?" Conversation in the compartment fell silent. "No skin irritation?" Nobody answered. "So who's going to turn next? You, Morey? You, Borgeson? And how many more of us is that person going to kill, if Jonesy ain't around to save us? To defend us?"

"I was only joking, Gary," Borgeson said.

"You idiots ought to be kissing Jonesy's ass," he said, quietly, but everybody heard him. "Don't you get that he's keeping you alive? How many of you would Scoot have killed? How many would Doc have killed, or Masur?" He finally looked down at Borgeson. "He's protecting you, and you just dumped a pile of shit on his head. You better hope he forgets it when the next one of us turns."

65

OS2 Amber Winkowski stood with her back against the wall in the Comm Center. Jackson Grabon, whom she'd never really liked, thanks to his arrogant indifference to anything or anyone who wasn't him, and whom she barely tolerated, thanks to his many and varied idiosyncracies, like his habit of chewing with his mouth open, had become a zombie.

He hadn't stripped off his clothes, thank God, because that was a sight she did not want to take with her to the grave, but he was, at the moment, trying to stalk and kill her. She had managed so far to keep the radio console between them, but she couldn't keep running laps around the COMMCEN forever. She needed to think. She needed a plan. She needed a weapon.

He/it started to climb up on the desktop, from which he could crawl over the top of the console, but she darted left and made it to the far end before he got halfway. He/it stopped climbing and instead started scrabbling down the desktop like a gerbil.

Behind her was a short corridor leading to the head. She could close the door on him and probably block it, but she'd be trapped in there, and all the food and water were out here. No choice, really. She feinted, as if to run back the way she'd come, and he/it hesitated in its imitation of a rodent. She turned and ran for the door.

66

Blackjack Charlie Carter watched as the RHIB disappeared into the distance. Most of his gang was in it: Old Joe, Joe-Boy, Hank Lazardo (whom Charlie thought was a fucking psycho, but you can't choose your associates in an apocalypse), Eddie Cochrane, the child molester who had latched onto the group when they made their break from Soledad, Skizzy Pete Hannity, the rapist, and Sugar Brown, the pimp (another goddamned pimp - he couldn't seem to get away from them), who had beaten one of his whores to death. There wasn't a whole brain between them, but they'd have to do.

He'd wanted to go along - should have gone along - but he couldn't be sure the *Daisy Jean* would still be here when they got back, in the event this attack didn't work. They were bastards, one and all, but they were not pirates, and if ever there was a situation that called for buccaneers, this was it. Only Old Joe had even known how to handle the RHIB.

This was one Hell of a dice roll, and he knew it. The odds of success were less than fifty/fifty, but Blackjack Charlie was both a gambler and a pragmatist. It *might* work, if whoever was on that other boat got caught by surprise, and if it worked, they'd have another boat, more supplies, and *vaccine*. Definitely worth the gamble. If, on the other hand, the other crew managed to fight off the attack, if they killed off a few or all of the men in that RHIB, well, then, there'd be six fewer mouths to feed.,

The three remaining: himself, George Potter, the mechanical engineer who'd murdered his wife in a drunken rage, and Felix Hoffman, the chemist for what had been the largest Ecstacy lab ever busted, could live on what stores were on the *Daisy Jean* for several months, if they augmented their larder with fish. Charlie didn't ,like fish, which was odd, since he'd been a Merchant Seaman, but if it came down to a choice between fish or starvation, he'd be a fish-eating motherfucker. So they had time. They could make do. And he still knew where the other boat was. If this attack failed, he could always wait, and try it again with better people and a better plan.

Besides, the murderous bastards he'd sent off in the RHIB might just kill a few of the other crew. That would even the odds a bit.

He smiled his devil's smile, and sat down to wait.

67

Jason Gilcuddy looked out to sea from his post on the *True North*. The sky was midnight blue, which fit, since it was, after all, midnight. He missed this. Civilian life had been okay, he guessed. He had a decent enough job, a little bit of money, and plenty of time - at last - to search for a wife. That had always been his problem when he was in: never enough time. They were always either underway, or repairing the ship, or getting ready to get back underway. And there were SAR cases, and

LE cases, and oil spills, and natural disasters, and whatever else the Coast Guard had been called upon to do. And then there were the transfers, always getting sent someplace new. He was never in any one place long enough to find that right girl.

Astoria, Oregon, had been as good a place as any to end up - and better than many others. He had friends there. John was there, and his family. And so were Gus and Jim, both of whom he'd met and worked with during his career. It was the one true advantage to being in a service as small as the Coast Guard: you were always running into people you knew, and Astoria was full of ex-Coasties. Not sure why. It was a nice enough place, and the scenery was breathtaking, but it hadn't provided the one thing he wanted most: a wife.

None of which mattered now he thought, as he stared at the 9mm pistol in his hand.

He'd been surprised (to say the least) when John handed it to him. He could see Jim going armed. The man positively *adored* guns. He could see John going armed. He had always been about protecting his loved ones, and with a heart like John's, that meant a lot of people. It even meant him, he supposed. He smiled at the idea, then frowned again as his gaze went back to the firearm.

Mick - the definition of a *man's man* - was a natural for a weapon. Even Lane - quiet, unassuming Lane Keely - seemed natural with a gun in his hand. But Jason Gilcuddy? Really? Not in this lifetime.

Yet here he was, on the boat deck of a ship at sea, preparing to defend her against Pirates. *No, seriously...Pirates?* Apparently so. There he was, armed and on watch, waiting for...what, exactly?

He didn't know, so he just continued looking to the East.

He'd have been much better of looking to the West.

68

YN2 Lydia Claire, dressed quite a bit like somebody in the midst of a zombie apocalypse, moved swiftly down the Boat Deck, heading forward from Fueling Position Six. It had been belatedly decided that since people in MOPP gear and gas masks could not coherently converse over the sound-powered phones, as would be SOP during fueling ops, and since using a comco was ill-advised while loading JP5 jet fuel (the risk of ignition from any radio transmission being too high to risk), then runners would be needed to carry information back and forth between the fueling stations and Main Control.

She slid down the ladder onto the Forecastle, then waited as SN Jennifer Collins let her into the hatch leading to the Mess Deck. Condition ZEBRA required permission for hatches to be opened, but the Captain, in the interest of speedy communication, had decided positive control of the hatches could be maintained by the presence of people at key points. In the interests of not allowing the zombie virus into the ship, however, a decon shower had been set up in the vestibule (with its strategically placed deck drain), which pelted her with chemical-laden high pressure water every time she entered any of the monitored hatches. It was getting pretty annoying, but at least she wasn't still locked in that hold.

A thick, rubberized sheet had been stretched from overhead to combing that prevented air from getting inside the ship, but did not restrict sound. Of course, the combination of rubber mat and gas mask didn't enhance clarity of communication, and so she had to yell.

"Position Six, eighteen feet, three inches!" she shouted.

"Roger," an equally muffled voice replied from beyond the rubber veil, and then she turned around and scurried her ass back to Position Six, just aft of the Starboard Boat Deck.

BM1/OPS Jeff Babbett was there, camouflaged in his protective gear, kneeling on the non-skid deck, and slowly feeding a weighted measuring tape up and down the fuel tank sounding tube. Anyone who could get out of the stifling hold had gotten out of the stifling hold, and all the other such antechambers of Hell created by MOPP Level 4. An oily rag sat on the ground next to him, and he wiped the jet fuel from its latest mark on the measuring tape, after he'd read it.

"Nineteen foot one," he said, and grinned at her through his gas mask. "Good cardio, eh Lydia?"

"Sure," came her muffled shout in return. "I'll have buns of steel, if I don't drop dead from running up and down that ladder," she added, then turned and retraced her steps.

The decon spray hit her like needles from a nail gun as she repeated the reporting process, was told Station Six could secure, and that she could move to Station Fourteen, and then, dripping wet, both outside and in (she was sweating profusely inside the MOPP suit), she headed back up the ladder to the Boat Deck to give Babbett the good news.

By pure chance, she happened to glance into the five foot gap between the air castle wing and the bow of the LCVP, and saw the pier, some fifty yards off their starboard side, lit up along its entire length by sodium arc lights. What she saw, illuminated in their brilliant glare, stopped her, dead in her tracks.

People - *hundreds*, maybe *thousands* of people - were gathered on the pier and waving madly at the *Polar Star*. They carried suitcases, they carried backpacks. Some of them carried babies or small children.

Refugees, she thought. And then she saw CWO4 Vincenzo and a crew of five Deckies setting up fire hoses along the rail aft. *What the Hell*? She thought, and then added: "What the fuck?" out loud, as she saw them pointing the hose nozzles outward, in the direction of the pier.

69

"Sir," Jonesy said, his voice straining against the urge to scream at the stupid son of a bitch. "I strongly recommend we have the crew tie themselves up and place gags in their mouths. At least when they're in the rack."

"No," Medavoy said - again. And again., he was being a dickheaded moron. "I will not allow it."

They were in the Wardroom, again, for another goddamned meeting, again, and Medavoy was being his usual obstinate, contrarian self - AGAIN!

"Sir," Jonesy's voice was cold as ice, as he tried to contain his growing rage and disgust. "Most of the crew sleeps in four-man compartments. Each person, therefore, has three roommates." *Christ! It was like explaining something to an idiot child!* "If one of them turns, if one of them goes full neurological in a compartment with three other sleeping people who have not turned, and if that person is not somehow restrained, those berthing areas will turn into slaughterhouses."

"You're exaggerating, Jones. And taking council of your fears," the CO said, his voice bland, and instantly infuriating. "Tisk, tisk." The *tisk, tisk* is what did it, the straw that broke the fucking camels back.

CWO2 Larsen stepped in before Jonesy could do anything stupid. "Sir, he does have a point." The CO scowled at him, but he kept on, unfazed. "If we don't do something, this problem could escalate."

"Into what, Mr. Larsen?" Medavoy snapped, derisively. "Tell me what you think is going to happen."

He's completely fucking delusional, Jonesy thought, but kept his mouth shut for fear that if he opened it, he might just explode and beat the living shit out of the prick. Kicking your Captain's ass - even in a zombie fucking apocalypse - would be bad, on a monumental scale.

The Warrant Boats sat heavily back into his chair and looked at the CO with stunned incredulity. Clearly, he wanted to say something, clearly he wanted to explain to the idiot. But just as clearly, he didn't want to mention the "Z" Word. Jonesy could see it in the man's face. CWO2 Larsen said nothing. Nobody uttered a word.

Whether you hated the person or not, whether you respected the person as a human being or not, whether you thought the person had his head so far up his own ass that it was a miracle he could even breathe, or not, there was nothing more like God on High as the Captain of a ship. And the one thing you never, ever did, was buck the Captain's authority. There was a word for it: *Mutiny*.

"I thought so," Medavoy said. "Meeting is dismissed. See to your duties." And so saying, he got up from the table and exited the compartment.

The remaining people there (all the officers, less Molly and Bloominfeld, who were on the Bridge, plus Jonesy) looked at each other in silence. Nobody said anything, but Jonesy could see it in all their faces. *Medavoy may have just sentenced us to death.*

70

CS3 Manny Manoa woke up feeling hungry. This was nothing new. He was a big boy. He was always hungry. What he didn't know (and soon he would be past the point of *ever* knowing), was why he should also feel *angry*. He sat up, careful not to give himself a concussion on the bottom of the bunk above him, and planted his feet on the ground. Why angry?

He shook his big head, flexed his dinner plate-sized hands, and farted. Above him, SNCS George DeGroot stirred. Across from him, SN David Duprovniak, and CS3 John Ryan slept on.

He'd been feeling bad for days, now. He knew about the Pomona Virus, of course, had seen the ultimate result when Doc turned in the middle of the funeral. But word was you had to catch the cold first, had to get the respiratory infection, and then the neurological would kick in, and he hadn't done either. In fact, he had *never* caught a cold, as far as he could remember. The problem was, he *couldn't* remember much of anything. His memory was fuzzy. His *mind* was fuzzy.

He looked into his rack and saw a spot of blood on the sheet, just below the pillow. *Blood?* He looked at his left arm. Nothing. He looked at his right arm and saw a raw patch of skin where there had been a small scab. Nothing big, no gaping wound, just a small cut that had been caused by...? He couldn't remember.

He lifted a large butt cheek and farted again. His head hurt, all the way across his forehead, as if someone had shoved a spike through his temples. It made him angry. His face felt flushed, like it had been wrapped in a hot towel, like that time...no...what time? He couldn't remember. That made him angry, too.

The room swam before his eyes. He could see the lockers on the bulkhead to his left, see the bunks across from him, and the two people in those bunks. *They* made him angry. But he couldn't remember their names, for some reason. He knew he *should* remember, knew somewhere deep inside that he had known these guys for a long time. So why couldn't he remember their names? That pissed him right the fuck off. He groaned - or was it a growl? He lurched to his feet and farted again.

Behind him, someone (who?) stirred. "Manny, go back to sleep, and quit fucking farting," a muffled voice said.

Rage filled him like hot liquid, oozing through his pores like lava. He had a fleeting moment of confusion, of wondering why he felt so angry, so goddamned fucking angry, and then it was gone, and only the rage remained.

He turned, saw the eyes of the thing behind him, and then he howled.

71

In the next compartment aft, along the Port side of the passageway, YN3 Gregory Haversham woke up. A noise had disturbed him, but when he opened his eyes, he found that he didn't recognize a thing about his surroundings, didn't know where he was. For that matter, he didn't know *who* he was. He only knew that he wanted to kill.

Two compartments aft and over on the starboard side of the passageway, Seaman Apprentice Tommy Barnes slept on, but things inside his brain were turning. Synapses were firing in his frontal lobe, but receptors weren't receiving the signals. His lizard brain, however, was wide awake, and it was *hungry*.

One deck above, in the single-occupancy Chief's quarters, BMC Bernie Adams woke up feeling like shit. He staggered to his metal sink and ran water into the bowl, splashing it on his fevered face. *Should go see the Doc*, he thought, vaguely. But then he remembered. The Doc was dead. He pulled on his uniform with trembling hands. Had trouble tying his shoes. Had trouble remembering how. He left them untied, opened the door with some difficulty (the door thing - how did that work again?), entered the passageway, and went in search of something to eat.

72

"Okay...Now what?" Amber Winkowski said to no one as she surveyed her new prison. The head smelled of disinfectant, and the blue shit they put in the toilet bowl water. There was a sink - not a very big one, not big enough to fill with enough water to help her survive more than a few hours, let alone days - and a shelf with cleaning supplies and (thank Dear God) seven rolls of toilet paper.

On the deck lay the obligatory swab and metal bucket, complete with strainer. This ubiquitous item appeared over and over again, in every unit, on every ship, in every building and warehouse and galley, everywhere, in every branch of the military. It was part of the scenery. She'd have probably noticed it more if it had NOT been there. But this time, she *did* notice it. Specifically, she noticed the long wooden handle protruding from the depths of the bucket.

She could make that into a weapon. She knew she could. But how? She examined the bracket where it connected the bottom of the shaft to the mop. Four small screws, two on each side, attached the metal to the wood. Okay...so...she needed a screwdriver. She knew they had one. Hell, they had several, along with all sorts of assorted tools in the Comm Center. None of them, however, were in the head with her.

She could break it. Hadn't she seen that done in countless movies? It would be simple, and then she'd have a weapon. She picked it up a bit clumsily, the heavier end with the swab portion making it unbalanced in her left hand. She raised it to chest height, raised her right knee straight in front of her, and brought it smashing down.

OUCH! That shit hurt! And it did nothing to break the wooden shaft. All she'd gotten for her efforts was a pain in the knee. Great! Just perfect! What else could go wrong?

She checked herself on the last question. Better not to ask.

Then she realized her mistake. *Idiot!* She chided herself, then dropped the swab end to the deck, took a firm grip on the opposite end with her right hand, and stomped down with her right foot. Pain shot up from her sore knee, and she staggered back, catching her balance at the last moment. She smiled. The wood had cracked. One more time...

She stomped, and with a splintering of sound and wood, the shaft snapped, leaving her with about a three foot makeshift spear. She examined the broken end. Yes. Plenty jagged enough. Plenty sharp enough to jab into that worthless jackass turned zombie in the Comm Center.

She steeled herself, and moved to the door.

73

BM1/Deck Dennis Hurdlika stuck his head inside the Crew's Lounge, checking on his babies. They were in there, his Deckies: John "Mad Dog" Kennedy, so named for his habit of turning every scenario into an episode of All-Pro Wrestling (*...and Mad Dog rips the turnbuckle from the post and smashes his opponent...*). It made Dennis laugh. It made everybody laugh. SN John "Big Balls" Fitipaldi, Seaman Siemen (that joke never got old - poor kid), BM3/DECK Eddie Brown, BM3/OPS Eric Hebert (not one of his Deckies, but still part of his crew), SA Pierre Milancent, from New Orleans (which he told people at every opportunity), EM3 Dan McMullen, MK3 Danny Maury; all were there, all were part of Dennis Hurdlika's crew.

He eyed the big screen TV and smiled. They were watching *Resident Evil: Apocalypse*. How appropriate - twisted, but appropriate.

In the corner of the compartment, Danny Maury went into a coughing spasm. It electrified the room. Everybody scattered, leaping out of the bolted couches, trying to get as far away from him as they could. Cups went flying. A half-empty bag of microwave popcorn spread itself across the compartment like gigantic, salt and butter-flavored snowflakes. A soda can, just opened by EM3 McMullen, sent carbonated liquid spraying like a brown geyser into the air.

Dennis saw the abject fear in their faces - felt it himself. The cold - the goddamned Common Fucking Cold; if you caught it, if you got the fever, you were zombie city.

Danny looked at everybody and shook his head, laughing. "Take it easy, you fucking idiots," he said in his Maine accent, waving his coffee cup at them. "Bug juice went down the wrong pipe, is all. Jeez, you're all so fucking paranoid!" He laughed again.

The crowd hesitated, looking at Danny, looking at each other. And then the laughter - nervous laughter, though it may be - started. Dennis laughed with them, declined the opportunity to bitch at them about cleaning the compartment, then turned, closed the door, and continued his nightly round.

They were all his crew, and he was their Boats. Most of them wouldn't have voiced the description, most of them would have been less likely to express the emotion than to turn into a turnip, but the fact remained. They were his babies, his kids, and he was their uniformed babysitter. He smiled at the idea. A movie poster flashed across his mind: *Adventures in Babysitting*. It's not just a job, it's an adventure. No, wait. That was the Navy. Fuck a bunch of squids.

He dropped down the port side ladder and into Crew Berthing Forward. The two Berthing areas were split by an athwart-ship watertight bulkhead, with a watertight door separating the two. Most of his Deckies slept in the Forward half, due to its proximity to the Buoy Deck and the God-awful racket they caused when working buoys. There were a few in the Aft section, but most were up there. All was quiet.

He turned Forward, went through the watertight door, and entered the Bosun Hold. Duke and Harold looked up, startled by the sudden *CLANK* of the hatch. They were clustered together by the table along the port bulkhead.

"Do I want to know what you're up to at this hour, or do you two need some alone time?" Dennis asked, half curious/half delighted in the opportunity to give them shit.

Duke gave him a *go fuck yourself* look. "We're performing brain surgery, can't you tell?" He asked, stepping away from the table to reveal six *Gerber Gator* Kukri Machetes laid out. Five were in their leather sheaths, and one lay with vicious-looking blade exposed.

"Planning on cutting a bunch of brush out here in the middle of the ocean?" Dennis asked.

They had gotten the rather unique implements as part of last year's Fallout Funds. Thanks to the unintended consequences of the Congressional well-meaning stupidity known as *Graham-Rudman*, any part of the budget not spent during the fiscal year would be removed from the following year's budget. As a result, any money not spent by the Fourth Quarter (which ended in September) would mysteriously disappear, then reappear as items they may or may not have actually needed. For example, the small workout room they had forward of After Steering, contained a *Stairmaster*. On the one hand, this was a useful item for maintaining crew fitness. On the other hand, they were on a ship filled with ladders, both inside and out. A *Stairmaster* was - at best - redundant.

The Kukri Machetes were another example. They often worked on fixed Aids to Navigation attached to land. This land was, by necessity, right along the shoreline, and since no civilian wanted a blinking light on their property, these Aids were frequently in remote places only accessible by bush-bashing through often thick brush. So a machete was a useful thing to have around. The specialized Kukri Machete, on the other hand, was a bit of an extravagance. But they were cool, and there had been Fallout Funds, and so they'd bought six. This still did not explain why Duke and Harold were sharpening them at eleven o'clock at night.

"Planning on cutting *something*, anyway," Duke said, guardedly.

"Do I want to know?" Dennis asked.

"Not really, Duke replied.

"Roger that," Dennis said, then turned, and started for the door, but then he paused and looked at what Harold had been doing. The young seaman had taken an aluminum baseball bat from the Morale Locker, covered the business end with a six-inch strap of leather, through which he'd punched ten-penny nails, and was now wrapping it with eighth-inch cotton line, tying small knots at the top of every wrap. This was ordinarily used as fancy work, called *coxcombing*, to wrap rails, or - in the Old Guard - the large brass helm that had been replaced by the modern joystick up on the Bridge, but this was definitely not decorative. The bat looked deadly as Hell. He stared at it for a moment, speechless, then shook his head and said: "I really don't want to know."

He turned, opened the watertight door, then closed it behind him as he continued his round.

He went back through Forward Berthing, then opened the watertight door leading to the Aft Berthing area, and stopped. It sounded like a brawl was going on in one of the four-man compartments. He went to investigate.

74

Jonesy climbed the ladder, dead on his feet. He hadn't slept since Scoot. That was, what? Two days? Three? He couldn't be sure. His head felt fuzzy.

But not feverish - definitely not feverish.

He passed the Captain's vestibule, outside The Cabin (as the CO's quarters were always called), flipping the door an insolent bird and mouthing the word *asshole,* as he went by. He needed to adjust his attitude.

He paused outside the Chartroom, just forward of the Radio Room, and thought about going in to make a pot of coffee, but decided to check in on the Bridge, instead. The red lights were on in all the interior spaces, to preserve the night vision of anyone going out on deck, but it was still damned dark when he entered the Bridge and looked around. He saw Medavoy over by the chart table (*his* chart table, god dammit) writing his Night Orders.

Jonesy could just imagine what they were: *Continue Box of Death on station, while the crew gets slowly but surely killed because I'm a fuck wit who refuses to do what's necessary to protect them.*

Okay...probably not. He doubted Medavoy was self-aware enough to accept responsibility for his idiotic orders. *Calm, Jonesy, calm...*

The asshole in question closed the Night Order book, slid it under the fathometer, as usual, then turned to head below. He glared at Jonesy for a moment, barely acknowledging his presence, then called "Good night," in the general direction of LTjg Bloominfeld and Ens. Gordon, and left the Bridge.

Instantly raising the general IQ of the compartment, Jonesy thought, disgustedly. He really had to watch this. If he accidently voiced what he was saying in his head, due to being so sleep-deprived, he'd be Court Martialed in a second. Might be worth it, though...

Fuck, Jonesy, adjust your attitude, he told himself, as he walked over to join BM3/OPS Jack Ross at the chart table.

"Are we having fun?" He asked.

"You know me," Ross said, in his laconic drawl.

Jonesy picked up the Celnav book, where watchstanders were *supposed* to record their celestial fix information. There were no entries in it for 2000 - 2400. There should have been, because Jonesy required his boys to take at least one per watch, if the sky was clear enough.

"Any stars tonight?" he asked.

"A few," Ross replied, hesitantly.

Jonesy closed the book, then lightly smacked Ross's forehead with it. "Take a wild guess who's going to be calculating sunrise and sunset for the next week."

"Yeah. Sorry." Ross said.

Jonesy turned, with the book still in hand, and looked at SN Borgeson, leaning against the starboard door. He was there as helmsman, but since the ship's autopilot was doing an excellent job of steering the ship, the seaman was pretty much just an extra lookout. Jonesy favored him with a smack on the forehead with the book.

"Hey!" Borgeson complained. "What?"

"If you ever call me Petty Officer Kevorkian again, I'm going to shove your head in the shitter," Jonesy said.

"Sorry Jones," the young man said. "It was only a joke."

"Yeah, whatever," he replied, then sidled up to the Bridge windows next to Molly. He looked down at her (since she was almost four inches shorter), then over toward LTjg Bloominfeld. The man did not look well. "Are we still in the Pacific Ocean?" He asked, sounding far more cheerful than he felt.

"Last I checked," Molly answered. The LTjg only grunted.

"Excellent," he said, then turned to go. "I'll be down in the Chartroom, if you need me." He reached the door and was unsurprised to discover Molly at his elbow.

"He doesn't look too good," she whispered.

Jonesy looked over at Bloominfeld, who was still staring out into the black night. "Watch your back," he whispered in return, then headed below.

75

The rubber-covered grapnel went over the rail and hooked so quietly, even Old Joe couldn't hear it from the RHIB. *Perfect*, he thought. Everything was going perfectly, without them even trying. *Fate.*

Fate had put him in that liquor store three years ago. Fate had caused a patrol car to roll by just as he was leaving, with gun and cash in hand. Fate had sent him to Soledad, caused him to meet Blackjack Charlie, and then served up a heaping helping of plague. Fate made the zombie guard slam the human guard into the cell release button in the C Block Guard Office. No other Block had been freed. Just their's. Fate.

And tonight, they meant to come out of the darkness, directly onto this boat's back end, and it had worked. Blackjack calculated the course to come up where they wanted to be, and Old Joe steered it, unerringly, for twenty miles, long before they could even see the ship. Blackjack had told him to come up slightly behind the boat, then loop into the South side. He'd said nobody would see them, and nobody had.. Fate.

The boarding ladder went up like a dream. Not a sound. "Go," he said, motioning to Hank Lazardo. "Get up there fast and stay quiet until everyone else is up. Clear?" Lazardo nodded and smiled. He was a wack-job, to be sure, but that shotgun he carried was real, and the man knew how to use it. Old Joe watched as he scampered up the ladder and over the rail.

76

Jim, on the Flying Bridge with his M-1 Garand rifle, and John, on the Bridge, didn't see the RHIB approach. They had expected it at sunset - had, in fact, been standing watch, staring into the empty sea since before the sun went down, more than four hours ago. To suggest everyone had lost their edge was an understatement.

Jason Gilcuddy, who had never found the wife he sought, in spite of having searched in all the undefined "nooks and crannies," didn't see the boat, either, because he was standing nearly amidships, at the aft end of the Boat Deck, looking to the north. None of them saw the grapnel go over. None of them saw the boarding ladder go up, or the man that followed it over the rail.

Mick Fincham and Lane Keely didn't see any of it, either, standing on the Buoy Deck, waiting for what they all hoped would not happen. Bob Stoeffel and Gus Perniola couldn't see any of it, since they were both on the Mess Deck, both fully armed (Gus with the .44 Magnum they had taken from Gilbert Farcquar, and Bob with a Remington 12 Gauge shotgun and a 9mm Baretta), and both stationed to protect the families. Teddy Spute didn't see shit, because he was below in the Lounge with those families, put there by a severely unhappy John and told to "Keep that stupid bitch from causing any more trouble."

The stupid bitch in question was sitting by herself in a chair, staring between Spute, (whom she blamed for putting her in this predicament) and the other wives (whom she despised, because they had gone from warm and friendly, to suddenly cold). The children did not know of her idiotic mistake, although Stephanie Barber, age nineteen and technically not a child, had her suspicions. Professor Christopher Floyd, also sitting by himself, and also getting the cold-shoulder treatment from the wives (because they all thought he was nuts and didn't trust him) knew what she had done, and thought her to be slightly above a low-grade moron, but he thought that of most people, so he didn't share in the rest of this new crew's animosity.

So nobody knew anything was happening when Hank Lazardo's feet hit the deck. They didn't know Blackjack Charlie thought the guy was a fucking psycho. They certainly didn't know that in a purely clinical sense, Blackjack was right. They didn't know that the prison dispensary had kept a supply of Thorazine ready for him. They didn't know he'd been told to take a daily regimen of anti-psychotic meds, to keep him calm and even. And nobody knew, except Hank Lazardo, that he hadn't had a dose in over a week.

Nobody knew that Hank Lazardo was delighted to be there with a shotgun in his hand. Nobody (particularly Old Joe, who had told Lazardo he must be quick, and above all quiet) knew the idea of killing somebody had given him a stone-hard erection.

But when Jason Gilcuddy, with his head in the clouds, turned and saw the intruder, and when Hank Lazardo, with the rocket in his pocket, blew a hole in Jason's chest the size of a bowling ball, suddenly a whole bunch of people knew that everything had gone seriously wrong.

77

YN2 Lydia Claire stared in anger at the team prepping the hoses aft of the Boat Deck, and then in horror at the crowd on the pier, as they started to run away from a spot about two-thirds down its length. At first, she couldn't see what had caused it. She glanced toward the hose team, toward CWO4 Vincenzo leading it, and saw that they had seen whatever it was, as well. And then she did, too.

Someone had turned zombie. This person (a man) had tackled the woman next to him and was ripping at her flesh with his hands and teeth. Nobody seemed to be trying to stop it. Everybody was running.

And then someone screamed directly across from Lydia's position. Another person had turned - or was turning, because this one (a woman this time) was tearing at her own clothes, and flailing at her body, as if to rid it of a thousand stinging insects.

A third person, a man, about twenty feet down from the second, had leapt upon another man, and was trying to rip the other's throat out with his teeth. The effect on the refugees of this triple threat was like a tornado touching down on a clapboard house. The crowd exploded outward in every direction - including into the water off the side of the pier. People dove or jumped or were shoved over the side. Screams filled the air, like a thousand fingernails on a thousand blackboards.

Even through the protective clothing and the gas mask, the tumult send daggers from the pit of Lydia's stomach, up her spine and directly into the pain centers of her brain. She dropped to her knees, covering her ears, and screamed. Jeff Babbett, the BM1/OPS who had been doing the soundings at Station Six, was to her in moments, kneeling beside her and ineffectually rubbing her back in an effort to sooth her terror. Didn't work. She continued screaming. And she continued watching, unable to tear her eyes away from the growing bedlam on the pier.

There were dozens of people in the water, some of them flailing, some of them drowning, some of them swimming toward the supposed safety of the *Polar Star*. "Stand by to repel boarders," she heard CWO4 Vincenzo shout, and it sent her world sideways.

She stopped screaming, shoved Roberts away with her left hand, and stood, staring at the hose teams as they charged the hoses and prepared to open them up on the fleeing refugees. "Stop!" she yelled. "You can't do this! We have to help them!" But Bobby V and his team heard none of it. They just charged the nozzles and started spraying.

She barely heard it herself through the muffling gas mask. Well, she could change that, right quick!

She stalked toward them, pulling at the bottom of her mask, but it wouldn't budge. The restraining straps at the back were too tight. They'd been bothering her the whole time, actually, but she hadn't even thought of loosening them, since she had no desire to get infected. None of that mattered now. She needed to get the mask off, needed to yell at the hose team, needed to make them stop this madness before it was too late. Those people were dying out there! They needed help - *their* help - the help of the United States Fucking Coast Guard! She reached behind her to the straps, but Babbett was on her in a flash, covering her mask at back and front with his large hands.

"Don't do it, Lydia,": he said into her ear. It was soft, almost a whisper, but undeniable, just the same.

Don't do it, Lydia. Don't do what? Don't save these people? Don't do their fucking job as the fucking "Lifesavers?" Don't do what she had joined the Coast Guard to do in the first place?

She could have gone into the Air Force. The recruiter had been relentless trying to get her to sign the contract. But she had wanted to do good, to help people, save people, not practice for what any sane person hoped would never happen - not to bomb the shit out of hundreds of people at a time, thousands of feet below.

Saving people was their job, their *purpose,* their whole reason for being; not pushing people away, not hitting fleeing refugees with fire hoses so they drown or get eaten by fucking zombies! They couldn't do this, they had to help them, had to save them. She had to make them stop.

But Babbett had her in a death grip, and wasn't about to let go.

Well, we'll just see about that!

Lydia had grown up a Southern Girl, an *Alabama* girl, to be precise, living in the country with three brothers who picked on her relentlessly, as brothers will. *Probably dead now* - the thought flashed through her head and was just as quickly shunted aside. She had learned how to defend herself. She kicked Babbett square in the shin.

"Ah fuck!": he shouted, and let her go - but only long enough to swing around behind and grab her in a bear hug, trapping her arms at her side. She struggled like a wildcat, but all it did was make his hand slip on the slick MOPP material, and grab her left tit in a vice-like grip.

"Ouch!" she screamed, and kicked her heels back to try his shins again, but he kept shifting back and forth, from one wide-spread leg to the other, avoiding her blows, lifting her feet of the deck, and grabbing her tit even tighter.

"Easy, Lydia," he said, softly into her ear, even through the muffling masks, as if she hadn't been struggling at all, hadn't been trying to kick his legs off. "Easy."

It was no use. He was too big. He was at least twice her size. She wasn't going to get away from him.

"But we have to stop them," she cried. "We have to rescue those people!"

"We can't Lydia," he said, his voice still soft, still soothing. "They're infected. We're not. We can't help them."

"But..." she started to protest again, but then the screech of a bullhorn rendered her attempts useless.

Roberts put her back on her feet, but didn't loosen his grip on her torso - or her tit. They stared up at the Bridge wing and saw the Captain, as he raised the bullhorn to his lips.

"Secure from Fueling Ops. Secure from Fueling Ops. Cast off all lines."

78

LT Richard Medavoy wasn't sure what he was seeing when he entered the Cabin. He was certain his wife was standing there with her back to him, but she looked a bit...*off*.

For one thing, she was standing funny: not her usual stance, either as Manic Marissa (which was a sort of jittery perpetual motion, even when still), or as Morose Marissa (which always seemed deflated). She stood with legs two feet apart, her back straight, her head down, and her arms in front of her body and out of sight, as if she were looking at something in them.

For another thing, the silouette created by the overhead lights showed that her body beneath the floor-length robe was naked, and that the robe was open. Odd as it might be, it would be fine, if she was in the sweet spot between manic and depressive phases. The sex was phenomenal at those moments, brief though they always were. It was pretty much the only reason he'd stayed married to her. Well...and Carson. Always Carson... But the sex-phase should still be a couple weeks away, if she remained true to her bipolar routine, which hadn't changed in seven years. Something else was going on.

"Marissa? Honey?" He said.

She didn't respond at first, didn't move, until two things happened at once, and Richard Medavoy's life twisted on its axis, as violently as if the magnetic poles had just flip-flopped. Her arms fell to her sides, and the scrawny body of their son - his boy, his Carson - fell to the carpeted deck with a *THUNK*.

He stared, gape-mouthed, feeling nothing, for perhaps three seconds, and then the horror of what it must mean hit him like a ball pein hammer. She turned, slowly, and the horror shifted into shear, unadulterated terror.

Her face was blank, though tears had been flowing freely down her cheeks. Her eyes were hollow, her mouth, slack. None of which caused his reaction. What did, was her left breast. Thick, red blood had coursed down her torso and onto her legs, like *Carrie*, after the bath from a drained pig bucket. The worst was the nipple. It was gone. It had been *eaten*.

He looked from his wife's face, to her breast, to her nipple, and then to the body of his son on the deck. Carson's face, his small, beloved face, was white. His mouth was slack and covered in blood and bits of flesh. But his neck was clear enough, clean enough, to recognize the strangle marks around his skinny throat. Medavoy looked at his wife's blank face again.

"Our baby was hungry," she said, her voice a sort of sing-song. "So I breast fed him."

His heart shattered into a million, razor-sharp shards of glass, shredding his mind and his soul. He opened his mouth to scream. Nothing came out but air.

79

OS3 Bill Schaeffer picked up his tray from the Mess table and brought it over to the scullery. The remains of the Midrats meal (Monte Cristo Sandwiches) looked as if he'd just moved it around on the tray - which was more or less what he'd done. Shame, too, since he liked those - especially when Gary King made them. The older black man peered out through the serving window, saw the nearly full plate, and nodded, understanding.

Nobody seemed to have much of an appetite. Bill looked around the Mess. Frank Roessler was there, swirling his fork through what had been mac and cheese. *Comfort food,* Bill thought. Gary knew his business.

EM3 Dan McMullen sat at a table nearby. Neither of the two engineers looked at each other. Neither of them spoke.

Mad Dog sat at a table with BM3/OPS Hebert, but they weren't talking, either. BM3/DECK Eddie Brown came in, grabbed a cup of coffee, then headed back out again. Not one word. It seemed to Bill as if everyone was waiting. For what, he didn't want to think. Neither did anyone else. The normally rambunctious Mess Deck, was silent as a funeral home.

It was broken when Mad Dog, looking around, said: "Shit! Forgot my cover. Hey Brownie!" He called out, and the BM3 turned from the passageway heading toward the Wardroom. "Tell them I'll be up in a minute," Mad Dog said, getting up from the table. "Gotta go get my hat." Mad Dog departed, heading toward the athwart ship's vestibule, and Brown continued on his way aft.

Bill deposited his tray in the scullery, then headed out.

The glare of white light on the Mess Deck had totally fucked his vision, so when he got into the red light of the port passageway leading to the Bridge ladder, he could barely see where he was going. It didn't matter. They had, from time to time, conducted Emergency Egress training, to prepare themselves for the possibility of having to move around in a ship with no lights, due to loss of power. For the people who worked below, it meant learning how to get from their work space to an exterior deck area, blindfolded. For those who worked above the main deck (all the OPS personnel) the blindfolded egress began in the berthing area.

When it had been his turn to stumble along, the XO had been monitoring and Bill took great pleasure in walking backwards up the ladder from his stateroom, through the passageway, and up the ladder to the Captain's Vestibule, which was where he exited (still walking backwards) onto the Quarterdeck. The XO had not been pleased, but Bill had done that same walk (forwards) while brain dead from sleep deprivation, every time he'd had the 0400 - 0800 watch, and so backwards up a ladder while blindfolded was child's play. He did so now, though it was 2330, rather than 0330. Since he hadn't slept in about a day and a half, for fear one of his roommates might turn zombie, the brain dead feeling remained the same, or worse.

He reached the vestibule, and thought he could hear something strange coming from inside the Cabin, but his give-a-shit level was about as low as it had ever been, and so he kept going up. He reached the door to Radio, keyed in his security code, and entered to discover that OS1 Carlton Bertram had become a zombie.

80

OS2 Amber Winkowski peered around the edge of the head door and found an empty corridor. She breathed a sigh of relief, but it was short-lived. The sound of shuffling feet said hello to her frightened ears, coming from the Commcen, along with what sounded like snuffling, as if some curious beast were trying to sniff out a tasty morsel.

She opened the door all the way and started down the corridor, then stopped, backed up, and moved a roll of toilet paper to hold the door open - just in case. Grabon was a skinny little fuck, and she didn't really think he'd give her too much trouble, but zombie fighting had never exactly been Amber's forte. Fighting anyone had never exactly been her forte, but it had taken her all of about three seconds to realize she wouldn't survive long, trapped in a head with no food and minimal water.

She couldn't run, because the world outside the Commcen door had become a scary place, getting worse by the moment, and she couldn't hide, because then she'd starve to death. Simple math: A, plus B, divided by C, equaled OS3 Gabon-Zombie needed to die. But she left the door open just in case this didn't work.

She stepped forward, creeping her way toward the junction of corridor and Commcen. Something wasn't right. She was making a mistake, and she knew it, but couldn't think what it might be. Then it hit her, and she smacked herself upside the head for being an idiot - or would have, if her hands hadn't been full of spear.

She didn't know where he was.

He was out there, somewhere. But was he to the left? To the right? Just around the corner, or halfway across the room? She didn't know, but suspected the answer to that question would mean life or death - quite literally.

But how to solve this? Obvious: bring him to her. How? Make a noise? Her hammering heartbeat should be loud enough to attract him from across the building, let alone inside the next room, but that was the abject fear talking. She thought for a moment, didn't like the solution her analytical mind came up with, but didn't see any better alternative. Reluctantly, she held out her makeshift spear, and smacked it against the wall three times.

The snuffling noise stopped. She gripped her spear in both hands and waited. Nothing happened.

"Hey! Jackass!" She called, and OS3 Jackson Grabon appeared at the end of the corridor. She screamed and charged.

81

Jim Barber darted to the aft Flying Bridge rail at the sound of the shotgun's boom. He couldn't see Gilcuddy, or the person who'd just ended his search for a wife with a blast of twelve gauge double-ought. What he did see was one man standing on the Fantail, near the port rail, and a second (actually third, though he didn't know it) man coming over the side. He didn't hesitate.

The M-1 Garand, semi-automatic rifle he brought to his shoulder was a storied weapon that no less an authority than General George S. Patton called: "the greatest weapon of battle ever devised." Its 30-06 round, held in an eight-shot clip, was designed with but a single purpose: to kill. Unlike the 5.56mm of the M-16 and, more recently, the M-4, designed with the idea that wounding enemies created a greater logistical difficulty than did killing them outright, the 30.06 and the M-1 were unquestioned man-killers. Jim put two rounds into the chest of the man crawling over the port rail. The body flipped over backwards and into the sea.

On the Buoy Deck, Mick Fincham and Lane Keely, the former with an M-1 Carbine (which also belonged to Jim, but the man wasn't going to get stingy when pirates were involved), and the latter with a Remington Model 870, pump shotgun, Lane had brought himself, heard the shotgun blast, then the two cracks of the M-1 from the Flying Bridge. They turned and looked at each other, hesitating. As if by some nonexistent pre-determined signal, they both started running aft. Mick went up the port side, and Lane went to starboard.

John thought his heart might stop at the first shot, but it didn't, and he raced to the port Bridge Wing, arriving just as Jim opened fire above him. All he had was his Colt 1911, retrieved from its case and cleaned free of the dust of neglect. The .45 was a great weapon, but firing from high ground, over and around parts of the *True North's* superstructure and Boat Deck, at a moving target, seventy feet away would have been a waste of ammunition, so all he could do was stare in horror. He could see Jason Gilcuddy's body, and wished, with everything he had, that he couldn't. There wasn't a single question in his mind. His friend was dead.

He heard Jim fire again, and in the booming echo, heard him curse his failure as the third round pinged off the deck, sending a chunk of non-skid into the air. The man he'd been aiming at skirted the end of the superstructure and disappeared from sight.

Lane Keely crept forward, past the black RHIB in its cradle on the starboard Boat Deck. He was mild-mannered as they come, had never seen the sense in getting worked up about this, that, or the other thing, because if it wasn't those particular things, it'd be something else. Why waste time? He did, however, take life seriously.

He'd been a Boarding Officer many times during his twenty-three years in the Guard, as well as a Cox'n on 41-foot, 44-foot, and 46-foot motor surf boats, and had done who knew how many hours of Law Enforcement Operations, so this wasn't his first rodeo. He'd never shot anybody - never came close to it - but never having done something didn't mean he wasn't trained and *ready* to do it. So he held the shotgun in a tactical carry position, with a round jacked into the chamber, and the safety off. And when Hank Lazardo turned the corner around the superstructure, holding a shotgun, stopped, ten feet away from him, and laughed, mild mannered Lane Keely blew that son of a bitch into the next world.

He stared down at the death he had caused, at first feeling nothing. But then the enormity of it hit him like a Mack truck. He sped to the rail and promptly lost his dinner. Just because he was ready to do something didn't mean he had to like it.

82

Teddy Spute was not a happy camper. Not at all. John had stuck him with the women and children. And perhaps John had a point, since it had been *his* girlfriend who'd placed them in this predicament. But, dammit! How was he supposed to know Clara would be so fucking stupid?

Had he been blinded by a really nice ass? Was he so far gone from rational manhood that he could be manipulated by pussy? He knew the answer before his mind finished formulating the question: *Of course he could.*

He felt sorry for himself, and he knew it. He looked at her, sitting alone in a corner of the below-decks lounge. The wives hated her guts. No. They didn't hate her, didn't feel *anything* that strongly about her, except maybe the disgust all good women feel when they come in contact with the rare (but not uncommon) example of their gender that seemed to make them *all* look bad. He understood their point, intellectually. He even recognized the double-standard. One bad woman made them all look bad, whereas one bad man was just an asshole. He often puzzled over it, the way men do, over anything that doesn't directly affect them. Or maybe he was just blowing self-justified smoke up his own ass. Either way...

His reverie was shattered by the sound of gunfire, and then destroyed when Marcie called out: "Where's Davy?"

83

BM1/DECK Dennis Hurdlika opened the door to the four-man berth and, for a moment, couldn't believe what he was seeing. He thought: *This has got to be a joke.* But it wasn't, and he knew it wasn't.

In the first place, the door wouldn't open all the way. SNCS George DeGroot's still form lay in the way. Dennis stared at his face. It looked wrong, *lopsided*, and the cook's right eye protruded, the white of it cracked like red lightening from burst blood vessels. More blood ran down his face and puddled on the floor, and his head lay at an odd angle, the neck twisted too far to the left.

The next thing he saw (and he felt oddly disconnected as he made these observations) was SN David Duprovniak. He lay on the deck past George DeGroot's crumpled form, face up. His eyes held a curious expression, as if he died wondering idly what a strange dream he was having. His throat was a mess of blood and tissue. Someone - some *thing* - had ripped it to shreds.

That someone (*thing*) was huddled over the lower bunk to the right, making slurping noises. The absurdity of the situation, the sheer unreality of it, sang through Dennis Hurdlika's synapses like a demented choir. This couldn't be happening. But it was, and deep down inside, Dennis knew it was, knew what he was seeing was true: members of his crew, his babies, were now dead, and some asshole was now eating - fucking *eating* - one of them.

"What the Billy Blue Fuck is going on?" he shouted, his voice on the edge of hysteria.

The hulking form eating CS3 John Ryan, stopped in his/its snacking and turned its head to look at Dennis. It no longer looked like CS3 Manny Manoa, but Dennis knew it was. "Manny?" he choked, the name struggling to make it up his constricted throat and past his numb lips.

He felt a momentary twist of vertigo as the Manny-thing, on all fours, spun a hundred and eighty degrees and lunged at him, yanking the door all the way open, shoving George DeGroot and David Duprovniak aside like discarded and broken action figures. Then all six-foot-five, two hundred and fifty pounds of zombie cook was on him, scratching, biting, ramming him into the opposite bulkhead. The back of his skull hit whatever material made up the false wall covering the pipes and conduits and steel I-beam frames, went through it in a shower of sparks inside his own head as the universe exploded in his mind. Blackness overtook him and he knew nothing more.

84

Bad things were happening on the USCGC *Sassafras*. In the After Berthing section, BM1 Hurdlika lay crumpled, half on the deck, half against the false bulkhead through which his skull had so recently been shoved. CS3 Manny Manoa lurked above him, as if trying to decide whether he was still hungry or not, his face and chest (clad only in a tee shirt, nowhere near white anymore) covered in blood. That blood belonged to SNCS George DeGroot, SN David Duprovniak, and CS3 John Ryan, who were now dead in their four-man berth.

SN John Mad Dog Kennedy headed toward that berthing section, because he had forgotten his hat. The lapse in memory, would soon cause his death.

In the Cabin, LT Richard Medavoy quietly, desperately strangled his wife. She killed his son - his sweet Carson - and now she had to die.

So intent was he on this macabre task, that he failed to notice the boy moving. Carson was not dead, and he looked hungry.

Down in the Wardroom Passageway, BM3/DECK Eddie Brown conducted his pre-watch rounds. This was routine. This was normal, even though nothing on board this ship had been either one of those things for days. He had tried to get in touch with his parents in Billings, Montana, but all the circuits were busy, and the e-mails he'd sent remained unanswered. It worried him, more than anything had ever worried him in his entire life, but he kept it inside, kept the panic down, and remained focused on the task at hand.

At first, it had been relatively simple. The ship was scheduled to go into Charlie Status for maintenance, meaning they wouldn't be going anywhere for at least a month. There would be time to get in contact. He would talk to his parents, they would be fine. They lived in Montana, for God's sake. As bad as this zombie bullshit was, how on Earth could it reach Montana?

But then the order came down. The Sass was getting underway. They were bugging out. The shit had gotten very, very real. If it was bad enough for the US Coast Guard to be effectively abandoning a major city like Honolulu, then what chance did anyone have, anywhere? Nevertheless, he'd tried to remain focused, tried to concentrate on the details of getting the ship supplied and underway. But then the Captain (LCDR Sparks, not that asshat Medavoy) abdicated, fearing he might be infected. And then Scoot turned, and Terry Proud had been killed. Then Doc, and Masur, and the questions of just who would turn next, who would become a zombie, and who would be the next to die, racheted up the paranoia to insane levels.

Nobody trusted anybody else. He didn't trust any of them, and that, more than anything, sent ice through his veins. He'd always trusted his crew, had always known they had his back. Not any more.

The Wardroom was empty, as he knew it would be at this hour. He saw a bowl of fresh fruit, secured for sea in its own cradle on a sideboard, and thought about swiping an apple. He was hungry enough. He hadn't been taking any meals on the Mess Deck. Not since Scoot. He'd grab bits and pieces of food: crackers, a banana, some coffee cake during break earlier in the day; but to sit in the compartment where Scoot turned, where Terry Proud had his throat torn out, where the blood from his dying body splattered the aft starboard corner like some sick painting by Jackson Pollock on LSD, was just too much. He decided against the apple.

He heard something back toward Chief's Quarters and headed to investigate. He should have stayed put, should have grabbed the apple and savored its juicy nutrition, but he didn't. He went to investigate, and found BMC Bernie Adams, scratching at a closed door. The Chief turned and regarded him with eyes so mind-fuckingly, so batshit-ingly insane, they left no doubt. Chief Adams was a zombie, and he was coming at BM3/DECK Eddie Brown.

Up on the Bridge, LTjg Craig Bloominfeld did not look good, at all. He kept tugging at the collar of his work blue uniform shirt, and it made ENS Molly Gordon nervous. She cast a glance over her shoulder at SN Borgeson, standing at the helm control. He saw it, too.

She stared out the Bridge window into the night. Clouds had come in, obscuring the moon and stars. It was dark out there, like the inside of a sensory deprivation chamber, and it gave her an odd feeling of claustrophobia - an absurdity, because she was as close to being outside as she could be, without actually being outside.

She looked over her other shoulder at BM3/OPS Jack Ross, who was leaning back against the chart table, staring at nothing. "Have you taken the weather yet?" She asked, snapping him out of whatever thoughts might be swirling around in his head.

Ross was a closed one. She'd figured out Hebert. He was like an open book, though she suspected he didn't think so. And she knew Jonesy - knew him far too well for her own good. But Ross was a bit of an enigma. A nice enough guy: friendly, respectful, even helpful. But he was so damned reserved, she could explode a firecracker under his butt and he wouldn't twitch an eyebrow.

He looked at her for a moment, as if trying to focus his eyes after the thousand yard stare she'd interrupted. Then he glanced at his watch and said, "No Ma'am. I was going to let Hebert do it. Should be up here in a couple minutes to relieve me."

Weather was something the Nav Watch did and recorded once an hour. They checked temperature, both wet and dry (to get the Dew Point), the anemometer (wind), the barometer (pressure), and they went out and looked into the sky to judge the type of clouds. Then they compared these findings to the previous recorded entries. Any drastic change would mean a violent shift in weather, which at sea, could spell disaster. Most of the time, there was no change, no cause for alarm. But if she had learned any one thing from her time growing up with Uncle John in a Coast Guard family, it was that Mother Nature could turn into a stone cold bitch in the blink of an eye. And so they checked weather.

At the moment, however, she wasn't thinking of temperature or wind or barometric pressure, or anything, other than getting away from LTjg Bloominfeld.

"I'll do it," she said, then turned and headed out the Port Bridge door.

85

The jagged end of the makeshift spear thrust into Jackass Grabon's throat, slamming him backwards against the Comms console. Amber put every ounce of energy, every gram of her own weight behind the thrust and it struck home, with a vengeance.

So why wasn't the fucker dead?

By all rights, he *should* be dead. He had a stick jammed through his windpipe, and probably tickling his spine. Blood coursed from the wound in a sheet, so how could he possibly, by all that's Holy, still be struggling against her? Yet he was.

He batted at the swab handle, the blows sending vibrations through her weakening arms, far in excess of what he should be able to do. The guy was a lightweight. Before he turned zombie, Amber would have sworn she could break him in two with a nasty thought, and yet it was all she could do to keep him pinned against the console.

She couldn't keep this up much longer. Her wrists and elbows were beginning to hurt from the strain, and her legs were starting to shake from the effort of holding him back.

She was in better shape than this. She worked out. Okay...maybe she didn't work out as often as she should, but she still went to the gym every week. Only, it had been three weeks since the last time, and maybe two more before that. Doesn't *thinking* about it count? Apparently not.

Yeah, but she was *busy*. She worked sixty hours a week, in five, twelve-hour shifts at the Comm Center, and went to college for another twelve. She had to sleep sometime, didn't she?

None of which mattered. She was losing this battle. Something had to give, and if that something was her, before she was ready to do...*whatever* she could do, then she was dead meat.

Think, Amber, think. Okay...thinking. He was bleeding. The human body only held so much blood. Sooner or later he would bleed out. And then he'd drop, and then he'd die, no matter how much stronger the Pomona Virus seemed to make him. Basic human physiology. Couldn't get around it. There it was: a stone cold fact. She could wrap her head around it.

So...what? Stand there until he bled out? No. That wouldn't work - as evidenced by the fact his attempts to swat the swab handle out of her hands seemed to be getting stronger while she was getting weaker. So...run. Back to the head. Lock herself in, and wait him out. Yes! That's it! That's the ticket.

With what seemed the last bit of upper body strength she possessed, Amber flung the Jackass-zombie to the side, and ran.

86

Jonesy sat at the Chartroom desk, waiting for the coffee pot to finish doing its job, trying not to think about Scoot, or Doc, or Terry Proud, or LCDR Sparks. He was definitely, *absolutely* trying not to think about Masur, and he was failing. How had it all gone so far south? How had he landed in this strange new world, where he could be called upon to kill his friends?

A week ago - less than a week ago - he'd been happy, if disgruntled at the abject stupidity of Coast Guard Bureaucratic bullshit. He was off the TACLET, but on a new ship, with a new crew who'd become his family. And now he was killing them.

Whiskey Tango Fucking Foxtrot?

All such maudlin thoughts, all considerations of his lot in life, all notions of anything, even unto the coffee he so desperately needed, flew out of his head like the Starship Enterprise going into warp drive, as he heard two things - two *commotions* - on either side of the Chartroom: one from the Bridge, one from the Radio Room. He stood, grabbed his helmet, and started to move.

87

BM1/OPS Jeff Babbett had finally released Lydia Claire's left breast, though it still stung and he still held her in a bear hug from behind. The whole scenario might be funny - just a bit of slightly ribald slapstick comedy - if not for the reason behind it.

A new group of Deckies, as well as a few Engineers (though she could only tell one from the other by what they did) were releasing lines and disconnecting fuel hoses as if their lives depended on it. Somewhere deep down inside her, she understood their lives *did* depend on it, but she wasn't about to give that knowledge any opportunity to shunt aside her righteous anger.

The other group of Deckies, Bobby V's original team, were still spraying full pressure fire hoses at the swimmers trying to find safety on the *Polar Star*. But there was no more safety there, than on the pier, where hundreds of screaming people were trying to escape the growing number of turning zombies. One person might narrowly escape death, but the one next to them would get dog-piled by two, three, sometimes four instant maniacs, courtesy of the Pomona Virus. This happened all over the pier, as first one, then three, then a dozen people started raving, or ripping at their clothes, or biting someone's throat in paroxysms of rage and lunacy and animal blood lust. Only, animals didn't attack with such ferocity for no obvious reason.

Animals could be savage, simply because the act of tearing flesh was, on its own, considered savage by the humans who observed it, but savagery, itself, was a wholly human condition. Animals would kill to eat or protect their young. Humans, throughout history would kill for any reason that suited them, and were only restrained by moral or legal limitations. But these creatures had no such restraint. They killed because they *could*; no morality, no law, no *reason*, just the lizard brain doing what it had always done, since the Dawn of Man.

She watched in numb horror as the zombie hoard multiplied, as did the escalating body count. She watched in anger and disgust and shame as one of the swimmers, who had found a dangling line to the ship, struggled to heave himself over the rail, and CWO4 Robert Vincenzo shoved him back with the cruel end of a boat hook.

This was humanity in all its raw power, in all its fear and rage and violence.

She had joined the Coast Guard to save people, to help people, but now all she could do was watch them die. It sapped her of all remaining strength. She hung in Jeff Babbett's arms. It was over. She was done. And as far as she could tell, so was humanity.

88

Jonesy flung open the Chartroom door and stepped into the passageway, in time to see Bill Schaeffer come flying out of the Radio Room door, backwards. His land-side roommate slammed into the opposite bulkhead and slid to the deck. His eyes were wide, but clear. He wasn't unconscious, he wasn't apparently hurt, but he was clearly freaked out.

The reason for Bill's change from his normal laconic manner followed him out of the Radio Room door - not flying, but stalking. OS1 Carlton Bertram had turned zombie.

"Hey! Zombie!" Jonesy yelled, and the Zombie-Bert turned his way. Jonesy didn't hesitate, didn't think, didn't bother with strategy or tactics or any of the bullshit they taught him at the Special Missions Training Center on Camp Lejeune. He just nailed the bastard with a tactical-booted snap kick, square on the chin.

The former Operations Specialist flew backwards into nothing but air. On a normal staircase (the kind found in a house), canted at an easy forty-five degrees, he/it might have cushioned his/its fall somewhat on one or two of the lower stairs. It was possible. It might not have done him any good, in the long run, but it remained within the realm of possibility. On the shipboard stair-type ladder, canted at a much sharper twenty-two-point-five degrees, however, there was nothing to slow or cushion his/its fall until he/it landed with head and neck and spine onto the hard tile deck of the Captain's Vestibule. He/it flopped over backwards, landing face down on the ladder leading to the 01 Deck.

Jonesy stared at his former shipmate, waiting for some sense of loss or remorse, but he felt nothing. And then Manny Manoa, in skivvies, covered with blood and bits of things Jonesy did not want to consider, stumbled by the bottom of the ladder, heading forward toward the galley. He gaped in horror and his heart skipped a beat, as he contemplated having to take on that big son of a bitch, but he took a step toward the ladder and the rag doll form of Carlton Bertram Zombie, anyway.

He stopped, dead in his tracks, as he heard another loud commotion behind and above him, coming from the Bridge. *Molly.* The name popped into his mind in an instant, and his heart skipped three or four beats, as the idea of her getting hurt cut through him like a Star Wars light saber.

"Get back in Radio and lock the door!" Jonesy barked at Bill, then he turned and ran up the Bridge ladder.

89

Davy Gordon crept down the passageway toward the Bridge Ladder. He needed to see his Dad. It was important. It was *Guy Stuff.*

He loved his Mom, of course. Who didn't love their Mom? Losers, that's who. He even loved his sister, Samantha, although he'd never tell her so in a million, billion years. And his cousin, Molly was just the coolest thing ever - especially when she was showing him that karate stuff. *HI-YA!* That was awesome! But they were all *girls.* In fact, all the people down in the Lounge had been girls, except the Nutty Professor (as Samantha called him), and Mr. Spute, who everybody seemed to be mad at for some reason.

There was George Stoeffel, admittedly. But he was twelve, and all he wanted to talk about was baseball (Davy liked football, because his Dad liked football) and - of course - girls. Davy was sure he had the hots for his sister, and that was just gross. He needed someone he could talk to about more important things, and he needed to talk to that someone now, because there was *Guy Stuff* going on now.

He could have slipped into the Mess Deck to talk to Mr. Stoeffel, or Mr. Perniola, but they were busy, they were nervous, and they weren't his Dad. He'd always been his Dad's "Little Man," and that was important. He wasn't totally sure what was happening (although somebody had mentioned *Pirates*) but whatever it was, it was not just Guy Stuff, but *Man Stuff*.

He was tired of being pushed aside and made to hang out with the ladies and other kids, and his sister. He wanted to prove to his Dad that he wasn't just his "Little Man," but a real man, who was able to be counted on and *included* when there was Man Stuff going on.

So he crept past the Mess deck and headed up the ladder toward the Bridge.

90

"Get your ass up there and take the Bridge," Old Joe yelled at the only two members of his so-called "gang" still in the RHIB. Eddie Cochrane, the child molester, and Sugar Brown, the whore-killing pimp, looked at him like he'd lost his damned mind. And maybe he had.

He'd known the plan was hosed the moment he heard Hank Lazardo - that crazy bastard - open up with the shotgun. He'd known it was totally fucked the moment he saw Joe-Boy do a reverse one-an-a-half gainer without a twist off the other ship, and land in the ocean with a belly flop. Two very large, very bloody holes were in the kid's back, as he floated face down, about a half-mile behind them. He could still see the body, in the loom of the moonlight cutting across the calm sea. It was a beautiful night for taking a ship that didn't belong to them in a zombie apocalypse. He didn't wonder at the morality of what they were doing. He didn't really wonder about the sense, though, at the moment, there didn't seem much. *Fucked all to Hell...*

Then he'd heard yet another shotgun blast. He couldn't tell if that was Lazardo doing something else stupid, getting his ass blown off, or taking out another member of the other crew. He had no idea where Skizzy Pete Hannity was, and now he was asking the only two remaining to get up there and maybe get shot. *Crazy.*

"Are you fucking nuts?" Sugar Brown asked.

Eddie Cochrane barked a laugh and said: "I'll do it," and started up the ladder. They watched him climb up and over. They didn't hear another shot. Old Joe looked at the pimp.

"Don't look at me," Brown said. "My ass is staying in the motherfucking boat!"

Old Joe held the RHIB steady beneath the ladder. The other boat wasn't moving very fast, and the sea was calm, so this was not difficult. *Never get out of the boat*, he thought, remembering the line from *Apocalypse Now*. If *that* wasn't appropriate.... He swore under his breath and tried to think.

He thought fate had brought him to this place. He thought it was all meant to be. But this wasn't fate, at all. This was a shit sandwich, and he had no choice but to take a big damned bite.

He heard another shot. *Never get out of the Goddamned boat.*

91

CS1 Gary King wiped at the flat metal surface of the grill, even though the thing had been clean for the last ten minutes. The whole Galley shined. So what was he still doing there?

Hiding.

The thought popped into his head, and he waited for the pang of guilt sure to follow, but it didn't. He was scared - more scared than he'd ever been in his entire life. Things were happening, very bad things, and he knew it, and there wasn't a single damned thing he could do about any of it.

The fear was like a living thing, clawing at his chest, shrinking his balls to the size of marbles. He was a man. He shouldn't be cowering in his kitchen like a little girl. But he was.

He wiped at the grill again.

Something big slammed against the galley door to his right, and he jumped - literally *jumped* - at the sound. *What the fuck is wrong with me?* He thought. *You're not an idiot*, the answer came. *You're not suicidal. But you are a cook.* He pondered that for a moment. He *was* a cook, just a plain old ship's cook, in a galley, filled with pots and pans and...*knives.*

He did have knives - a shitload of them. He went to the stainless steel drawer and opened it. The first thing he saw was the cleaver. There was another bang at the door, but he didn't jump this time. Instead, he picked up the cleaver and looked at it. He went to a cabinet below the prep table and selected one of two, six-inch cast iron skillets, hefted it in his left hand, then looked at the chopper in his right. This was more like it. This he knew. This he could do.

There was a loud grunt outside the door, then a growl, and the sound of something sliding along the bulkhead, heading forward. His balls were still crawling somewhere up into his chest cavity, but he was no longer paralized with the fear. He wasn't wiping at an already clean grill. He wasn't hiding any more. He was ready.

He saw the face of insanity at the serving window, and decided he wasn't ready for this, at all.

Manny Manoa stood there, all six-foot-five of him, his face covered in blood. Chunks of flesh hung from his once-white tee-shirt. Another hung from the left corner of his mouth. He was growling. The thing that used to be one of Gary King's Culinary Specialists lunged its head in through the serving window.

Gary took one step, then two in rapid succession, building momentum. He used that momentum in a great overhand swing as he brought the cleaver down onto Manny Manoa's forehead. It stuck there, with a sound that might have come from a casaba melon. The result was far, far bloodier. He retreated even faster than he had come forward, backing up until his butt slammed into the pristine grill.

"Holyfuckingshit!" he swore the oath in one continuous word. The Manny-thing teetered for a moment, a confused look on its face. It slowly - ever-so-slowly - toppled over backwards and out of sight.

"That's enough for me!" he said aloud. Or maybe he screamed it. He didn't know. He didn't care.

He spun around, took a chef's knife from the drawer - the long sucker, with the nine-inch blade. He tucked it in his belt, then reached into the cabinet and grabbed the other cast iron skillet. He hefted them, one in each hand, and gave them both practice swings. Then he got the flying fuck out of the Galley.

92

MK2 Frank Rosseler and MK3 Danny Maury stumbled down the ladder to the Engineroom. It was hot, it was noisy (even through the industrial headphones), and it stank. But it was also home. Being inside the engineroom of a ship was like crawling inside the hood of a car, while the engine was running, and shutting the hood. Of course, there was more room to move around, and the engines (two of them) were a whole lot bigger. But he was used to this; it was familiar; it was *home*.

They entered Main Control, and found DC3 Mike (Ski) Kiepelkowski chatting with the EO. CWO4 Kinkaid, the Engineering Officer was an odd discovery. Frank almost never saw him down there at this late hour, unless there was some emergency. Officers need their beauty sleep, and this one, in particular, needed all he could get. Frank chided himself for the disparaging thought, then forgot all about it.

"Evening, sir," he said, removing the hearing protective headphones. "Couldn't sleep?"

The EO coughed and replied: "No," but didn't elaborate. He looked flushed. This observation sent a cold slice of fear through Frank's spine. Then again, it was getting towards midnight, and maybe the man *hadn't* been sleeping. He could sympathize. Frank hadn't slept in at least two days. Of course, the heart palpitations he felt with every sip of his *somethingth* cup of coffee probably weren't helping, either.

"Where's Moncrief?" Danny asked. He was Moncrief's watch relief, and so had to get all his information from the young Fireman.

"Doing PM on Number One Main," Ski said. PM was *Preventative Maintenance*.

Danny nodded, re-donned his headphones, and exited Main Control, shutting the door on a blast of engine noise. Frank watched him go, then returned his attention to Ski.

"So, what fun are we having tonight?" He asked.

"Number Two MDE is on line, making turns for a blistering nine knots," The Damage Controlman began. "Number One is on One Hour Standby. The Plant is green across the board. Fuel State is at eighty-nine percent. The bilges are dry as a bone, the shit tank is about one-third full, the gray water is slightly over half, and you get the great pleasure of doing PM on the Evaporator!"

"I can barely contain my excitement," Frank replied, with no attempt whatsoever to hide his sarcasm, in spite of the presence of the Engineering Officer, his boss, who seemed to be looking worse by the moment. He stared at him for a bit, before looking back at Ski.

"As usual," Ski said," try to get it back on line before people start getting out of the rack, so we don't have to listen to them bitch about sea showers all day."

"Roger that," Frank said, having had to listen to such bitching more times than he cared to count. As long as all the mechanical things were doing what they were supposed to do, nobody said a word - especially not the word "thanks." But God forbid anything should break down. If anything did, the EO became the Designated Asshole, and the shit rolled downhill from there.

Frank looked at the man, who appeared to be mumbling to himself. He couldn't hear what the EO was saying, at first, but he began to catch snatches of it, and the more he heard, the more his balls tried to catch the Last Train to Clarksville.

"...against me... ...know they are... ...behind my back..." Kinkaid looked first at Frank, then at Ski, his eyes wild, yet furtive, as if he was trying to hide his paranoia and fear. The attempt was an utter failure. The EO seemed to fixate on Ski, as if the young man were somehow his mortal enemy. "He's the one..." he said, nodding. "He's always been the one. Lurking. Behind my back. Stabbing me in the back. Bet he'd like to do that now. Stick me. Stick me right in the back. Stick the knife in and give it a good twist."

Frank took a couple steps back, his upper thighs slamming into the counter top. Ski, however, just looked amused. It was the worst thing he could have possibly done.

"Thinks it's funny, eh? I'll Show HIM!" he shouted, the final sentence getting louder and more like a scream with each word. He leapt at Ski, his fingers curled into claws.

93

EM3 Dan McMullen stretched and yawned. He hadn't been sleeping, either. There was a lot of that going around. He picked his tool bag off the table in the EM Shop, and started aft, idly scratching at his balls through the material of his work pants.

Tonight, even though he didn't have watch, he'd been directed to take the Stern Thruster offline so he could work on the panel for it. Why, exactly, it needed to be done in the middle of the fucking night, he had no idea. It could have easily have been done mid-day, but *noooo*. After all, they weren't using it. They weren't maintaining station, like intelligent and sane people who didn't have any idea when or where they'd get fuel again. Instead, they were steaming the Box of Death at nine knots, slowly but surely sucking their fuel tanks dry.

They'd topped off before they got underway...what? Four days ago? Five? *Time sure flies when you're in an apocalypse*, he thought. But the supply was not unlimited. Sooner or later, they'd need more. Sooner, if they kept wasting it.

None of which mattered. What did, was the work he had to do. He yawned again, scratched again, then opened the door to the crew's lounge, intending to pass through on the way aft to Thruster Control.

That, however, was before he saw the bodies, and the blood, and the two crew-turned zombies headed straight toward him.

He ran, as if his life depended on it - because it did.

94

Teddy Spute ran onto the Mess Deck, where Bob Stoeffel and Gus Perniola were standing, guns raised, waiting to respond if any of the pirates got in through the locked watertight exterior doors. He vaguely grumbled to himself that they were wasting their time. No one could get in through those doors without the master key card or the key fob John kept with him.

He didn't know about Gilcuddy, didn't know his shipmate was dead. What he did know was that John had exiled him to the shameful position of babysitter, and he failed.

"Have you seen Davy?" He asked, almost yelling.

"John's kid?" Bob-Bob asked.

"How many Davies do we have on board?" Spute snapped. "Have you seen him or not?"

"No... I..." Bob-Bob stuttered.

Where could that little fucker be? Where would any kid go at the worst possible fucking moment? To their Mommy. But she was below, frantic over the fact she'd lost her little boy. So where does that leave? *To their Dad.*

"Where's John?" He barked, already knowing the answer, and heading in that direction.

"Bridge," Gus said, pointing.

Spute sprinted toward the far passageway. *He better be up there*, he thought. If he wasn't, Spute's life wouldn't be worth spit. John was a friendly man. He was a kind man. But if his kid got hurt because Teddy Spute had failed to keep an eye on him, then Teddy Spute was a dead man. He reached the bottom of the ladder and began to climb.

95

Molly heard the commotion on the Bridge, and knew what it was: LTjg Bloominfeld had turned. She'd gone outside to "check the weather," precisely because she knew he would be turning. She couldn't have known *when*, but it didn't change the inevitability. And in so doing, in abandoning the Bridge, abandoning Jack Ross and Seaman Borgeson, she'd become a coward. A pang of shame sliced her heart, as she realized she didn't even know Borgeson's first name. But she had readily - eagerly - abandoned him to the fate that had become all-too familiar in the last couple of horrible days.

She was a coward, and she was compounding her cowardice by staying outside, instead of investigating the commotion *inside*. Forget that she already knew what it was. Forget that members of her crew were being killed as she was wallowing in self-absorbed guilt.

Fuck that. She said to herself. *Grow a pair, Molly Gordon.*

Ignoring the anatomical impossibility of her admonition, she thrust open the watertight Bridge door and ran inside.

96

EM3 Dan McMullen burst through the watertight door onto the Buoy Deck, running faster than he had in his entire life. He'd escaped the crowd of crewmen-turned zombies in the Crew's Lounge, slipped past the two others busy killing Seaman Siemen and Seaman Apprentice Pierre Milancent (from New Orleans, don't you know), in the passageway through After Berthing. He'd managed those without pissing his pants (or worse), but now he had four more zombie-crew behind him. DC1 Devon Holdstien led the pack, followed by EM1 Darius Sinstabe, his boss - the fucker who'd told him to take down the Stern Thruster at fucking midnight, for no rhyme or reason. FN Gabriel Carnegie was behind him, SN Peter Donelly behind him, and bringing up the rear was SKC Duane Robinson, a new arrival, making it five fucking zombies running after him.

He didn't bother trying to close the watertight door. There wasn't time. He turned around the end of the port ladder, grabbed the rail to swing himself onto it, and kept right on running. The zombies ran with him.

He had to think, had to do something to slow the fuckers down, or he was going to be zombie-chow. He snapped a look over his shoulder, saw Devon Holdstien's face level with his right boot, and kicked out, without thinking, without planning, and - most importantly - without missing. The Damage Control-zombie screamed in rage and pain, and pin-wheeled its arms to stop itself falling backwards, so Dan did the only sensible thing he could do, and kicked the fucker again. It did the trick.

Like dominoes on an incline, one zombie fell back into another, and into another, and the creatures bent on Dan McMullen's death cascaded downward and backward onto the Buoy Deck. He didn't wait around to verify the fruits of his labor. He kept running.

97

BM1/DECK Dennis Hurdlika awoke in agony. The back of his skull felt like, well, like someone had smashed it through a false bulkhead. His shoulder hurt, and a cursory examination (because cursory was the best his pain-addled brain could manage) showed him a bloody bite mark where his left shoulder met his collarbone. He'd been bitten. Somewhere in the back of his mind, he knew this was bad, knew this was the worst possible thing. But his brain didn't seem to be working right.

He felt fuzzy-headed. This was most likely the result of cranial trauma, he reasoned, gingerly touching the back of his skull, and feeling immense relief when his probing hand did not come away covered in blood. At least he had that going for him. With a groan (which may or may not have sounded more or less like a growl), he slid upward along the bulkhead until he stood on unsteady legs. He looked around.

The first thing he saw was a long smear of blood. It looked black in the red light of the passageway, but he knew it had to be blood. He knew this, because the smear ended in what could only be a handprint - a very large handprint. *Manny Manoa*, he thought, then couldn't connect the thought to any specific memory. His head wasn't working right.

The next thing he saw was John Mad Dog Kennedy, lying in a heap on the deck, ten feet down the passage. His head looked like a smashed pumpkin. Glancing the other way - aft - he saw two more bodies, lying four feet apart. He couldn't tell who they were; didn't really want to know. All he did know was *rage*. These were his boys, his babies, his crew. Someone or some *thing* had killed them, and oh my dear God did that piss off BM1/DECK Dennis Hurdlika.

The crew was in danger. The ship was in danger. And what did you do when the crew and the ship were in danger? You defended it.

He strode to the nearest berthing compartment door and thrust it open. "Everybody up!" He yelled. "Roll out! General Quarters! Man your Battle Stations!" Without waiting to see if the occupants obeyed his command, he strode to the next compartment and the next and the next, repeating the process each time, rousing the crew.

It was the most boneheaded thing he could have done.

In his defense, it should be noted that Dennis Hurdlika's brain was malfunctioning. While he was unconscious, the infection from the bite on his shoulder had worked its way through his bloodstream, and was now zipping and zapping from synapse to receptor in his frontal lobe, cooking it, as if it had been thrown into a microwave. At the same time, his hypothalamic region was dumping hormones directly into his lizard brain, jacking it up as if someone had attached a big ass pair of jumper cables to it, while injecting an insane dose of methamphetamine. In short, Dennis Hurdlika was becoming a zombie.

He did not know this. He could not know this, any more than a psychotic axe-murderer would know or realize or care that he was batshit crazy.

This lack of knowledge, however, did not alter the fact that by opening all the doors and rousing the men, he was making certain the uninfected members of the Cutter *Sassafras'* crew would now be mingling with those who had become zombies. He didn't know this, *couldn't* know this, as he made his way forward toward the Bosun Hold,

98

Lydia Claire stared at LTjg Amy Montrose in shock and anger, and more embarrassment than made any real sense. "What did you say?" she demanded.

"Strip down to your skivvies," the officer replied, calmly.

They were standing just aft of the superstructure on the fantail, behind a tarp, strung to provide some semblance of privacy as the four female crew members who'd been involved in Fueling Ops stood under the Decon Shower. It had been a good thing, both in that it cleared them of any possible contagion, and the cascading water had hidden Lydia's tears

Her heart was broken, as was her faith in the crew, the Captain, and humanity, in general. How could they have shoved those refugees away? How could they have turned their backs on people when they were most needed? *How could they?*

Yes, she understood, somewhere in the recesses of her wounded, traumatized mind, that doing what they did saved their own lives. Yes, she knew they couldn't help anybody if they allowed themselves to get infected. She understood, rationally, logically. But rationality and logic didn't make it hurt one bit less.

Herself, Montrose, Seaman Jennifer Collins and Seaman Titsy McGangbang had started by being doused with the chemically-treated water in their full MOPP gear, then took those off and were doused again in their uniforms. Now they were supposed to strip down further to just their underwear.

Being in the military and being housed with other women in a variety of settings, from open bay berthing areas containing thirty or forty of them, as in bootcamp, to the four-person berth she shared on *Polar Star*, made undressing around other women a thing so common, she scarcely thought about it anymore. But walking around the ship, soaking wet and in her underwear was not something she commonly did, although she suspected it was something Titsy McGangbang at least *thought* of doing.

That wasn't the Seaman's real name of course. It was Tara McBride. She'd been given the unfortunate nickname because of the rumors surrounding her transfer from one of the High Endurance Cutters homeported in Seattle that shared dock space with the *Star* and the *Healy*.

Supposedly, the well-endowed nineteen year old redhead had allowed the entire Deck Force to use her as a morale boost. This was almost certainly bullshit, and anyone with a brain knew it was, but nicknames, and sexual innuendo, and cruelty knew no intellectual master, and so the rumors had flown like a flock of salacious seagulls, and *Titsy McGangbang* had been born.

Lydia usually felt sorry for the young woman, but when SN McBride wordlessly stripped off her work blue uniform to reveal a skimpy bra and even skimpier thong, (both of them white, both of them transparent, thanks to their waterlogged condition) her empathy took wing and headed for parts unknown. It was evident from the wet cloth covering her private parts that the woman shaved. Completely. It was also evident from her suddenly see-through bra, that she also had a pierced nipple.

"Oh for Christ's sake McBride! Could you at least try to not act like a slut?" Jennifer Collins said. She was a friendly young woman - also nineteen - who was cute, in that purely Irish sort of way, complete with freckles and sun-dappled brown hair. Unlike her fellow Deckie, her reputation was solid, both in terms of her perceived virtue (the boys tended to treat her like their kid sister - even the ones who were younger than she was), and in her work-ethic.

"Fuck you, Collins," the redhead snapped.

"Both of you give it a rest," Ms. Montrose said. Lydia liked her well enough. Didn't really know her, in the way most of the crew didn't know the officers, but at least she wasn't a bitch like some of the female officers she'd met. "And you two strip down. The sooner we get this done, the sooner we can get dry," she added as she began to strip off as well.

Collins' lingerie choice had been wise. They were rose-colored, which made them both pretty, and good at concealing her attributes. Ms. Montrose had worn a white sports bra and dark blue panties. The panties covered herself well, but the bra clearly showed her prominent areolae. Lydia looked down at her own fashion choice and immediately had to quell the irrational desire to cover herself. She might as well have gone commando, for all the good her white underwear was doing, but it hardly mattered, as long as it was just the four of them. This brought up a rather important subject.

"Uh," she began, looking around the tarp-enclosed area. "What are we supposed to wear when we head below?"

Montrose looked at Lydia, then the other two, then herself, then the surrounding area, where there was a decided lack of anything to conceal their near-nudity. "Shit," the LTjg said. "Hey!" she yelled. "Who's out there?"

"Tis I," Wheeler said in his strong Boston accent.

"I know I'm the Morale Officer and all, but I don't think a wet tee-shirt contest would be an appropriate morale event," she said.

The Assistant OPS Officer didn't say anything for a pregnant moment. Lydia could just imagine the not-at-all appropriate thoughts going through the man's head. She hated him for it. She hated all of them, at the moment.

That wasn't exactly true. She didn't hate them. She didn't like them very much, but she didn't hate them. What she hated was the callous brutality of mankind, in general, which could label a young woman a slut, just because she wore her sexuality on her sleeve; which could leave four women uncovered in wet underwear on a ship full of testosterone-laden men; which could abandon hundreds of refugees, just to save their own asses.

"Right you are," Wheeler said, finally. "I'll take care of it."

Would he? Could he? Could he "take care" of the black despair filling her heart like cholesterol? Could anybody? Ever? Lydia doubted it. But she did know one thing for sure: as soon as she could get off this ship, she would.

99

Skizzy Pete Hannity checked the Ruger .357 he carried for the umpteenth time, making good and damned sure the thing was loaded. It was, just as it had been all the other times he'd checked. He was nervous. *No. Let's call a spade a spade, Pete old boy. You're scared shitless.*

He was, too. He'd never gone in for guns before. Oh, sure, he'd used them a couple of times when he'd needed to threaten some of the bitches he'd banged. You had to do that sometimes with bitches. His father taught him that. And, yeah, a couple of them accused him of rape, and the jury agreed - those goddamned liberals in California. But the guns he'd used had never been loaded. This fucker most definitely was, and he was most definitely going to have to use it, which scared the living shit out of him.

He'd never hurt anybody - not really. The bitches complained, but of course they did. That's why they were bitches.

They *acquired* the pistol from a liquor store they'd *visited,* following their escape from Soledad. Charlie had constructed another one of his signature blackjacks using a leather drawstring bag he'd shoplifted from a specialty store, which he filled with quarters stolen from a vending machine Old Pete jimmied. It served its purpose well, to judge from the liquor store clerk, whose unconscious body they'd moved before emptying the cash register. They found the pistol and a short, double-barreled shotgun behind the counter.

Skizzy Pete was there for that robbery, as well as the three others, on the way to the Marina, where they'd commandeered the *Daisy Jean.* They had been exciting - even fun. This, however, was not.

He crept across the deck toward the left side of the boat. He didn't know from Port or Starboard or any of that shit, and he didn't care, either. He wanted to be off this motherfucking boat, for damned sure. But Blackjack Charlie made him come, and Old Joe made him climb the ladder after Lazardo. Now Lazardo was dead, and Joe-Boy was dead, and there he was with a gun in his hand that might as well have been his dick.

He heard something - some *one* - coming from around the corner. He cocked the pistol, ever-so slowly, ever-so quietly. He saw the barrel of the rifle before he saw the man. His first instinct was to run like a scared little bitch, but he knew it wouldn't work. There was too much open deck, too much space with nowhere to take cover. He'd get a hole through his back before he got three feet. He waited, holding his breath.

The moment he saw the man's face, he opened fire.

100

Seaman Borgeson lay dead, folded backwards across the center console, his spine at a right angle to his legs. It might have been possible he was an accomplished contortionist, if not for his missing throat. The wind pipe, larynx, part of his esophagus (*and good dear God, is that his tongue?*) hung below the bloody mess like a sick necktie made by a thoroughly insane member of the Hermes family. Borgeson's blood covered the compass and helm controls, the pooling liquid falling in fat drops onto the deck in front.

The thing that had once been LTjg Craig Bloominfeld was trying to do the same to BM3/OPS Jack Ross. He had the young man pinned against the deep fathometer, trying to shove his head through the readout screen. Molly Gordon, brand new boot Ensign, so petite, so soft, so feminine, so far beyond her realm of experience, so far out of her depth, and so scared she felt as if she might wet herself, snapped a solid kick into Bloominfeld's right kidney.

Might as well have tried to tickle his ass with a feather, for all the good it seemed to do. The newly-turned zombie maniac grunted, but kept right on slamming the back of Ross' skull into the large, gray bulk of the fathometer.

She moved by instinct, not thinking, not planning, just falling back on her years of training at the various *Krav Maga* studios she'd attended as a teenager, first in Alaska, then Oregon, then in Connecticut, near the Academy. She did a reverse spin into an elbow strike at the back of Bloominfeld's head. That, at least stopped his attempt to turn Ross' head into a depth sounder, but it didn't stop him from strangling the poor navigator. She shifted into a front kick to the same kidney, then a back kick with a spin to the side of the zombie's head, and that made it break contact. Ross' insensible and probably dead body fell to the deck, where it stayed, unmoving.

The Bloominfeld-thing turned on her, lunging for her throat, but she batted away its clutching hands, and retreated to the far side of the console, almost tripping over Borgeson's feet. In the brief time it took her to maintain her balance, it was on her again, piling into her back, shoving her forward against the Bridge windows.

The one thing you could never do in defense was to stop moving. An opponent couldn't subdue if he/it couldn't grab, and so she twisted and ducked, and threw an elbow into the zombie's blessedly still-clothed groin.

Basic male physiology 101: if the mere mention of getting hit in the testicles will make a man cringe at the very idea, then an actual blow to said testicular region will have an adverse effect. Screw a bunch of zombie bullshit. An elbow to the nuts can and will cause excruciating pain.

It did.

Then again, however, stories of PCP cranked bad guys going apeshit, even after being hit with multiple tasers were legion, and so her respite from zombie wrestling turned out to be brief, indeed. No sooner had she spun away from the Bridge windows and escaped his/its grasp, then he was on her again - this time pinning her against the chart table so hard, it knocked the air from her lungs like a hammer blow. She managed to turn herself so she faced him, and could use her hands and arms, but that was all. Her strength had departed with her supply of oxygen.

Krav Maga was all about aggressive defense - with emphasis on aggressive. She'd learned all sorts of defensive measures against choke holds: from the side, against a wall, from behind, from the front, while pinned to the ground - every conceivable scenario where she might have to fend off a choking attacker, or so she thought. She'd never learned what to do when a zombie had her pinned, bent backwards over a chart table, after slamming her diaphragm against that table so hard that all the available air in her lungs departed for destinations unknown.

She tried to bring up first one knee, then the other, but Bloominfeld insinuated himself between her legs, as if he was trying to boff her while strangling the life out of her. She tried lifting her one arm straight up (which in this case was straight out toward the bulkhead behind the chart table), but her one-time OPS Boss had his elbow in her armpit while he continued to throttle her, and that particular hold-breaker proved unavailable. Her other arm was trapped as well, shoved under Bloominfeld's jaw, keeping the zombie's teeth from rending her face.

Its grip on her throat felt like a bear trap snapping closed on her neck. Her arms flailed, the blows having no more effect than a piece of paper might. Her vision began to close in - red, then gray, then black around the edges. Stars winked in and out in front of her dilating pupils. She had to do something! She was going to die.

Her flailing arm went to the chart table, trying to find a weapon, trying to find anything that might save her life. Her numbing fingers felt a pen or pencil (she couldn't tell which by touch alone). She flicked whatever it was aside and kept searching, kept probing the damnably empty table.

There! A sharp pain in her finger. She didn't pause to contemplate the incongruity of this fact, didn't wait to puzzle out just what in the fuck pricked her. She grabbed for it.

101

"What the fuck are we doing here?" Harold asked. They were still in the Bosun Hold. Duke had put away the kukri-machetes, but Harold still had his "special" bat.

"Waiting," Duke replied. He'd taken a pair of eight-pound sledge hammers, with twelve-inch carbon fiber handles out of a cabinet below the table, and was hefting them, as if testing their weight and balance in his hands. He took a practice swing with each and smiled. Harold didn't like that smile one bit.

"What are you planning to do with those?" he asked, then amended his question. "Never mind. I don't want to know."

Duke just shrugged and tried another couple of practice swings. The hammers didn't make a sound as they sliced through the air. Harold

287

found it strange. Such big and massive and deadly things should make at least *some* damned sound.

"So what, exactly, are we waiting for?" He asked.

As if in answer, the dogging arm of the watertight door swung upwards with a *CLANG*. Both men turned toward the door, and it seemed both knew they were jumping at nothing. Zombies didn't open doors. At least, that's what they'd heard. Harold held his bat at the ready.

Dennis Hurdlika stumbled through. His eyes were wild, and his normally pristine hair was mussed. There was a big blotch of blood on one shoulder, and more on his hands. He held the door for support.

"Zombies," he gasped. "Behind–"

But his words were cut off as the unholy creatures shoved him into the compartment on their way through the hatch. Seaman Tommy Barnes (or what had been the young man) led the way, followed by YN3 Greg Haversham, SK2 Al DeBenedetto, SN Stanley St. John, and FNMK Ronald "Bart" Simpson. Both Simpson and DeBenedetto stepped on the prone form of Dennis Hurdlika. The rest ignored him. They were focusing on Harold and Duke.

"Oh shit! Oh shit! Oh shit!" Harold said, in rapid succession. He saw Duke snap a look in his direction, and yelled: "Don't look at me! Kill those motherfuckers," and raised his bat like Hank Aaron standing at home plate.

It was all Duke needed. The large Bosun Mate waded into the zombie flash mob, swinging both hammers like John Henry in a railroad tunnel. The one in his left hand smashed into Haversham's shoulder and sent the ex-Yeoman flying into Stanley St. John, who fell back, tripping over Hurdlika. The one in his right took DeBenedetto square in the forehead. It was as if the young Storekeeper's skull imploded in blood and bone and brain matter.

"Fuck you!" Harold screamed, and swung his bat at Tommy Barnes. He missed his former co-worker, but the swing carried the bat around and smacked the nail-covered end into Simpson's left ear. The impact landed with a resounding *THUNK*, and blood covered the fancy knot-work he'd spent an hour adding to his makeshift weapon. He tried to yank it free, but it stuck, and instead pulled the falling zombie toward him.

Either from surprise or from the weight of the dropping former-man, the bat fell from Harold's hand and went clattering to the deck, with Simpson on top of it. Barnes made a lunge for him, but Duke ended it with a massive, bone-cracking blow directly between its shoulder blades. It must have smashed the spine, because the young man - their friend - dropped like, well, quite a bit like someone who'd just had their spinal column crushed by an eight-pound sledge hammer. Harold stared at him in shock and horror, and might have stayed that way, had it not been for Dennis Hurdlika's screaming growl.

Their BM1 had become a zombie.

102

In quieter, less chaotic, less fraught with murdering shipmates-turned zombie times, MK2 Frank Roessler had, on occasion, voiced, with some jealousy, the opinion that the Deckies stole the Engineers' thunder by laying claim to the term "Big Fucking Hammer," (BFH). That they used said implement to work on the chains for the buoys that were the Sass's stock in trade, was entirely beside the point. It had been discussed at great length during the annual extended deployment down to American Samoa, with Deck Force insisting *their* claim took priority, and so the Engineers couldn't use it. This was absurd nonsense, of course, but a ship full of bored men on extended deployment with lots of time on their hands, generated such nonsense like a wind turbine generates electricity. Heated arguments had been made with raised voices, and the potential for fisticuffs had not been beyond the realm of possibility, and so (in the interest of crew harmony) the Engineers had acquiesced - sort of.

The thing about engines on something the size of the Sass, was that they were big. Not as big as, say, those on an oil tanker, but pretty damned big, nonetheless. Naturally, therefore, many of the nuts and bolts holding those engines together were also pretty damned big, and thus required the use of wrenches that were just as damned big. In fact, they were deemed *fucking* big, as in *Big Fucking Wrench*, an example of which (its handle emblazoned with the letters BFW in bright red paint) was currently being used by MK2 Frank Roessler to cave in the skull of his Engineering Officer.

The man had gouged out the eyes - *gouged out the fucking eyes* - of DC3 Mike (Ski) Kiepelkowski, who was lying on the deck with his face in a pool of his own blood. Frank had seen it happen, had *watched* it happen in dumb horror, too shocked to move, until the EO turned his/its attention onto him, at which point, Frank moved with speed and agility, spurred on by abject terror. He'd seen the wrench on the table near where Ski had been sitting, grabbed it and swung in that disconnected, otherworldly way that sometimes happens when someone acts on pure instinct. His aim had been true, the blow had been solid, and now CWO4 Kinkaid, his head misshapen and bleeding like a Las Vegas fountain, lay on the deck, his own blood mingling with Ski's.

Frank stared at the bodies on the deck, his heart beating like a Keith Moon drum riff, his breathing sharp in his lungs. The wrench - its handle long enough to reach the deck - hung loosely in his hand.

For one moment, then two, then three, he thought of nothing. In the fourth moment, however, he thought: *Where's Maury?*

103

The .357 kicked like a son of a bitch as Skizzy Pete fired it at the head of the man he saw coming around the corner. The recoil and noise of it shocked him, and his aim sucked. The first bullet slammed into the man's shoulder, the second ricocheted off the steel wall in front of him, and the third went sailing over the side of the boat. The guy dropped like a stone, but he was still trying to bring the rifle around toward Pete, and so Pete shot him again, this time hitting the flesh of his gut. Blood squirted from the belly wound, making Pete want to puke, but his gag reflex was interrupted by a shout from behind him.

Another guy came around the opposite corner, carrying a shotgun. Skizzy Pete ran like the scared little bitch he was, leaping over the fallen form of the man he'd just shot. He did not run fast enough.

The roar behind him followed by searing pain in his right butt cheek combined into the thought: *I'm shot in the ass*, but he kept right on running - now hobbling - just as fast as he fucking could. More by instinct and self-preservation than by any sort of skill, he snapped a couple shots of his own over his shoulder. He doubted any of them found a target, but astoundingly, they seemed to work. No other blasts from the shotgun followed.

Ahead, he saw two ladders: one close, going up, and another further along, going down. The one up was closer, so he took it.

A third man (*how many of these fuckers are there?*) popped into view at the top of the ladder. He was carrying a pistol. Skizzy Pete paused. The man above paused. They looked at each other for a suspended moment, then both pointed at the other and fired.

There was one final kick from the .357 in Pete's hand, followed by a *CLICK, CLICK, CLICK*, as the hammer fell on empty chambers, and Skizzy Pete Hannity knew he was well and truly fucked.

The first bullet struck him high on the left shoulder. The impact swung him around, and he started to fall backwards. He flailed with his right arm, dropping the pistol, and trying to grab the ladder rail, but it did him no good. The second round hit him in the leg, the third missed completely, then the fourth, fifth and sixth hit him square in the chest, and Skizzy Pete was no more.

104

OS2 Amber Winkowski sat on the porcelain throne and waited. She considered herself to be a patient woman. She wasn't flighty, wasn't headstrong (most of the time), and wasn't reckless. But sitting on a toilet with the seat and lid down waiting for a zombie to bleed out in the next room was about to drive her right out of her ever-loving mind.

She looked at her watch. It had been at least an hour. Or was it two? She couldn't remember checking the time when she locked herself back in the head after skewering the Zombie-Jackass. Her butt was getting numb; she knew that much.

Okay, so, think... The human body held how many liters of blood? She didn't remember that, either. And a single, horrifying thought brought gorge up into her throat:

The virus causes memory-loss.

Her heart stopped beating, as if her arteries had suddenly clogged with every single piece of cheese-laden pizza she'd ever eaten. It was trying to beat, trying to push the blood through her veins, but it couldn't quite seem to make it move, as if her life-fluid had turned to ice.

Could I have it? Could I be turning? If I was, how would I know? Would I know?

There was the age-old question: If you were crazy, would you know it? She didn't *feel* crazy. She felt fine (her numb butt notwithstanding). She hadn't caught the cold. She hadn't caught any cold in years - a decade or more, come to think of it. She was alarmingly healthy, although her diet sometimes made her wonder how that was possible.

She hadn't felt feverish before, and didn't feel so now. She felt fine, all things considered. Her situation sucked, and the seating arrangements in this head left something to be desired, but she didn't feel the least bit sick. So why the memory loss?

Stress, you idiot.

The internal condemnation popped into her mind, was considered, agreed upon, then shunted aside as having no more significance to the problem at hand. And the problem at hand was that she was going stir crazy.

She contemplated that lovely thought for a moment, and realized this was only the beginning. Sooner or later the zombie in the Comm Center would bleed out, would be dead, and she could leave the porcelain throne behind and give her butt a rest. *However*, even after she was able to access the Comm Center, she'd still be trapped inside a locked and windowless room in a building filled with unfriendly used-to-be people who would gleefully tear her to shreds. She didn't know from stir crazy - yet.

With a small groan, she rose on half-asleep legs. Her joints hurt. This was an after-effect of the adrenaline rush that had enabled her to become a spear-wielding warrior goddess. The incongruity of the juxtaposition of Amber Winkowski and Warrior Goddess made her chuckle. Then it made her guffaw. Then it made her laugh with a hilarity tinged with just a little bit of hysteria. She was losing her grip, and she knew it. She got herself back under control.

Screw this, she thought. Time to take the bull by the horns and wrestle that nasty dilemma to the ground. Time to check on the zombie.

105

Jonesy burst through the Bridge door in time to see Molly jab a pair of stainless steel dividers into LTjg Bloominfeld's left eye.

Dividers of the type they used on *Sassafras* were six inches long, and ended in two sharp pins, instead of a pin and a pencil of the variety normally found in high school geometry classes. They were used for measuring distances on paper nautical charts.

They also, it appeared, worked just fine as a way to kill a zombie.

The thing that had been Craig Bloominfeld reared back off of Molly, staggered a couple of steps, ineffectually swiping at the metal implement sticking from its eye, then fell to the deck, after tripping over the still and blood-splattered form of Jack Ross. It groaned and cried and writhed for a few moments, twitched a couple times, and stopped moving altogether.

Jonesy surveyed the carnage. Borgeson lay bent backwards over the console, his chest a mass of gore, his blood pooling on the deck below the helm. Ross lay slumped over, facing the bulkhead, his neck craned at a horrible angle, the back of his skull looking as if someone had taken a jackhammer to it. Above him, the readout screen of the deep fathometer was cracked in three places and smeared with brain matter and small chunks of bone and hair. Molly watched him taking it all in. He saw her looking, saw her hold her breath, as if in anticipation of a blow he had no intention of delivering.

He looked at Bloominfeld again, at the dividers protruding from his eye socket. How many times, he wondered, had he dreamt of doing that to one of the Junior Officers? Not Bloominfeld, though. He'd been one of the good ones, but Jonesy knew plenty of boot Ensigns who'd come up and snatched the dividers right from his hand, while he was in the midst of taking a fix, and every time it happened, he'd had brief visions of snatching them back and stabbing them into the arrogant fuckers' eyes.

He looked at Molly, and tried to giver her a reassuring smile. He could tell it wasn't working, and was about to add a few comforting words (or at least what he hoped were comforting words - pathetic though they may have been), when he saw her own eyes dart toward something behind him.

"Bridge door!" she shouted, pointing over his right shoulder.

He spun and saw DC1 Devon Holdstien (clearly a zombie due to his complete lack of clothing and blood-smeared face) lurch through the open portal, with wild eyes, gnashing teeth and outstretched clawing hands. Fireman Carnegie loomed behind Holdstien, also nude, also smeared with gore. And it looked as if there was someone (or some *thing*) else behind him.

Jonesy strode forward and planted a straight kick, flat onto Holdstien's chest, sending the creature slamming back into Carnegie. They both collided with EM1 Sinstabe, whose presence stopped them from falling back through the hatchway. Jonesy tried a snap kick into Holdstien's jaw, which connected, but did nothing to free the zombie-jam at the door. He kicked the DC1 again for good measure and to provide a bit of breathing room, then backed off a step and reached behind him to the two sheaths at the back of his harness belt. He fumbled a bit with the velcro, but managed to remove the two LE batons, and with a practiced snap of both wrists, extended the rods to their full length.

He had trained for this. Not this, specifically, not fighting zombies on the Bridge of a ship, using LE batons, but he had spent many hours learning *Kali* and *Escrima*, on the mat or in the park, smacking trees with his ratan *Baston* sticks and annoying the local squirrel and bird population. He had sparred with other people, of course, but never, in the hours, and hours, and hours of sweat and busted knuckles, did he expect to actually have to use this shit to kill crazed zombies from Hell who used to be his shipmates. This went way above and beyond, and he might have paused to consider the absurdity of it, but he was simply too goddamned busy trying not to get killed.

"Molly!" he called, without looking, but got no response. He snapped a look over his shoulder and saw her standing, stock still, her mouth open in stunned horror, staring at the zombie swarm trying to enter the Bridge. "Ensign!" he snapped, and that got her attention. He darted forward and swatted Holdstien in the left shoulder and right ear with the two batons, in a maneuver called *The Blessing*, oddly enough -

not hard enough to do any real damage, but it did back the thing off. "Is the other door clear?"

He didn't see her check, busy as he was with the battle, but he took it for granted when she answered with a quick, but clear: "Yes!"

He attacked the swarm with a fury of blows, called the *Redonda*, or *Whirlwind*: a series of right and left swings to ears and elbows and heads, hitting both Holdstien and Carnegie. The howling things backed away, but the press of zombie flesh from behind kept them from going very far.

He couldn't keep this up much longer, and it wasn't doing much good. Something had to change. "Head to the Flying Bridge!" he shouted. "We need room to fight!"

106

"Fuck me!" Harold said, diving for the end of his bat. It had become trapped under Ronald "Bart" Simpson's dead body after it had made an absolute mess out of - and became stuck in - the Machinist Mate Striker's ear. Duke was dealing with BM1/DECK Dennis Hurdlika, their "Boats," who'd just turned zombie, leaving Harold to deal with YN3 Greg Haversham and SN Stanley St. John.

Haversham was getting to his/its feet. His/its shoulder slumped downward, making him lopsided, and he/it didn't seem to be able to use the arm attached to it, but that didn't stop the diseased lunatic from lunging toward the nearest non-infected human: one Seaman Harold F. Simmons, jr..

Harold grabbed the end of the bat and yanked, the effort pulling the dead weight of the dead zombie whose ear didn't seem to want to let go. He jammed his foot into the side of the zombie's head and pulled harder. The bat came free with a disgusting and indescribable sound, and Harold backpedaled several steps, trying not to fall on his ass. But he had the bat, and just in time.

Seaman Stanley St. John had been trapped beneath Haversham and was now free to roam about the compartment doing whatever damage and mayhem suited his/its fancy. Naturally, what suited its fancy was Harold Simmons, who had always enjoyed a certain popularity amongst the crew, but would have traded it all for anonymity at this particular moment. He didn't, however, seem to have a choice. The two shipmates-turned drooling, snarling, homicidal zombies advanced on him.

He couldn't run, couldn't hide, couldn't wish away the reality, and he couldn't think of a single smart-assed remark, so he took a batter's stance and waited. His heart pounded the blood of his body straight up into his freaked out head, as if his skull might explode with the pressure, but it didn't stop him from thinking. A wild swing had missed its intended target (SN Tommy Barnes) before and ended up lodged in the ear of FNMK Simpson, whose weight had dragged his one and only weapon from his sweat-slick hands. It would not do to have it happen a second time. In a split second of survey and assessment and decision, he noticed the naked ex-Yeoman's "toy soldier" dangling between the advancing zombie's legs, the testicles hanging low and swinging. The idea sickened Harold, but it didn't stop him from taking a mighty underhanded and upward swing, as if aiming at a slow pitch softball he intended to hit into next fucking week. The bat connected with a sick, squelching slap, and the creature stopped dead, as *I've been terribly struck in the balls,* made it from the junction of the thing's legs to the recently-cooked brain. Harold didn't wait for the message to get through. Planting his booted foot on the young man/zombie's chest, he yanked the bat back and away, then took two shuffling steps to the side, as the body fell in a heap into the space he had just occupied.

Stanley St. John barely noticed as he stepped onto the still-writhing form of Haversham and continued to advance on Harold. He, at least, was still clothed, sparing Harold the never-to-be wiped-from-his-brain vison of yet another naked shipmate covered in blood, with his dick hanging out as he headed to do damage to Harold's favorite Seaman: himself. He hadn't liked St. John much. The kid was too opinionated, too self-absorbed and self-important, and always seemed to be pointing out flaws in the orders of his superiors. That was Harold's job, dammit. He didn't need some new boot fucker coming in and getting in the way of his rightful position. He swung the bat at St. John's chest, stepping into it. It struck home with a crack of what had to be ribs, but it didn't seem phase the new zombie, who swatted it away and kept coming. Harold stepped to the right, quickly regained his stance, and swung with everything he had at the zombie's head.

This time, it didn't matter that the bat got stuck in flesh and bone and brain and blood. As St. John fell, Harold looked up in time to see

Duke's mighty hammer blow crash into Dennis Hurdlika's left temple. The thing's head cracked like a hairy egg, and the former Bosun Mate fell to the ground, joining the bodies of Haversham and St. John, DeBenedetto and Simpson and Tommy Barnes.

He looked at Duke, who stood there, panting and surveying the carnage. The Bosun Mate looked into Harold's eyes.

"Well..." he said. "That sucked."

Harold boggled. "You think?"

107

Davy Gordon, age ten, who liked football, not baseball, and who didn't like girls (except for some of them, like his Mom and his sister and his cousin - but that was different), heard the gun fire and didn't hesitate. He sped up the ladder toward the Bridge. His Dad was up there, and his Dad needed him. It was time for Davy to show that he could be a man his Dad could count on.

This was important.

The slide on the .45 locked back. The pistol was empty. Its contents (most of them anyway) were on display at the bottom of the port side exterior ladder to the Bridge, in the body of the asshole who had tried to storm up it. John, his own body tense and feeling sick, felt for a moment as if he might puke, but the gorge receded back down his esophagus, and seemed as if it might stay there. He swallowed to be sure.

The radio inside the Bridge crackled. Lane's stressed-out voice came up through the light static. "Mick is down! Mick is down!" the radio voice shouted. "Oh, Christ, there's a lot of blood."

John keyed the mic. "Where?"

"Port side. Boat Deck. Fuck, he's bleeding bad," the voice came back.

John ran to the rear bulkhead, keyed the 1-MC and shouted "Doctor Floyd to the Port Boat Deck. Doctor Floyd to the Port Boat Deck, on the double!" He reached across and keyed the radio. "Lane," he said, trying to keep his voice calm. "There's nothing you can do for him at the moment. Doc Floyd his heading there, and there's nobody else left on the fantail. I need you to keep watch. This ain't over yet. There could still be more of them." He wasn't entirely sure their Mad Doctor would go where he was told, but that didn't change things. Whether Mick lived or died was out of John's hands, and they were still in real trouble.

"But..." Lane's voice protested.

John heard the key release on the other end, so he stepped on any further disagreement. "Just do it, Lane. Keep watch so this doesn't get any worse."

And as if he had tempted fate with that statement, and as if fate had replied with a resounding *fuck you*, the interior Bridge door opened, and his ten year-old son entered.

"Davy! What the Hell are you doing here?" he shouted, rushing to his son and grabbing him in a bear hug. Whether to protect him or to strangle the little idiot, John wasn't entirely sure.

The boy snapped a decent salute and smiled, saying: "Reporting for duty, sir!"

John's heart filled with shock and wonder and pride and love and no small amount of growing hysteria as he looked at his son. "What...?"

But he didn't get a chance to finish the thought, because that bastard Murphy with his fucked-up, ever-present, ever-dangerous Law came to call in the form of a new threat, a new enemy, a new pirate coming through the starboard Bridge door, wielding a shotgun.

108

If MK3 Danny Maury wasn't dead, then he was having one Hell of a bad day. *Night*, Frank corrected himself, the thought floating through his mind with an unreality matching the circumstances of his current situation. He stared at the young man's crumpled form, swimming in a pool of his own blood, and went through the catalogue of recent insanity.

He had just caved in the skull of his Engineering Officer with the BFW (*Big Fucking Wrench)* he held in a twisted sort of port arms in front of him, after watching the man/zombie tear the eyes out of Kiepelkowski's head. His co-worker. Maury, lay mangled at his feet, and there was another fellow crewman wandering somewhere in the Engine Room, dreaming the dreams of the fucking insane. Talk about a shit sandwich!

I went back to my Mother, and said I'm crazy, Ma, help me / She said, I know how it feels, son, 'cause it runs in the family...

The words to the Pete Townshend song, *The Real Me*, from The Who's *Quadrophenia* album (one of Frank's favorites) ran unbidden through his head. It seemed appropriate to the situation. If the crew of a ship at sea was a family (and Frank felt certain it was) then insanity most definitely ran through this one.

He looked around, at the roaring Number Two Engine, and at the silent Number One, where Danny lay. No sign of Moncrief. The Fireman had to be here, somewhere.

Frank was wearing the industrial headphone-type hearing protection, which might have been a problem, since he was searching for a man-turned homicidal maniac somewhere in the depths of the Engine Room, and hearing might mean saving his own life, but he couldn't have heard anything over the engine noise, in any case, so he was better off with the headphones. He compensated by keeping his head on the swivel, trying to look everywhere at once. *Just because you're paranoid, Frank, doesn't mean the zombies aren't out to get you.*

And as if on cue, Moncrief appeared. He'd managed to strip off his Coast Guard-approved dark blue coverall, but had only managed to get it past one still-booted foot, so the clothing dragged behind the Fire-zombie, in a comedic parody Frank might have found hilarious, if not, well...

It saw him, and charged.

109

LT Richard Medavoy, new CO of the USCGC *Sassafras*, opened the Cabin door and peered out. He saw the body of OS1 Carlton Bertram, folded half-on the vestibule deck, half-on the ladder leading below. He ignored it. The effort it would take to acknowledge a fallen crewman, or, for that matter, the death of a fellow human being, was beyond his capacity.

He stepped out, closing the door behind him. He didn't want to think of what he'd left inside, but the thoughts came, anyway. His wife was there, in the middle of the carpeted deck, where he'd left her after strangling the life out of the woman. He'd wanted to do that for years, truth be told, but wanting to and doing it were two entirely different things. She was his wife, and he had taken the marriage vows seriously. *Til death do us part*, meant what it said. Now she was dead, and now he was free - not that it would do him any good.

He was finding it hard to think. His head was fuzzy, as if someone had filled it with one of the ubiquitous gray military wool blankets. Why had he killed her? He remembered.

His son, Carson, his little boy, lay on the bunk, his cherished face hidden from view by the pillow Medavoy used to suffocate the poor kid. Now why had he done that? He looked at his left forearm, at the white cloth wrapped around it, acting as a makeshift bandage to cover the torn flesh, and knew the answer at once. Carlton had bitten him.

When he'd finished, he'd taken the boy in his arms and laid him on the bunk, trying to make him as comfortable as possible. This was absurd, of course. His son was dead, but the thought counted, right?

Thoughts were getting harder and harder to create, to concentrate on, to hold. He un-dogged the exterior hatch to the Boat Deck and exited. The night air felt cool on his burning forehead. *I have a fever.* The thought bubble appeared in his mind's eye. *That means something,* he thought. *Something bad...*

110

Jonesy gave the zombie hoard at the Bridge door one more whirlwind of LE batons, then spun and followed Molly out the starboard door. He slammed it shut behind him. *That ought to keep them busy and confused for a bit,* he thought. Then, out loud: "The Flying Bridge is that way!" he shouted, after seeing her bypass the ladder leading to first the Signal Bridge, then the Flying Bridge. She ignored him.

Instead, she ran aft to the center of the superstructure, heading straight for the fire axe cradled on the bulkhead. She grabbed at it, but it stuck, having been there for months since the last time anyone thought to check it out. With a growl of frustration that at first scared the crap out of him, thinking that maybe she was turning, she smacked the handle end with the upturned palm of her left hand, once, twice, a third time before it broke free of the salt and rust holding it in place. She snatched it off the bulkhead in triumph, and said: "I needed a weapon."

"I'm mildly turned on," Jonesy said.

"Shut up," she snapped in return, reaching the bottom of the ladder. Molly looked from it, to the large axe in her hand, then to Jonesy. "Hold this," she said, thrusting it into his hand.

He fumbled the grab, encumbered as his hands were with the two batons, but managed not to drop it on his own toe. Tossing it onto the deck above after she'd scurried up the ladder, he followed.

Scooping up the axe, he tried to hand it to her, but Molly's attention was on the Flying Bridge. He glanced upward and saw why.

Seaman Ronald "Saigon Ron" Wilson had been acting as lookout. The man had been in the Army, once upon a time, but got out after six years, having realized the level of bullshit was too high for his delicate sensibilities. That's the way he always put it whenever someone asked the inevitable question. He also boasted: "Yeah, I was in Nam," and when people balked at the obvious inconsistency of time and his age, replied: "I played second base for the Saigon Tigers." Hence, the nickname.

It was all a pile of bragging horseshit, of course. He'd never been to Vietnam - had never been anywhere near it. The closest he'd gotten was Bremerhaven, Germany. None of which mattered, because Saigon Ron had become a zombie. He launched himself off the Flying Bridge, straight at Molly.

Jonesy learned a lot of Martial Arts philosophy during his years of training in Malibu, and then at the various *dojos* he'd managed to find in the far-flung places the Coast Guard saw fit to send him. *Jeet Kune Do,* Bruce Lee's creation, had been chock-full of it (pun intended). But the best defensive advice he'd ever heard, came from the Seventies TV show, *Kung Fu*. *The best defense is not to be there.*

Molly embodied that advice when she sidestepped the diving ex-Army zombie, who landed in a belly flop upon the Signal Bridge deck. Jonesy tossed her the axe, which she deftly caught, raised over her head, and slammed down onto the prone, but still-moving former seaman. The blade and pick of the implement were both covered in leather, so as to protect the edge from salt and corrosion, and so the blow did not cut, but when the skull of their would-be assailant shattered, they both discovered that blunt force trauma worked fine in a pinch.

Jonesy watched Molly stare at her handiwork, her face white, in spite of the recent effort, in spite of the high blood pressure-inducing stress of recent events. He worried about her; worried she might not take this well, at all.

Killing wasn't something the average human being experienced in the course of a normal life. He would have been perfectly content if he'd never had the dubious pleasure. But he was wired differently than the average bear. Maybe that's what LCDR Sparks had seen in him. Maybe that's why he'd been so sure Jonesy was the right man for the job of killing some of his shipmates to protect others.

You did a bang up job of that, didn't you, Jonesy? He thought, bitterly. But such self-absorption was a waste of time. There were more important things, like whether or not Molly could deal with the guilt and shame of what she'd just done - twice, now. He needn't have worried.

She looked at him and gave a wry smile. "That was easier than it should have been."

111

This is almost too easy, Eddie Cochrane, escaped convict, newly-minted pirate and full time (whenever he could so indulge himself) child molester thought, as he entered the Bridge and leveled the shotgun at the man and - *oh goody* - child he found there. The shotgun had been lying next to the body of that fucking wombat, Hank Lazardo. The.38 revolver he'd brought on board remained tucked into his belt. A shotgun was so much better.

The man, his back to Eddie, was sheltering the kid with his body. That would not do, at all.

"Move away from the kid," he said, trying to sound tough.

He'd never been very good at it. Truth be told, he had always been picked on by the bigger kids: the bullies and jocks, and various other Neanderthals during his years at public school in Schenectady, NY. They called him "wussy," and "fag," and "homo," and a dozen other variations on the homosexual theme. And maybe they had a point.

He'd always been a bit effeminate, never masculine, never good at sports or chasing girls, or fighting. And he'd enjoyed - *really* enjoyed - getting buggered, as the schoolyard slang called getting done up the old poop chute.

The first time had been by his "uncle;" some loser his mother was banging, but who, it seemed, had been more interested in her little son. And he'd heard all the shrinks talking about how that led to his own "affliction," as the more liberal of them called it. But it was all so much self-serving bullshit, voiced in an effort to understand what made him rape those three young boys. They couldn't deal with the notion that he'd done it, because he liked it - a lot. It didn't fit their suburban fantasy about the essential good in all human beings. Eddie Cochrane had been a homosexual, child molesting rapist because he *liked* it. There needn't have been any deeper, more philosophical understanding than that.

"Please," the man begged. "Not my son."

"Move away from the fucking kid," he repeated. "I promise I won't hurt him. Not till I've had my fun."

The man was truly cowed - by him. Eddie Cochrane had finally become intimidating! Would wonders never cease?

"Move away from him, or I swear I'll kill him sloooow," he said, drawing out the last word. "I'll take my time. I'll make it hurt." *Damn! This was fun!*

But then, wouldn't you know it? Everything changed. Everything got ruined. Same as it had always been. Same as the first time he'd raped a boy and had to flee Schenectady, same as the second, when he'd had to stop before finishing, because the kid had started to scream. Same as the third - and final time - when those dock workers in Oakland found him in the abandoned warehouse he'd used to have his fun. They kicked the living shit out of him, then turned him over to the cops. Not even his Public Defender had said a word about that. Same as always. Eddie Cochrane just couldn't get a break.

The internal Bridge door slammed open, and Eddie's world went away for good.

112

Teddy Spute was freaking right the fuck out. John was going to kill him, for sure.

The man had given him responsibility for that stupid bitch Clara, and he failed. Then John gave him the responsibility of watching over the families - of watching over his children - and he failed there, too.

Hearing the gunshots, he raced up the Bridge ladder, hoping against hope nothing had happened, that Davy Gordon had just slipped away to take a nap, that they'd find him curled into a ball under a table or a bed or something when this was all over. But deep down, he knew it was a fool's hope. Davy was up there, and he knew it. John was going to kick his fucking ass.

Teddy pondered the 9mm pistol in his hand. It was loaded, cocked and off safe. Maybe that would give him time to explain. Maybe that would make John hold off from turning his face into a pile of goo.

He burst through the Bridge door, saw John shielding Davy, saw the man with the shotgun and knew why. He didn't think. He didn't plan. He opened fire.

113

"What the fuck are you doing?" Harold asked, deeply concerned as he watched Duke gearing up into his full tactical rig.

They'd stacked the bodies into one corner of the Bosun Hold, a task Harold planned to never think of ever again. It had been a nightmare, at the end of a series of nightmares. Fighting his shipmates was bad enough. Killing them had been even worse, but that was self-defense. No choice. If he hadn't killed them, he'd be Zombie-Chow right about now. He'd done it without thinking, allowing his instinct for self-preservation to take over and do the nasty deeds without any conscious involvement on his part. But moving those bodies - looking at the faces of his friends - sucked more than anything had ever sucked before.

Now it looked like Duke was getting ready for more of the same.

"We're going out, Harold," Duke said. His voice was calm, but left no room for discussion or debate. "Get some gear out of the LE Locker and put it on."

"Why would I want to do that?" he asked. "We did our bit." He waved toward the corpses. "We killed the zombies. What more do we need to do?"

Duke paused in donning the body armor, and stared at him, as if surveying an interesting, yet inexplicable insect. He pointed at the bodies. "Do you think that's all the zombies on our ship?"

Harold didn't answer.

"They've taken over," Duke said, shrugging into his Tactical Harness and slipping each of the two hammers into the waste belt on either side. He bent and searched the clothes of BM1 Hurdlika. Harold soon found out what he was looking for when Duke stood back up, bouncing a large set of keys in the palm of his hand.

"Fuck Medavoy," he said. "I'm arming up. Are you coming or not?"

"We're getting guns?" Harold asked.

"We're getting guns."

"Fuckin' A," he replied. This was more like it!

"Time to take back our ship."

114

Petty Officer Jackass was dead. Amber refused to call him by his actual name, as if using the name would require her to acknowledge that he had once been a human being, and she had killed him.

Obviously, she had. The ex-Operations Specialist lay in a pool of his own blood, leaving a mess behind in death as he had often done in life. The guy was a pig. She couldn't quite make herself go to the *dark place* and suggest he deserved to get a swab handle shoved into his throat, but facts were facts. She and the world were better off without him.

Gorge rose in her throat and she thought she might have to race back to the head and barf her dinner into the toilet, but she managed to keep it down. *Some warrior princess*, she thought, then chided herself for wasting time to wax self-effacing. She had a job to do, and standing there feeling sick and morbid and just a little glad the fucker was dead, wasn't getting the sheep shorn, as her Grandmother used to say.

She held her breath as she stooped and grabbed him by his shirt collar, not wanting to smell the blood and urine and shit created by the recent violence. No, she really didn't need that at all. Thankfully, the jackass had been a scrawny little pain in the ass, instead of some behemoth, and so he came away from his swimming pool of blood with little effort.

She got to the door, let go of the dead jackass, and paused, feeling sure she was forgetting some important fact. The zombie was dead. *Check.* She would be safe inside the Comm Center now, there being no more zombies in the room. *Check.* The body would begin to decay, thus causing rot, bad smells, insects, nastiness and all manner of unpleasant health-related stuff if she didn't somehow dispose of it. *Check.*

So what was she missing?

She stared at the door and contemplated the dilemma.

What's on the other side of that door?

A very good question, the answer to which could mean life or death - her death, to be precise. There could be nothing. There could be a hoard of homicidal maniacs bent on turning her into *Amber Tartar.* Nope. That wouldn't do, at all.

She leaned in and put her ear to the door, then mentally smacked herself upside the head for being an idiot. This was a soundproofed room. That was a security door, meant to keep people out and secrets in. Of course she wouldn't hear anything. Or if she did, it meant she was more screwed than the most screwed person in the history of being royally fucked. So how could she find out what was on the other side without opening it onto the aforementioned crazed and hungry hoard?

She actually did smack herself upside the head. There was a security camera.

"Pull your head out, Amber," she said aloud, then shook her head at the potential psychological ramifications of talking to herself in an empty (corpse notwithstanding) room. She could be here like this for a very long time. Talking to herself was the pathway to madness, and she'd only been there a few days. She paused, wondering how many days it had been: four...? Five...? More...? What would she be like a week from now? Or a month? Sheep, comma, not shorn, comma, one each. *Get your ass moving.*

She skirted the front side of the console and strode to the monitor that showed a view of the outside corridor. It was empty - the corridor, not the monitor. The monitor showed a hallway utterly, blissfully devoid of zombies, naked maniacs, creatures from Hell, or any other denizens of her worst nightmares.

Okay...So...Now what?

She could open the door fast as possible and drop the body right outside. It would solve the first problem. No zombie, no zombie rot, no potential health hazard. On the other hand, if she just left it there, it would provide a tasty and readily accessible snack for any other zombies wandering around in the building, thus bringing them quite literally to her doorstep. Would they eat and go? Or would they eat, decide they liked the ambience of the place, decide there might be some other future morsels tossed their way, and wait till Hell freezes over, or they drop dead from hunger and/or thirst?

Sometimes she really hated having such a great imagination.

She was going to have to drag the body and dump it well away from the door, preferably in some other empty room. She was going to have to go *out there*, beyond the scope of the camera. Her great imagination conjured up a schematic map of the Comm Center building. On it were written the words: *Here there be Dragons.*

115

The light of the three-quarter moon cut a swath across the calm sea, giving lie to the tumult within Jonesy's chest. It felt like John Bonham, Buddy Rich, Neal Peart and the entire percussion section of Carlos Santana's band were jamming inside his heart muscle. And yet, nothing was happening. That was the problem.

During the battle inside the Bridge, and the rush to get onto the Flying Bridge so they'd have room to fight, and even watching Molly take out Saigon Ron, his heart remained relatively docile, under the circumstances. Training and adrenaline and the need for action kept him from thinking about what was happening. He'd just reacted, going from one problem, to the next, and then the next, because it wasn't like he'd had any other choice. Now that they had a bit of breathing room, however, the total fucked-up-ness of their situation began to take its toll.

"Nice night," he said to Molly, trying to test his voice, to see if it had risen by several octaves into a girlish soprano. It had not. He sounded normal.

"Oh, yeah," she said, her voice dripping with sarcasm. "I'm having the time of my life."

She seemed calm, which was just *wrong,* on so many levels. She was a *girl.* Okay... Political-Correctness check...she's a *woman...* But damn it! He was the man, here. The masculine one, the tall and brave and strong one. Wasn't that how it was supposed to work? How in the fuck, then, was she so calm?

He was babbling inside his head, and he knew it. The problem, it seemed, was that nothing was happening. There they were, ready for action, armed (as best they could be) and ready to fight off the zombie hoards. But there were no zombie hoards. There was no enemy. There were no creatures from the bowels of Hell trying to kill them, and it was driving him out of his ever-loving mind.

"I wish they'd show up and get this over with," Molly said.

"I know, right?" he said, relieved he wasn't the only one feeling the strain. "You'd think zombies would be less rude."

"I blame TV," she said.

"And the media, and video games," he added. "Don't forget them."

"Might as well add the AIDS Quilt, while we're at it."

"And the War on Christmas."

She snapped her fingers as if she'd finally gotten the answer. "Global Warming," she said.

"Gotta be," he replied.

He walked to the port edge of the Flying Bridge and looked down. The crowd at the door had vanished, presumably inside the Bridge. He didn't like to think of what damage they might be causing in there.

Movement caught his eye: something down on the Boat Deck, milling around near the bottom of the ladder, just out of view. He glanced over at Molly, saw that she was looking at him, expectantly. He shrugged.

"Might as well invite them to the party," he said, then flipped his right-hand baton over and started banging on the rail with the thicker handle. "Hey, Zombies! Hello Zombies!"

Two things happened, almost simultaneously: SKC Robinson, his uniform shredded, but still more or less intact, and his face and hands covered in blood, popped his head out the Bridge door; and LT Richard (Dickhead-fuckface-asshole, and whatever other nasty epithets might come to mind) Medavoy peered up from the bottom of the Boat Deck ladder. Both of them were zombies.

Of course, from that distance, Jonesy couldn't say with absolute certainty that Medavoy had turned, but he discovered (with a mildly gut-wrenching feeling of glee) that he *hoped* the arrogant prick had - if for no other reason than it would give him a reason to kill the son of a bitch. Time to get the show on the road.

"Are you assholes waiting for an engraved invitation?" he yelled.

Robinson moved first, snarling to start the festivities. He was followed by Seaman Donely, Fireman Carnegie, and EM1 Sinstabe.

DC1 Holdstien did not, at first, put in an appearance. A quick glance down below the ladder caught Medavoy heading up, as well. Jonesy looked at Molly and gave her a wan smile.

"Be careful what you ask for," he said.

"Because we might get a gang of zombies, instead?"

"Exactly," he replied. If he hadn't already liked her, hadn't already had the hots for her, and hadn't already admired the living Hell out of her, he certainly would have then.

They backed away from the rail and each took a stance, and waited.

And waited...

And waited...

Nothing happened. No zombie heads appeared above the combing. No deranged fiends climbed the ladder to do battle. They waited in silent anticipation.

Finally, Jonesy uttered: "Whiskey Tango, Foxtrot, over?" Then he moved back to the rail and looked down. The hoard of would-be attackers looked back up at him, then at the ladder, then at him again, and growled. The straight ladder from the 02 Deck, so unlike the stair-type ladder any idiot could fathom, seemed to be beyond their capability.

"Oh for fuck's sake," he said.

Molly joined him at the rail and peered down. "Huh," she said, in wonder. "Will you look at that?"

"Never thought I'd *want* a bunch of bloodthirsty zombies to get closer, but..."

"Yeah," she replied.

"Come on..." he said to them. "You can do it. Hand over hand. Easy as pie." He demonstrated the maneuver, pantomiming his hands reaching upward toward an imaginary rung and pulling on the air.

Sinstabe - who seemed to be the leader of this band of flesh-eating Village Idiots - gaped at Jonesy, slack-jawed, then slowly brought his gaze to the ladder in front of him. He looked up at Jonesy, down at the ladder, up at Jonesy, down at the ladder, and then reached out and grabbed the rung just above his blood-covered head.

"That's it," Jonesy said, unable to believe he was *encouraging* a zombie. The idea was insane, on the surface of it. But if they couldn't get them to come up, they would have to go down. Up on the Flying Bridge, they had the high ground, the zombies would have to squeeze thru the gap in the rail to get at them, and so Jonesy and Molly could engage them one at a time, without getting swarmed. As crazy as it sounded, they *needed* the zombies to climb up. "You can do it," he encouraged.

"You sound like you're talking to a puppy," Molly said.

He looked at her. "Thanks. I really needed that image."

"Just trying to help." She grinned at him. There was a touch of hysteria in that grin.

"When this is over," Jonesy said, marveling at the idea there might actually *be* an end to all of this, "I do believe I'm gonna need to get shitfaced."

"I'll buy the first round," Molly replied.

"Deal," he said, as Sinstabe finally figured out the complex intricacies of a vertical ladder, and began to climb. "Oh, and look who decided to join us!" Medavoy arrived, and yes, he was infected - or, at least, he looked thoroughly insane - which was confirmed when Robinson growled at him and he growled back. Yep, definitely batshit.

"So..." Molly began. "Do we salute, or...? Not sure what the protocol is in this situation."

"I think we just kill him," Jonesy said. "And if you would... Let me do it."

Sinstabe's face appeared at the gap in the railing leading to the Flying Bridge. Jonesy did his best to punt the zombie's head into next week with his steel-toed boot. The head remained more or less intact, but the former Electrician's Mate's nose splattered like an overripe pomegranate, spraying blood as he/it flew backward into Donelly, who staggered, but retained his footing and charged at the short ladder. Carnegie joined him, and both tried to climb it at once, which might have been hilarious, except that the combination of four clutching hands managed to block Jonesy's next kick, and sent him tripping backwards, where he landed on his ass.

This, too, might have been a bit on the funny side, since pratfalls were as old as comedy itself, but his flailing attempt to stop his fall, knocked Molly aside, leaving the ladder wide open. Donelly and Carnegie were up it in a flash, both headed straight for the brand new Ensign. She shoved the still leather-covered axe blade forward, hitting Donelly with it's flat end just under the chin. He/it gave a strangled cough and took one step backward, but he was far from out of the fight.

She launched a solid front kick into Carnegie's chest, sending him into the rail, but by then, Robinson had arrived, so she now found herself facing three zombies, with what was effectively a blunt instrument. She swung it at the SKC, smacking him just above the left ear, and then Jonesy was by her side.

He sent one baton swinging into Robinson's knee, the other into his/its elbow, and the first into almost the same spot Molly had hit - *whap, whap, whap* in rapid succession. It proved to be too much for the large ebony zombie, who dropped like a stone onto the deck at their feet.

Molly dodged Donelly's crazed attempt to rip her face off with his clawed hands, but the spin brought her straight into Carnegie. She avoided his bite toward her ear, then slammed her head back into a reverse head butt, plastering his nose much the same way Jonesy had rearranged Sinstabe's face, but with less deadly effect. She side-slipped, then jabbed the axe handle straight back into the Fireman's gonads. The young zombie whimpered, but did not stop trying to bite her ear. She spun away from him and found herself face to face with LT Medavoy. This was for but a moment, until Jonesy punched their new CO right in the eye, snapping its head back.

He followed with a combination of rights and lefts, driving the despised ex-man into Donelly, who stumbled backward, hit the rail high on his/its thigh, and tumbled over the side and into the sea. Medavoy crashed into the signal light, but the blows didn't seem to be doing him/it any harm. Jonesy felt a mad rage building inside him. He dropped the batons, wanting to feel the impact with his own hands, wanting to pound the son of a bitch into putty.

The fucker had been crawling up his ass since the day he reported aboard. He'd given him every shit detail he could think of, made him take duty on the first day of every single liberty port, and the last day of all five of the AtoN trips they'd taken in the past six months. He missed not a single opportunity to make some snide or otherwise derogatory comment, and had been as much of an asshole as he possibly could. At least, that 's how Jonesy saw it, as he kept pummeling the bastard he'd come to view as his nemesis aboard the ship he had grown to love. Plus, the stupid motherfucker refused to take any steps to insure the safety of her crew. He should die. He *deserved* to die. And Jonesy wanted to be the one to do it.

Molly nailed Carnegie in the nuts again - this time with a kick, and the zombie-kid dropped to its knees. She brought the axe, blade first into the top of its skull, with exactly the same result as with Saigon Ron. The skull splattered and the zombie crumpled. But this time, the axe penetrated the bone, and the falling zombie took her weapon with it.

She glanced at Jonesy in time to see him execute a maneuver straight out of *The Karate Kid* - just without the silly arm waving. He brought his left knee up, then sharply down again, using it to power his right leg's kick square into the bottom of Medavoy's jaw. The XO/CO/ pain in the ass zombie flew into a back-flip, straight over the starboard rail and out of sight.

And then it was over. All the zombies were dead.

Jonesy came to her side, but kept glancing toward the starboard rail, as if half-expecting to see Medavoy climb right back over. He looked at her and gave her a half-guilty/half-sheepish grin.

"I think I enjoyed that just a little too much," he said, looking to starboard again. Then he stiffened, hearing the sound of movement below. *No! It can't be! He can't be coming back!*

He wasn't - at least not Medavoy. DC1 Holdstien's face appeared at the head of the ladder from the 02 Deck. "Oh for Christ's sake!" Jonesy swore, looking up toward the Heavens. "Enough is enough, already!"

He pulled his large Bowie knife, with its eight-inch blade from the sheath on his right thigh and hopped down onto the Signal Bridge, holding the blade flat against his forearm. Holdstien-Zombie's head, shoulders and chest were now in view. Knocking aside the grasping hand with his foot, as if nudging away an annoying puppy dog, Jonesy squatted and stabbed the knife into its chest twice, in rapid succession. Blood spurted from both wounds and the Damage Controlman-Zombie's mouth opened and closed like a bleeding goldfish, before the former shipmate slipped down the ladder and onto the deck below with a finality of sound, signalling the real end to their battle on the Flying Bridge.

He looked up at her, and she looked down at him. A moment passed in silence, then two, then three.

Finally, Jonesy gave a shrug and a smile and said the last thing she could have or ever would have expected: "What are your orders, Captain?"

116

"...Doctor Floyd to the Port Boat Deck on the double!" John Gordon's voice boomed over the *True North's* PA system, and Stephanie Barber saw the mad scientist look up at the speaker and frown. But that's all he did - just frown. He did not jump to his feet and go rushing off toward whatever emergency awaited his attention. He did not start barking orders and taking charge like any doctor on any medical TV show. He just sat there, staring at the now silent speaker.

"Professor Floyd," Marcie Gordon began. She was white-faced with worry about her missing son, and clutching her teen-aged daughter as if to prevent her from getting out of her sight ever again, but still collected enough to see a problem and want to fix it. "They need you on the Boat Deck."

He flicked the statement away with the back of his hand as if swatting at an annoying insect, but still did not move.

Stephanie Barber was nineteen, tall, slim, pretty, and had no real idea what she would eventually be majoring in at NYU. At the moment it was (or had been) Journalism, but she'd been thinking of maybe switching to the Film School, or perhaps Psychology. That last was what she told her father she was studying, partly because she knew it would annoy him, and partly because she wasn't entirely sure a career in the arts was really what she wanted to do. On top of all that, what she had *actually* been taking classes in was Biology, Chemistry, and Human Anatomy, because she had also been playing with the notion of becoming a doctor. This may or may not have had something (or everything) to do with a certain James O'Bannon, who just happened to have also been taking those same classes, but the strategy had gotten her exactly nowhere with the toothsome young New Yorker, and now - given the zombie apocalypse - it never would.

But it had also caused her to take a course in Advanced First Aid. She might have been head over heals in unrequited love or (more likely) lust, but nobody had ever accused her of being stupid. Since she was toying with the idea of Medicine as a career, she'd taken the course to make sure she wasn't, ultimately, too squeamish for the profession. Turned out, she was not.

This autobiographical stream of consciousness flashed through her mind in but a moment. She'd heard the call, and the sense of urgency behind it. Somebody needed help. Floyd wasn't a doctor, but he was the closest thing they had to one, and she was the closest thing to a nurse. She rose and walked to him.

"Come on, Doc," she said, gently but insistently grabbing his arm. "They need us topside."

Another thing Stephanie Barber was, was a hottie. She knew it, and had found it both annoying, and occasionally useful. Men were such pushovers when you goosed them with even the slightest glimmer of a hope of the possibility of maybe getting laid sometime in the as yet to be determined future. She was wearing a skimpy bikini top that did nothing to hide her boobs, and an almost skimpier pair of shorts that did the same for the other important bits. She'd done this - again - to annoy her father, but also because they were on a tropical cruise and it seemed the right thing, the natural thing. That it was also the perfect thing for a bit of male manipulation was not lost on her.

She leaned in and gave Professor Floyd an indecent view of her breasts. He couldn't help but notice them, since they were a scant six inches from his nose. His eyes at first flashed with annoyance over the apparent affront of having someone actually deign to touch him, but then they drifted to the cleavage, then shifted slightly to the left, where she knew he was staring straight at her all-but exposed right nipple. She tugged at his arm. "Come on, Doc," she said. He came.

117

Old Joe heard the flurry of shots on the far side of the ship. It sounded like a .45, but he couldn't be sure. Thing was, though, none of his men had been carrying a .45. He did not share this with Sugar. The pimp was nervously walking back and forth across the solid deck of the RHIB, making Joe nervous. He heard the second flurry of shots, and they were definitely .9mm, which he was sure none of them had been carrying.

The .357 Skizzy Pete held hadn't made a sound since the first flurry of .45, and while there had been a shotgun blast, Old Joe was pretty sure that fucknut Lazardo, who'd gone up there with a shotgun, was now deader than shit. He didn't mourn the man.

"What the fuck is taking so long?" Sugar asked, for the fifth time in the last six minutes. Old Joe was about ready to shoot the fucker himself.

"Do I look like I know?" Joe asked. "Why don't you go up there and find out?"

Sugar apparently didn't think much of that idea, because he shut right the Hell up, which suited Joe just fine. He should have been more careful what he wished for, however, because the silence gave him time to think, and what he thought was that maybe they should just get the flying fuck out of there, right now. Fuck Skizzy Pete. Fuck that child molesting piece of shit, Eddie Cochrane. Lazardo was certainly dead, Joe-Boy was absolutely dead and still floating out there somewhere in the dark. This left just Old Joe and the pimp. The pimp could go fuck himself, as far as Joe was concerned, but he didn't feel inclined to do anything about it, since Sugar still held the other shotgun.

Blackjack Charlie would be pissed, but fuck him, too. This whole thing was a mistake, and it had been that bastard's idea.

"Fuck this," he said, reaching his decision. "We're leaving."

"Fucking right!" Sugar agreed.

Blackjack Charlie could go fuck himself. Old Joe was going to save his own ass. He cut the line to the grapnel with his buck knife and slammed the throttle forward.

118

Frank dumped Moncrief's bloody and wrench-battered body onto the pile at the aft end of Number One MDE. That made four. Danny, Ski, the

EO and Moncrief were dead, and Frank was alone in the engineroom of a ship which may or may not be totally overrun by zombies.

He returned to Main Control and shut the door, cutting off the loud thrum of engine noise. He sat heavily onto a chair as far away from the pools of blood on the deck as he could get and dropped his headphones onto the counter top. Out of habit, he checked the gauges and readouts, ensuring all was still in the green. It was.

He was a veteran, a sailor, and an engineer on this third ship. He could walk all the mechanical spaces blindfolded, if he needed to, and was stupid enough to try. He did not, however, need to, but he wasn't exactly sure what he *did* need to do.

The Engine Room was free of zombies. The hatches and watertight doors were all shut and dogged tight. He was safe, for the time being, anyway. Nothing could get at him that wasn't wholly, one hundred percent human. Number Two MDE was running fine, the board was green, the bilges were dry, and there wasn't anything that needed his immediate attention. He could breathe easy.

Except he couldn't. He had no idea what was happening in the rest of the ship, no clue about the rest of the crew or what was going on anywhere but within the confines of his compartment. He looked at the telephone handset on the wall.

Who ya gonna call? The *Ghostbuster's* jingle popped into his head. That's all he needed right now - movie themes. He better not start thinking about *Titanic*. Oops. Too late.

"Get ahold of yourself, Frank," he muttered, then leaned over, picked up the phone, and dialed the Bridge.

Nobody answered.

On the list of not-good things, that one stood right up there at the top. No answer on the Bridge meant no *body* on the Bridge - at least not any reasonably sane ones, anyway. Anybody who survived this cluster fuck was going to be at least a little nuts. He already felt the fringes of his own sanity beginning to fray. But nobody up there meant there was nobody steering, nobody looking out, nobody to pull back on the throttle or turn the helm if something like, say, a supertanker stumbled into their path.

There. That was something he could do, some action he could take. He could stop the ship's motion.

The old ships of yore had an engine telegraph system, where the people in the pilot house would signal the engine room to go from All Ahead one-third to All Back full, if the situation warranted. And then somebody (or, more likely, bodies) in the engine room would make it happen. In these modern times, however, the bridge had direct throttle control, and the Engine Room personnel only had to make sure the engines kept running. They could, however, manipulate the throttle from right there in Main Control. He did so, bringing it to All Stop.

He heard the pitch of Number Two MDE drop as the load reduced. Okay. Problem solved - for the time being, anyway. What now?

Well, Ski said they needed to do PM on the Evaporator. He didn't have anything else to do, at present. Might as well get to work. He stood, grabbed his headphones, and headed toward the door, but before he could even grasp the handle, the phone rang. He snatched it off its cradle.

"Main Control, Roessler."

"Frank?" the voice on the other end said. "Good to hear your voice, man. It's Jonesy."

A wave of relief washed over him like he was rolling in the surf at Waimaia. "Dude! What the Hell is going on?"

"You okay down there?"

"Yeah," Frank replied. "But it's just me. The rest are..." he let the sentence fade.

"I know the feeling," Jonesy replied. "I'm on the Bridge. Was that you who shut us down?"

"Yep."

"Good thinking. Are you safe down there?"

"Yeah," Frank replied, surprised to actually feel safe.

"Stay put. I'm going to check the rest of the ship."

"Anybody else up there?" Frank asked.

"Ms. Gordon," Jonesy said, a bit cautiously. "She just got promoted to Captain."

"The Hell you say?"

"All the other zeroes are dead, Frank. She's our new CO."

He thought about it for a bit, then - rather chagrined - said: "Gotta be better than the last one."

"I agree," Jonesy said. Frank could hear the pleasure in his voice, which seemed weird, but at that particular moment, he did not care. He wasn't alone, anymore.

"Stay put," Jonesy repeated. "I'll call you when I know."

"Roger that," Frank said, and hung up the phone.

119

Jim Barber raced down the ladder from the Bridge to the Port Boat Deck in time to see his daughter drop the over-large First Aid kit down onto the deck next to Professor Floyd and the bleeding body of Mick Fincham. "Christ! This thing's heavy," she said, then saw her father and smiled. Her face was flushed with the effort, but her eyes looked dull, almost dead with shock.

He glanced at her, did a double-take and scowling assessment of her near-lack of clothing, decided now was not the time for a fatherly lecture on decorum, and kept running. Then he was past and headed for the rail, chasing the sound of the speeding small boat engine.

The RHIB carrying two men sped away from the *True North*, bouncing on the mild swell as it picked up speed. He brought the rifle to his shoulder, aimed, and fired twice. The one not conning the boat went down, fast and hard, and Jim saw the shotgun fall from his hands and drop into the sea. He shifted aim and fired at the helmsman, who jerked to the right, but kept on his feet. He fired again and missed as the RHIB sliced left and away, then missed again, as it cut right, zig-zagging into the night. He brought the sight to his eye again, but released the trigger without firing. No point. The boat was out of range, and in any event, it was leaving.

The fight, it seemed, was over. He watched the pirate bastard disappear into the distance for a while, then turned and headed back to his daughter and the carnage that had been left behind.

Mick was in horrible shape; his shoulder a bloody mass of exposed bone and ripped tissue, but the belly wound was much, much worse. "He needs blood, Dad," Stephanie said, her voice trembling. "Lots of it. And Morphine, but the cabinets in the Sick Bay were locked. So I brought this," she babbled, the words coming fast, and pointed at the First Aid kit, now lying open, with Floyd searching through it, picking up something, then tossing it back, then again, then again.

The Nutty Professor shook his head in apparent disgust. "No. No. This won't do. It's not what I need." His voice was almost conversational, except for the tone of disdain, but that was normal, from the few discussions he'd had with the man. He looked at Jim and shook his head again. "There's nothing I can do for him."

"What do you mean nothing?" Jim demanded, getting angry and letting it show in his tone. "You do something, God dammit, or I'll..." Stephanie stopped him with a hand on his knee.

"I think he's right, Dad." She'd been listening to Mick's heartbeat with the stethoscope from the kit. "His heart's got a bad rhythm. Not sure what it means, but it can't be good. And he's lost a lot of blood."

"If we had a real doctor," Floyd added. "Not me, but an actual MD, with an operating room at a trauma center, with all the available equipment and drugs and anaesthetic, and sterile protocols..." He let the words trail off, then shrugged. "I still think they'd lose him. The damage is too severe. Looks like this was point blank." He pointed to Mick's ravaged abdomen. "Haven't turned him over yet, but from the position of the entry wound, I'd be surprised if the spine wasn't damaged." He shook his head again. "And I'm not an MD."

Mick gave a shudder, as his body went into violent spasms. Blood spurted from his mouth as his head rolled side to side. He coughed a great, crimson gout, all over Christopher Floyd, who gave a sharp, short scream, and backpedaled away like a crab. Their shipmate twitched a few more times, then fell still and silent.

Stephanie stared at him in horror, her mouth hanging open, her face white as Floyd's shirt had been, moments before. Her hands trembled and tears welled into her eyes as she turned them toward her father. He wanted to take her in his arms, to comfort and soothe her, but something inside told him it would be a bad idea. She wanted his comfort, clearly, and she needed it, too, but she needed the strength of knowledge in having dealt with this on her own, more. *I am a cold bastard,* he thought to himself, but he also knew his instinct was right. She would be better off in the long run, and this brave new world was going to be a long run, indeed - long and almost certainly bloodier.

"Check his heartbeat, Steph," he said, softly. Her eyes held a mixture of pain and shock as she stared at him. But he saw them change, shift, harden in resolve as she took a deep breath, nodded, then put the earpieces into their proper place and the scope to Mick's chest. She listened for a moment, moved the scope, listened again. She did it twice more and sat back, shaking her head.

Mick Fincham was dead.

120

Molly watched Jonesy pass through the interior Bridge door and head below. *What are your orders, Captain?* Those five words sent her world well and truly sideways. Was it possible? Was she now the Captain of the USCGC *Sassafras*? It couldn't be. But it was.

LCDR Sparks had stayed ashore, fearing he would turn and endanger the crew. Medavoy had turned, had endangered the crew, and had gone back-flipping over the side. Bloominfeld now lay with the bodies of Borgeson and Ross on the port wing, and Ryan had gone down in a plane crash, which left exactly one Commissioned Officer aboard ship: her. CWO4 Kinkaid and CWO2 Larsen may or may not still be alive, but she, technically, outranked them, so she, technically, was now Captain of the ship.

Oh Hell no! The thought stabbed through her brain and her heart the way Jonesy stabbed DC1 Holdstien. She couldn't do it! She wouldn't do it!

Did she have a choice?

Of course she did! Larsen or Kinkaid were more qualified. She could hand it off to them. Hell, Jonesy was more qualified than she was.

But Jonesy wasn't an officer, and Kinkaid and Larsen could very well be dead, or worse.

Controlling Legal Authority.

The phrase entered her mind like a stately liner entering port, escorted by tugs and fireboats, with all hoses shooting sea water into the sky. The Coast Guard, for all the military in-jokes about Puddle Pirates and Shallow Water Sailors, and Navy Lite, was part of the Armed Forces. They carried heavy weapons. She had the authority to arrest people, seize their boat, fire on them, if necessary, kill them, if necessary. The Captain of a ship - *any* ship so armed, and commissioned by the US Government, or any responsible government - held the Controlling Legal Authority. That was the Law.

But this is a Zombie Apocalypse, dammit!

Yes, it was - most definitely was - and that, ultimately, made the law so much more important. When all social order collapsed, which had either already happened, or was on the verge of happening, then the law was the only thing holding utter chaos at bay. She'd seen the messages, read the reports of cities falling to the Infected, one by one being over-ridden by zombies. But pockets of survivors had to still exist, didn't they?

They existed - she and Jonesy and MK2 Roessler and OS3 Schaeffer, and hopefully at least a few more were alive and uninfected. It stood to reason, therefore, that others would have survived. This may or may not be fuzzy logic, coupled with wishful thinking, but she had to believe in it - she *had* to - or otherwise, what was the point?

So...Okay...She was the Captain. What did that mean?

It meant she was in charge. It meant she was responsible for the lives of however many crew members survived. And if she was responsible, then it was damned well about time she got off her procrastinating ass and did her job.

She picked up the chart table phone (careful to avoid the pools of blood on the deck) and punched the number.

"Radio, Schaeffer," the answer came immediately, as if the young man snatched it off its cradle before it had even started ringing.

"Schaeffer, this is Ms. Gordon," she began.

"Yes, ma'am," he replied, seeming glad that somebody was in charge, that somebody could tell him what to do.

"This is far too complicated to explain at the present time, but I have assumed command of the ship." She waited, breathless, her heart pounding as Schaeffer processed the information. It did not take long.

"Yes, ma'am," he said.

"Have we got comms with anybody?"

"Not directly, ma'am," he said. "Haven't heard from COMMSTA Hono, or any of the other cutters in several hours. Couple days, come to think of it. BBC is still broadcasting, so are a few other stations, and there is still some chatter on the civilian channels, but nothing official."

"Very well," she said, taking it all in. "Try and raise the COMMSTA. Failing that, try each of the cutters. If you reach any of them, let them know we are in distress but still in control of the ship. Will follow with details when we get them."

"Yes, ma'am," he said. "And if I can't?"

She thought about her answer for a few moments that seemed to stretch into infinity. If they couldn't connect with Coast Guard assets, then what? Did they try the Navy? Did they send out a general distress? No. They were still in control, still in command, and were not in any immediate danger, so far as she could tell. She cast a glance at the three points of access into the Bridge: one interior, and two exterior doors. All closed. No immediate danger. Roessler was secure in the Engine Room, she was secure on the Bridge. The rest would sort itself out.

"Ma'am?" Schaeffer asked, popping her out of her thought bubble.

"If you can't raise any Coast Guard assets, then just maintain a watch and listen for any official government forces. Do not let any civilians know our condition, if for no other reason than we don't yet know it ourselves." "Ma'am?"

"Look...Bill's your first name, right?" she asked.

"Yes, ma'am."

"Look, Bill...We're in a bad situation, here. I'm not going to soft soap it. But we don't want to make it worse. We don't want to bring anything down on us to add to our problems, understood?" She was thinking about pirates, but did not want to utter the word.

"Yes, ma'am."

"We're alright for now. I want to make sure we stay that way, understood?"

"Yes, ma'am."

"Get to it, and keep me informed."

"Roger that," he said, and hung up.

And now, all she could do was wait. She moved to the forward windows, picked up a pair of binoculars, and began to scan the darkness. *Come on, Jonesy. Give me some good news...*

121

BM2/OPS Socrates Jones found what was left of CWO2 Larsen in the Wardroom Passageway, on the port side. He had not died well. In the berthing spaces, the next deck down, he found chaos and blood and death. Bodies were strewn throughout the passageway, in the berthing compartments, and in the Crew's Lounge, which looked like an abattoir. The big screen TV, home to so many gory and gratuitously violent movies on cruises past, looked like a grotesque version of modern art gone horribly wrong. He stared at a bloody handprint on the left side of the screen, his mind numb, then he smacked his helmeted head, as if to clear it, and kept moving.

As he was walking cautiously (both for stealth and because there was so much bloody mess) forward toward the Bosun Hold, the watertight door swung open. He tensed, knowing that all he had for weapons were his two knives - the Bowie, and his dive knife, held in a sheath on his left calf. The batons had both been bent by the Flying Bridge battle to such a degree that he couldn't retract them into their carry positions. He'd left them up there.

He took a stance, left leg slightly forward, Bowie held against his right forearm and down, dive knife in his left, held aloft. The door creaked open.

The first thing he saw was the barrel of a twelve gauge shotgun. The next thing he saw was Duke's face, his lips cracking into a crooked smile.

"Nobody here but us zombies," he said.

"Fuck a bunch of zombies," Jonesy replied, happier than shit to see his friend and shipmate, and then even happier to notice none other than Harold F. Simmons, jr., poke his head around Duke's shoulder.

"What the fuck, Jonesy?" the young man said, grinning. Both were dressed in full LE rig, as was Jonesy. They, on the other hand, were armed to the teeth.

"I see you raided the Armory."

"Medavoy can book me later," Duke said, with supreme unconcern.

"No, actually, I don't think he can," Jonesy said.

"Is he dead?" Harold asked.

"Yes, sir," Jonesy replied.

"You?" Duke asked.

Jonesy nodded. Duke grinned. Harold pumped his right fist up and down.

"How'd it feel?" Duke asked.

Jonesy theatrically looked around to see if there was anyone within earshot, which of course there wasn't, since - aside from the three of them - everyone else appeared to be dead.

"It was awesome!" Jonesy said, breaking into a wide smile. "You should have seen it."

\   "Wish I had," Harold said. "Fucker needed to die."

Jonesy's face darkened at that. Make no mistake, he'd wanted to kill the bastard almost since the day they met. The prick had been universally hated and reviled by the crew - and that was before he took command and proved what an absolute fuckstick he actually was, but saying that he "needed killing," brought the reality of what happened home, straight to whatever humanity and morality remained inside Jonesy after all the death and killing. Ultimately, technically, and (most important of all) legally, what he'd done was mutiny. Yes, okay, Medavoy had turned zombie, and anyone with a lick of sense would have done what he'd done in response - though probably without such violent relish. But common sense and reason didn't apply to the Headquarters weasels who might be sent to investigate this after it was all over. They, like the half-wits who'd comprised his after-action hearing on the LE shooting, might not be so ready to take into account certain things like self-preservation and a zombie fucking apocalypse. Best not to be so cavalier about killing their Commanding Officer.

"Let's not get carried away, shall we?" he said.

"So what's the what?" Duke asked.

"We control the Bridge, the Engineroom, and I guess the Radio Room. You guys are alive. I'm alive. Bill Schaeffer is alive. And Ensign Gordon is now our CO."

"No shit?" Harold asked.

"None whatsoever," Jonesy replied. "Oh, and Frank's alive, too. He's the only one left in the Engine Room."

"Anybody else?" Duke asked.

"Don't know yet," Jonesy said. "And it's high time we found out."

122

Amber steeled her nerve, one hand on the COMMCEN door, one on the tattered collar of OS3 Jackass. Her heart hammered in anticipation of going *out there*, into the Great Unknown, where there may or may not be Dragons. Adrenaline pumped into her bloodstream, preparing her for fight or flight or abject terror, whichever came first, last or in between. She took a deep breath.

Then damned-near jumped out of her skin as she heard: "COMMSTA Honolulu, COMMSTA Honolulu, this is USCGC *Sassafras*, USCGC *Sassafras*, two-one-eight-two, over.'

She dumped Jackass back onto the deck and ran around the console, because diving over, while certainly quicker, could just as certainly result in a broken neck, and since she liked it in its current condition, she refrained from leaping and just ran, instead. As it was, she almost tripped over one of the chairs getting to the GSB 900 handset.

2.182mhz, or 2182khz, was similar to Channel 16 on the VHF band, and similarly used as a distress frequency, but the Upper Side Band nature of 2.182 gave it a much greater range. It also made the voices coming through it sound as if they were calling from the bottom of a well, using one of those *Scream* voice scramblers, but that was hardly the point. It was all she could do to keep *herself* from screaming when she said into the handset: "Cutter *Sassafras*, Cutter *Sassafras*, this is COMMSTA Honolulu, over." In fact, she was quite surprised to hear her own voice sounding like a radio announcer, instead of like some scared idiot.

There was a pause, then the voice replied: "Can we go secure? Over."

Now that was interesting. Not necessarily the desire to go secure - that was normal in normal times. 2.182 was supposed to be monitored by everyone - military and civilian - and so anyone at all could be listening. But it's not like they were keeping secrets from anyone...or were they? "Roger," she replied. "Current key, this date."

They had a wide variety of cryptological gear at the COMMSTA - more, in fact, than most of the cutters. Face it, Buoy Tenders rarely needed to be involved in top secret missions, but they did have secure radios, accessed by a numerical key, which changed daily. These changes were promulgated by Top Secret messages with the key information disseminated weekly. As luck or fate would have it, the last change was less than a week ago. She went to the appropriate piece of gear, consulted the appropriate message on the TS Board, and keyed in the code.

In a few moments, the now even more distorted voice came through the speaker. "COMMSTA Honolulu, Cutter *Sassafras*, Over."

"Good to hear your voice, *Sassafras*," she replied, throwing standard comms procedures out the window. "What's your status? Over."

"We've had an outbreak. Bad one. Most of the crew is dead. But we still control the Bridge and Engine Room, and are currently assessing the extent of the problem. How about you? Over."

"As near as I can tell, I'm the only one left in the COMMCEN," she said, and it sent a stab through her heart, as if uttering the words brought the reality home like nothing else could. "Honolulu is gone, the Base is gone, and I think I'm the only one in the building who isn't infected. The generator hasn't kicked in yet, so we still have shore power, but no telling how long that will last. I have enough food and water for about a month, but that's about as good as the news gets. Over."

"Have you heard from the other Cutters? Over."

"Negative," she said. "But then I've spent most of the time locked in the head, waiting for the zombie that was in here to bleed out. Far as I know, however, you and I are it. Over." Listening to herself voice the litany of disaster, things really did sound like it was over - maybe for good, maybe forever.

"Roger that," the voice on the other end of the ether said, sounding strangely calm. Her own voice sounded the same, oddly enough, but the steadiness of their respective tones belied an incongruity of colossal proportions. Things were not calm. Things were not steady. Things were totally fucked, when it came right down to it, and the fact they were both relating this information to each other as if it were a normal conversation was just *wrong*. But what else could they do? Start screaming and crying and begging for God to take this poisoned cup from their lips? Hardly. If there was a God, if there was some Supreme Being in charge of this current cluster fuck, then He, She or It, had some serious explaining to do.

"Not sure if we can help, but we'll see if we can work something out," the voice continued. "Don't hold your breath. Over."

"Roger that," she said, in return.

"*Sassafras*, out."

123

Jonesy spun the wheel on the Dry Stores scuttle and heaved it open. "Any zombies down there?" he yelled.

"Nobody here but us chickens," came the voice, and then the head of CS1 Gary King. He was holding two frying pans, and had a big assed knife stuck in his belt, which, ordinarily would have looked bizarre as Hell, but this had been no ordinary day.

After hooking up with Duke and Harold, they'd gone back to the Armory, where Jonesy gleefully armed himself to the fucking teeth, with two .45 pistols (one had been his own and the other belonged to CWO2 Larsen), with thigh holsters for each. He'd also grabbed an M4, which he now had strapped to his chest, on a retractable rig. He complained about losing the LE batons, but Duke presented him with something much better: a seriously sharpened kukri-machete, the sheath for which was currently stuck through the left side belt of his harness, along with ammo-filled magazines for all of his firearms. "Anybody else down there with you?" he asked.

"Not a soul," Gary said, climbing up through the round scuttle. It didn't look easy, since the man clung onto the frying pans, as if he might never let go. The Culinary Specialist looked from Jonesy, to Duke, then to Harold. "Please tell me this isn't all that's left."

"Pretty close," Harold said.

"Frank's in the Engine Room, Bill's in Radio, and Ms. Gordon - who's now the CO, by the way - is on the Bridge," Jonesy said. "Other than that, we haven't found anybody."

"Well slap me nekked and call me Bubba," Gary muttered in disbelief.

"No thanks, I'll pass," Jonesy said. "But you can accompany us on the rest of the sweep, if you like."

"Pass," Gary said, vigorously shaking his head.

"Wimp," Duke chided.

"Damn right!" Gary agreed.

"Head on up to the Bridge, then," Jonesy said. "Tell Ms G... - The Captain - we're continuing the sweep." He closed the scuttle and spun the wheel again to secure it, then stood and looked to Duke and Harold. "Let's go."

124

Old Joe felt dizzy from blood loss, in agony from the wound in his right shoulder, and scared, because he was also lost. On the way to the boat they'd tried - and failed - to hijack, he'd steered due South from the *Daisy Jean*, and if they had been attacking someplace on shore, all he'd have to do was head due North to get back, because on shore, things like buildings didn't move. But they hadn't been attacking on shore, they had attacked on water, and water did move, just as the boat they'd attacked had been moving.

He'd kept an eye on the compass, and their course had been just South of due West, but he wasn't sure how long they'd been there, or how fast the other ship had been going, so he had no accurate way to judge how far he was now off course, as he continued to speed northward. He had no idea where the *Daisy Jean* was, and he was running out of time.

The RHIB steering console once held a marine radio, but Blackjack Charlie removed it, saying he didn't want the other boat to be able to do what they had, which was follow their radio signal right back to them. It wouldn't have mattered, if the plan succeeded, but it had not, and Old Joe held the sinking suspicion that Charlie had gone into this - had sent them on this fucked mission to begin with - knowing it would probably fail.

He'd stopped to toss Sugar's body over the side as soon as he was sure he'd gotten out of range, and the other boat wasn't following. It had been agony, and uncoordinated as Hell, with only one good arm, but he'd managed, primarily because Sugar had fallen onto the inflated sponson, half-on/half-off the boat. It had still been a bitch.

He scanned the horizon, but it was dark, the RHIB was low to the water, which didn't give him much range, and even if it had, his vision was blurry from fatigue and blood loss. In short, he was fucked, and he knew it.

Fate.

Fate brought him here, all right. Fate, the California State Department of Corrections, the Pomona Zombie Virus, and Blackjack Charlie Carter, had turned Old Joe's life into a world of pain and blood and shit.

Fate.

Once upon a time, he hadn't been a bad guy. Oh, sure, he'd stuck up a few liquor stores, but the owners were all Pakistanis and Iranians and other kinds of probably terrorist assholes. There was that one Korean place, but they were probably North Korean, so again, what did they matter? Old Joe had been alright, though. He'd been a good friend, a solid man to have at your back in a fight. And he'd paid his taxes, dammit; taxes that paid for his trial by jury and inevitable incarceration, because he wasn't rich enough to afford a good lawyer. Wasn't that a stone cold slap to the face?

Fate.

Something, some flash of movement caught his eye off to the right. He lost it, found it, lost it again. His head swam, as he tried to concentrate. Then he saw it again: the *Daisy Jean*, big and beautiful and coming toward him, less than a mile away.

Fate.

Maybe the fickle bitch wasn't so bad, after all.

He tossed the line to Blackjack Charlie, who stood alone at the back of the motor sailor. Strange that he didn't have at least one of the others helping, but what the fuck?

"Didn't think I'd find you," Old Joe said, taking Charlie's outstretched hand up and out of the RHIB.

Blackjack didn't say anything at first, but Joe figured he was just busy making sure the small boat was tied off. Finally, the man looked at him and said: "Saw you on radar."

"Thank the blessed mother for that," Old Joe replied with relief.

"What happened?" Charlie asked, leading him toward the absolute back of the *Daisy Jean.*

"Cluster fuck," Joe replied. "They were waiting and armed to the teeth. Everybody is dead."

Blackjack Charlie Carter nodded. "Too bad," he said, pulling a 9mm pistol out from behind his light jacket. He pointed it at Old Joe. "For you," he concluded, and pulled the trigger.

The last thought passing through Old Joe's dying mind as the bullet slammed into him and as he toppled over the side was: *Fate.*

125

With a heave, Amber shoved the body into the corridor. It fell with a muffled *thump* as it hit the carpet. *That was more work than it should have been*, she thought, as she struggled to catch her breath, which seemed to want to run away and never come back.

The problem had been figuring out how to get Jackass out of the COMMCEN and through the door without having the door shut behind her, and thus lock her out. The building still had power, the security door would still work, as long as she didn't suffer severe memory loss and forget her code, but Amber believed in Murphy's Law, which guaranteed that as soon as she had three or four bloodthirsty zombies on her tail, the power would cut out and she'd be royally fucked.

In short, she didn't want to get locked out, and so she contrived a way to wedge the door open. Of course, there being only one of her, and her having only two hands (both of which were occupied getting Jackass's body through the door), putting said wedge in place had been an exercise in weight, balance and contortionism she never wanted to have to repeat.

She leaned against the door jam and drew a large, slow breath. Her heart resumed its less rapid normal rhythm, and her temples no longer throbbed with an excess of blood rushing into her skull, but she wasn't quite ready to begin the next phase of her mission.

No sound greeted her ears; no telltale growling or howling or insane vocalizations indicated the presence of any infected personnel. She was - as near as she could detect - alone.

Two options - three, if she included saying to Hell with it and just locking herself back in: she could leave the body where it was for the time being and reconnoiter the area to find a suitable place to dump it, without dragging the thing all over the building, making noise, and bringing all the zombies down upon her head; or, she could just risk it and drag the body, thus reducing the amount of time she had to spend exposed. Neither option filled her with puppies and bunnies. Then again, standing there thinking about it wasn't going to do her any good, either, so she pushed off the door and made her way down the corridor, *sans* Jackass.

The COMMCEN building was shaped like a squashed sort of "H;" long in the middle and short on both ends. One end held the offices and conference rooms, etcetera, of the Admin portion, where the officers hung out and looked busy. The other end held the Communications Center itself. The officers had windows, the enlisted scum in the radio room did not. Of course, this was for security reasons, but it seemed to fit the downtrodden lot of enlisted pukes everywhere, and so that was the excuse everybody gave, sometimes calling her workspace, the "Depravation Chamber."

The immediate pathway to and from the COMMCEN was narrow and lined, on one side, by the Executive Officer's office (empty, but too close for her comfort), the COMMS Officer's office (ditto), the OSC's office (locked), the YNC's office (also locked) and then the main exterior glass-doored entrance. Beyond, were other offices and a cafeteria, of sorts, for those few who brought their own lunches, rather than availing themselves of the Base Mess Hall. The opposite wall held maintenance closets, an equipment room, housing all the gear for the myriad antennae on the roof, another set of glass doors leading to the back of the building, and the fire and sound-protected Emergency Generator room. None of these rooms immediately seemed like a great place to stash a body.

The corridor appeared empty, clean, and quiet, which seemed *wrong*. This was an apocalypse, wasn't it? There should be bodies and debris and stuff laying all over the place. It shouldn't look so *normal*.

She reached the corner of the entrance atrium and peered inside. *This is more like it*, she thought, upon seeing the carnage. She might have lost her lunch if she had eaten any in the last twelve hours. A body, that had apparently been used as a battering ram to shatter the glass outer doors, lay mangled and covered in congealed blood three feet into the space - just far enough to have been invisible from the corridor. Flies buzzed and crawled around and on it. Another two bodies lay just outside. They appeared to have been...*chewed*. A fire axe hung embedded in the near wall. *Be careful what you wish for, Amber...*

She cocked her head around to look at the crumpled form of Jackass laying outside the slightly open COMMCEN door. She should really just leave it there and get the flying fuck out of this corridor. She felt exposed, vulnerable. Glancing into the rear atrium, she saw nothing out of the ordinary. The glass doors remained closed. No bodies lay on the floor. No axes hung suspended in the walls.

"This is just too fucking weird," she muttered to herself, in what she thought was an inside voice, meant to carry no further than from her mouth to her own ears. But in the silent and empty corridor, it echoed, and in her heightened state of abject terror, it sounded as if she had been using a bullhorn. She slapped both hands over her offending mouth and cursed her stupidity.

Nothing happened for a moment, then two, then three, then four. Her heart banged on the inside of her breastbone, as if to say *Let me out of here!*

There came the sound of a chair or something scraping down at the far end, where the cafeteria sat in what she foolishly hoped was dust-swirling emptiness. Something banged. Something else fell over. And something *moaned.*

A face appeared at the far doorway - crazed and demented and covered in blood. Its eyes turned to her, registered her presence as *dinner*, and it let out a hungry scream of rage, as it lunged into the hallway, followed by another, and another, and another. They began to lurch toward her, like a gang of drunks, stumbling home from the bar; some were naked, some in tattered remnants of uniforms, one (a woman) in a stylish, but conservative suit, now covered in gore.

Amber turned and ran.

126

Duke banged on the DC Shop hatch, heard nothing in response, and opened it, with Jonesy and Harold covering. They'd used this method throughout the ship, searching for other crewmembers. Mostly, they found dead bodies. The one exception had been BMC Bernie Adams, whom they'd found wandering around the wide-open ship.

If the fact his uniform was tattered and just as covered in blood as had been his face hadn't informed them that the Chief had turned, then his growling charge at them sealed the deal. They couldn't risk weapons fire, because they didn't want to destroy the laundry, where they'd found him, and which they were going to need, but Harold had left his bat behind, in the Bosun Hold, and Duke's hammers were stuffed in his belt, so he couldn't get to them in time, which gave Jonesy the Golden Opportunity to try out his kukri-machete, which proved to be simply outstanding at beheading infected people. Any people, really, but they found it easier to use the word "infected," or "zombie," or some other damn thing, to keep from reminding them what and whom they were killing. It didn't work.

They were going to need to come up with suitable nomenclature to talk about this stuff, in Jonesy's considered opinion. He favored "zombie," but Harold kept insisting they weren't the living dead, so perhaps a new name was needed. Or perhaps not. Harold could just shut the fuck up. That certainly worked best for Jonesy.

The DC Shop held nothing - at least nothing living, or formerly living, or twisted into a pile of mangled guts, so...*bonus*. Jonesy had decided small blessings were what was important in extreme situations.

They dogged the hatch closed and paused to consider. The sun was coming up on what looked to be a really nice day. Jonesy said so.

"Nice day."

"Except for the end of the world," Harold added.

"Always so negative," Duke said, giving Harold a mild shove. "You really need to adjust your attitude."

Harold seemed about to retort with what Jonesy felt sure would be a perfectly sarcastic remark, when they heard a noise coming from within the Lifejacket Locker. The glorified closet sat at the rear of the superstructure on the fantail, but they hadn't considered it as a possibility. It was a lifejacket locker, filled with Type 3 PFDs and Survival Suits. Why would anybody be in there? *Hello...zombie uprising*...but still...

They each took a defensive posture, with Duke and Harold pointing their shotguns and Jonesy pulling his right-hand .45. Slowly - ever-so slowly - the hand-sized dogs on the hatch came down, one by one. Whoever or whatever was in there, was being cautious, which should have been a clue the size of Nebraska that the occupant was not a zombie, but Jonesy didn't feel the need to take any chances, and neither, it seemed, did the other two.

The hatch cracked, and a brown eye peered outward, followed quickly by the smiling face of EM3 Dan McMullen. "Holy fuck am I glad to see you guys!" He said with glee. "What took you so long?"

"We stopped for coffee break," Jonesy said, droll as could be.

"I forgive you," Dan replied, grabbing Harold's hand and shaking it.

"That's everybody," Jonesy said. They had kept a list of whom they'd found, checking off shipmates one by one. McMullen was the only one unaccounted for. He keyed the mic on his comco. "Bridge, Search Team."

"Go," Molly's voice came up in a moment.

"All accounted for. Found one more alive."

"Very well," came the reply. "Is he ambulatory?"

"Big words," Harold quipped. Duke shoved him for his troubles.

"Affirmative."

"Bring him and yourselves up here," Molly's voice said. "Time for a crew meeting."

"Roger that, Captain," Jonesy said, then cocked his head at McMullen, who stared at him in disbelief. "She's our new CO. Deal with it," he added, then turned and started heading to the Bridge.

127

John gazed at each of his remaining crewmembers, gathered around him on the fantail. They were floating on the dawning sea - under power, but not going anywhere. He stopped the ship so they could hold the burial ceremony for Jason Gilcuddy and Mick Fincham. The mood was not great.

As with the crew meeting before they left Astoria, everyone looked bleary-eyed with exhaustion. He always seemed to hold these gatherings when everyone was about ready to drop from sleep deprivation. *Brave new world...*

They dumped the bodies of the pirates before stopping for the burial. There had been no ceremony for them, and only Jim, Gus, Lane and Bob-Bob had been involved.

Spute had been green around the edges after he'd emptied his 9mm into the bastard who threatened Davy, but he seemed more relieved that John wasn't going to kick his ass for losing track of the boy, in the first place, than remorseful for having shot the fucker full of holes. He'd also managed to shoot up the starboard side of the Bridge, and they were going to have to replace one of the windows, but John had stored spare everything for the journey: spare engine parts, spare line, spare supplies and dry stores, spare food, and, yes, spare window glass for each of the standardized sizes. *Always Ready* meant what it said, and John took the concept to heart.

Of course, he didn't think the people who came up with the Coast Guard's motto had a zombie apocalypse in mind when they did it, but he forgave them their short-sidedness. There were just some things you could never be ready for.

As, for example, being ready to give a pep talk to his crew in the aftermath of a pirate attack. That hadn't been on his list of possible contingencies, and he mentally kicked his own ass for making the mistake. John believed - or tried to, anyway - in the basic good of people. He'd always felt it best to give everybody the benefit of the doubt, but it ignored the basic fact of what Jim said before the attack: *There will always be assholes.*

At the moment, everyone was treating Clara as the *Designated Asshole*, and they had a point. Mick and Jason were dead as a direct result of the boneheaded mistake she'd made. But it had been done out of ignorance - monumentally stupid ignorance, but ignorance nonetheless, and not malice, which was the important factor he now had to convey. He took a calming breath, and began.

"We've lost two shipmates," he said, stating the obvious. "And that is tragic. It is terrible. It is heartbreaking." He looked at each of them, including Clara who was staring at the deck. "And if anybody deserves the blame, it's me." He saw multiple pairs of eyes shift from him, to Clara, then back to him again. "That's right. Me. And only me. I didn't plan for this. I didn't allow for piracy and I should have. I screwed up. Me. And what happened was a direct result of it."

"John..." Jim began, but he stopped him with a hand gesture.

"I am to blame," he repeated. "I accept full responsibility. And I have every intention of learning from my mistake." He gazed out to sea to give himself a moment to gather his thoughts before continuing. "This is a new world, we're entering. A dangerous world. A world filled with hazards and enemies and fear and death. It's not a question of whether or not we will have to face anything worse. It's a question of when." He gestured toward the starboard side, where they'd committed their shipmate's bodies to the sea. "We've seen the result. We feel the pain and the loss. But we must all learn from it. We must all steel ourselves for the challenges and dangers of the future. And that future can be bright. There can be hope. There can be light at the end of the darkness. We must face it together. And together we can." He shook his head and gave a wry laugh. "Hate to use a cliche, but they are occasionally appropriate. Ready?"

He looked at them, caught a few smiles and many more nods.

"United we stand. Divided we fall," he intoned. "And I have no intention of falling. Are you with me?"

Davy took a step forward, separating himself from his Mom and sister. He stood to attention, snapped a parade ground salute that would have passed muster at the strictest boot camp, and said: "Yes, sir!"

John nodded and returned the salute with all solemnity. "Set the watch," he said. "Let's get back underway."

128

"...All Officers, your presence is requested in the Cabin. All Officers..." BM3/OPS Eric Riechert said into the 1-MC. He turned and addressed BMCM Wolf. "He said to include you too, Master Chief."

BMC/DECK Dan Huffman, who currently had the Deck and Conn, glanced at the Master Chief and shrugged. "Sucks to be so popular," he said.

BMCM Philip C. Wolf grumbled his way off the Bridge. Riechert could have sworn he heard him say "Fucking Officers," under his breath, but he was neither brave, nor stupid enough to comment. The Master Chief was an entity unto himself. Normal rules of decorum simply did not apply.

"What do you suppose that's about?" Eric asked, after Wolf closed the interior Bridge door behind him.

"No idea," Chief Huffman replied. "Apparently, we're not qualified to know."

Capt. Gideon Hall sat behind his desk, waiting for all the officers to arrive. He was not a happy man, but he took solace in the fact that his unhappiness had nothing to do with his officers. They had done their job. They had done their duty. They saved the ship. Now he must ask them to save the crew, as well.

LT Wheeler was the last to arrive. He looked as if he had just woken up, which made sense, because he'd had the midwatch last night, after being up all day in Guam. The Captain stood, and left the other officers standing as well.

"We have a problem, gentlemen, ladies, Master Chief," he began. He hadn't meant it as a joke, but that's how it went over. Chuckles flitted through the compartment, and the assembled officers relaxed, just a bit. They knew what he'd said was true. He hadn't, in fact, needed to say it, but sometimes stating the obvious was a good way to enter into difficult areas.

"The Captain of a ship should never explain himself," he continued - also obvious, as anyone with any training or experience in command would know. "But just this once, I'll explain it to you." They stood there, looking at him, not nodding, not shifting, not glancing at each other, their eyes fixed upon him. Good.

"Guam was a tragedy. There are times in this profession, if you're in it for long enough, when you are faced with a situation for which there are no good answers. When that happens, the only real choice is to fall back on your orders. That is what I did." He paused, both to let it sink in, and to gather his thoughts.

"Our orders were to top off fuel, under conditions which would not risk infection any more than necessary. We are to act as a beacon in the darkness for whatever remains of our fleet and our forces. We could not and cannot do that, while also fighting the spread of a plague more disastrous, more dastardly than any before in history. To that end, what you did, Mr. Vincenzo, what your boys did, was essential." He clasped his hands behind his back and began to pace. This was old and hackneyed and seen in countless movies about sea Captains and men in positions of authority in extreme circumstances. But cliche had its place, as well. Sometimes a bit of theater, no matter how familiar, was necessary, precisely *because* it was familiar.

"The crew is understandably shaken. They are shocked, they are wounded to their souls, and sooner, rather than later, they are going to start looking for someone to blame, if it hasn't already started." He looked at Bobby V. "They're going to want to blame you, sir, because you are the one they saw give the order. We cannot allow that to happen." He looked at all of them, each in turn, making certain they understood. "Therefore, I want you to tell them it was all my fault. I want you to convince them that it was entirely my responsibility and that I am the one to blame - the *only* one. Were I to try and do it myself, it would put me in a position where I'd have to explain myself to them, and as we've already discussed, that cannot be. You must do this. Each of you. All of you."

He stopped his pacing directly in front of the center of his desk, giving it that final touch of theater. "They are going to grumble, they are going to grouse, they are going to bitch, and they are going to hate me for this. Let them."

"Sir," Commander Swedberg tried to begin, but Hall cut him off.

"Just this once, XO, just this once, all of you, I want you to let this go on. Do not stomp on it. Let them focus their anger on me." He looked toward Wheeler and Montrose, who were standing next to each other. "How goes the plan for the Crossing Ceremony?"

Wheeler - for once - was momentarily speechless. The abrupt change of subject and colossal non-sequitur, made him pause, but only for a moment. "More or less ready, sir," he said. "All we need to do is pick a time."

Hall nodded, then looked at the Engineer. "EO, how much fuel did we get?"

LCDR Douglas Chezku stiffened a bit, as if coming to attention. "Topped off on JP5. That's the good news."

"And the bad?" Hall asked, patiently.

"Three-quarters on DFM," he said. "We had to leave before..."

"Yes," Hall said, nodding. He looked to Wheeler again. "I'm afraid the "X" is out of the question, then. Can't afford to waste fuel."

"Yes, sir," the Lieutenant replied, his expression neutral, but Hall had long ago learned to read men's eyes, and Wheeler's registered a touch of disappointment.

"Having said that," Hall continued, "We will still be crossing the Date Line, and there are many among us who have not had the pleasure." he said. "The Ceremony will go on." He breathed in - almost, but not quite a sigh. "Some of them may not want to participate. Encourage them otherwise."

"Should we make it mandatary?" LTjg Montrose asked, the skepticism evident in her tone.

"No," he replied, simply. "At least not overtly." This was met with more than a few raised eyebrows. "Nudge them in the right direction. We need them to blow off steam, or we risk an explosion."

129

"Good to see you're still breathing, Petty Officer McMullen," Molly said, as they all gathered on the Bridge. The ship was maintaining station with the Dynamic Positioning System doing the work. The only one they were waiting for was Bill Schaeffer, still down in Radio.

Jonesy admired the way she was holding up. No, it was more than that. She carried herself differently. In spite of her new and awesome responsibility, and the insanity that had swept the ship during this bloody night, she was now calm, and solemn and utterly professional. It didn't make what he had to say any easier.

"As a reward for having survived," she continued addressing McMullen, "I'd now like you to do a survey of all the electrical systems throughout the entire ship. We need to make sure everything works, and keeps working. Understood?"

"Yes, Ma'am."

"Ma'am?" Jonesy said, reluctantly.

"Jones?"

"If I may, there's something we should probably do first," he said. "A matter of security."

"Which is?" She asked, looking at him with cool eyes.

He hesitated, really not wanting to go there, but knowing he needed to. "We need to ensure that all of us are infection free," he said, hedging.

She stared at him for a moment longer, then nodded. "Very well."

"Unfortunately, we don't have a corpsman," he said, still hesitant.

"I'm aware of that," she replied, her tone held just a tinge of annoyance.

He took a deep breath. "The only way I can think to do this is to give each other a visual examination," he said, pausing. "For bites."

She stared at him and blinked.

"It would require us all to...strip, Ma'am."

She blinked again, her skin tone flushing pink. Jonesy flicked his eyes to the others and saw they were pointedly looking anywhere but at their new CO. She looked at him a moment longer, then gave a small grunt of frustration - whether with the situation in general, or with him in particular, he did not know.

"Oh for Christ's sake," she said, moving toward the interior Bridge door. "Chartroom, Jonesy," she barked. "Now."

He followed, obediently. As he was closing the Bridge door behind him, he heard Harold mutter, "Lucky guy."

"Shut your fucking pie hole," Duke snapped. "You heard the man. Strip people. And if anyone grabs my ass..." the voice cut off as Jonesy closed the Chartroom door.

Without a word, he began to de-rig. Slowly, but surely, he un-clipped the M4 and set it on the desk, then removed the machete in its sheath from his harness belt, then undid the straps of the harness. He ripped the velcro from first one thigh holster, then the next, then the first calf-sheath, then the next, and placed all his guns and knives and ammo next to the M4. He shrugged out of the body armor and added it to the pile, then turned around.

Molly was facing the chart table with her back to him. She was not disrobing.

"If you'd rather somebody else did this..."

She stiffened, then her shoulders began to slump, bit by bit. "No," she said in a very quiet voice. Finally, she turned to face him. "Jonesy," she said softly. "We can't..."

"I know," he said, just as softly.

"Ever."

"I know."

She stared at him for a moment longer, then her lips quirked into a crooked smile. "You said that a little too easily," she said, then turned her back on him again and began to get undressed.

"You know me," he said, chuckling, then he, too, turned his back.

"Yes, I do," she said, and Jonesy thought he detected a touch of sadness in her voice.

They disrobed in a silence weighted down by an unresolved past that he wasn't sure he wanted to remain unresolved. At the same time, however, he also recognized the impossibility of the situation. The words he'd uttered to his subordinates so many times over so many years - *you ain't gotta like it, you just gotta do it* - came back at him with a vengeance.

Finally, he heard her heave a heavy sigh. "Why didn't you ever call me?" She asked. "No, wait. Forget it. I don't want to know."

He laughed, and tried to keep it to himself, but ultimately it slipped into audible range and danced around the room. "Don't strain you brain, Molly. The answer is simple," he said. "You told me not to.":

"And you believed me?"

They still had their backs to each other, but he knew what the expression on her face would look like: that mixture of exasperation and humor and anger and amusement he'd always managed to get out of her, both before and during their affair. "Yeah, I'm funny that way," he said, pulling off his tee shirt. "I tend to do what people say they want me to do."

"You're an idiot."

"Yes, Ma'am."

He dropped his trousers, then his underwear, then turned to face her. As if in some rehearsed and intricate ballet, she turned at the same time. They stood, facing each other, neither of them saying a word, and both of them stark naked. He watched her eyes slowly, inexorably descend from his face, to his chest, to his abs, and finally to...

"Why do I think you're enjoying this?" she said, her gaze lingering on his half-erect penis.

"Because my eyes are open?" He quipped.

"Wasn't thinking about your eyes," she said, and finally looked at his face again.

"Oh just ignore that," he replied.

"Right," she said with a tanker truck full of sarcasm. She sighed again, and said: "Let's get this over with."

Jonesy eased open the interior Bridge door and called: "Everybody decent?" He heard an affirmative reply at almost the same moment he heard the door to Radio click open behind him. Bill popped his head out.

"Got something," he said, as he headed past them and onto the Bridge. He took a look around at the assembled crew, some of whom were still partially undressed. "Did I miss something?"

"Whatchya got?" Molly asked.

"An EPIRB," he replied (referring to an Emergency Position Indicating Radio Beacon), going over to the GSB 900 on its rack near the remnants of the deep fathometer. He said it as a word (*eeperb*), rather than a series of letters. That always drove Jonesy insane when he heard it pronounced as letters on TV by people who supposedly should know better. That went double for SAR (search and rescue), which always seemed to be said as S-A-R. Didn't the idiots in Hollywood understand that acronyms were created for brevity? Didn't they make the connection that other such acronyms like FUBAR, SNAFU and BOHICA, were said and not spelled out?

A dim and distant, but still clear and readable beeping came through the speakers as Bill tuned the GSB to 406mhz. He reached over and did the same tuning on the Radio Direction Finder. The relative direction indicator pointed slightly to the right of straight ahead.

Jonesy glanced at the gyrocompass and checked the bearing. "About two-nine-zero," he said. "Somewhere towards Midway, I think." He lifted the top of the chart table and rooted around until he found a smaller scale chart. He glanced at the GPS in its rack above him, roughly plotted their position using his fingers, then slid the Wheems Plotter into position in the direction of the signal. He nodded, then looked at Molly. "Two-nine-zero will do, till we get some better information." She gave him a subtle but clear questioning look. "We only have one bearing. We need three."

She stared at the deck for a moment, mulling it over, then said: "Can you blow this up onto a maneuvering board?" she asked, indicating the chart that covered such a wide area. To get three bearings that would make any sense on a chart that covered so much ocean, they'd have to move fifty or sixty nautical miles in one direction, then turn around and go a hundred in the opposite direction. By blowing up the scale onto a maneuvering board, however, they reduced that distance to maybe ten, depending on how far the source of the signal actually was.

She turned to Duke. "You and Simmons get in the RHIB (pronounced "rib"), head ten miles south, get a bearing with the RDF, then turn around and go ten miles to the north. We'll maintain position right here." She glanced at Jonesy, who nodded.

"Yes, Ma'am," Duke said, then turned and headed below, adding: "Move your ass, Harold."

Jonesy looked at her and smiled. "Looks like we got us a SAR case."

130

They located the signal roughly six hundred and eighty nautical miles from their original position, using the method Molly devised. In theory, they shouldn't have been able to pick it up at that range, but every now and then (or so Bill explained) you could get an atmospheric bounce that would spread any signal for a thousand miles or more. Jonesy remembered sitting at the PACAREA Command Center, in Alameda, CA, and hearing radio chatter from Sector Honolulu on VHF, which should only have been line-of-sight, so it was within the realm of possibility. Of course, the world was pretty damned empty, these days - of live, sentient people to talk on a radio, at any rate, so maybe that had something to do with it, as well. Whatever the case, Jonesy would take it. They needed some good news.

While Duke and Harold had been taking their little boat ride, the others began the grizzly task of removing the bodies of their shipmates. Those below deck were moved to the Forward Hold, and once Duke returned, they popped the Buoy Deck hatch with the crane and hoisted them up on pallets. It was gut wrenching, heartbreaking work, but it had to be done, and so they had done it.

The worst part, however, was cleaning the blood and guts and shit from the compartments where the various fights had taken place. Three of the staterooms were so bad, Jonesy almost recommended welding the doors shut, but decay and rot spread insects and disease, so if they wanted to survive the aftermath, they had to clean it all.

Frank had taken the Engine Room, and Molly had taken the Bridge, which left Jonesy, Bill, Dan, and Gary to clean the worst of it, until Duke and Harold returned to give them a hand. By the time they neared the EPIRB signal, two and a half days later, the worst of it was over - except for dealing with the emotion..

Jonesy had thought he was becoming hardened, and could no longer feel *anything* like a normal human being. All the killing, all the senseless death, all the guilt and horror, should have made him desensitized, numb, immune. It had not.

When this was over, he really was going to have to get shitfaced.

The signal turned out to be a sweet little sailboat, the *Pretty, Pretty*. It bobbed on a calm sea, apparently empty. But appearances, as they used to say, could be deceiving, and so Jonesy went armed to the teeth, and since they might be able to salvage the boat, or at least take the fuel and some of the parts, Molly decided (at Jonesy's suggestion) to send Frank along, instead of Duke.

The boat had already been moved to the rail, so Jonesy and Frank climbed aboard and sat on the sponson as they began to lower it onto the sea. Jonesy brought along a gym bag, which he put on the deck at his feet.

They were away in less than three minutes, thanks to Duke's practiced handling of the drop, and in a bit more than two, were tying off onto the Transom Deck of the S/V *Pretty, Pretty*. It was an apt name, for it was a pretty boat - or had been before the Fall, and however many days it spent adrift. She was blue and white and forty-five feet long, with nice lines and a straight, but empty mast that reached toward a windy sky that would never propel it onward again.

They tied off and climbed aboard to eerie silence. The sound of the *Sass* could be heard in the distance, but it was subdued and almost covered by the breeze. Tackle slapped against the aluminum yard arm. Nothing moved. No one came on deck to greet them.

They found the EPIRB, its light flashing in its rack on the bulkhead just forward of the steering console. A cast metal car (a Trans Am, to be precise - black, like something out of *Smokey and the Bandit*) sat just to one side.

An abandoned child's toy...

Jonesy and Frank looked at each other. A chill ran up Jonesy's spine.

He opened the gym bag and pulled out two respirators, a can of disinfectant spray, and a jar of *Vapo-Rub*. He handed one of the respirators to Frank, then tucked the spray can under his arm, opened the jar and offered it to his friend.

"It's gonna stink in there," he said.

He had seen people in movies use the stuff to mask the smell of corpses, most famously in *The Silence of the Lambs.*, a movie that had scared the shit out of him. Apparently, so had Frank, who dipped a finger in the jar, and wiped a glob of it beneath his nose.

"It puts the lotion on its skin, or else it gets the hose again."

The chill was back, doing wind sprints along Jonesy's vertebrae. He wiped some of the sharp, medicinal-smelling stuff beneath his own nose, then dropped the jar into the bag at his feet and donned the respirator.

"Let's get this over with," he said, his voice muffled by the mask. *Before I lose my nerve*, he added - but only inside his own skull. He re-fastened the helmet, dropped the face shield, then opened the outer hatch and stepped inside, holding his .45 at the ready - just in case.

131

Molly and Harold watched from the open Bridge door. She supposed at least one of them should be paying attention to the radar, but the Dynamic Positioning System was holding them on station, they were two hundred and forty-three miles from the nearest point of land (Midway Atoll), and there hadn't been a single contact in days, until they found the sailboat. She glanced down onto the Boat Deck, and saw Duke and Gary also watching their shipmates disappear into the bowels of the unknown vessel.

She felt like she should be doing something - issuing orders, acting like a Commanding Officer - some damned thing, *any* damned thing, other than watching two of the eight survivors of the *Sassafras* disaster vanish into God Knew What was waiting for them. But she shoved the thought down and locked it away, tight as a bank vault.

This was the job. Like it or not, want it or not, she was in command - their *Glorious Leader*, for good or ill.

Uncle John had once told her a quote from Admiral Chester Nimitz, the man in charge of all Naval forces in the Pacific, during WW2: "If put in a position of leadership, lead." She'd nodded sagely at the time, as if she understood - which she hadn't. She might understand it now. It meant, make a decision, stick by that decision, take responsibility for that decision, and watch as others got on with the business of executing that decision - even if it meant putting them in harm's way.

But they could die.

She shoved that thought into the vault, as well, and spun the combination.

The moments ticked on. The DPS maneuvered the ship. The engines and generator chugged away below. They waited.

The hatch popped open with a bang, sending a bolt straight into her heart as Jonesy and Frank staggered out onto the deck of the sailboat. Frank fell to one knee and stayed there, bowing and shaking his head. Jonesy paused in the hatchway, then stepped toward the rail on the far side, pulling off his helmet and respirator as he went. He leaned his free hand on the rail, leaned his torso over the rail and convulsed, as if he were about to vomit. He did not, but it looked as if it had been a near thing.

Molly glued the binoculars to her eyes, willing them to make sense out of the tableau. They didn't. Something had happened. Something bad.

After a period of that odd sort of time that could be moments or could be hours, Jonesy straightened and moved back from the rail. He seemed to wipe at his eyes before he turned . *Were those tears?* She couldn't tell, but something was clearly wrong. And all she could do to help her shipmate, her friend, her (former) lover, was wait.

He said something they obviously couldn't hear to Frank, who looked up at him, then raised a hand toward him, as if in supplication.

But no. That was just Molly's imagination getting the better of herself. Jonesy grasped the offered hand and pulled Frank to his feet. They stared at each other for a moment, then Jonesy slapped his friend on the side of the helmet, and reached for his radio.

"Sass, Boarding Team, over..."

Molly stared at the comco in her hand, scarcely remembering that she had brought it with her when she and Harold exited the Bridge. She brought it to her lips.

"Go Boarding Team, over..."

"Three dead," Jonesy's voice said, sounding flat and emotionless over the radio. "Two adults and..." he paused. "One child."

He didn't say "Over," but she'd heard the faint electronic pop as the handset key was released.

"Understood," she said. "Over..."

He took a deep breath she could see, even without the binoculars, then continued. "Vessel is not worth recovering," he said, not explaining. "But it is filled with fuel and stores. Recommend we strip it of everything..." he paused again. "Then burn it to the waterline. Over..."

132

Jonesy made a slicing motion across his throat, signaling Duke to shut off the pump sucking all the diesel fuel from the *Pretty, Pretty.* He disconnected the intake hose, then watched as the large Bosun Mate pulled it onto the buoy tender.

They'd covered the bodies of the mother and...*child...*, but left the father where he was. Hadn't seemed any point in moving him.

Frank set a large cardboard box heavily onto the bar. "This is the last of the dry stores." He peered into it. "Pasta, mostly, but a few spices. Gary ought to be happy."

"What's left?" Jonesy asked. They had been at it for hours. Duke and Harold had both offered to come over and help (Harold reluctantly) but he turned them down. Two people with nightmares would be plenty, he'd thought. Besides, they'd needed to stay aboard for the fuel offload. Dan needed to stay in the Engine Room, Bill needed to remain locked in the Radio Room, and Molly needed to be on the Bridge. That would have only left Gary to handle the fuel transfer, and Gary was a cook. Competent, yes, absolutely, and certainly capable, but still a cook. Fuel Ops were not in his job description - nor did he want them to be.

"Just the booze," Frank replied. They had both taken off their helmets and respirators some time ago.

The interior still stank of decomposition, but they opened all the port holes and exterior doors, closed the husband into his stateroom, and then Jonesy sprayed the fuck out of the main cabin, using the entire can of disinfectant. They still had the globs of *Vapo-Rub* beneath their noses, and, after a while, they'd just gotten used to the stench.

Amazing, the shit you can get used to, Jonesy mused.

From what they could tell of the scenario they'd discovered on entering the interior, the child - a boy of perhaps ten - caught the virus and turned. He'd *mangled* the mother. Looked like something out of *Jack the Ripper*, but without the knives. The father had then, apparently, killed the child with a knotted length of nylon line, then used more of that line to hang himself from a beam in the Master Stateroom.

Jonesy wondered if there was enough alcohol in this entire fallen world to blot the memory of it from his mind. He doubted it, but looking at the bar, he thought they might be able to make a really good start.

There were excellent (and expensive) bottles of scotch, rum, gin, vodka, bourbon, and (gods be praised!) even a full case of *El Tesoro de Don Felipe*, Jonesy's favorite *Anejo* tequila. There were also numerous bottles of various liqueurs, including, he saw with a pang of loss, BM2 Masur's favorite: *Cointreau*. The man had drunk nothing but the orange liqueur, every chance he got - which was often - and he usually ended up face down in some inconvenient gutter as a result. Many was the time Jonesy or Frank or Duke or Harold or Bill or (name pretty much every other enlisted crew member) carried the poor bastard home.

Now he was dead, and nobody would carry him home ever again.

They loaded several boxes filled with bottles into the RHIB. When they were done, and with barely enough room in the small boat to hold the two of them, they returned to the main cabin to take care of the final task.

That poor family on that poor sailboat had suffered true tragedy. Jonesy had never seen anything so tragic, and he was sure he'd remember it for the rest of his days. Simply scuttling the boat and allowing the ocean to swallow it whole didn't seem to be enough, somehow. They needed to burn the tragedy out; to scour it from the earth, to leave no trace - not even at the bottom of the sea.

He picked up the bottle of *Cointreau* from the bar, where they had set a half-dozen bottles they'd known none of them would ever drink. He stared at it for a moment, silently remembering his shipmate, then pulled the cork and sniffed it. The shit smelled like kerosene.

"Masur," he said, lifting the bottle toward the heavens. He took a swig, and nearly gagged. "Good God that's foul," he swore, took another drink and passed it to Frank.

"Revolting," he choked, took another drink, then passed it back to Jonesy.

"Let's hope it burns better than it tastes," Jonesy said, and heaved the bottle across the compartment to smash against the far bulkhead. Alcohol fumes instantly filled their nostrils.

Frank picked up one of the other bottles. "Butterscotch Schnapps?" He asked, incredulous. "Who the fuck drinks this shit?" he asked no one, then tossed the bottle over his shoulder, where it smashed against a different bulkhead.

A bottle of rotgut vodka Jonesy had seen at several of the seedier bars he'd frequented went crashing into the galley. Another of disreputable bourbon went sailing through the open door of the smaller stateroom. They both ignored the NASCAR decorations and child-sized bed.

Soon, only two bottles remained: one of some unpronounceable Greek shit smelling of licorice, and a full bottle of *Everclear.*

Frank pointed to it and asked: "What?"

"No idea," Jonesy answered. "That couch, however..."

They both stared at it, at the strange, blue paisley sort of pattern, bordered by green, yellow and purple flowers.

"Hideous," Frank said.

"Truly," Jonesy said, pulling his eight-inch Gerber from the sheath on his left hip. It looked like he could use it to carve a cow. He motioned with his head toward the Master Stateroom, where the Master himself hung swaying in the gentle swell. "Take the Greek shit and douse the bed and carpet, then leave the door open." He added, as he began to shred the couch cushions.

The red flare shot a nearly flat trajectory from the RHIB to the sailboat, ricocheted off the superstructure, and bounced on the after deck, where it met the puddle of *Everclear* trailing from the deck, through the door, and into the trashed main cabin. Nothing happened for a moment. Then two... Then three... With a muted *whump*, the alcohol fumes ignited, and flames leapt out of the open port holes.

Jonesy turned the RHIB toward the *Sassafras*, and left the S/V *Pretty, Pretty* to its fiery, and watery grave.

133

Lydia Claire stood to one side of the Flight Deck, watching some of the Golden Dragons set up the chute that would eventually be filled with assorted garbage that had been fermenting in the Engine Room for days, thus turning it into the Whale's Belly. She was not participating.

She hadn't joined in during the Fashion Show, nor the Talentless Show, which word on the Mess Deck said was hilarious. She hadn't had the desire; hadn't had the heart. Truth be told, she didn't have the heart for much of anything, and it sort of worried her.

She knew the root cause, of course: Guam. What happened there, what they had done, what she, by extension as a member of the crew, had done, filled her mind and her heart and her soul with a sickness that wouldn't go away. She cried herself to sleep each night - when she could sleep, which wasn't often, and wasn't much when she did.

The Captain accepted full responsibility, took the blame upon himself, and that was right, that was true. It *was* his fault - but it wasn't his fault alone, in spite of every officer and chief she talked to insisting it was.

That seemed real odd. She'd been in for quite a few years, this being her second enlistment, and she'd never heard of such open hostility and disrespect being not just allowed, but encouraged. It didn't make any sense. Only, it did.

By accepting sole responsibility, by encouraging the crew to direct their anger at him, and him alone, he was keeping it from becoming a general sense of rage and hatred, that could, if given its head, eat away at the crew until there was nothing left but the darkness. That wouldn't do anybody any good.

So she understood it, intellectually, but that didn't change a single thing. *They* had done this. The crew of the USCGC *Polar Star* had not just refused to help those in distress, but actively repelled them when they were screaming to be rescued. Those screams haunted her nightmares, which was why she didn't sleep much. But that had its own price tag. The dreams needed to be dreamt, the system needed to be cleansed, and so if she wasn't allowing it to happen in the normal manner, if she wasn't sleeping and allowing herself to dream, then the dreams would come of their own accord while she was awake - if for no other reason than she went through the motions so tired, she might as well have been sleepwalking.

As if to provide proof, she felt, rather than heard, one of those screams swelling inside her mind, growing and pulsating, like a living, breathing thing, which was why she let out a tiny scream of her own, when somebody tapped her on the shoulder. LT Wheeler stood there, looking at her.

"Lydia," he said, in a bemused tone, the corners of his lips curling into a smile. "Somebody walk over your grave?"

Yeah, she thought, as her heart raced away to who knew where. *The entire fucking world.*

"You...startled me," she said.

"Sorry about that," he replied, giving the obligatory response. "I've been wanting to talk to you."

"Oh?" was all she managed to say, as her heart finally dropped from her throat and resumed its rightful place in her chest cavity.

"I've been talking to some people," he began. "People who care about you."

Her heart began to sink, now, heading toward her belly or her nether regions or just looking for another way out. She didn't respond.

"You aren't participating in the festivities. People have noticed."

Anger began to swell within her. What right did anybody have to talk about her behind her back - to an officer, no less? This was betrayal! This was bullshit!

He seemed to sense what she was thinking. "You have friends on board, you know," he said. "Quite a few of them. And they are concerned," he added. "So am I."

"I'm fine," she said, giving an obligatory answer of her own.

"Bullshit," he said, flatly. She looked at him. "You're not fine. I'm not fine. Nobody on this whole damned ship is fine." She continued to stare at him. This wasn't officer talk. Sure, the Coast Guard was far less formal than the other services, but there had always been some sort of separation. You didn't make friends with them, you didn't hang out with them. If you met them on liberty in some foreign port, it was always uncomfortable, always strained. And you never *ever* heard them suggest that the world was swirling down the toilet, and yet he just had.

She didn't reply, so he kept talking. "What happened was terrible, but you understand, we had no choice. It was quite literally them or us."

"So we chose ourselves," she said, her voice low, almost a whisper.

"Yes, we did," he said. "And for one simple reason."

"Which is?" she asked, her tone bordering on outright insubordination. He ignored it.

"We are the Lifesavers, Lydia."

"Yeah, we did a great job of that!" she spat.

"We did the only thing we could do," he said. "The entire world needs saving, in case you haven't noticed." She cocked an eyebrow at him, but didn't respond. But she wanted to. Oh boy did she want to. She wanted to give him a piece of her mind that would drop him like a punch from Mike Tyson. He didn't give her the chance. "As far as we know, we're the only intact Coast Guard platform left. We haven't heard from anyone else in days. Not PACAREA, not Honolulu, not any of the other ships. Not from the Navy, or from some headquarters in Cheyenne Mountain, or wherever the Command structure is hiding and waiting this out. We are alone, and the entire world needs saving."

She locked eyes with him, trying to spot the lie, trying to sense the bullshit that must be there, but she saw nothing.

"What good would we have done anyone if we allowed ourselves to get infected?"

She said nothing. She knew this stuff, logically, at any rate; knew that what he was saying was true. But that didn't make the horror of it, the wrongness of it, any less harsh, any less heartbreaking.

"Are you familiar with the Serenity Prayer?"

She nodded. It was her mother's favorite. The memory stabbed at her heart, but on top of everything else, it felt like a pinprick. Her mother was dead, most likely. Everybody she knew or cared about back in Alabama was probably dead. But added to all the rest, it seemed insignificant, somehow, as if her brain couldn't fit any more bad news, bad thoughts, bad feelings into it.

"Grant me the Serenity to accept the things I cannot change," he said. "You remember that bit?"

"Yes," she said, her voice feeling small and insignificant.

"We can't do anything about the plague. We can't do anything about all the death and horror and tragedy. It's there, it's real, and there's nothing we can do to change it."

She nodded, as she felt tears begin to well in her eyes.

"The next part is the important bit," he said. "The Courage to change the things we can." She nodded. "What we can do, what we *will* do, is rescue what's left. But to do that, we first need to survive. Can't save anybody if we're dead."

"No," she said. He hadn't asked for her opinion, but it felt right to give it, anyway.

"So the last bit, the Wisdom to know the difference, says we did exactly what we had to do. No dishonor, no betrayal, no failure. We did the right thing, the only thing. And because we did that, we can get on with the rest of it." he said, and then took her by the shoulders. "To do that, we need each and every one of us, and that includes you."

"What does swimming through garbage have to do with saving the rest of the world?" she snapped, gesturing toward the now complete Whale's Belly.

"This crew needs to blow off steam," he said, simply. "I need to. *You* need to. We need to clean out the pipes, as it were. Purge ourselves of the past, so we have the strength to face the future. Can you understand that?"

"Yes, sir," she said, automatically, though she wasn't at all sure that she did, or could, or ever would.

134

Molly pulled the throttle to All Stop, and engaged the DPS. The Bow and Stern Thrusters kicked in with an almost imperceptible whir.

"Looks like Midway," Jonesy said laconically, scanning the atoll with binoculars.

Laysan Albatrosses (commonly known as gooney birds), flitted about the shoreline of Sand Island, dotting it with moving specs of white. There were hundreds of them. Molly knew - both from conversations with her Uncle John and from reading the Sailing Directions - that there were, in fact, *thousands* of them throughout the Atoll. Why the birds picked this remote bit of rock in the middle of nowhere, she did not know. What had once been the scene of the most significant battle in the Pacific War, during WWII, was now a bird and wildlife sanctuary.

The Entrance Channel, between Sand Island and Eastern Island was clearly visible, and it would have been a simple matter in the past to steam right in and tie up at the pier. But, number one, the Coast Guard, who used to maintain the Aids in this area in days gone by (with the original, 180-foot version of the *Sassafras*), pulled the last of them out in the mid-Nineties, and the last Naval personnel departed the island in Ninety-Seven. There were supposedly Marker Buoys and Range Boards within the channel and harbor, but supposedly didn't cut it when the alternative was grinding to a stop on some rocky shoal. The second problem, of course, was the possibility of zombies.

"Midway Harbormaster, Midway Harbormaster, this is United States Coast Guard Cutter *Sassafras*, United States Coast Guard Cutter *Sassafras*, channel one-six, over," Molly said into the radio mic. All she got for the oxygen expenditure was static. It's all any of them had gotten for the last three hours.

"Well, shit," Jonesy said.

"Couldn't have said it better myself," Molly replied, in an offhand way. "Better get Duke and Harold into the RHIB."

"Be a good idea to make it Duke and me," Jonesy said. She gave him a questioning look. Jonesy nodded toward the atoll. "Just in case." She nodded. He picked up the 1-MC. "Duke, contact the Bridge," he said, and she could hear the pipe echo both through the bowels of the ship and into the quiet of the summer's day from the loudspeakers on the superstructure.

She caught movement out of the corner of her eye. At first it just looked like a flurry of gooney birds, but she quickly saw the reason for it: a human figure stepped out of the brush and onto the sandy beach. The birds seemed to avoid him like the plague.

"Either Midway just became a nudist colony," Jonesy said, pointing to the naked man.

"Or there are zombies," Molly said, finishing the thought and the sentence.

The phone rang and Jonesy picked it up. "Duke," he said, without waiting for the usual exchange of greetings. "Gear up. All the toys. And get the RHIB ready," he said. "You and I are going hunting."

135

Blackjack Charlie peered into the distance. He'd once heard a quote somewhere (wasn't sure where, and it really didn't matter) about the sea and sailors: *The sea to a sailor is like a blank page to a writer: filled with adventure and endless possibilities.* It seemed apt, in the current situation. He had no idea where they were going, no idea what they were going to do when they got there, but the possibilities seemed infinite.

He glanced back over his shoulder at his two remaining crew. Felix Hoffman, the chemist, and George Potter, the Mechanical Engineer (one, a drug dealer, the other, a murderer), who joined him on the Bridge because they - not surprisingly - wanted to know the plan.

"What are we doing, boss?" Felix asked. At least he was still being respectful. At least there didn't seem to be the imminent threat of mutiny. That was good. He'd hate to have to kill them.

"And where are we going?" George asked, although his tone wasn't so polite. *Have to watch him,* Blackjack thought. The man was drunk - had been drunk, pretty much since they'd set sail. The booze would last longer now that there were fewer mouths to feed, as it were, but he really should take tighter control of the supply.

None of which negated the validity of the questions, for which he had very few answers. He had goals, he had concepts, but no actual plans to back them up. *When in doubt,* he thought, *baffle them with bullshit.*

"Well, me boyos," he said, affecting a theatrical accent. "Tis the life of Pirates, for us."

"That didn't work too well for Joe-Boy and the others, now, did it?" George said, derisively.

"That didn't work," he snapped, "Because we didn't know what we were heading into." He turned to face them. "I'll admit it," he continued. "That was my mistake, but it's not one I'm likely to repeat."

"Especially if we don't give you the opportunity," George replied, looming toward him.

Quick as a rattlesnake, Blackjack Charlie whipped out his namesake and smashed George just over the left temple. The drunken bastard dropped like the proverbial puppet with cut strings. He turned to look at Felix. "Any problems?"

"No!" he yelped, backpedaling. "Sir," he added, to Charlie's great pleasure and relief.

"First thing you do," Charlie said, "is gather up all the booze and put it in my cabin."

"All of it?"

"Don't worry," Charlie soothed, adopting a friendlier tone. "It may be a while before we get more, and so it's high time we started rationing." He looked at the unconscious form of the Mechanical Engineer. "Don't think he'll be arguing much after he wakes up."

"No, sir," Felix was quick to agree.

"I do have a plan," he lied. "But I'm still working out the details." He was about to elaborate, had a really good line of bullshit just waiting to come out, when the VHF radio interrupted him.

"...Mayday," the voice crackled through the static. "Uh, Mayday. This is the *Point of Order*. Anyone up on sixteen?"

Blackjack Charlie smiled. *Chance favors the prepared mind,* he thought, as he reached for the radio.

136

"Alright, Harold. Take us in. *Carefully*," Jonesy said, waving in the general direction of the entrance channel.

He and Duke were fully rigged up this time. They wore the standard black tactical uniform, plus the addition of a firefighting hood, tucked into the shirt, with the shirt collar buttoned all the way up. Their pant legs were tucked into, and taped to, their boots, and their long shirt sleeves were taped to their full dexterity tactical gloves, which were themselves worn over nytrile medical gloves they'd gotten from Sick Bay. Over the uniform, they wore full MOPP gear, with yet another hood, over which they placed their helmets, with ballistic face shields, and carbon fiber mouth and chin guards, equipped with integrated, voice activated microphones, tuned to channel twenty-one. Over all of this, they wore knee and elbow pads, plus body armor.

Naturally, of course, they were also wearing sunglasses. It was, after all, important to look cool.

Feeling cool, however, was not on the menu. Taped up and sealed in, then wrapped in MOPP Level Four gear was like standing in a sauna upon a volcano in the middle of August during a heatwave. But given the choice of sweating for a (hopefully) short while, or becoming either dead or a zombie after being bitten, they chose to perspire.

Jonesy wasn't completely, absolutely, one-hundred percent guaranteed sure all these precautions would keep them from getting bitten, but if they didn't work, it would not be from lack of trying. Heat stroke, however, might be a different kettle of fish, so they both carried water bottles.

On top of everything else, they wore the tactical harness and carried both weapons and ammo, but also an assault pack, containing more ammo, as well as line, flashlights, and various other items they thought might prove useful. Duke carried two 9mm pistols in thigh holsters, a kukri-machete in a sheath, and his two hammers. Jonesy questioned the addition of the hammers, but Duke had said, simply, "They work." Couldn't argue with that. He also carried a 12 gauge riot gun.

Jonesy took arming to a whole new level. He wore two thigh holsters, with two .45s, a double shoulder rig with two Baretta nines, his Bowie knife and dive knife in calf sheaths, and two - count them, two - kukri-machetes, one strapped to each side of his pack, so he could pull them over his shoulders and use them as he had the batons. He also held the M4, on a retractable chest rig, and a shitload of magazines for everything.

Molly hadn't questioned that he had enough weapons and ammo to start a small tribal war, but she had cocked a questioning eyebrow. He'd shrugged and said: "Always Ready."

"If Midway is an island in the middle of nowhere," Harold shouted over the wind and engine noise of the RHIB, of which he was the cox'n. He was in his normal uniform, with the addition of a light, dayglow orange float coat. He wasn't going ashore. "How could they possibly have gotten infected?"

That was a damned good question Jonesy had been asking himself since they first started getting no response from the Harbormaster. When they made the ninety degree turn toward the inner harbor, they got their answer. Three sailboats, ranging in size between forty and seventy feet lay at anchor on the south side of the basin.

"Ain't that a bitch?" Jonesy said.

"What?" Harold asked, as if he'd missed something important.

"Those boaties thought they were coming to a safe haven. Someplace they could wait out the plague. And the people on shore thought they were doing the right thing helping them out." Jonesy explained.

"So?" Harold asked.

Jonesy shrugged. "Nobody knew they were letting death come through the front door."

"How fucking poetic," Duke jibed.

"Feel free to blow me," Jonesy replied.

Insults thus given and duly returned, they began to scan the area, looking for the best approach.

"Head for the seaplane ramp," Duke told Harold, pointing to an old and chewed-looking square of concrete just shy of the dividing line between sand and trees on the western side of the harbor.

Jonesy turned on the radio he had tucked underneath his armor and signaled Duke to do the same. "Sass, Sass Two, Over," he said, using the designation for that particular small boat. Sass One was a Motor Surf Boat, of roughly the same size, but without the inflatable sponsons.

"Sass Two go," Molly's voice came over the airwaves.

"Making the approach to the beach. Over."

"Roger," she replied. "Don't get killed. Over."

"That was my plan," he said, standing and readying himself for the jump onto the ramp. He knew, without thinking, that Harold would waste no time in getting the flying fuck away from shore just as soon as they were off. It happened exactly as he thought it would. They hit the concrete, and the RHIB roared away. The evolution took maybe fifteen seconds.

Once Sass Two was away, they stood on the slab in near total silence. Jonesy could hear the deep thrum of the RHIB engine, but it was distant, and somehow disconnected. He knew the wind was blowing, because he could see its effects on the trees to their right, but he couldn't feel it or hear it inside all of the gear. They stood there, waiting.

Nothing happened.

And then it all happened at once.

137

"...so I discovered I'm the only non-insane person left in the building," Amber said into the secure radio set. She was talking to *Sassafras* again, which, as near as she could tell, was the only ship out there. Or at least the only Coast Guard one. She knew the Navy had to have assets out there. The *Ronald Reagan* Carrier Group had been returning from the South China Sea, after joint operations with the *Theodore Roosevelt* Group off of Korea, and the *George Washington* was supposed to be somewhere near San Diego, as was the *Carl Vincent*. All of which was speculation, of course, because the Navy didn't tell the Coast Guard where their fleet was.

"At least you've got that going for you," the electronically-altered voice of whom she now knew to be Bill Schaeffer said.

"Lucky me!" she replied. "What's your status?"

"There are eight of us left." Amber couldn't tell for sure, given all the cryptological crap happening with the signal, but it sounded as if he were simply stating a fact - no opinion, no feeling. *Just the facts, Ma'am.* "Thirty-nine dead. Forty-one, including Medavoy's wife and child."

"That...sucks," she said.

"Yes it does," he replied.

"How can you still run the ship?" she asked.

"Nobody is sleeping much," he replied. "Plus, we caught a SAR case. EPIRB on a sailboat, two-hundred fifty miles East of Midway."

"Survivors?" she asked, hoping for some good news.

"Three aboard," he said. "All dead."

Her heart, which had been bouncing enough to be considered a basketball, sank yet again. It did not rebound. The crowd did not go wild. There were no cheers. There weren't even any tears.

If she started crying, she might never stop, and that wouldn't do her any good. She'd never been much of a crier - even when she was a little kid. Oh, she had a temper, alright. Her mother had taken great delight at regaling family gatherings with tales of her outbursts, but tears had not been her normal response to anything. Lately, however, it was looking like a good idea. But once it started, Niagra Falls would look like a leaky faucet in comparison.

"What's your–" She had been meaning to ask for their plan, when the lights blinked out. No warning, no flicker, just darkness. One moment. Two. Three. Her heart apparently decided the pit of her stomach was no longer a suitable location, and was seeking accomidations elsewhere at some higher elevation within her torso as she waited for the Emergency Generator to kick in. Four. Five. Six.

At least the emergency lighting should turn on, but it wasn't. Was this it? Would she now be trapped in darkness?

Seven. Eight. Nine.

At *Ten* she heard a decided *CLICK* as the generator came on and the lights flickered back into blessed brilliance. *Thank God, Buddha, Krishna, Nebakenezzer, Noah, and any other religious figures that might be listening*, she thought, as she waited for all the systems to reboot.

She should have spent her time shutting down all the equipment so it didn't fry when the power came back up, but, number one, it had been really damned dark, and, number two, she was scared out of her damned wits. One by one, however, all the gear came back up without any increase in the ozone levels. No sparks, no smoke, no electronic screetching; just the light *beep, beep, beep* as it all came on line.

She re-keyed the code into the secure radio set and picked up the mic. "Cutter *Sassafras*, COMMSTA Honolulu. Over."

Silence. Just static. Nothing more.

"Cutter *Sassafras*, COMMSTA Honolulu. Over," she repeated, adding insistence to her tone, as if that would somehow work. It didn't.

Think, dammit, think! She thought. The antennae on the building were pretty tall, but the building itself was at sea level, which limited the range. There were repeating antennae atop Ka'ala, on Oahu, Moana Kea, on the Big Island, and Haleakala, on Maui, but if the power was out, then the power to any or all of those repeaters could also be out. The

Sassafras was a good eleven or twelve hundred miles away. Without the extra boost, the odds of reaching her weren't even worth calculating.

Amber Winkowski was alone.

138

Jonesy and Duke moved forward, slow and cautious. They were on a rocky stretch of sand on the western edge of the harbor. To the left, stood a stand of trees, then a greenbelt of sorts, filled with various grasses and a shitload of gooney birds - only a few of which had bothered to waddle out onto the sand. A road stretched northeast on the western edge of more trees.

A small, rectangular shed sat on the near edge of the first stand of trees. The door stood open, swinging slowly in the mild breeze. No one - neither person, nor zombie - poked their head out to discover the source of the boat noise.

What had once been the seaplane hangar, but was now (judging from the several cars and pickup trucks parked on the side they could see) converted to some sort of office building or workshop area, sat off to their left and inland. With no better plan, they headed toward it. Jonesy kept wondering when everything was going to go to shit, and it kept not going there, which was driving him nuts.

"Okay....," Duke said, his voice coming through the radio earpiece. "What the fuck, over?"

"Shore team, this is Sass, over." Molly's voice came through loud and clear. She didn't sound nervous, but he knew her, and knew she'd be biting her lip - internally, if not visible to the viewing public.

"Go," Jonesy said.

"What's you status, over?"

"Approaching the seaplane hangar," he replied. "No contact yet."

"Roger," she replied, and seemed about to say something else, but then apparently decided against it. "Over," she added, and Jonesy had to hand it to her. If ever there was a fish out of water, it was Ensign Molly Gordon. No amount of training at the Academy could have prepared her for what she now faced, and yet she seemed to be facing it just fine.

They approached a man door, next to what had clearly been a large overhead bay door, now rusted and decrepit. He doubted they could open it with a forklift. The man door, however, opened easily inward.

"Flashlight," he said, reaching his hand back toward Duke, who handed him one, already turned on. It was dark as fuck inside the place even with the brilliant shaft of light. Shadows loomed out of the blackness, and had Jonesy been more prone to histrionics, he might have imagined all sorts of Lovecraftian creatures waiting for them, but he wasn't, so he didn't. He didn't see much of anything else, either, except the vague shape of a large panel truck off to one side, its hood up, and its windows reflecting back into his eyes.

"Where are all the people?" he asked. There wasn't any point to the question, because Duke couldn't have any more answers than he did, but asking felt right. They moved across the vast expanse of concrete floor toward the offices at the back, judging by the glass partition sitting there, waiting for them. No heads popped up, no sounds reached their ears, no zombies arrived to attempt beheading them or rending their flesh.

The offices were as empty as the cavernous warehouse, though these, at least, showed signs of there having been live people in them at some point in the not-too distant past. A trash can lay un-emptied, a desk held papers spread out to be read, along with a mug, half-filled with cold coffee, and emblazoned with an insipid cat picture and the caption: *Hang in There, Baby*.

They opened doors, looked in closets, found nothing. It was eerie. It was annoying. Jonesy kept thinking about the fight on the Flying Bridge, as he and Molly waited for the zombies who weren't showing up to start the dance.

They located an exterior door, opened it, and found themselves at the back of the building, facing a paved road. Up ahead, they could see a crossroads, with one paralleling the shoreline and the other heading inland. They made their way to it, saw nothing in the direction they were heading, and turned inland.

At the corner, there were a series of Japanese markers. They were written in Japanese, and so incomprehensible, but Jonesy was sure it had something to do with the battle. It seemed odd, since the Japanese never made it to the island, itself, just flew over it and blew shit up, but thinking about it was an unnecessary distraction, so they kept going, past trees and grass that had been mowed within the last week or so, maybe two.

They came to a road sign at a T-junction and discovered they had been walking down Nimitz. To their right was a large building, carrying the sign: *Midway Mall*.

"Wonder if there's a Starbucks," Duke said.

Down Peters Avenue, to their left, and set back from the road maybe thirty yards, sat a series of narrow buildings that formed either an "L" or a "T." They couldn't be sure which, since they could only see the parts of it they were facing, and even then could only catch glimpses of it through the trees.

Then they did see something - or, rather, some *one* - down Peters, stumbling out onto the road in pursuit of a gooney bird. They watched, fascinated, as a naked zombie caught the bird, wrung its neck and began to tear into it with gnashing teeth. It hadn't bothered to pluck the feathers, which hung out of its mouth and floated away on the light breeze.

Jonesy looked at Duke, who shrugged. He raised the M4 to his eye, then paused, thinking better of just opening fire.

"Sass, Shore Team," he said.

"Go," Molly's voice said.

"One person in sight. Infected. Opening fire. Over," he said, then took aim and took the shot.

The crack of the 5.56mm round echoed through the silence so loud, he might as well have been using a fifty caliber black powder buffalo gun. The naked male zombie with bad table manners staggered backward, but did not fall as the bullet struck home, center mass. It stepped back, steadied itself, then looked down the road, directly at them.

Jonesy knew he hit the thing, if for no other reason than the growing blossom of blood on its chest, but apparently, the ruined brain of the poor infected bastard - whoever he had been - needed more encouragement to register that it had just received a mortal wound. He fired again, hit again, and the zombie toppled over. The second shot echoed, just as the first had done. Birds squawked somewhere in the distance, then the silence returned. He looked at Duke, then back down Nimitz the way they had come, then back at the now dead body in the middle of Peters Avenue.

A keening howl began to rise, directly behind them.

139

Blackjack Charlie eased in toward the M/V *Point of Order*, using some of his dwindling supply of diesel, rather than coming in by sail. "Get ready, but keep your guns out of sight," he said to Felix and George, as they headed out onto the port deck to handle lines.

George had not been thrilled, to say the least, when he regained consciousness with a massive headache, but he had not voiced any more objections, except when he discovered that the alcohol had been locked away in Blackjack's cabin. He was, however, keeping a hawk's eye on the man for as long as he carried one of the remaining 9mm pistols.

A lone man, in what appeared to be a yellow sweater vest stood on the foredeck of the ninety-foot Broward Motoryacht. The vessel floated on the calm ocean, not under power. Charlie hoped like Hell it wasn't because they'd run out of fuel. He needed that fuel. He needed that yacht, come to think of it. The *Daisy Jean* was a good boat, for what it was, but it wouldn't do in the long term. He needed to upgrade, and he had set his sights on this newcomer. The fact there was only one man in view, he took to be a good sign, but he was not counting his chickens.

"Ahoy!" the man shouted, waving his arms, and Blackjack Charlie shook his head.

Who the fuck said "Ahoy?" Morons, that's who. Morons and people who had no idea what they were doing upon the sea. He couldn't count the number of suicidal idiots who'd bought great big yachts, convinced they could handle them, simply because they could afford them. The bottom of the world's oceans were littered with their carcasses.

Problem was, nobody - no matter how stupid and arrogant - could have handled a ninety foot yacht this far into the Pacific without help. So where were the other people? Where was the crew? Where was the captain? He sincerely doubted Mister Sweater Vest could be anything but the walking wallet. So were they all dead? Had they all turned zombie? Or were they waiting somewhere below, planning to do to Blackjack Charlie what he was planning to do to them?

Inquiring minds want to know, he thought.

140

"...Shore Team, this is Sass, Over," Molly's voice crackled over the radio.

"Little busy!" Jonesy shouted, letting the M4 snap back to his chest as the firing pin clicked on an empty chamber. How the Hell had he gone through a thirty-round magazine that fast? Duke popped off two rounds of twelve-gauge, as Jonesy pulled his right-hand .45.

"Need to reload!" Duke shouted. Jonesy stepped in front of him and started walking backward in a three-point shooter's stance. The zombies had come from nowhere, and now they were simply *everywhere*.

There were only forty to sixty people who lived on the whole damned atoll at any one time, and it looked like all of them were pouring out of the *Midway Mall*. The building itself, wasn't much to look at, and didn't seem to be a mall at all, in any sort of traditional sense - just a large building, made of wood and aluminum, and maybe some concrete, here and there, with a peaked, shingle roof on top of it. Windows dotted the face, and a double door, half glass/half wood sat in the middle. Zombies poured out of it.

They were also coming from around the near corner, as well as through the trees, almost *behind* them as they backed down Nimitz toward the harbor. Jonesy and Duke had already killed a half-dozen of them (which Jonesy might have felt shame about, considering his shitty marksmanship, if he hadn't been too goddamned busy), but there were plenty more where they came from.

"Shore Team, what's your status? Do you need help?" Molly's voice said into his ear.

The slide locked back as he put two final rounds into the chest of a pretty, young, female zombie, wearing a tee-shirt that said: *Mama Like!*, who had come out of the woods to his right. Duke signaled he was reloaded by taking the head nearly off of a small, naked, oriental man coming down Nimitz from the Mall.

Jonesy holstered the pistol and puled the nine-millimeters from his shoulder rig. He opened fire with both at a portly guy in cook's whites, spraying most of the rounds into the surrounding trees.

Calm down, asshole, he said to himself. He was panic-firing, and he knew it. He had only fired dual pistols a few times, and then only in the controlled environment of an indoor range. This was neither indoors, nor controlled, and he was blasting away like some untrained rent-a-cop who'd seen too many action movies. He willed himself to get his shit together.

Duke fired twice more, killing first a naked elderly woman, then a clothed young man in board shorts and a pink wife-beater with tiny sailboats on it. He, at least, wasn't spraying and praying.

Jonesy snapped a look behind him, down the asphalt road they had so recently traversed. Nothing was coming that way, and the so-called "hoard" of zombies had suddenly turned into about half-a-dozen scattered individuals staggering toward them from the Mall. He holstered one of the nines - mainly as a way to resist the temptation to go all *Lethal Weapon* like an idiot - and put three rounds into the nearest attacker: a middle-aged man, wearing a *Buffy the Vampire Slayer* tee-shirt and a Speedo.

"Shore Team, report!" Molly's voice snapped.

"Large concentration," he said, sort of amazed that his voice didn't sound shrill. "Coming from the *Midway Mall*," he added, though he doubted she had any idea of where he was referring to.

"Do you need assistance? Over."

"Negative," he said, looking around, as Duke took out two more with two shotgun blasts. There were now only three zombies left in sight, and they were the slow ones, who stumbled down the road, as if dragging their tired asses home at the end of a very long day.

He holstered the remaining nine and calmly ejected the magazine from his M4, then replaced it with one from the right-side ammo pouch on his belt, and tucked the empty into another pouch on the other side. They continued walking backwards down Nimitz, but there really wasn't any great hurry. The three remaining insane inhabitants in view looked emaciated, as if they hadn't eaten in about a week, which he supposed was possible.

He pulled the charging handle, took aim and fired once (head shot), twice (another head shot), a third time (left shoulder), and finally a fourth time, with a final head shot. All three remaining zombies in view were now maggot food.

He stopped back pedaling, and Duke followed suit. They both looked around. Nothing in either direction down Nimitz, nothing coming from the turn down Peters, nothing coming at them through the trees - not even goonie birds, who had all decided there were better parts of the island to be.

"That was...*interesting*," Duke said, reloading the shotgun from his own ammo pouch.

"They should create a ride at Disneyland," Jonesy replied, in his most laconic voice.

"Zombies of the Carribean?" Duke quipped.

"Wrong ocean, dude," Jonesy said.

"Whatever," Duke replied. "Everybody's a critic."

141

"Don't mean to be critical," Lane Keely said, pulling the binoculars from his eyes and looking at John. They were on the Bridge, and the *True North* was steaming ever-westward at a sedate twelve knots. "But is there some plan beyond just going to Hawaii?"

"Yes," John said.

"And it is...?"

John looked at his friend and shipmate. They'd known each other for well over a decade. Nearly two, now that he thought about it. They'd served together on the original, one-hundred and eighty-foot *Sassafras*, and then again at Group Humboldt Bay, in the California Redwoods. Both ended up in Astoria - John, as the chief on the two-hundred-ten-foot Medium Endurance Cutter *Alert*, and Lane as an instructor at the National Motor Lifeboat School, where they intentionally made the forty-four foot MLBs capsize, as training, which John always considered to be suicidally insane.

He looked out into the setting sun, and marveled at the interplay of light and shadow and color on the mare's tail, cirrus clouds painting the sky in hues of orange and red and purple and deepest blue. He loved this time of night.

He turned to his friend. "Molly is out there," he said. "She's aboard the Sass, she can take care of herself, and she's alive."

Lane scratched his bald pate and uttered a sound that was half-sigh and half-grunt, but said nothing.

"Out with it," John said.

"Are you sure she's alive?" Lane asked.

"Yes," John replied.

"Why?" Lane asked. "How?"

That was a good question. He didn't have a clear, definable answer, but he knew the answer, anyway - sort of. He exhaled through his nose and said: "I know, because if she's not alive, if she's dead, if they're all dead, then there really isn't any point, is there?"

"Well, yeah, that makes sense," Lane said, the sarcasm just a smidge away from being written in flashing neon.

"Fine," John said. "If that doesn't satisfy, then leave it at this: Do you have any better ideas?"

"Nope," Lane admitted. "No, sir, I don't."

"Then this is the one we're going to run with," John said. "Keep calling the Sass on the GSB. Do it on the hour and the thirty, just to give you something to do." Lane nodded. "And let me know if you hear anything."

With that, John turned and headed below, praying to all the gods he didn't believe in that he was right, that Molly was alive, and that there was hope.

Please let there be hope...

142

"Henry David Goddard, at your service," Mr. Sweater Vest said, hopping onto the port side deck of the *Daisy Jean*. Blackjack Charlie knew the name from somewhere, but couldn't quite dredge up the memory. Then the newcomer did it for him.

"I am the United States Representative from the Forty-Fourth District in California," he said, reaching out a hand to shake.

Blackjack took it and shook, connecting the name. Goddard had been elected a year-and-a-half before, during the sea change that was the ascension of Donald Trump. He had been, at the time, just another Republican, from the primary bastion of conservatism in the ultra-liberal Golden State. There hadn't been anything remarkable about the man - at first. Slowly, but surely, however, the crazy began to peek its head out in various speeches and attempts at legislation.

He was, if Charlie recalled, anti-abortion (no surprise), anti-gays in the military (or anywhere else, for that matter), pro-pray the gay away, anti-vaccination, anti-climate science, anti-Evolution, pro-Creationism in schools, pro-prayer in schools, pro-Second Amendment (as if a Republican could be anything else), a Birther, a racist, and finally - and this had been the nail in his coffin - a vociferous proponent of the flat-Earth theory. None of these would have been fatal, in, say, the Bible Belt, or the Deep South, but California was a different matter. Even the most hard-line right-winger in California was nevertheless fairly well-educated, and the idea that somebody in such a position of power could actually believe - in the Twenty-First Century - that the Earth was flat, simply did not fly. When he tried to put forth a bill requiring the teaching of that theory in public schools, he effectively sealed his own fate.

The Forty-Fourth District had been Republican since time immemorial, and the party leadership wasn't about to risk losing the seat to a Democrat by running someone who actually believed something so patently batshit, and so they put forward a Primary challenger, who promptly wiped the political floor with one Henry David Goddard. He would not be getting re-elected in the next cycle - if there ever were a next cycle. Until such time, however, he was still a sitting member of the House of Representatives.

"Sir," Charlie said, affecting a tone of respect he did not feel, and then got straight to business. "What is the status of the rest of your crew?"

"All dead, I'm afraid," he said, as if commenting on the weather. "Tell me," he continued. "Have you heard anything from anyone else in authority?"

"No, sir, I have not," Charlie said, easing his hand under the untucked hem of his shirt. *Time to drop this motherfucker in the ocean,* he thought, grasping the butt of the 9mm. The last damned thing they needed was some political wack-job thinking he was in charge. He was about to pull the weapon and put a round in the asshole's forehead, when the man said something that changed everything.

"Well, then," Goddard said, clasping his hands behind his back and bouncing lightly upon his toes. "It is quite possible, under the Succession Act of 1947, that I am now the President of the United States."

143

"There are eight of us, Jonesy, " Harold said, waggling five fingers on his left hand and three on his right. "This is fucking nuts."

After the fight at the Mall, Jonesy and Duke had commandeered a pickup truck. At least it was a truck in the technical sense. In a very real sense, it was an absolute piece of shit, with rust, and bald tires, and a wonky suspension that bottomed out whenever they hit a bump or pothole - which was to say, about every thirty seconds. It had one advantage, however: they found the keys in the ignition. They used it to cruise the rest of Sand Island's 20 miles of road, finding only two more zombies and no survivors. They'd used it to pick up the dead bodies.

"Of course it's nuts, Harold," Jonesy replied. "But when has it not been?" He looked at each of them in turn. "Let's do the math, shall we? Pre-Plague, the PACAREA AOR, all by its lonesome, was eleven million square miles, right?"

"I'll take your word for it," Dan McMullen said.

They brought the Sass in, using the RHIB as a guide, and tied her off to the pier on the North side of the harbor. Gary King whipped up a delicious, fire-grilled dinner of steak and aluminum foil-baked potatoes, and they had eaten it in relative comfort on a strip of sand near the ship. And then they broke out the booze, taken from the *Pretty, Pretty*.

"Good idea," Jonesy replied, continuing. "And there were maybe twenty thousand of us in uniform to cover it. Of that, around half were in support, admin, or supply positions. Those are important, don't get me wrong, but that left ten, maybe eleven thousand of us to physically cover that eleven million square miles. Ten thousand of us to do Law Enforcement, Drug Interdiction, Immigration, Port Security, Homeland Security, Fisheries Enforcement, Marine Environmental Response, Boating Safety, Search and Rescue, and Aids to Navigation. Plus a bunch of whatever other bullshit they threw at us. And we did it, day after day, three hundred and sixty-five days a year."

"I get tired just thinking about it," Duke quipped.

Jonesy took a healthy swig from the bottle of premium tequila before resuming. "And we did it all while being the red-headed bastard stepchild of the Armed Forces. It was always, 'Thanks guys. Great job! Oh, by the way, fuck you, we're cutting your budget. Again.' Tell me I'm wrong." He pointed the bottle at Gary King. "You been in, what, twelve years? How many times have you seen that?"

Gary nodded. "Three or four."

"But we kept right on doing it, every single damned day."

"Your point is?" Harold asked.

"My point is, that this is no different."

"You *are* insane," Harold said.

"Of course I am," Jonesy agreed. "So are you. So are every one of us. We did this every day, because we were insane enough to volunteer and stubborn enough to want to do it right." Nobody disagreed. "But we didn't do it for country or flag or honor, or any of that esoteric bullshit."

"Big words," Frank said, grinning.

"Fuck you," Jonesy replied, grinning back. "We did it because it needed to be done, and we were the ones who stepped up. This is no different."

"There are eight of us, Jonesy!" Harold repeated, waggling his numerical digits again. "We're not going to cover eleven million square miles with eight people."

"Nope," he replied, shaking his head. "We're not. But we can cover ten thousand." He looked at each in turn again. "We can say, right here and right now that in this patch of ocean, everybody who needs to be rescued is going to be rescued. By us. Because there's nobody else stepping up."

"I'm with you Jonesy," Dan said, after a silent pause in which everybody seemed to consider Jonesy's words. "But how are we gonna do it?"

"Fuck if I know," he replied. "We figure it out, like we always have." He shrugged. "Damn near everything I've learned in the Coast

Guard, I learned because somebody dumped it in my lap and said: deal with it." Frank, Duke and Gary all nodded their heads.

"Been there," Frank said.

"Done that," Duke said.

"Bought the tee-shirt," Gary completed the triplet.

"I'll tell you this, though," Jonesy said, pointing at Molly. "I'll bet you she's got a plan."

All eyes turned to her. She blinked in mild surprise, then smiled, ruefully.

She chuckled,. "I'll be honest. I'm so scared I might just wet myself at any moment." This drew a few snorts of laughter. Her face turned serious, and she continued. "I'll say this: If I gotta be stuck in a zombie apocalypse, I'm glad I've got you guys watching my back."

"Cue the emotional music," Dan joked. Jonesy pelted him with a pebble, and Frank shoved at his shoulder, toppling him to the side. He sat back up and looked at her, a little sheepishly. "So...Do you have a plan?"

She nodded. "I've been thinking of one. Haven't worked out all the details, but yeah. I do." She had everyone's rapt attention. "We start by doing the same thing we'd do in any disaster."

"Which is?" Harold said, then hastened to add, "Ma'am," before Duke could carry out his evident threat of physical violence.

"Duke," she said. "You were at a small boat station in California, right?"

"Yes, Ma'am."

"Did you ever go through an earthquake?"

"Of course!"

"What's the first thing you guys did?"

Duke thought about it for a second, then smiled. "We made sure our own shit was good to go."

"Exactly," she said, waving her finger in the Bosun's direction. "The *Kukui, Assateague,* and *Galveston Island* are all out there, somewhere. Their crews are probably in the same mess we're in - or worse." She looked at their surroundings. "We're not in bad shape."

"Are you nuts?" Harold blurted, and was promptly smacked upside the head by Duke's large right hand. "Sorry..."

She nodded. "Yes. We've lost thirty-nine crew members. Yes, that's a tragedy. More than I can express without bursting into tears - which I absolutely will not do." Molly smiled at them all. "But look around. We're on a secure island, free of zombies. We have food, water, fuel. And we have each other."

"Could be a whole lot worse," Jonesy agreed.

"We find those other ships, consolidate our resources, and then we start rescuing people," she concluded. "We can figure the rest out later."

They all looked at each other, the light dawning in their eyes. These were good men - good *people* - in extraordinary, impossible circumstances so far beyond their experience, it couldn't have been seen with the Hubble, but they weren't giving up. Not by a long shot.

Jonesy raised his bottle of tequila. "A toast," he said. "The Coast Guard's unofficial motto:" He theatrically cleared his throat. "We, the unwilling..."

"Led by the unknowing..." Molly said, waving the hand not holding a bottle of rum, and drawing a roar of appreciative laughter.

They all chimed in. "Have been doing so much, with so little, for so long, that we're now capable of doing anything with nothing!" A cheer went up, along with several bottles of premium booze. The laughter died when Dan McMullen said:

"I hate to be a buzz-kill here," he began.

"Then don't," Gary said.

Dan ignored him. "Harold's right. There are only eight of us."

"Not any more," Bill Schaeffer said, coming up from the direction of the ship. He walked to Molly, and announced: "You've got a phone call, Ma'am."

144

"...Cutter *Sassafras*, this is M/V *True North*, two-one-eight-two. Over," John said into the GSB 900. Barber had gotten through to somebody, and the first thing he'd done was call John, who raced to the Bridge, barely pausing to get dressed. His hair was mussed, his shirt was untucked, and his eyes were red and puffy, but he was smiling.

"*True North*, *Sassafras*. Over," Molly's voice - distorted by distance and weather, and whatever other crap the communications gremlins might be throwing at them, but still perfectly, blessedly recognizable - came though the tiny speaker and went straight to John's beating heart.

"Hey, Molly," he said. "Over."

"Good to hear your voice," her voice said.

"What's your status?" he asked, trying to maintain some semblance of radio protocol.

"Alive," she replied. "Got knocked down. Got back up again," she said. "You? Over."

"Same," he said. "Where are you? And before you answer, be advised. There may be unfriendly ears listening."

"Not taking any chances?" Jim asked.

"No, sir, I am not."

"Will she understand your cryptic message?" Jim asked.

"She's smart," John replied. She'll figure it out."

As if to prove the point, there was a definite pause at the other end of the transmission. It went on for mere moments, but as they ticked by, John began to worry. He needn't have bothered.

"We're at your favorite golf course," she said.

"What the fuck?" Jim blurted. "What the Hell does that mean? You don't golf."

John thought about it for a moment, at first just as confused as his friend. Then he got it and smiled. "I've played golf exactly once," John said.

"Where?" Jim asked.

"Midway."

145

"Roger that," John's voice said over the GSB. "See you soon. *True North,* out."

Molly smiled and placed the radio mic back into its bracket.

"Favorite golf course?" Jonesy asked. He'd followed her up to the Bridge, every bit as enthusiastic about hearing from John - about knowing that somewhere, out there, other people survived. Truth be told, he'd begun to think they might be alone.

He knew that was foolish, of course. Simple math told him there had to be other people somewhere. He didn't need statistical probability or actuarial tables, or anything other than his own mind to tell him so. But numbers had no life, no animus, no soul. They were just numbers, just figures on an imaginary piece of paper in his head. This was real. He smiled at her. He smiled at Bill. Hell, he was ready to smile at the whole goddamned world.

Molly turned to him and smiled back. "Please don't take this the wrong way," she said, and then to his great delight, pulled him into the best hug he'd ever had. And then she also hugged Bill, of course, but Jonesy took heart and pride, and just the slightest erotic thrill in the knowledge that she hugged *him* first.

"What was that for?" he asked, looking the gift horse firmly in the mouth. He wanted to kiss her, but that would have been going a bit too far. He could dream, though, couldn't he?

"We have a purpose," she said, stepping away from Bill. Jonesy thought this may have been the first time he'd ever seen his friend flustered. He turned his attention back to Molly.

"We have each other," she added, then pointed at the radio. "And we just got the thing we needed most."

"Which is?" Jonesy asked.

"Hope."

To be continued...

Made in the USA
Monee, IL
23 September 2021